The Ghost Dancer

The ghost dancer had come clear of the forest and was crossing the open plain toward the Thunder-tree men. Unobstructed by trees, he blazed blue, a hot piece of noon-sky running toward them through the night.

"Why does he burn?" Vran asked, transfixed.

"He's not burning," the priestess said. "He carries the spirit-fire of the sky. He is but an animal. The spirit-fire makes him something more."

The ghost dancer entered the gully beyond where the travelers had stopped for the night, and disappeared. Only his weird glow rose from the ditch like a starlit fog.

Then his head appeared out of the gully . . . until the ghastly apparition loomed over them, silent as smoke, and the men moaned.

Vran let fly his spear—and the projectile hurtled through the giant's chest and clattered among the rocks of the gully behind him. . . .

Other titles by A. A. Attanasio

WYVERN

*KINGDOM OF THE GRAIL

Published by
HarperPaperbacks

*coming soon

A. A. ATTANASIO

HUNTING THE GHOST DANCER

HarperPaperbacks
A Division of HarperCollinsPublishers

HarperPaperbacks   *A Division of* HarperCollins*Publishers*
10 East 53rd Street, New York, N.Y. 10022

A hardcover edition of this book was published in 1991 by HarperCollins*Publishers.*

Cover illustration by Kang Yi

First HarperPaperbacks printing: March 1992

Printed in the United States of America

HarperPaperbacks and colophon are trademarks of HarperCollins*Publishers*

10 9 8 7 6 5 4 3 2 1

For Mary Evans—
sister on the woundward journey

Fifty thousand summers ago,
the world was stranger than we remember—

CONTENTS

PART 3
MASTERINGS OF THE BEAST

HUNTING
THE GHOST
DANCER

Prelude

Sun sparked on the wings of a dragonfly. A lone figure watched the flitting insect disappear in a sunny mist of rhododendron and barberry. Squinting against the late afternoon glare, he stared north across the flat terrain at the blue star of a distant glacier. The shadows of several woolly rhinos marred the level distance as they selected their resting spots for the night, and a herd of yaks mulled along the rocky bed of a tributary stream that shone like ice in the hard light. Otherwise, the tundra appeared empty. A few flakes of snow, dropping from mare's tail clouds, glittered gold in the sun's slanting rays.

The figure squatted alone on the spine of a ridge that marked the northern limit of the Great Forest. Behind him, a dark wall of shaggy pine and stout cedars admitted only fibrous sunlight, and when the wind backwashed off the dense trees, the resined air inspired memories of the thirty-five winters he had sheltered there. Those were the winters he had counted. At the end of each, as now, when the snow lifted and the silver lichen again crept out of the crevices in the tree barks, he had cut a notch on his clan belt. His clan had cut seven for him before he had earned the right to mark his own time.

Using a wooden knife, he cut a nick in the leather of the belt just above his left hip. Then he untied the thongs of the elephant-hide belt and removed it from his waist. He sheathed the knife in the furry cuff of his boot so that he could pull the belt taut in both hands and hold it against the western horizon. With one eye squeezed shut, he matched the notch he had just cut to a cleft in the tree-stubbled landscape, where the sun was setting. This was a custom he remembered from his childhood. Each year at the coming of the warm winds and the flowers, the old ones held high the belts of all the clan members, one at a time. But now there were no old ones. There was no clan.

Winter done, summer already pushing up from the dark earth, the tundra looked beautiful to the wanderer, fiercely so, for he knew this would be his last warm season before he rejoined the People, who had gone ahead. He was old and he was entirely alone, had been for eight winters now. Like an ancient lonely elk, he had wintered in the Forest, proud under the heavy antlers of his memories. That pride was hard to bear even in the most clement weather. But in the snow and biting ice-winds his absentminded daydreaming had almost killed him. Once, he had been a great hunter; his clan were the Spear-Throwers. But too often now he curled up among his remembrances of the People when he should have been hunting, and he had survived only because the spirit powers had pitied him. He knew he could not rely on the compassion of those benevolent spirits another winter. He had to find others of his kind before the harsh winds came down again from the cold plateaus. One more winter alone and he would fulfill the promise of his given name, Baat, which meant "Hollow Bone."

Baat yearned to share what he had learned in his seasons of solitude, to hear once more the music of his youth, to huddle with the others, to talk and laugh again before the journey with no return. And so he had found his way to the edge of the Great Forest earlier than usual to hold his year-notch up to the last sun of winter.

Baat lowered his arms and fastened the belt about his waist. He purged his mind of sorrow: He would be with his clan soon enough. Almost certainly this was his last summer, his last opportunity to savor the bounty of life, even if alone.

Looking out over the tundra to the way north, the traditional summer path of the People, Baat felt a deepening nostalgia for the perfections of summer. How easy the days of flowers were. That he might never again wander with the herds, never fish among the boulders with the cranes, or smoke bees from their bracken hives and chew their sweet combs was a loss that ached in him. Most of all, he would miss walking up to the glacier, staring into its blue depths, hearing its shatter rock songs, feeling its cold under his feet while the day's styptic heat tightened his skin.

His reminiscence snapped from his mind at the sight of thin shadows appearing out of the glare of the glacial stream. The yaks casually lumbered away from the sudden figures. Baat crouched lower. The slim shadows were people, not the People, his race, but the smallheads, the narrow ones, whom he often saw in the Forest and on the tundra. They were dangerous by day, for they traveled always in bands and were cunning hunters—and they hated him and his kind. Their hatred was murderous envy, because they could not share the cold fire that came down from the night sky—that cold fire which, with all its strength, voices, and pain, belonged only to the People.

Against the sun's red fire, the smallhead band stood out in sharp relief. Four men and a woman moved slowly along the stony margins of the stream. At first Baat thought they were carrying a hunt prize among them, but looking closer he saw that the object trussed and hoisted between two of the men was another smallhead. They were carrying someone injured. On the flat tundra the litter could be dragged, but over the stream rocks the wounded one had to be lifted. With their burden, they would not reach the Forest before nightfall.

At that thought, a sexual flurry troubled Baat. He recognized that as an urgency of the cold fire. Night was near enough for the cold fire to feel its way to him. Ul udi was what the cold fire called itself. But the name was hard for him to speak, even silently to himself. Much of what the ul udi said to him when their cold fire descended from the night and furred him in chill brightness he had no way to fit to his breath. Yet that hardly mattered, for he carried their cold fire, as all the People did. And in those cool, bright flames was far more than speaking or understanding. The ul udi wanted rapture and blood.

Baat considered moving on, away from the smallheads. Far better for them if he slipped off now, back into the Forest. But the erotic flimmer in his muscles protested with a hot craving. Even if he left now, he could not go far before nightfall. And once the night came and the cold fire descended, the ul udi would bring him back for the blood of the smallheads.

He crouched, making certain that he had not been

spotted. Though it seemed futile, he had to try to get away before the night claimed him. If he stayed, there would be violence and more smallheads would come. Bent over, he edged slowly backwards. Once the cool shadows of the Forest closed around him, he turned and loped through the dark tree tunnels. He knew well in which direction the smallheads' winter camp lay and where they journeyed in spring to set up their summer residence. Those were choice places in the Forest, near clearwater springs and salt holes, where the People had once dwelled. The smallheads had driven off the People and made those places their own.

Baat ran hard away from there, into the dense thickets, where the wild pigs rooted and the Great Bear slept and the smallheads were afraid to go. When he could, he leaped from one root-arch of the giant trees to another and swung from the thick lower limbs. More often, he crawled among bramble and clawed his way through winter-killed curtains of dead ivy and dodder, ignoring the scratches on his face and bare arms. If he could get far enough away from the smallheads, the ul udi would not smell them and would lose interest.

But he was already too late. The erotic flutter he had felt at the edge of the Forest only steepened in him. The cold fire had already come down from the sky. In the darkness of the Forest, he could see it glowing like moonmist on his limbs. Soon the voices would begin. Soon he would wonder why he was running, why he was letting the little claws of the Forest cut him when the smallheads were the ones who should be fleeing. Were they not the ones who had intruded on him and the People? Had he forgotten that they were the ones who had drawn first blood, who had murdered not only the hunters but the old ones, and the women, and the children? Did he not remember his own children, twisting in his arms with pain from the poisoned water they had drunk?

He stopped running. His breath chuffed loudly from exertion, yet he could hear his blood thrumming even louder in his ears, his heart knocking hard at the root of his throat, where a cry coiled.

The smallheads are your enemy, a bitter voice spoke. That was the ul udi. They were with him again. They had come down from the sky to live the life of the earth through him.

Baat held his hands up in front of his face. The space between his fingers webbed brightly with the radiance of the ul udi. The glow pulsed with his breathing.

Kill the smallheads, an ul udi voice said. And in the cold fire that he held in his hands he saw again the faces of his children, their large, bright eyes staring at him through the pain, expecting him to help them, as he had always helped them. He watched them die again. Their faces closed around their suffering, hot with tears and pain, not comprehending his helplessness. *Da!* they cried to him. *Da—it hurts!*

Baat's hands fisted, and the cry twisting about his heart uncoiled to a howl.

Kill the smallheads!

On the tundra, where the wanderers had stopped in their trek to build a fire against the night, the howl from the distant treeline sounded deathly. Two of the men rose from where they hunkered by the juddering flames, and shook their spears at the Forest. The two women, one sitting in the litter, the other kneeling at her side, feeding her from a wooden bowl, shared a knowing look of apprehension. The other two men hugged themselves tighter beside the fire, and looked to the woman in the litter for directions.

"Deadwalkers begone!" the larger of the spearmen shouted, and the two began a dance to ward off phantoms.

"Have those fools sit down," the woman in the litter spoke.

"Sit down!" the squatting men yelled.

The dancers stopped; the large one said, "The dead are crying. We must drive them away."

"That is not the cry of the dead, you dolts," the woman in the litter said. "That is a ghost dancer."

The spearmen exchanged surprised stares. "You're mistaken, priestess," the big one said. "The Grandfathers have killed all the ghost dancers."

"Not all." The priestess waved away the bowl her attendant still held before her, and signed for her shoulders to be covered. The kneeling woman placed the bowl by the fire, got up, and draped the priestess' white shoulders with a bearskin.

"None of the Thundertree has ever seen a ghost dancer," the smaller of the spearmen said, while the other tentatively shook his spear over the fire. "Maybe you're wrong, priestess. Maybe these are our dead—unhappy that we're bringing you, a Longtooth priestess, to our people."

The priestess shared a mocking expression with her male escorts. "The Thundertree are fools, all of you, fools. You've lived too long in the Forest hiding like squirrels. You've forgotten the Ways of Wandering. That's why there are no great hunters among you. You've forgotten how to be human. And that is why you need this." She lifted the fertility rock from her lap, where it had to remain to stay potent.

The Thundertree men looked away from it, afraid

it would steal their virility and wither them to old age before their time.

The priestess laughed. She lowered the round, smooth stone to her lap and placed her fingers in its cleft. "Only what is in here can save your people. Without the rock of fertility to call great souls into the wombs of the Thundertree, your people will become more foolish with each generation—and soon enough not even the animals will talk with you. Only this rock can save you." She cooed to it as to a child. "And only I can carry the rock. So do as I say. Douse the flames, quickly, and carry me into the darkness."

The Thundertree men turned away. "No," the smaller one objected. "In the darkness the night beasts will feast on us."

"In the light, the ghost dancer will tear you limb from limb. We must hide. Quickly, do as I say."

"No, priestess," the larger hunter spoke. "For days we've done all that you told us, carrying you as you wished, stopping when you wished, eating what you wished. But now we see the Forest. Now the Thundertree know the ways. You will obey us. Have your Longtooth men gather more kindling and feed the fire."

The Longtooth men rose, spears in hand, and moved threateningly toward the fire. The priestess stopped them with a raised hand. "Fight each other and we'll all die out here. The ghost dancer knows we're here. He comes for us."

The Thundertree men clacked their spears together. "Then we will kill him as our Grandfathers killed the ghost dancers in their time. Feed the fire— and let this ghost dancer dare enter the light of our circle."

The Longtooth men looked urgently to their priestess. She signed for them to be calm.

"You came to the Longtooth for help," she said to her Thundertree escorts.

"Many among us don't want your help. We'll call forth our own great souls."

The priestess tossed her head with exasperation. "Then why have I been troubled to make this long journey? Why must I endure the rigors of winter's end, keeping this rock warm between my legs? If the Thundertree don't need us, why have we come this far?"

The Thundertree men conceded with weary nods. "You are needed," the short one admitted. "The hunt has been difficult for many years now. There has been little meat. The women have provided most of our food. We alone are the two great hunters of our people."

"As they have reminded us since they came for us," the priestess smirked to her attendants.

"But"—the larger Thundertree hunter spoke up— "we are now in sight of the Forest. Our Grandfathers watch us from there. We can't cower in the darkness. Let this ghost dancer come for us if that's what's out there."

"Oh, it is a ghost dancer out there, bravo Thundertree hunters. It most certainly is. Look for yourselves." The priestess pointed to where the crest of stars ended abruptly at the bristly horizon of the Forest. In the darkness there, a blue light blinked. "He is still among the trees. Soon, he will break for us."

The female attendant gasped and began whimpering.

"Be still, Shala," the priestess ordered. "It's too late to hide now."

"The crystal will stop him, surely," Shala whispered.

"No. There is no moon tonight. The crystal is too weak."

"What are you speaking of?" the big Thundertree hunter asked.

"Shut up, Big Kell, and prepare to fight for your life," one of the Longtooth men snapped. "You didn't want to hide, so now let's see your courage."

"You've killed ghost dancers before, Teshuk?" Big Kell asked.

Teshuk looked to his partner, and they grinned without humor. "Cort and me killed our share, eh, brother?"

"But not like this," Cort said, his grin suddenly gone. "They got to be killed asleep. When they sleep deep. Better to poison 'em, then jump 'em while they're cramped up. Never like this."

"Mudman! Look at that thing."

"Forget asking the Mudman for help, Vran," Teshuk grumbled. "Mudman isn't going to rise up to save your shivering shanks."

"What makes it burn like that?" Big Kell wanted to know.

The Longtooth men shrugged, looked to the priestess. She was staring at the Forest with half-lidded eyes and did not appear to have heard them. She was not really watching the blue light winking brighter and nearer. She was thinking about what was to come. The ghost dancer would certainly kill the men. But for her and Shala, if they were submissive—no, more than submissive, willing—they might survive yet. The Thundertree were not far. Two women could travel that distance alone.

Shala knelt beside the priestess and pressed a cold glass blade into the woman's hand. With tear-bright eyes and a sob in her voice, she begged, "Kill me, priestess. Be swift. Don't let it get me."

The priestess threw the black-glass knife into the

fire and seized Shala by her hair, pulled her face up close. The priestess' stare was fixed with fierce intensity. "For the men there is only death," she whispered to the girl. "For us there is yet hope. But you must give yourself to him. You must pretend he is your wished-for lover."

"No!" Shala cried and pulled away.

But the priestess jerked her close again. "Do you want to die? Do you prefer the Mudman for your lover? Are we not women? Does not the Mother shine in us? Let Her shine brightly, dear Shala—and we may yet live!"

"Priestess—" Teshuk called. "Look!"

The ghost dancer had come clear of the Forest and was crossing the open plain toward them. Unobstructed by trees, he blazed blue, a hot piece of noon-sky running toward them through the night.

"Why does he burn?" Vran asked, transfixed.

"He's not burning," the priestess said, watching intently. "He carries the spirit-fire of the sky. The cold fire comes down from the sky and it carries him. He is but an animal. The spirit-fire makes him something more."

"Make brands!" Cort ordered, and the men began binding dried shrub to thick brush-limbs.

"Yes, make brands," the priestess chortled and lay back to wait.

When each of the four men had a torch in one hand and a spear in the other, they spread out, two to each side of the fire and shouted their battle cries. The ghost dancer advanced silently. Now they could see his shape, his legs pumping, arms flailing, as he sped across the uneven terrain, the eerie light of his body illuminating the ground around him, flickering off the tundra grass and the bramble bushes.

Clearly, he would be exhausted from such a run by the time he came upon them. The men's shouts echoed defiantly and their torches swung wide, waving the monster closer.

The ghost dancer entered the gully beyond where the travelers had stopped for the night, and disappeared. Only his weird glow rose from the ditch like starlit fog. The hunters braced for him. "Don't throw!" Teshuk shouted. "Hold your spears. We'll stick him like a pig as he comes at us."

Then his head appeared out of the gully—a boulder with a grimacing face bashed out of it, the hair short, bristly as a hog's, and streaming blue fire. Giant shoulders followed, burnished like sunshot fronds, hackled with flames. Long glittering arms, a prismatic torso strapped with pelts, naked muscled legs, and furry boots tufting sparks. The ghastly apparition loomed over them, silent as smoke, and the Thundertree men moaned.

Vran let fly his spear—and the projectile hurtled through the giant's chest and clattered among the rocks of the gully behind him. The men hooted with surprise and confusion. The ghost dancer lurched toward Cort, the ul udi within him touching flesh, feeling the rage and the fear, the heat and the cold competing in Cort's nerves. Cort jabbed with his weapon, but again the spear cut emptiness; the flames of his torch flapped green as they passed through the blue ghost. Then the wraith swept over Cort, and the Longtooth hunter cried out in anguish.

From out of the darkness behind the hunters, Baat slinked back. While his body of light swirled about Cort, he advanced into the firelight, a rock in each fist. Shala saw him first and screamed. By then he had moved close enough to hurl a rock and strike Big Kell a crunching blow at the back of his head. Even as Big Kell dropped, Baat flung the second rock, and hit Teshuk on his temple as he turned.

Vran attacked, obsidian knife held low. Baat snatched the wooden bowl by the fire and heaved it at the charging man. The bowl caught Vran full in the face, and he spun and crashed into the fire. He twisted swiftly to his feet with a howl, stumbling into the ghost dancer who grabbed his head and shoulders and with one mighty twist snapped the man's neck.

The ul udi capered with delight in Baat's mind, a chorus of chittering devil voices. *Kill the smallheads!* The stink of blood ignited the cells of his brain, making the inside of his skull a luminous pulp, an interior mirror in which every tremor of the dying smallhead, every swell of fecal stink and the soft croon of last breath, reflected again and again. The Dark Ones' appetite for detail was insatiable—and the killing, which had been terrible in its swiftness, went on inside him, repeating itself over and over.

Hot with murderous frenzy, Baat faced the last of the men. Cort stood transfixed. Numbing shivers coursed through his muscles, while his head whirled with crazy voices jabbering in a language he did not understand. Every effort he made to move creaked slowly. Vision belled, blurred at the edges, where he saw the Thundertree men sprawled on the ground in the graceless postures of the dead; and there, below him, even Teshuk on his back, staring up with blood-spattered face and lifeless eyes.

Terror swirled through Cort, and the gnattering voices flurried louder, so that he thought his ears would burst. Two spear-lengths away the ghost dancer stood, a head taller and a hand's span wider than the biggest man he had ever seen. He looked much like the other ghost dancers he had come upon after they had been poisoned—ruddy-haired, with long green eyes under bulging brows—an ugliness as if hacked from rock. Only this one was standing, striding closer until he was only an arm's reach away. Cort smelled the forest duff on him, saw the dried leaf-mulch in his stiff hair, a crescent-moon scar parting the whiskers on his right jaw. He gazed up into those long, slim eyes, met the fury there, and went cold in the hollows of his bones.

Burn him—burn him! the ul udi cried—and the scarlet pulse in Baat's skull hammered. He tore his attention away from the exploding voices and shouted, ''No burning!'' His shout sounded like animal noise to the smallhead, made the man's tiny eyes flare and his quivering lips lift from his teeth.

Baat opened his palm before the smallhead's terrified face, and the blue fire lifted up from Cort, balled in the air above him, and vanished.

Suddenly, the voices were gone from Cort's head, and his muscles unlocked. Immediately, the Longtooth hunter drew back his spear. But before he could raise it, the ghost dancer grabbed his arm in a grip so ferocious that Cort's arm broke at the elbow. The torch in his other hand fell, and he crashed to his knees, mouth open around a soundless scream. Baat swung his fist hard against the smallhead's ear, and ended his suffering.

The blue fire played briefly over the corpse, moved away, and returned to Baat. The ul udi voices bleated with ecstasy. The hot smell of blood, the crunch of shattered bone, the sharp apex of pain, and the fluting gasp of last breath reflected endlessly among the interior mirrors of his brain. He had not killed smallheads in a long time. He had forgotten the sodden joy it gave the ul udi. They flashed brightly in him, savoring the bloodsmoke and dreaming they were flesh. He felt their unslaked appetite: He had killed these smallheads too quickly. He had had no choice, but the ul udi would have relished more suffering, more bloodsmoke, more death.

Kill the smallheads! Kill the bitches! Kill the sows!

Baat turned toward the female smallheads. One had lifted her robes to show the white of her thighs, pink in the firelight, her legs spread and a large stone pressed against her genitals. The other cowered behind her, backing off into the darkness as he approached.

Kill them! Spill their blood! Let us smell their death heat! Kill the smallhead bitches!

The fleeing one made the death voices wriggle louder in Baat's head. *Kill them! Kill the sows!*

But studying the other one, the one with the rock between her legs, her breasts open to the firelight, overrode the pain-hungry voices, started a new strumming going in his head with its own echoes in his body. She murmured to him, seemed to be smiling in a sickening way. The other backed off, frightened, and her fear fed the hateful violence in him.

Baat knelt before the open legs of the priestess, summoned by the new melody of the ul udi. Only the fear of the other smallhead spoiled the strumming in his groin, jangled it with the competing need for bloodsmoke.

Shala saw the giant kneel between the priestess' legs, his large, hideous face gleaming. The blue fire had almost entirely vapored away. The killing was over. She backed away, her heart banging, almost gagging her. Then she spun and sprang into the dark like a rabbit.

The ul udi guided Baat's hands. He did not have to think, not even have to try. With wide-splayed fingers, he lifted the rock of fertility and exposed the priestess' slewed cleft. She whispered him encouragement, filling him turgid with the ul udi's new melody. He heaved the rock of fertility out of the way, and it flew into the dark with the ul udi's murderous accuracy. But when it smashed Shala's skull he heard nothing, the new melody was that loud.

Kirchi startled awake, a cry widening through her body, a cry already too large for her voice, too big for her lungs. The cry had pushed out silently through her gaping mouth, right through the walls of her chest, and left her wrung and weak. The cry went on, beyond her, out through the cave wall into the night, through the Forest, out to the tundra, where, right now, the beast heaved his engorgement into the priestess, while in the dark Shala lay, her brains naked to the starlight.

"Wake up, child," a familiar voice spoke. "It's over. Tell me what you saw."

Kirchi's eyes strained wide, locked in a stare bent on a small tallow flame before a crystal lobe as big as her knee. It amplified and scattered the light into enormous shadows on the cave wall. In the shadows, she still saw the beast, his broad naked back hunched over the priestess. And all the while those tiny, evil voices in his head singing shrilly in rhythm to the fire's elemental vibrations, as if the fire itself were pushing and pulling the beast over the priestess. And with each thrust, her legs jerking straight up and a slurred cry rising from her—

"Wake up, I say!"

A thorn pricked Kirchi's cheek, and her whole

body winced and curled up on itself like a torched moth. The old woman who had jabbed her placed a knobby hand on the back of the young woman's neck, feeling through the bright red hair for the pulse behind her jaw.

"There, there," the crone clucked. "You've had a fright. Remember what I've told you about frights. Remember, now. Feel your heart. Feel her drumming in you. Be the drummer. Be her—and slow the drumming down. That's good, child. That's very good. Now sit up."

The hag grabbed Kirchi's coarse hair and pulled back her head till she was sitting upright. In the tallow light, her pale skin reflected all the hues of the flame, and her gray eyes spun color like the lump of crystal on the moss-mat before them. Sensibility had returned to her stare. But her fright still showed in the small quivers at the corners of her slack mouth. She was a handsome, not a pretty girl, with a ferocious fox-keen face, a pallid, lithe, small-breasted body braced by the proud bones of the sybil who had birthed her. The Mothers of the Longtooth had been happy to let her go to the witch, for the girl lacked the breadth of hips and the fullness of teats to serve them. Yet, with a sybilline mother, she was too noble to spend her days digging tubers and mashing acorns.

"Tell me now, Kirchi-girl, what did you see?"

"A ghost dancer," she muttered.

The hag's long, sullen face brightened. "Five moons in front of the scry crystal and you've found your first ghost dancer! Ha-ah! I was a full year staring before I saw my first. Who was it?"

Kirchi blinked, trying to remember the names and characteristics the witch had taught her. "I'm not sure."

"Not sure? Child, there are no more than a dozen ghost dancers in our domain. You know all their names and traits. Think. Was it female?"

"No. A man. Big, with bristly hair like red hackles."

"All the men are big, child, and all, here, have red hair. But most are not tall and some trim their hair in odd ways. Come, now. Was it one-eyed Moruc? Or Toothless Talman? Gray Pindal with the black mole on his nose?"

"He had a scar on his jaw, curved like the new moon."

"Baat!" The crone sat back with surprise. "I thought he was dead. He must be very old—forty or more summers. Nearly my own age." The witch thumbed her chin reflectively. "It's been almost seven years since I've seen him; that was the year after he lost the last of his tribe. It maddened him of course. I was sure the loneliness had killed him when I stopped scrying him at his ancestral grounds. Now he's the last of those that lived at this end of the Great Forest. Yes, they were tall ones. The others—Moruc, Talman, Pindal, Cark, all the rogue women—they're short-legged. They've wandered up from the south. Baat, alone, belongs here. It was our tribe, the Longtooth, killed his people."

Kirchi was not listening. Now that her fright had dulled, the weariness of the scrying-brew saturated her.

The witch again pricked the young woman's cheek with her thorn, and Kirchi snapped alert. "Where did you see Baat? What was he doing?"

"On the tundra, in sight of the Forest. He burns blue with spirit-fire."

"Dancing?"

"No. Not dancing."

The crone's face creased with worry. "Not dancing? Then the Dark Ones have him."

"Yes, they have him. They filled him with killing-strength and he has slain four men—two Longtooth men from my father's cult, Teshuk and Cort, and two Thundertree hunters, Big and Little Pell or Gell—I couldn't hear their names so well, the Dark Ones jabbered so."

"He killed them with his hands—or with the fire?"

"With his hands."

The old woman swung her face toward the black night in the mouth of the cave. "Bless him, Mother of Darkness, he's trying to control himself. Still trying after all these years. No wonder he yet lives."

"There were two women—one a priestess."

"Women!" the witch wailed. "What were women doing on the tundra at night?"

"They journeyed to the Thundertree. The priestess carried a rock of fertility."

The witch threw up her hands in despair. "Superstitious children. Politics, not wisdom, brought them there. Every priestess knows those rocks are useless. So now the Longtooth women are playing the silly games of their men and trying to influence the primitive Thundertree."

"Only one woman is dead," Kirchi spoke, staring down at her lap, not wanting to look into the crystal or face the shadow wall and begin the trance again. "Shala ran and Baat broke her head open with the rock of fertility. And now he ruts with the priestess."

"Oh, Mother, Mother!" the witch cried out, and her outburst folded into echoes far into the cave. "Why do You give Your daughters to the beast?" She shook her head, weary with grief. "A moonless night. No crystal could have spared her this indignity. The Dark Ones will not be denied tonight. She is fortunate, at least, to be under Baat. Once he is spent, he will not let the Dark Ones kill her.''

Kirchi shut her eyes, wanting to blot out the horrid memory. The crone gripped her behind the neck.

''Don't fall asleep yet, child. You must purge the scrying-brew or you'll fly and maybe not return. Go out to the spring. Drink a full gourd at least. Wait for the cat star to set. Then sleep. Tomorrow we will have to find Baat. The Longtooth men are too wise to want a ghost dancer's blood for Teshuk and Cort, but the Thundertree will want vengeance for their dead. They will be hunting him now. Blessedly, they are sloppy hunters. Still, we must protect Baat. He has come back to his ancestral grounds. He has come back for only one thing. He wants to die. We must see he has that with dignity.''

Kirchi lugged herself to her feet and swayed out of the cave and into the night. The chill air cut through the drowsiness of the trancing brew. A breeze shuffled the branches of the giant firs with a sound like a stream of water, and the femur bones hanging on the skeleton-poles beside the spring clacked.

She followed that noise under a vast hive of stars until she came to where water sluiced from a fissure in a hillock. A mist soaked the fern brambles around the spring, frosty against her bare legs. She knelt and felt for the drinking gourd, found it nestled between two smooth rocks. As she drank, the cold water hurting her teeth, she prayed to the Mother to be free of this, not to have to drink the bitter scrying-brew again and see the horror she had seen tonight.

Never had Kirchi wanted to be a sybil, or even an important mother. She would be happy, she knew, to be one of the simple mothers in the tribe, foraging with the others, smoking the meats, watching her children grow.

She finished drinking and gazed up at the stars crackling in the darkness, her yearning harsh as malice in her after what she had witnessed this night. Her wordless prayer to the Great Mother spun in her, though it was empty of hope. How could she ever be free of the witch? If she fled, the beasts would devour her within a night. If she stayed, in time she would become the witch herself. Her only hope was that someone would come to take her place—a great woman better suited than she to serve the Mother—a woman of caring and enormous power, who would happily take her place so she could return to the Longtooth and live as a simple mother. But that hope was no hope at all, for no such great woman existed. The witch chose her successor. This had always been so. No thin wordless prayer would change that.

The cold tightened her flesh against her bones, and tears wet her cheeks, though she was far past sadness. She wept in despair, not only for herself but for the young woman whose brains lay on the tundra nibbled by ants, and for the priestess under the beast, and for the beast himself, his people dead, alone forever now under the smoldering stars, enclosed by a night black as venom.

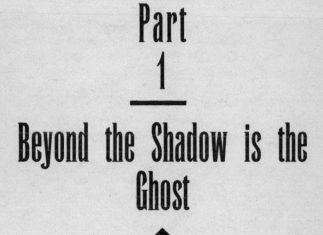

Part
1

Beyond the Shadow is the Ghost

Life's greatest danger lies in the fact that people's food consists entirely of souls.

—Eskimo shaman

1

Blind Side

An arrowhead of white cranes hurried north through the red air. Duru stood in the cave-mouth and watched them wing silently overhead, carrying her heart joyfully into her ninth spring. Winter had seemed interminable, moaning outside the caves, numbing the land and the people, graying the sky, and peeling the ocean to whitecaps that made fishing impossible. No birds to hunt, no fish to net, no berries to gather. She had long ago wearied of pecking the dust in the back of the caves for insects and eating the stale acornmash and dried meat from autumn. Now there would be fresh food again. The sea mirrored the blushing sky, and already the fisherfolk sculled out into the bay in their dugouts, while their women waded the tidepools. And not long ago the last of the great winter storms had thrashed the Forest more fiercely than ever and had driven numerous flocks of birds out of the trees and into niches of the sea cliffs, where they were easily hunted, even by children. Meat abounded yet again. Spring had returned, and the honking of the cranes chorused in the fragrant sea-air.

Duru looked about excitedly for someone to share the news of spring's arrival. She waved to one of the fisherfolk far below on the beach, stringing his net between two limbs of driftwood, and he waved back from under the wheeling gulls. To left and right ran the ledgepath, strewn with small bones the cats had dropped. One of the family's old yellow dogs slept at the juncture where the path bent upward to the high fields, too tired for the climb yet still eager to partake of the mice and snakes the children brought back from above.

Today, or very soon from today, there would be cress and berries, cattail sprouts and orange mushrooms. She skipped into the cave, singing, "White cranes—white cranes—spring is flying overhead!"

Biklo, the family slave, squatted in the moon of morning light that came through the roofhole, where the water-gourds were lowered. He was stringing the gourds together for that morning's hike, and he smiled laconically at her little song, his good eye sad, his blind eye bright as a shell. He mimicked her song: "White cranes, white cranes, spring is flying overhead—and when they fly back who among us will be dead?"

"Biklo!" Duru frowned at him. "Don't tease."

"Life comes and goes like the cranes, little sister."

Duru clucked at him and ordered him back to work. Long ago, before she was born, Biklo had been captured by her Grandfather Scom in a war with the Walnut Hands. Most of the men of the Walnut Hands had fought and been killed, their brains eaten and their skulls stacked in the sea-cave where the boys became men and the women could not go. Biklo had submitted without fighting, and Grandfather Scom had spared his life. Every summer, on the longest day, Biklo gathered field flowers and placed them on the bonehill where Grandfather Scom now lay and sang a song to the Mudman to watch over the man who had given him a new life. Duru loved Biklo for doing this and for his amusing and sometimes scary stories that whiled away the long winter nights.

"White cranes—white cranes!" Duru sang, parting the grass curtain that muffled the wind from the cavemouth. The dimly lit cavern rang with her joy. Mother and her sisters sat toasting nuts with the Firewatcher, the crone who sat up all night singing breathy songs to the embers. The small children chivvied the shells about, playing scuffle.

"Get your basket," Mother said, offering her a toasted almond. "We're going soon enough. And find your vest. There's still a chill in the air."

Duru snatched the almond and bounded across the cavern to the ladder that mounted to her sleeping niche. Feeling mischievous with excitement, she detoured on her way up the ladder, stopping to poke her head through the moss veil of the chamber where Timov lay with the older women. Most of the women had gotten up already and gone to the back vaults to freshen themselves at the stream that rilled through the rockwall there. But Timov, who as the only uninitiated man in the Mothers' cavern was obliged to sleep with the old women, would still be there satisfying one or more of them.

"White cranes—white cranes!" Duru sang into the old women's chamber.

"Aw, so what?" Timov griped from the dark.

Duru could just make out his silhouette rising and falling between the stocky legs of Kwyn, whose raspy breathing sawed loudly in the dark with her pleasure.

A boot thudded against the wall beside Duru's head, and she pulled away with a laugh.

"Leave Kwyn alone," a young woman's voice chided Duru from the chamber above. That was Aradia, Duru's older sister.

Duru hurried up the ladder and parted the curtain of ribbon grass. "White cranes, Aradia! I just saw them."

"Kwyn's bones have been aching her all winter," Aradia said. She sat in the dark on her pelts stroking her long, soft hair with a bristle-brush. She stopped long enough for Duru to crawl into her lap. "Let Timov give her some pleasure. You know he hates doing what he must, so why do you trouble him?"

"Because he hates his work." Duru pouted. "He eats our food, takes the best pelts after the Mothers, and what does he do but complain all the time? When are the men going to take him?"

"When it pleases them."

"But there are boys two years younger who have already been initiated and live with the men. Why can't he?"

"He'll be among them soon enough. Does he trouble you that much?"

"He puts thistle-burrs in my bed, steals my food, and never does what I tell him. He even barks at Mother."

"If not this summer then next, the men will take him. If Father were alive they'd have initiated him by now. He has no one to sponsor him."

"What about Father's brothers? They do the Father-rites for you and me."

"For the boys it's different. Father's brothers have their reasons."

"Hamr will do it."

"Hamr is a Tortoise man. Timov will be a Panther man."

"Tell me again about the two cults." Duru squirmed in her sister's lap, intrigued by the men's mysteries.

"You know all this already. Why are you acting like a baby?"

"Please, Aradia. Tell me again."

"Once, long ago," Aradia began, wearily, continuing to brush her hair while she spoke, "the Tortoise men knew nothing of hunting. They were just fisher-folk—and they were our enemies. They raided us Panther people for pelts and hides. We raided them for shells and fish. But the women of the two tribes convinced the men to join together and share their skills as one tribe—the tribe of the Blue Shell, named for the Great Tortoise whose shell is made of two halves."

"But the two cults would never have stayed together with only the skills of the men to bind them," Duru recited.

"That's right, little sister. Men compete—women complete."

"And so the Blue Shell has two cults of men—the hunting Panther men and the fishing Tortoise men—and one tribe of women who bind them." Duru smiled proudly. "That's why when you take Hamr for your own, he will no longer be a Tortoise man but will become a Panther man, and then he can sponsor Timov. Hamr is brave."

Aradia sighed. "Too brave, I think, little Duru. Hamr has great dreams—and I'm afraid what happened to Father may happen to him."

Father had been gored by a boar three summers ago, and the children remembered the long time he had lain dying, growing weaker each day, fading like an echo.

Duru sat up, put her hands on her sister's knees. "You *are* going to take Hamr for your own, aren't you, Aradia?"

"If he'll have me."

"Why wouldn't he? You're the most beautiful of the Blue Shell women." Aradia pouted at this but did not contradict her. "And besides, Hamr brags about wanting to be a hunter. He doesn't want to fish, so he'll have to marry some Panther woman. How could he refuse you?"

"You know, Duru. We've talked about this before."

"The horse."

"Yes. He wants a horse, like the great men of old had. He won't marry until he has one. And if what you say about the white cranes is true, then today is the day he will try."

Duru leaned closer, her heart suddenly high in her chest. "Today? This very day, Aradia?"

"That's the sign he's been waiting for."

"Why didn't you tell me?"

"And have you tell everyone? He doesn't want a crowd watching him. So I don't want you telling Mother. Or anyone. Go up to the fields with them today. I'll join you there later and tell you what happens. Now go and get your basket, and don't forget your vest."

Duru slipped through the plaited ribbon grass and bumped into Timov. "You don't belong up here," she said. "The old women's chamber and no higher, Timov. You know that."

"Shut up, Toad. Mother let me hang my birds from the cope-beam so the mice wouldn't spoil them. I'm getting them now." He nudged past her and made his way over the dark shelf to where several tree limbs had been lashed together and laid across the open space at the back of the cavern. There, visible in the smoky light from the fire below, several pelts hung as well as a raft of birds dangling by their legs, wings open. Timov used a tined pole to hook the raft of birds and lower it to the cavern floor.

"I see hawks," Duru said. "You've killed many."

"Six hawks, three falcons," Timov said proudly. "More than most of my friends, though the others got their share."

"Why so many?"

"Hawks and falcons, they're the only birds whose feathers are useful in the dance."

"But why kill so many? You don't need that many feathers."

"All the boys are doing it this year," Timov answered, nonchalantly. He returned the pole to its notch in the wall and pushed past her. "The seals came ashore too far west this winter."

"Because of the storm," Duru said. "The same one that beat the birds out of the Forest and onto the cliffs. The men should've left the birds alone and hiked up the beach for the seals."

Timov twisted his mouth derisively. "What do you know? It's easier to climb the cliffs and stone birds. Everyone's doing it."

"That's not good."

"Why not? The Fathers are glad enough for the feathers—and I see you've been eager enough to eat your share of their meat."

"They're already dead."

"Greedy, greedy."

"I'm not. You're greedy. You kill them just for the feathers."

"Greedy toad."

"Greedy saphead!"

Timov dismissed her with a backhanded wave, clambered down the ladder and picked up his birds. He had taken them down sooner than he had planned, but he had not wanted his righteous little sister to know that he had actually been eavesdropping on Aradia. He had heard Hamr's name, and he had wanted to hear what they were saying about him. He knew Hamr was Aradia's favorite, and that annoyed him, for Hamr was the most boastful, arrogant, and self-centered of the Tortoise men. Hamr thought the Beastmaker had personally chosen him to benefit the Blue Shell and to become a great man.

All the boys and young men laughed at Hamr behind his back, to think that he or anyone could be a great man in these modern days. The great men lived long ago, when the earth was young and the spirit powers still tried out different shapes. Nowadays, the powers had found their forms and men were simply men and beasts and plants no longer talked or changed their shapes. How could anyone think he could be a great man in these changeless times?

None, however, not even among the men, would taunt Hamr about his bloated ambition to his face. Those who did got their mouths smashed and their balls kicked back up where they came from. He was big and tough—and crazy. He talked out loud to the Beastmaker, as if the sky and all its paraphernalia awaited his next breath. He laughed at the warnings and omens of the old men, fishing beyond the smoking breakers when no one else dared, sharing his catch with anyone who would meet him as he came triumphantly to shore.

When the dead were laid out for the tears of the women and the awe of the men, Hamr smiled faintly, as if he knew something about death no one else did. He had smiled like that when Father was laid out. That was when Timov began to hate him.

Sooner or later, the swaggerer would fail at something, hurt himself lame or dead, and then the whole tribe would laugh. Timov did not want his sister inviting so certain a tragedy into their family but could think of no way to stop her. As an uninitiated male, he had no authority in the family.

Timov dropped the raft of birds before Biklo, who had just finished stringing the water-gourds for his daily trek to the spring. "Pluck them and separate the feathers," he ordered. "Give the meat and the small feathers to the Mothers but save all the pinions for me."

Biklo nodded and began untying the birds. "The white cranes are flying, Grandson Scom."

"Yeah, yeah." Timov stepped onto the ledge path. The sun crowned the eastern mountains and flimmered below on the sea in golden flakes. He squinted his eyes and breathed deeply of the sea and the calm smell of ice from the distant peaks. Today looked like a lovely day for Hamr to wrestle with a horse. In the last few days, the herd had moved into the meadow above the sea-cliffs, following their ancient, narrow trail from the south. He had seen them, their flanks shivering with energy, power jetting from their nostrils in silver clouds. Timov smiled smugly. After today, Aradia would have to find someone new to fill her womb.

Timov ambled past the cave-entrances of several families, stopping to pet the dogs and to tell the friends he met that he had to get bog-mud for Biklo's aching joints, a messy chore he knew he would be left to do on his own. He did not want any companions, for he knew Aradia would be meeting Hamr soon, and he wanted to follow them alone.

At the ledge-trail that mounted to the top of the cliffs, he climbed into a dense pine shrub clinging to the rockface and startled a flurry of mice. He marveled that they were everywhere this year and shook the branches to see them scatter pell-mell into the rock crevices. Then he waited. He watched a young girl gathering molted feathers while her mother hung a patch-pelt rug over the ledge and thrashed the dust out of it with a wicker sheaf. Soon the Mothers' singing lilted above the birdchatter. A band of women came sauntering along the trail, gathering members from each cavemouth. He saw his mother and aunties and the old women he serviced at night and behind them the youngest children who could walk, with Duru and her girlfriends to mind them.

Aradia was not among them, so Timov lingered in the pine bush until the Mothers' band had climbed past and their singing and prating dimmed with distance. The blueflies rose with the morning thermals and began harrying him, and he was about to swing down from the pine when Aradia appeared on the ledge-path.

In the brilliant morning light, she looked as beautiful as the panther that the men of her family worshiped: She had tied her sleek jet hair atop her head in a fan-crest and wrapped a black rabbitskin mantle under her arms, tucked up around her waist with a sash of pink shells, so that the pelt dangled above her knees. Nut-oil glossed her limbs and shoulders, and her lissome muscles shimmered as she mounted the uneven notches in the trail to the top of the cliff.

Timov climbed down from the pine bush after she was out of sight, scrambling up the cliffwall. At the top, the trail cut through a bluff of yellow grass and opened into a knolly field. To the left, the land sloped west through stands of bare trees to hummocky meadows, the haunt of the red deer, through brambly groves of hazel shrub and thornapples to the bog. Ahead were the hills, replete with skeletal groves of fruit trees, berry swatches, chuckling creeks and icy rills galloping down from the purple mountains of the north. The Mothers had gone that way to forage the first tender shoots along the brooks and rivulets. But Aradia had turned right, and he could see her moving east among the leafless scrub oak along the cliffedge toward the migratory trails—more like ditches—that cut the land into a patchwork of hawthorn shrub and clusters of laurel and black birch, all still without foliage, wiry and haggard. On the other side of the migratory ruts a cedar forest began, rising dark green and majestic toward the mist-tattered highlands, where the Eyes of the Bear, the Blue Shell's ancient enemy, lived.

The wind slicing over the cliff top rattled the naked oak branches, and Timov did not have to worry about keeping quiet or even staying very far behind. He was virtually Aradia's shadow, ducking back and forth among the oaks. At the first migratory trail, she turned inland, picking her way carefully among the leafless blackberry bramble on the trail ridge. The ridge climbed toward the towering clouds, became a hill of coppery grass crowned with spires of poplar.

Crouching among the slender trees, Timov watched Aradia descend the far side of the hill toward a dark hollow of spidery trees. Beyond loomed the wind-sheened grassland, where the horse herd grazed. Now Timov advanced slowly, since somewhere around here Hamr lurked. He crawled under a soapberry bush and scanned the hollow until he found the man. He was not alone. An older man stood beside him, gesturing at the herd, obviously instructing him.

Timov, seeing that the men were intent on the horses and Aradia on Hamr, rolled out from under his cover and boldly pranced downhill into the hollow. He ran in a crouch behind the cluttered trees to outflank his sister and curled up behind a blue willow, naked of leaves but dense enough to hide him. He had gotten close enough to hear the two men talking.

"Wind'll turn before midmorning," the older man said. Timov recognized him now as Spretnak, Hamr's sponsor among the Tortoise men. Hamr's father had drowned years before, snatched away by a giant wave while harvesting urchins on the slippery rocks. "You can move in closer then."

"You sure?" Hamr looked nervous, which delighted Timov. The man had only three more summers to Timov's fourteen, but his strong cleft chin made him appear older. In the fashion of the Tortoise men, he was beardless, the hairs plucked from his face with tweezing shells. Even so, his mien was as manly as any of the full-whiskered Panther men. Timov was amused to see his dark eyes blinking anxiously above his small, hawk-bent nose, a tuft of his unbraided hair in his mouth.

"See that shear up there in the ice clouds? The sea wind is rising with the day. Probably rain late this afternoon. But it will certainly turn the wind long before midday. So be patient. Don't get any closer before then or the herd will close around him."

"Hamr." Aradia had come up behind the talking men.

Hamr took a moment to fix the cloud pattern in his

memory, then turned casually to take Aradia under his arm. His relaxed intimacy with Aradia irritated Timov.

"You shouldn't be here, Aradia," he spoke earnestly and brushed his lips against her brow, inhaling the nut-scent in her hair.

"The white cranes arrived this morning," she answered.

Spretnak greeted the young woman with an awkward nod and said to Hamr, "I'll start making my way to the other side of the grove. When the wind changes and you're ready, give your call. I'll approach the horses from the side, and they'll move away, onto the ancient path. You know what to do then. But remember, if you hear my call, run. The Eyes of the Bear are swift when they raid."

The name of their enemy pricked Timov's attention, and he cast a nervous glance to the distant hills. The Eyes of the Bear ate horses and would be very displeased to find Blue Shell taking from the herd. But neither Hamr nor Aradia seemed alarmed at that prospect. Before the old man had limped out of sight, they were hugging and cooing at each other.

"Let the horses alone," Aradia said and nibbled on his ear. "Come back with me."

Hamr caressed her neck with his lips and, ignoring her plea, picked her up and sat her on the elbow of a bent tree. "There, at the edge of the herd, you can see my horse. It's the one browsing closest to the ditch."

All the horses looked the same to Timov. They were dun-brown with creamy-white bellies, stubby tails, and bristly manes that stood straight up. The one Hamr indicated seemed to lift its head more often than the others to sniff for predators.

"Hamr, you'll never get near enough to take one," Aradia said.

"Spretnak and I have been watching them for a long time. We think—"

"Spretnak was lamed when he tried to take a horse."

"He was. But he chose the wrong horse."

"And how is yours different, Hamr?"

He smiled, sadly. "He can't see. Look at him, Aradia. He never prances like the others, and he's constantly tasting the air. He's sightless. I've named him 'Blind Side of Life.' "

Timov strained to look and saw that, indeed, the animal's eye-sockets were darker than those of the others. Hamr had found a blind horse. No wonder he was so cocky, so confident of doing what none of the other Blue Shell men had done. Blind Side of Life—what kind of name for an animal was that?

"Sightless or not," Aradia said, "you're risking your life with a beast that big. And for what if it can't see?"

"He can smell. Once I tame him, he'll help with the hunt. I'll track the biggest game. I'll bring you ivory and bear claws."

"I want only you, Hamr."

"But I want these things for you."

Aradia lost her fingers in the long hair at his shoulders. "I'm afraid for you, afraid I won't see you again. The hunt killed my father."

Hamr met her imploring gaze with his fixed expression. "You're beautiful and wise, Aradia. There are others, perhaps better than myself, for you."

Timov nodded with agreement, hoped his sister would not contradict him. She was going to speak, but Hamr lifted her off the bough and silenced her with a nuzzle. His hands unfastened the shell sash and opened the mantle she had wrapped about herself. It fell to the ground, and they began nibbling at each other.

Timov choked back a groan, then looked about for pebbles. By the time he had gathered a small handful, the lovers were naked and lying in a nest of grass between two treeroots. Mischievously, he waited until Hamr mounted her before pelting him with the sharp rocks.

Hamr slapped his stung buttocks, and jerked about with a ferocious glower and a shout.

Timov laughed like a jackal, danced briefly before them, wagging an imaginary penis, and darted away. He did not dare to glance back until he had attained the poplar grove atop the hill. Hamr and Aradia had disappeared deeper into the hollow, and he sat down to catch his breath. For a while, he stared out over the shimmering waves of grass at the horses. They seemed small and fragile among the clouds' running shadows. Soon Hamr's come-cry would spark out of the hollow, the wind would shift, and the hunt would begin. He rose and ran off to tell the others.

Spretnak had worked his way slowly through the hollow, down one side of the migratory ditch and laboriously up the other side. He sat now in the shade of a gnarly tree. His gimpy leg throbbed from the effort, but he ignored the pain. For him, this was a small sacrifice, well worth the coming joy of seeing his son ride a horse into the settlement.

It was true that Hamr was his son. But in the autumn when Hamr was born, Spretnak had been thrown from the horse he had wanted to master and had broken his leg. And though the leg had mended badly, his dream of becoming a great man had not. He could no longer hunt, fish from the dugouts, or climb the sea rocks for mussels. So instead he mended nets, studied the mysteries of the Tortoise, and gave his son to a good friend so that the boy might be reared by a whole man. He never told Hamr the truth, and the few other people who knew the truth were dead now. Yet the dream lived on and had been passed whole.

From the time Hamr was old enough to talk, Spretnak had fed him the faith that he was to be a great man. He did so quietly, secretly, only to the boy and in such a way that the boy believed this fate had risen from within him. Never telling him the words outright, he let Hamr discover for himself that he was different, able to listen deeper, run harder, eat more food and endure more pain. And, to Spretnak's satisfied amazement, the boy grew tall, strong, and certain of his fate, some would say arrogant—and even Spretnak had come to believe he was merely a sponsor to the boy's destiny.

Spretnak lifted his gaze into the wide morning sky, noticed in the clouds that the day's heat had turned the wind. Men were like the clouds, he thought, moved by invisible forces that rose out of the earth and descended from the heights. The clashing of those forces shaped men as wind shaped clouds. Great men learned to read the wind and to partake in their own shaping. No one, not even the greatest of men, could choose their way. Acceptance, and with it participation, were the only choices beyond ignorance. He thought this good. Life was simply as one found it, beautiful and terrible in its simplicity.

His thoughts were interrupted by a clattering among the briars in the trees behind him, and he twisted about in a fright, half-expecting to see rushing toward him the brawny hatchet-faced men who called themselves the Eyes of the Bear. Instead, he spotted

the glossy black wings and red legs of a chough exult-
ing in the briar over its capture of a large mudbeetle.
Spretnak blew a relieved laugh at this demonstration of
what he had been thinking: Life gave no choices to the
chough or the beetle, to the Eyes of the Bear or to him.

He nervously scanned the dark treeline that un-
dulated with the hills, saw no movement at all. A deer
or drifting wolves would have reassured him that the
woods were empty of his enemy. Now he could not be
certain. Surely, the Eyes of the Bear knew the herd was
here, since the horses had to trespass their territory to
reach this valley. He hoped that the hunters had already taken all the horsemeat they wanted.

Hamr's call warbled from across the hollow.
Spretnak pulled himself to his feet, the fright of a moment ago shifting to exhilaration. The time had come
for a lifetime of resignation to be justified. For seven-
teen years, he had trained his son for this morning,
teaching him everything he had learned from the mis-
ery of his own blunder. This time, he would see a Blue
Shell man master a horse.

He limped a short way toward the herd. When they
saw him, he stopped. He did not want to frighten them
into bunching, the mares and foals inside, the stallions
ringing them. He simply wanted to move them on their
way. They would have gone in another day or so anyway, once the grass had thinned, but better to cut out
the one they wanted now while it was still hungry so
later it could be gentled with food.

From the hill's brow, he waved his arms, and the
horses watched him. Like a slow dream, they began to
move out, drifting single file into the ditch that thousands of springs and autumns of migration had cut into
the land. They moved unhurriedly, nose to tail, occasionally glancing up at him or maybe past him to the

deep rows of cedar from where predators might descend.

Spretnak followed the herd, not close enough to spook them but sufficiently near to see that they were not tempted to clamber out of the deeply worn trail and favor themselves with the early and tender shoots of the hollow. The horse he and Hamr had selected, Blind Side of Life, marched in the middle of the herd, with the mares.

The appearance of a sightless horse two summers earlier had been accepted by Spretnak as one of those offerings by the invisible powers. Every moon since the first sighting, he and Hamr had made offerings to the Beastmaker, throwing into the ritual fires bundled grassheads, each with a seahorse at its center. Hours ago, they had shaped a tiny horse from mud. Hamr had tied a strand of his hair about the mud-steed's neck and had buried the icon on the migratory trail with only the hair sticking out, so that he would have the right to lead the horse away from the ancient path. Now if only Hamr would remember everything he had been taught. Ahead were the dunes where the horses would have to wend. Hamr would be waiting there, remembering but, at last, able only to trust himself.

Spretnak sighed deeply and slowed into the hurt of his walk. There was nothing more for him to do. At best, if all went well, he would be the secret half of a proud story. And he would spend the rest of his life accepting that—or whatever happened.

Hamr knelt at the crest of a dune alongside the trench where the horses would be passing shortly. He could see, above the coppery beach grass, the silver haze that was their dust. The haze blurred his view of the bosky hollow with Aradia at its center. Though, of course, she had left there when they had parted, gone back the way she had come, he imagined her still there. Their moment together was a perfection he did not want to let go until after this trial was over. Her love for him was the faith he needed to accomplish what before had just been a boast.

He knew the others in the tribe thought him insolent and boastful. No one would say it to his face, but he read it well enough in their measuring glances, studying him for his flaws. If he failed now, they would be happy, remembering they had gauged him a fool. And if he survived his failure, he would spend the rest of his life wintering in pain, like Spretnak.

That was the one man who believed in him, but only because he was halt and useless as a man and could no longer believe in himself. The haze rising from the herd was all the dust of the summers he had sat on the ground with Spretnak, watching him draw pictures in the dirt to illustrate his ideas of the hunt, the capture of the horse, and war. Though they were flat, the drawings were sharp and rich; horses moved, hunters ran, spears flew, and ideas took shape, so that time was no longer invisible but a line that turned back on itself and spun round through the seasons. A wheel, Spretnak had called it. He had made one once from the shell of a tortoise, put a hole in its middle and a stick through the hole and spun it round, like time, always returning to where it had begun, night to day, winter to spring. But what good was a wheel? What use did drawings in the dirt have? These were the makings of a useless man playing games. If Hamr succeeded now, Spretnak could sincerely believe all those games were more than games. The horse would make it so.

Hamr's reverie snapped as a hooting laugh

whooped overhead. He looked up, toward the seacliffs that loomed to his left on the far side of the defile, where the horses would pass—and he saw Timov, small as his toenail, staring down at him and pointing. At the boy's side, other figures stepped forward. Hamr recognized them all but fixed on one, Gobniu, the chief of the Blue Shell. The fact that he was there, summoned by a boy, meant that what was about to happen was important. Gobniu should have been with the dugouts, finding food. But he, stout and commanding even at this distance, stood there with the other men, leaning on their fishing spears, watching him.

What did they expect to see? His death or maiming, of course. None of them believed he could take a horse. Why should they believe—he was just Hamr the braggart, after all. Gobniu and the others did not like him, for he did not care to spear or net fish with the others. And though he obligingly did both every day that Gobniu called the men to the sea, he did so dreamily. Now they had gathered to see his dreams shattered.

As the first of the horses came around the bend, the men on the seacliffs frightened them, and they moved faster than he had expected. Quickly, he reviewed what he had to do. The rocks he had piled atop the dune days earlier were in place; the fishnet clotted with horse dung lay furled at his knees; his heart beat strong and calm, trusting in the clarity of his plan.

The first mares passed. He continued to lie flat on the dune, downwind and unseen by the horses, but his hand strayed toward the twined hemp that was tied to the wooden stake holding the rockpile on the crest. When he spotted Blind Side of Life following the mare ahead of him—the horse's head high to catch the scent of her, eyes sunken, the shape of the skull showing through at the sockets—Hamr jerked on the rope. The stake flew out, and the rockpile crashed into the trench, nipping the back hooves of the mare that Blind Side followed.

The mare bolted. Blind Side reared and stumbled into the rocks. The mares behind him were already up the sides of the ditch and scattering when Hamr slid down the duneface and cast the fishnet over the horse's head. The stallion reared again, but Hamr held fast to the net. As Blind Side came down, Hamr rushed forward, pulled himself up by the net onto the animal's back, and clung to its neck with all his strength.

Blind Side of Life bucked, banging his front legs among the fallen rocks. Hamr feared the creature would break its hooves or legs, but the next moment the horse was up the side of the ditch and twisting to shake him loose. A sighted horse would have rushed at full gallop down the beach, but Blind Side reared, capered, and bounded. He could hear the cries of the other horses fleeing down the strand and he sprang toward them.

On the cliff, the men howled and shouted encouragement and derision. Timov, agape at Hamr's mounting the beast, was certain he would be flung off at any instant.

The other horses had galloped out of sight, their scent thinning away in the seawind. Blind Side, frightened and confused, continued to thrash but he was tiring. Each time Hamr tried comforting noises the horse started bucking again.

Drawn by the din of screaming men, the women had hurried back from their foraging and now gazed down from the cliff. Aradia was among them, and she watched with arms outstretched, as if she could project her strength into him. She had not expected this. She had made herself believe she would care for him if he was lamed or remember him if he was killed. But this was unbearable, watching him clasping a frenzied animal fighting him across the beach.

Spretnak hobbled up the side of the ditch, and stood gaping at his son astride the stallion. Emotion welled up in him, at once proud and frightened; he had taken this wild ride once before.

Only panic kept Blind Side of Life moving finally. He heard the pounding sea very close now. A wave splashed his fetlocks, and he reared halfheartedly. There was no pain, just the weird weight of this creature holding him tight, its stink muted by the safe, good smell of the herd's droppings. The animal paused, breathing hard, now more afraid of the water sloshing around his legs than the weight on his back. He edged back onto the shore, sniffed for the herd and—frightened anew not to find any sign of the others at all—bucked again and again. Fatigue pulsed in him, and he ambled up the beach.

Hamr, his shoulders contracted with pain, his hands fused into fists on the fishnet, dared not relax. He tried gentling noises again. The horse did not object. Blind Side moved away from the pounding surf. As soon as he shuffled among the dunes, Hamr slipped off his back; the horse reared again, but Hamr held to the net still firmly wrapped about the steed's head. With the net, he gently, slowly, guided the horse among the dunes to the cliffwall. There, in a recess bounded on three sides by the cliff-face, he let the horse go.

Blind Side wandered about the enclosure. Hamr and Spretnak stood in the depressions between the dunes on the open side and made comforting noises to keep him inside. Spretnak pulled tufts of grass from the bale they had harvested the day before and scattered them in the enclosure while Hamr closed off the open side with bramble and rocks.

For a long while, the horse wandered round and round, first one way then the other, trying to find the scent of the others. They were always nearby. Where had they gone?

Gobniu and the fisherfolk were the first to climb down the clifftrails. The women hurried down after them, trilling and clicking their amazement. Gobniu clapped his big hand on Hamr's shoulder and looked up into his gleaming face. ''Don't think because of this big catch your net-fishing days are over,'' he joked, and all the men laughed and pressed forward to touch him and rub some of his lucky power into their own hands and hair. Spretnak, too, was embraced despite his protests, and the men hoisted them both into the air as the women poured off the clifftrail, shouting and laughing.

Aradia's face glowed the brightest among them. Hamr swam down from the embrace of the men and took her in his weary arms. To the excited throng, he announced, ''This woman has asked me into her family. Now that I have something more than my bare hands to give her, I gratefully accept.''

The women trilled loudly at his eloquence, and the men cheered. Even Timov, whose displeasure with Hamr had softened during the jubilant rush down the clifftrail, shrugged his acceptance and whistled with the crowd.

The noise startled Blind Side of Life as he paced back and forth in the enclosure, crying out for the herd and the freedom they had taken with them.

Purple spears of crocus pierced the meadow where the Mothers had erected the wedding bower, an arbor of alder limbs jeweled with buds like clusters of jade and hung with yellow plaits of lemon grass and seaweed in scarlet ribbons. Conch shells gaped like pink mouths at the sides of the bower. A panther-skin wrapped the bride, who otherwise was naked but for sparks of tiny red blossoms in her untressed black hair.

The bride stood alone in the bower for the last hour of night, watched over from the bluffs by the Mothers. The Mother Mysteries decreed that the women stand apart until the moon fell through her last station and the sun rose into his first. But this year, the field mice had proliferated. Swarms of them drifted like cloud-shadows in the moonlight, nibbling at whatever blossoms they could reach. So the Mothers thrashed at them with bundled switches until the last possible moment.

Alone, Aradia thought about her childhood, the playfriends she would leave behind and that lonely night long ago when she bled for the first time and was locked inside the cramped reed hut of First Blood. Hanging from the inside of the bower was the Hair of the Mother—the valerian bines, tannis roots, nettle berries, drake nuts, and strips of resin-beaded bark— whose uses she had been taught beginning that night. She reviewed each carefully, not wanting to slight any of them for fear of losing their potency. She recalled the ills and aches she had seen the medicinal plants heal in herself and in others, and as she did so, she gathered them in the bride's wallet of many pouches given her by the Mothers.

She fingered the acorn shells she implanted as cervical contraceptives, which she had been using faithfully since First Blood, and thought of the boys and men she had favored since her womanhood. There had been others before Hamr, blown off now like seedtufts into the sky.

As a girl, she remembered, she had feared Hamr. He had been a bully, always fighting and taunting the other boys, ignoring the girls. But as the two of them had grown, both had come to stand apart from the others—she by her beauty, which the tribe honored, and he by his strength, which the tribe feared. She herself had not favored him until recently. He seemed so aloof and strange, talking aloud to himself, braving seastorms when no one else would fish, as if spirits did indeed ride him. But he was too strong to be possessed. Many of the women favored him and bragged of his stamina and erotic cunning. The summer before, when she had finally mustered the courage to call him into the bushes, he had surprised her with his gentleness and his humor. They found they could play together, chasing butterflies and diving for starfish. It surprised her to find that he was still a boy in a man's body. As she put aside the acorn shells, she remembered the times he had made her laugh, which was truly why she wanted him for her own.

Last came the nuts and bark whose paste she could use to choose the gender of her children. For herself, of course, and for the Mothers, the first would be girls. But the Mothers, the oldest of them wise to the needs of the tribe above the desires of the families, had sworn her to birth at least two boys. The man she had chosen had the marks, at least superficially, of a great man, and his boy children would strengthen the hunt.

When the bride's wallet was full, Aradia trilled her beckoning cry. By now the moon neared the horizon, the first full moon after the time of equal day and night that began the season of spring in the sky. Iris light purpled the east as the Mothers began filing down from the bluffs and assembling around the bower. Aradia's mother stood behind her daughter, and Duru meticulously plucked fallen blossoms from her sister's panther wrap.

Then came the men, the hunters of the Panther cult and the far more numerous fisherfolk of the Tortoise clan. All were decked in feathers. The seal hunt had been poor this winter, so the fisherfolk as well as the hunters had killed instead many more hawks, owls, and eagles. Now they displayed their trophies in hair-crests, capes, bands around their elbows and knees.

Timov walked at the head of the Panther procession, taking Father's place, holding high a belt of white and red feathers that Father's friends had made for the bride. He presented his offering and took his place beside Duru, who thought he stood too close and gave him an elbow jab. Mother frowned at him for whining, and he glowered at Duru.

The Tortoise men carried gifts: seal furs, narwhale horns, baskets of brilliant shells, coils of edible seaweed, wet pouches of mussels—all the sea's treasures, in gratitude that their son, Hamr, had been chosen worthy of a bride.

Last of the men to arrive was Spretnak, the groom's sponsor. He hobbled proudly to the threshold of the bower and presented Aradia with a rainbow necklace of the rarest abalone shells and polished discs of sea-amber. And then, from under his tunic, an odd object, a small round plate of tortoise shell with a reed lancing the bore hole at its center. Timov had often seen Spretnak and Hamr playing with that toy, and he leaned closer to hear what the old man said. Spretnak spun the wheel as he handed it to the bride. "Give this to your husband if he should ever act childish," he said softly, for her alone to hear. "It will remind him of everything good I have taught him."

Duru shoved Timov aside to hear better, and the boy was about to step on her foot when Spretnak lifted a conch shell from the base of the bower. The old man blew long and deep before stepping back among the Tortoise men.

As the green filaments in the east brightened to red, Hamr came up from the sea. He rode Blind Side of Life, a tall, majestic shadow against the brightening sky, climbing the long trail that wound through a cleft in the giant seacliffs and trotting between the eastern knolls to the meadow, where the tribe and his bride waited. At the sight of him, the drummers in the throng beat a cadence to his advance—a new rhythm in time to the horse's stride, unheard before at any Blue Shell wedding. None among the tribe had ever seen the likes of this, and an excited murmur flashed through the gathering as he slowly approached.

In the month and five days since he had captured his horse, Hamr had lived with the animal, feeding him tender shoots, filling a large basket he had lined in octopus-skin with fresh water twice a day. For a long while he had not mounted the stallion again but instead laid blankets atop him. Slowly, as the horse had become comfortable in his presence and had begun to anticipate his feedings and the songs Hamr would sing to him, Hamr had increased the weight with rocks wrapped in pelts. Only after Blind Side came to him for his food when he called had Hamr put the rocks aside and hoisted himself onto the steed's back.

Over the last ten days, Hamr had taught Blind Side of Life to take direction from the pressure of his knees. They had wandered miles along the beach. Spretnak, too, had mounted Blind Side and at last felt animal strength muscling under him, his will melded to animal power, clopping along the firm sand, his heart mute with the wonder of his dream made real.

The horse had already worked for the tribe: Hamr had fastened a fishnet across the stallion's chest, strung braided lengths of hemp from the net, attached them to another net dropped into the bay by the dugouts, and with Blind Side's strength, had trawled to shore large caches of fish. In like fashion, they had made new tidepools by moving boulders, a labor that would have been unthinkable by men alone.

Hamr's legend was assured, and he rode proudly to his wedding. The faces, like pale petals in the early light, stared up at him in awe. He noticed all of them but acknowledged none—his attention reserved for the lone figure of his bride, who watched him with a demure joy from under the blossomy bower. Gobniu the chief did not gawk, though Hamr noticed the hard stare of amazement in his face and the nod of acknowledgment as he rode by. Hamr ignored him as he had the others. He looked down only once, when Spretnak swung into view, to stare him full in the face and receive the old man's beneficent smile and salute.

Hamr dismounted at the bower, palmed a sweetroot to Blind Side to keep him still, and joined his bride. The drum-throbbing stopped.

Duru kicked Timov, then deflected his anger by pointing behind him to an antelope pelt folded on a reed mat. He hurriedly picked it up and glared at his sister, but she held his stare easily. The antelope should have been hunted by him, the pelt flensed from the hot animal by his own flint blade. But he had no flint and had never killed anything bigger than a hare. One of Father's friends had presented the pelt and Mother and Duru had tanned and tailored it.

Timov should not even be under the bower, Duru thought. He should be with the children, except that Aradia had insisted he offer the wrap. The older sister expected some of her husband's greatness to pass to her diffident brother and, no doubt, some of Timov's idleness to pass the other way and keep her Hamr close to home.

Hamr removed the seal-fur loinwrap and jerkin and stepped out of the tortoise-leather thongs with their fishskin toppings to stand naked before Aradia. Gobniu, as head of the Tortoise clan, took the doffed garments, and Timov, as the bride's eldest clansman, offered the groom the antelope-skin. Hamr wrapped the pelt about his nakedness and fastened it with a bone clasp. At his feet, Duru placed boarskin sandals, bristles standing straight out from the straps. He stepped into them and into his new life.

The crowd broke into song, and drum flourishes and conch bleats announced the end of the wedding ceremony.

Agog with the focused excitement of the gathering, seeing as one that their lives would—again—never be the same, Timov and Duru stepped back. Father's going had weakened them all, but now Hamr's coming would give strength to everyone. They clasped hands and moved closer to Mother, to share the tribe's joy for their family.

Blind Side shuffled nervously under the burst of sound, until Spretnak gentled him with a reassuring pat at the neck and another sweetroot. Patiently, the horse hung his head and chewed the root, stopping suddenly to lift his long face. The noise had stopped. Warmth touched everything.

Hamr and Aradia embraced, and the sun cast his first light over them. Then Hamr mounted Blind Side and offered a hand to Aradia. Though Hamr had told her days before that he planned to carry her off on his horse, she hesitated. Until they wed, the Mothers, ever wary of ill-fortune, had forbidden her to ride, for there was no precedent. Better, they had reasoned, to wait until she was ritually joined to Hamr and could partake of his power. But now she felt no more powerful, and the beast looked so large and restless, its sightless sockets dark and frightening.

Hamr smiled down at her, his long hair falling past his shoulders, his eyes radiant in the first light of their first day as one. She placed her hand in his and was hoisted into his strong arms. He turned her about so she sat facing forward, scared and giddy. Awkwardly, she leaned back on him and straddled the beast, then clutched at its bristly mane. Blind Side pranced side-ways, disturbed by the unfamiliar double weight, but Hamr's hands at his neck calmed him.

Hamr leaned to the side and tugged at the stal-lion's mane to turn him around. Spretnak handed him a satchel stuffed with food and a water bladder. And then, in a graceful saunter, smelling and feeling his way, Blind Side carried the couple into the rising sun.

Hamr directed Blind Side of Life through the hum-mocks past the green-dotted hazel brambles and bud-ding thornapple shrubs, along the tall sedge margin of the bog, where spring already bloomed with churlish red flowers and white-tufted grass fluttery as feathers. On the far side of the swale, they arrived at a fern grove, where butterflies bobbled and bees hummed. Here, while Blind Side browsed happily, Hamr and Aradia spent most of the day erecting their own wed-ding bower, one sturdy enough for them to reside in while the moon waned and then grew full again. Under this roof of lashed beech branches thatched over with eelgrass slick enough to repel the spring rains, they would make their first child.

By day's end, they sat together in their hut on a mat of fern and white moss and shared the wedding food that Spretnak had gathered for them—roe kept damp in fennel grass, dried fish, a leafpouch of honey ants, and smoked seal-meat wrapped in seaweed. The last bees were lugging their amber burdens home, and the sky above the wide sward glowed with the fires that made the world.

"Now that we're married," Hamr said, "I can tell you what I've never told anyone else, not even Spretnak."

Aradia lay with her head in his lap, nibbling on a twist of dried meat, half-listening, watching Blind Side of Life shining gold under the black trees.

"I dream of the Beastmaker, Who is the Great Mother's husband and son," he began, looking at her closely. "He's entered my dreams since I was a boy."

Aradia sat up. "Hush," she said sternly. "It's not good to talk of these things."

"I want to tell you what I've seen."

"No. I don't want to hear any more."

"And why not?"

"These are secret things."

"So that is why I must tell you. The Beastmaker has shown himself to me. I've seen his hidden face. He has antlers, like an elk, and eyes like moons filled with blood. But his features are human. He has a human mouth, and he has told me secret things that I can tell you."

"I don't want to hear these things, Hamr."

"The Beastmaker says that I am to be a Beastmas-

ter, so I must know these things. And since you're my
wife, I can share them with you.''

"Don't, Hamr.''

"Why are you afraid? We're together now. I won't
let any harm come to you. The Beastmaker says we are
made from pieces of the sun. That our bones were
baked in the sun the way we bake clay in the fire. Our
blood, too, was made in the sun, for our blood grows
out of our bones. And when we die and our flesh goes
to worm-dirt, we do *not* die. We become like the sunlight, something bright and warm that we can feel but
can't hold.''

Aradia stood up. "Hamr, be quiet. If you say any
more, I'll leave.''

"But night is falling.''

"I don't care. The Great Mother does not want us
to know these secrets or they would not be Her secrets.
The Mother gives—but she also takes away. She's
given us each other. I fear if we say too much about
these things, she may take us away before our time.''

"But the Beastmaker tells me—''

"Hamr! I tell you, if you want to be mine, you must
never again speak of these things, to me or to anyone.
Do you hear me?''

Hamr stared hard at her, then nodded. Aradia visibly relaxed and knelt beside him. "Far better, my
Hamr,'' she said, removing the bone clasp from his
antelope-skin, "to live the secrets of our lives than to
talk of them.''

While the red evening climbed the sky, Hamr
kicked at a sponged log, watching the worms pearl and
shine. Aradia awaited him in their bower, but he was in
no hurry to go to her. The moon would rise late tonight,

seven nights after their first night. True to her word, she had not once wanted to hear his prayers, his thoughts, his dreams of the Beastmaker. Eating and rutting passed their nights, foraging and rutting passed their days. Playing, while they foraged and rutted and ate, was all she wanted to do. Her laughter intoxicated him, made him feel light in his bones, so he was glad to splash with her in the rivulets, to catch crickets, to couple in the mud. But that was all she wanted! Nothing was serious to her, except her hopes for their children. That he had tired of hearing about, and they had begun to quarrel, first about the Beastmaker, then about his doting on his horse. Dearly as he regarded her, there was much they disagreed about.

With a mighty blow to the dead log, Hamr kicked loose wafers of light. *Beastmaker!* he cried in his mind, not daring to speak that name aloud. Two nights ago, after overhearing him talking to the Beastmaker, she had curled up to sleep and would not let him touch her; though, the next morning she woke him by slipping a toad into his loinstrap, and laughed as if nothing had happened.

Beastmaker—what now?

The red evening climbed the sky and was gone. Frogs spat and creaked while mating. Fireflies blinked among the rushes with the cool radiance of courtship. And out of the darkness, Aradia called his name. He shrugged and turned to go to her. From shreds of clouds among the stars, a slur of rain fell, and he felt the Beastmaker's answer rise in him with the odors the earth gives the sky, *What did you think?*

"Saphead!"

Timov threw another pebble at Duru. She was supposed to be gathering dead grass for kindling, which she could do anywhere, but she insisted on doing it here, on the knoll where he had come to watch the hunt. "Get lost, Toad. You're a girl. You're not supposed to watch. You want to kill him?"

Duru made an ugly face. "You're mad because you can't hunt. You're still a boy—Saphead."

"Get out of here." He threw several more pebbles, harder, driving his sister into the tall grass at the toe of the knoll. Soon as she was out of sight, he peered down the knoll through a stand of green-budded trees to the far end of the bright meadows, where Hamr and some of the Panther men had taken the hunt. They were just visible at the shimmery edge of the canebrake, lazy clusters of men slouching on their spears. They had been waiting there since midday, when Hamr and Blind Side of Life had entered, following a trail beaten down by a large boar.

From his vantage, Timov could see Hamr pacing back and forth through the clacking husks of last season's growth, his head just visible above the green furls of the young plants. The boar he stalked moved invisibly among the traps and obstacles of the sedge. Father's friends called out advice from the branches of overlooking trees when they spotted it. Other hunters, returning with fallow deer slung between them and a dozen hares strung on a spear, jeered.

Timov gloated with relief that he was not Hamr, hot with mosquito bites, icy with fear, tensely reading the shadows for sharp tusks and a bristly stare. When he became a hunter, he would go with the other men, after hare and deer. Why had Aradia married this reckless showoff? Each time Timov ran back to the summer camp for a drink and a snack of nutmash or salted fish, he found her cool as a berry, helping the other women skin the animals their men had brought in. Not once did she ask how the hunt went. He wanted to tell her she should be worried: The hunt had gone on too long, the horse would be tired, the boar enraged. But her gaze kept slipping off his.

Father had died on the hunt—slain by the Boar. Now Hamr would die. Timov felt the certainty of it. This was not a time of boldness but of common sense. Hamr had defied common sense too long. His time was up. Grimly, Timov watched as Hamr's shadow drifted back and forth through the field. Every now and then, one of Timov's friends, the sons of men who had returned to camp with prey, whistled, wanting to catch his attention and wag proudly. He ignored them, and wondered what they would think when they saw him smiling at Hamr's funeral.

The boar crashed through the canes and burst into the field of marshgrass. The hunters who had gathered there—young men drafted by the Bride-Father's friends to help the newcomer—were chatting wearily about the deer and the many hares the other hunters had caught. When the bristling, humpbacked swine, big as three men, charged toward them, they scattered in a panic. Shouting confused orders at each other, they quickly regrouped, however, spears lowered, to block the giant boar's escape.

Hamr charged out of the canebrake in time to see the boar turn sharply before the jabbing spears and bolt for a gap that the clustered men had left at their flank. He kicked Blind Side to a dash, and the sightless horse lurched forward a few quick strides, enough to reach spear-range. Hamr threw his spear underhand,

and it struck the boar's back but lacked the force to pierce vitally.

Hurt and infuriated, the boar turned, tried to shake the spear loose, then heaved itself toward the horse that had dared to hurt it. Hamr stiffened with alarm, and Blind Side, feeling his fear and hearing the enraged squealing, skittered nervously. By scent and sound, he measured the boar's lunging attack and reared as its tusks thrust for his front legs.

Hamr, unprepared for the boar's assault, lost his grip on Blind Side and went flying. The sedge grass softened his fall, and he sat up in time to see the boar bearing down on him, head lowered, tusks glowing with dawnlight. His provision sack had fallen beside him, and he clutched it desperately, knowing it was a useless gesture but unable to stop himself. Above the grass, he saw the heads of the hunters and their spears, too far away to help him. Grunting with fury—the impaled spear waving from its back—the boar flashed toward him. The wisp of a scream squeaked in Hamr's throat.

Blind Side trotted into view, reared up, thrashing the air with his front legs, and came down on the angry noise in the grass, striking the boar's skull with his hooves. The beast collapsed with a squeal, and lay unmoving. Blind Side backed away and ambled off as the hunters rushed toward him. Their spears stabbed at the boar, but it was already dead.

Breath gushed into Hamr's lungs, and he got to his feet. He waved the hunters off, looking down at the still boar and the socket of blood above its eye, where Blind Side's hoof had crushed its skull. Its legs stuck straight out from its thick black bulk. Its dark lips revealed sharp teeth set in a permanent snarl, and its tusks gleamed. Its rage still rang in Hamr's ears.

He thumped it hard, but it lay still. The men had begun to apologize for not killing the creature as it came out of the canebrake. Hamr silenced them with a hard stare. "Truss it," he told them, and pulled his spear from its back.

Blind Side had drifted to the firmer land above the sedge. Hamr called to him, and he reluctantly stepped back onto the softer ground and came, head waving side to side, smelling for more danger. Hamr rewarded him with several sweetroots from his sack and whispered his gratitude in the horse's ear.

Burnt umbers of cloud released a soft rain as the trussed boar was dragged through the tall grass and over the hummocks toward the Blue Shell's summer camp above the seacliffs. Hamr had tied the rope about his waist.

The dead weight of the beast pulling behind him as he clung to Blind Side was his own death. He had died back there in the sedge. His soul had squeaked in his throat on its way out. But the Beastmaker had forced his soul back into him and had saved him from the boar by the power of the Horse. The other hunters had seen it. He heard them muttering among themselves as they walked behind him. Blind Side of Life was Hamr's soul-animal. They were one life in two forms. The Beastmaker had joined their souls, fused them together in the space where Hamr would have died, and made them one.

At the Blue Shell camp, the hunters spoke excitedly to the others about what they had seen. The whole tribe gathered to view the boar. Even the fisherfolk climbed up the clifftrails from their summer beach camp to see the fierce creature Hamr had killed with his horse. It was a huge boar, big enough to provide some meat for each of the families.

The tusks, of course, belonged to Hamr. He promptly gave them to his wife; it caused a stir among the Panther men who had expected him to honor their cult with the trophy. But Hamr was more intent on securing his marriage than his rightful place in the Panther cult. During their moon together in the fern holt, he and Aradia had often quarreled. She had been continually annoyed with him for spending time with his horse. He had tried to explain to her that Blind Side of Life had never been separated from him since the fateful day that he had ridden the wildness out of the animal and made him his own. They were to be thought of as one—a thought that repelled Aradia. She sharply informed him that she had married Hamr and not his horse. Time and again she made her displeasure apparent by refusing to ride with him. When he had gone ahead and ridden without her, she wandered off alone, and once he spent the better part of a day looking for her, only to find her in a tree near their bower, weeping disconsolately. On their return from the fern holt, Aradia had walked and, not wanting to enrage her, Hamr had walked too, leading Blind Side with a rope around his neck.

Now that the entire tribe had acknowledged the soul-bond of Hamr and his steed, Aradia could no longer object to the attention her husband lavished on his horse. The tusks mollified her somewhat, for with them came a great deal of prestige within the tribe, especially among the Mothers. The tusks were shaped like the crescents of the New and Old Moons, and the Mothers proudly installed them behind the Throne of the Elder, with the blessings of the Great Mother redounding to Aradia. Surely, now her childbearing would be easier and her children would be great souls.

After that, Aradia was more tolerant of Hamr's

doting care of Blind Side of Life. She even took time to help prepare the horse's daily feed, sifting through the sheaves of wild barley and oats for strands of milkweed and thorngrass. When Hamr went riding, she was content to see him go and to attend to her duties as a Young Mother, for the first signs of pregnancy had already appeared in her.

Her younger sister, Duru, eager to learn the Mother mysteries, shadowed her everywhere. Except when her new brother, Hamr, let her ride with him. Unlike Aradia, she enjoyed riding, feeling the muscular strength under her, smelling the good animal heat. She was always the first to greet Hamr each day when he returned from his time with the men, and he always pleased her by taking her on a slow circuit about the camp.

Timov watched with feigned indifference from behind the hut, where he and the slave Biklo gathered kindling for the night-fire. Timov, amazed that Hamr had not died hunting the boar, began to believe that the hunt was not all common sense. He began resenting the time that Hamr spent with Duru. She was a girl and belonged with the Mothers. He, however, needed a sponsor to be initiated among the Panther men. But Hamr could not be his sponsor until he himself had been initiated, which would not happen until Hamr had crafted the pelt of the boar he had killed into a ceremony-vest. And the more time he spent amusing Duru, the less time for him to work on the vest, which he alone could do.

Hamr knew that Timov was anxious to be free of the women and to join the men, but his time with Duru was important for him. Soon after his father had drowned, his mother had chosen another man among the Tortoise men, a man who had insisted that the young Hamr leave his mother's clan and join the men in the dugouts. Hamr had never liked the dugouts, where the men had to work together closely to spear and net fish, gossiping and joking the whole time and not at all interested in his dreams. He had much preferred being alone, lifting rocks for hours on end, trying to pack their strength into his muscles, running all day between dunes and sea, fitting the wind itself to his breath, or, if he had to work, wading through the tidepools collecting mussels and seaweed with the women, who sang their songs and left him to ponder the thoughts Spretnak had taught him and to dream of how he would become a great man. His time with Duru reminded him of those earlier days, when the women had given him the chance to think about the Beastmaker and the ways of power. When he rode with her, he felt free of the Panther men's judgments and Timov's expectations.

Still, every night, no matter how tired he was from accompanying the men on their hunts, Hamr worked on the boar hide. He chewed the margins, where the bristles had been plucked, gnawing the boarskin to leather. He pierced the softened hide with a bone-awl to stitch feathers and shells to the edge with plant fiber.

Timov helped him in the only way he could, by talking with him to help pass the time. He talked about how many birds-of-prey he had killed at winter's end and boastfully displayed the feathers. And he observed how, without the birds to eat them, there were many more mice and hares for him to kill with his slingshot. He had achieved skill with the sling, and he related the tales of his rabbit hunts with his friends.

Hamr smiled to himself as he chewed the leather and stitched the white owl's feathers to the boarskin's edge. Last season, Timov had hated him for being a pompous fool. The whole tribe had thought him an intimidating bully. And now here he was, crafting his ceremony-vest, his wife proud to be growing her first child for him, Gobniu, the chief, so envious of his power he was glad Hamr had married out of the clan. The boys who had feared him and mocked him behind his back were now avid to win his attention. Everything had changed for the better in his life. Just as Spretnak had promised, the wheel had turned. He had turned the wheel of his life himself, by his own dream and his own bravery.

And all this bounty he now enjoyed—sitting here by a Panther cult fire, the Panther women feeling safe to have him near, the Panther men pleased to consider him their own—all this he enjoyed because his life had once had a hole in it, an emptiness, a lack of greatness into which he could fit an axle that had let him turn his life around. That axle, Blind Side of Life, had filled his emptiness, had made him whole.

Later, when his jaws and fingers ached from his work on the boarskin, when the fire dimmed and the old woman fire-watcher was wakened to attend the embers through the night, he got up, as he always did, and went out to where Blind Side of Life was tethered to a stake. Together, in the underworld of darkness beneath the floating river of stars, they comforted each other: Hamr with sweetroots and a quiet song for the horse, and Blind Side with his sleek, shouldering power-body that the Beastmaker had lifted up from the earth for the man.

◆ 2 ◆
The Doom of the Blue Shell

Hamr and Spretnak sat on the slipface of a dune, gazing at the moonless night, a black snake glittering over the candescent breakers. For a long while they said nothing, simply shared the pleasure of watching Blind Side of Life facing into the salt wind and blowing sighs from the verge of sleep.

Presently, the old man broke the susurrant silence: "You know this'll be the last time I can talk to you about the wheel. The coming moon will see the longest day. And now that your ceremony-vest is finished, the Panther men will make you one of their own."

Hamr agreed with a nod, not sure what to say.

"Your ties to the Tortoise clan will be broken. If they catch us talking about our mysteries, they'll think you're divulging their secrets. Men get nasty when they think their secrets are betrayed. So we won't be talking anymore." Spretnak shook his head remorsefully, muttered, "Secrets. What else makes us important? We're such pitiful creatures." His chest rattled with a deep laugh that constricted to a cough. "Only the animals have real secrets, eh?'' He nodded toward where Blind Side had turned his back to the wind and drowsed. ''How's your animal?''

''He's fine. Caught a burr in his left hind hoof four days ago and hobbled for a day after that. But the Mothers made up a nettle mudpack that healed it almost overnight. He's himself again.''

''And Aradia? You treating her as well as your horse?''

Hamr's sudden smile flashed in the dark. ''Since the boar, she considers Blind Side of Life one of the clan.''

''The Panther men were unhappy you gave the tusks to the Mothers. That's why they made you chew leather. You don't need a ceremony-vest. They've initiated boys of fifteen summers with no vest, just a two-point antler. And you've killed Boar.''

''I had to give the tusks to Aradia. Blind Side had come between us, and she was telling me to go rut my horse. Now a night doesn't go by she doesn't favor me.''

''My gimp leg spared me the blessings of a wife. But from my younger days, I remember how cunningly they use our need to fulfill their own. Surely, the Mother is Great.''

Laughter swept the two men, and Spretnak curled up on himself in a fit of hacking coughs.

''You're not well,'' Hamr said, steadying the old man with an arm about his shoulders.

Spretnak answered through a gasp, ''Forty-three winters.'' He rubbed his face with both hands. ''I've lived long enough to see you become a Great Man. I'm ready to die.''

''It's just a muscle chill. The Mothers will heal you.''

"There's no healing at my age, Hamr. Be great while you're young. There's no greatness in growing old."

"Let's go to the fire and warm up."

"You're a Panther man now. You can't sit by a Tortoise fire."

"I'll take you there. You need to warm up."

"No." He laid a firm hand on Hamr's shoulder, felt the muscled strength there and nodded to himself with pride. "There's something more of the wheel I must tell you."

"You can tell me later. First let's warm you up."

"There may not be another chance. If I've done well by you, then listen to me now." He paused, searching for the strength to speak, then began with the cadence of an oft-told tale, "At night, in the spring of every fifth summer, the tortoise climbs out of the sea to lay her eggs . . ."

Hamr laid the old man back against the dune. The younger man took off his antelope-hide tunic and draped it over Spretnak. Then he lay down beside him and listened to the story he had heard many times before, of the wheel of life, of turning seasons and returning stars, and animals journeying endlessly around the wheel of their migrations.

While Spretnak recounted the mysteries of the wheel, Hamr explored the old man's face. Clouds hooded the stars and the wind uncovered them again, drifting starlight and darkness across the familiar features and highlighting characteristics Hamr had never noticed in brash daylight. The old man's squared-off temple bone and the mating of nosebridge to the overhang of brow looked suddenly very similar to what he had seen of his own face in rainpools and the black reflections of volcanic glass. A soundless joy swelled up in him at the thought that this man could be his father.

He dismissed the thought with a frowning flinch and gazed up at the spectral sky. He was just seeing his wish. The man had been as a father to him, not only sponsoring him in the clan and transmitting the mysteries, but also wanting more for him than the drudgery of the dugouts and the fishing nets. Spretnak had remembered the Grandfathers, who had ridden horses. They had reared them from foals captured from the herd. But that was no longer possible, not since the Eyes of the Bear had settled close to the Blue Shell. The Eyes of the Bear ate horses; they believed the Blue Shell were stealing the food of their children. It had been Spretnak's vision to tame a grown horse.

Hamr returned his attention to the old man and noticed he was shivering as he spoke: "Men, too, turn with the wheel, just like and yet different from women, animals, and stars. Women turn from blood to blood to make their children, the animals turn from north to south to make the herds and flocks, and the stars turn through the sky to make the seasons. Men turn, too, but what turns us is invisible. Not blood, not direction nor season. The invisible power that turns us is destiny. And because it is invisible, most men ignore their destiny, are not even aware they have a destiny. It turns them old—otherwise it does nothing for them."

"You're shivering, old guy. Come on, let's go get warm." Hamr pulled Spretnak till he sat upright, then wrapped the antelope-skin full about him.

"Listen, Hamr—destiny is never chosen. It can only be recognized, then accepted. You must see that your destiny is to serve the Beastmaker."

"I understand, old man. Let's go."

"Wait." Spretnak put his hands to the sides of

Hamr's thick neck. "You must be equal to the silence to meet Him. We all meet Him in death. But to meet Him in this life, you must be equal to the silence from which we have come and to which we go. This is the final mystery I have called you here to tell you. Whoever speaks of the Beastmaker, speaks lies. Only silence carries His power. Tell no one what He reveals to you. Destiny is invisible. It can never be spoken. It can only be lived." Spretnak coughed violently, shuddered with his eyes squeezed closed. "Now take me to the fire. The damp is in my bones."

Hamr hoisted Spretnak to his feet. What the old man had just told him, it paralleled what Aradia had said the first night of their marriage, when he had tried to share his vision of the Beastmaker.

This insistence on silence troubled Hamr. He wanted to talk about how the bloodnoise in his ears sometimes spoke to him, how the busy darkness behind his closed lids sometimes made scenery, a lavish landscape of red earth and fat leaves and an oily sky of swirling rainbows—and sometimes out of that mischief behind his lids, he saw the Beastmaker with His wide antlers and moon-eyes filled with blood and His black elk shanks and hooves holding erect a manbody, a manface, packed with muscle, yet bright, carefree, a deity with a laugh in his heart.

The edict of silence left Hamr with a weight of longing, a frustrated need to boast and to share both the wonder and the fear of his vision. At the edge of the Tortoise camp, where the dogs barked at them, they embraced, and Hamr defeated the urge in him to ask Spretnak to explain his vision.

"You'll be the best of the Panther men," Spretnak said, "so long as you live what you dream."

The old man turned, shuffled toward the wincing campfires, and left Hamr alone in the darkness.

Though Hamr yearned to boast, he had little time to be troubled by Spretnak's insistence that he be silent about his visions. His childhood days had ended when he captured Blind Side of Life. Now he was far too busy laboring for his rightful place in the tribe to make fireside chat about his dreams. Besides hunting with the Panther men, tending his horse, and spending time with his wife and her family, there was fighting to plan.

Each year, at the height of the spring mussel-harvest, the Eyes of the Bear raided the Blue Shell, marching down from the cedar forest to meet the Blue Shell men among the dunes. Atop a dune selected for its majesty, the Blue Shell chief left a cache of mussels, pelts, and shells. If the Eyes of the Bear were satisfied with the offering, they took it and left. If not, they attacked the Blue Shell men on the beach, striving to reach the Tortoise camp where they burned the huts and stole women and children. On the way back to the cedar forest, they did the same to the Panther camp in the fields above the seacliff.

Seven summers had passed since the Eyes of the Bear were dissatisfied with the offering. Then, Hamr's mother and sisters had been among those carried off. Hamr had not yet been made a man then, but he had sworn he would never allow the Blue Shell to suffer that way again.

At the council held on the first evening of the new moon, the night before the Eyes of the Bear would come down from their forest camp, Gobniu reviewed the offering. The mussel trove was bountiful, kept alive in nets left in the tidepools. But the seal-fur bundles were small, since the seals had beached farther north than usual this past winter. The feather-sprays from the birds-of-prey that had been taken in place of the seals seemed less impressive than the usual pelt-bundles.

''We must prepare to fight,'' Gobniu announced.

Murmurs of agreement seethed from the circles of men surrounding the council fire. They were not far from the Tortoise camp but hidden by dunes, where the women could not hear their deliberations. The initiated men composed three circles, the inner one Panther men, the outer ones Tortoise. On the flanks of the surrounding dunes, the uninitiated men sat, Hamr among them. Not long ago, he had been a part of the Tortoise circles, and he felt odd to be excluded from this important council. He sat farthest from the others, where he could be near his horse, whom he had tethered to a ghostly log of driftwood.

Patiently Hamr listened to the men plan their defense; but inwardly he squirmed. When he closed his eyes, he saw the luminous face of the Beastmaker, a tender smile beneath the terrible moons of his eyes. Little skulls hung around his neck, human skulls clicking against each other with a sound like a cricket's chirping. He understood: The dead belonged to the Beastmaker. He opened his eyes and saw the heads of the men bobbing as they schemed to defend themselves. But there was no defense. All fury was false. All fear was false. Only a man's destiny was true, and it could not be seen, touched, or talked about, only lived.

Then he noticed that among the men, near where he once sat as an initiated Tortoise man, one was gazing directly at him. It was Spretnak, huddled in a woolly hide, his pallid face drawn and intent. He nodded once and looked away.

Hamr took the old man's cue and stood up, speaking loudly enough to be heard above the mutterings in the fire-circle: "There is no defense."

The men fell silent for a moment, saw who was speaking, then muttered their protests. Gobniu quieted them, addressed Hamr: "You are not free to speak, Hamr. You're here only to witness. The initiated men alone may counsel the tribe. Be silent, listen, and learn."

"I'll say only this," Hamr said again, louder than before. "There is no defense. You know the Eyes of the Bear will attack tomorrow. I say, there is no defense. Let's attack them first."

Deploring groans and shouts erupted from the gathering. Gobniu again quieted the men, and stood for a silent moment regarding the defiant youth. "You speak from outside the circle, Hamr. You speak without experience. Be silent or be removed."

"Not long ago, I sat in the circle. My advice was good then."

Gobniu scowled at him. "You were a Tortoise man then. Until the Panther men initiate you, be a good boy, Hamr, and sit down. I swear, I'll drag you out of here myself if you say one more word."

Hamr sat down. A few mocking hoots sounded from the circle, with some snickers from the uninitiated men; and then the deliberations continued. But Hamr was not silent in himself. Since he knew his destiny was to attack the Eyes of the Bear, he planned the best way to do that, mentally preparing himself to die as a lone warrior.

The next day, as the men arranged the offering atop the most noble of the dunes, Hamr groomed Blind Side of Life. Timov, who had sat beside him at the council gathering and had laughed into his hand when Gobniu rebuked him, went with Biklo to fill the water-gourds, so as to avoid Hamr and not have to see his humiliation. After the gathering, Timov's friends, who had been silent about Hamr since he had become a horseman, jeered at Timov: "Are you going to lead the attack with Hamr?" Now he wanted to help somehow, but he was afraid Hamr would guffaw at him.

From the rill where they gathered their water, Timov and Biklo saw the Eyes of the Bear emerge from the shadows of the cedar forest. Forty men moved casually down the slopes and across the migratory gullies toward the beach. They carried spears and axes.

Timov ran far ahead of the aged and half-blind Biklo, shouting to warn the others. But the sentinels on the clifftop had already seen them. Abalone shells flashed the warning to where Gobniu stood with the elders before the offering. The chief reviewed the stack of pelts and feather-displays and the seaweed-swathed baskets of mussels, then turned and made certain the men he had positioned among the dunes were not visible. A spearhead appeared here and there, and he shouted orders for those men to lower their weapons until the attack began.

As the Eyes of the Bear approached the beach, they began to prance truculently, jeering at the Blue Shell's uninitiated men, who had gathered on the clifftrails to watch. Gobniu and the elders had retreated from the offering dune and stood before the tribe's dugouts, where their weapons were hidden. None of the Forest tribe directly mocked Gobniu, though as they mounted the dune to claim their prize, they stared with scorn at the chief and his men.

At the crest of the dune, the Forest men picked over the offering. Holding up the few seal-pelts they kicked the rabbit hides and feather bundles into the sand with disdainful shouts. Other Forest men below the dune brandished their weapons as their leaders with angry cries proclaimed their dissatisfaction.

The Blue Shell elders drew together behind Gobniu. "Out to sea with you," the chief ordered. Several of the men responded instantly, and shoved their dugouts into the waves. Those who remained took their fishing spears from their dugouts and lined up firmly at the chief's side. He nodded his approval, prepared to give the signal that would bring forth the men he had hidden among the dunes.

The sight of the fleeing elders and the appearance of fishing spears incensed the Eyes of the Bear. Angry yells from atop the dune began the attack. Screaming their battle cries, the Forest men charged down the dune and across the beach toward the dugouts.

Gobniu gave his signal, snatching his fishing spear and battle ax from behind his dugout. The Eyes of the Bear did not falter when the sand hills around them suddenly bristled with spears. They had expected this, for this was what had happened seven springs earlier. The Blue Shell were great fisherfolk, but the Eyes of the Bear were hunters and accustomed to coordinating themselves to take down large prey. While the fisherfolk attacked haphazardly, from every direction, with varying courage and ferocity, the hunters had bunched into battle groups, backs to one another, moving as one.

The fiercest of the Blue Shell were the first to engage the enemy, and the first to fall. They knocked spears with the invaders and hacked with their axes. But while each of these vehement warriors engaged one hunter, the other Forest men at his side closed in. They clubbed and speared the courageous Blue Shell, while his companions yelled with dismay from a distance.

Gobniu and the fighting elders, with their dugouts

between them and the invaders, shouted for their laggard spearmen to press harder. Some responded, and were cut down. Most bawled with anger and fear, threw their spears futilely, and backed away out of spearthrust.

Timov and the other uninitiated men hurled rocks from the seacliff, but they were too far to be effective. Though the battle had raged for only moments, six Blue Shell lay dead and not even one Forest man was injured. The rout was nearly complete. Only Gobniu and the handful of courageous elders stood between the Eyes of the Bear and the shore camp.

Timov looked for Hamr to share his grief: Mother, Aradia, and Duru were in the field camp above the cliffs, which would be the second objective of the victorious Forest men. What could they do? But Hamr was gone. Timov scanned the clifftrails and could find no sign of him. The other boys on the cliff with him had clearly not seen him, either; their faces, wrought with desperation, were fixed on the slaughter below, fearfully anticipating the plunder to come.

Hamr had not waited for the attack. He knew it was certain. As soon as the Forest men reached the shore, he had led Blind Side of Life away from the steep clifftrails and down the long path in the cleft of the rockwall, reaching the dunes as the fighting began. He had seen all this before, when he was a boy and had stood, like Timov, with the other boys on the clifftrails and had watched the slaughter and the plunder. The fisherfolk and the handful of Panther men had behaved then just as now: The brave died swiftly, the others screamed, danced, and wept. Soon, the chief and his elders would flee in their dugouts, and the women and young children would be taken, the huts would burn, and the invaders would make their way laughing up the trails to the Panther camp.

But before that happened, the Eyes of the Bear would have to kill him. Hamr had no doubt he would die now. Forty hunters, used to slaying and eating horses, would make quick work of him and his blind steed—but he well remembered what he had seen seven springs ago: He knew the leaders by the bear-claws they wore at their shoulders; he was determined to kill at least one of them before his destiny was fulfilled.

As Hamr had foreseen, Gobniu, recognizing that the battle was lost, heaved his spear uselessly against his attackers and rushed with his dugout into the waves. No one pursued him but his own elders. The few who remained behind were quickly slain. With a triumphant howl, the Eyes of the Bear lifted their spears to the sky and marched boisterously down the beach to claim their prizes. From the camp ahead came the shrill wails of the women.

Hamr, mounted on Blind Side of Life, had loaded his slingshot and hoisted his fishing spear. He would not see the women taken. He would return first to the Beastmaker. Goading his steed with his heels, though his insides churned with fear, he went forward to complete his destiny.

The carousing Forest men pulled up short at the sight: a horse mounted by a man! Some were confused by what they saw, thinking this was one beast, a horrific fusion of man and horse. Most were simply awed. Well they knew the wildness of Horse, and thus assumed a great spirit power was possessed by this man who rode one. But the leaders felt only anger that anyone—or anything—would dare block the way to the prizes they had won with blood.

Blind Side had often ridden on this shore, and he recognized the firm sand footing and the lapping whisper of lowtide. The driftwood would be higher on the beach and the way ahead clear; when Hamr signaled him to go forward, the horse did not hesitate. He liked to run when he was sure he would not trip.

The Eyes of the Bear, astounded and befuddled, scattered before him. Only the leaders stood fast, spears raised, shouting for the others to come back.

Hamr pointed his charge directly at the men with the bearclaws at their shoulders. He slowed Blind Side when he was within slingshot range, then let fly his rock. The missile arced true, and struck one of the bearded men in his eye, felling him. The others cried out, aghast.

Eager to meet his death—and be done with the fear twisting in him—Hamr urged Blind Side forward again, pressing him to run. The horse lurched forward but, hearing the alarmed cries of the Eyes of the Bear, faltered and stopped. Two spears slashed through the space where he would have been. Hamr snatched one of them from where it stood straight up in the sand and trotted the reluctant Blind Side toward his enemy.

The Forest men who had thrown their spears attacked, battle axes whirling over their heads, screaming doom at the man-horse. Hamr returned their cry, lying flat against Blind Side's neck, both spears thrust forward, kicking hard at the ribs of his animal, expecting him to rear at any instant.

Alarmed by Hamr's yelling and kicking, Blind Side abruptly leaped forward. The unexpected rush caught the attackers head on, and impaled one of them on a spear that snapped in half with the impact. The collision startled Blind Side; he reared, sending the second attacker staggering backwards. Hamr clung to his steed with his one free hand and heaved his spear at the easy target below him. The spear pierced the hunter's chest, and he fell thrashing into the sand.

Amazed, Hamr hugged Blind Side's neck, and the horse sidestepped nervously until he felt the sea sloshing at his legs. The Eyes of the Bear, anguished at the swift deaths of their leaders, were fleeing toward the dunes. Now the Blue Shell pursued; two more of the Forest men were speared before the others disappeared into the ravines that led back toward the cedars.

Hamr watched, suddenly very far away. He sat tall on his horse and gazed out on the world as though he had never seen it before. The joy in his people's faces and their jubilant cries were new. Dunes dazzled, the sea's dark body gleamed, grasses bowed shyly beside the bodies of the men who would have killed him—and, experiencing all this, he felt he understood now the ancient stories of men returning from the dead. With his legs, he hugged Blind Side, until he felt again the immediate strength of his life. All his fear had passed and had left him pure, possessed of a divine secret, a holy simplicity only he could bear within himself: He *was* alive and he knew fear—yet he also knew, with utter certainty now, he was not afraid of death.

The Blue Shell who had chased off the enemy returned jubilantly to the beach, followed by the boys from the clifftrails. But their laughter died off at the sight of their own dead. Gobniu and his elders, humiliated to have fled before the fight was done, wore baleful expressions. Hamr walked Blind Side to the dugouts and dismounted. Gobniu surveyed the dead, and refused to meet his stare. But the others gazed admiringly at him. Today his legend had become secured. He would be remembered for generations to come. He was not yet initiated among the Panther men, but he was already a Great Man.

Timov recognized the pride flushing Hamr, and expected to hear his customary boast. But when Hamr did speak, it was merely to name those who had died. The initiated men shouldered around him, to touch him, to take some of his power, and the uninitiated men grinned and gaped at him, wanting to look into his eyes and gain his favor. When the women came, they threw red seaweed on him and on Blind Side, the emblem of the hero, and sang his name loudly.

Aradia knelt before him to the cheers of the women and the gasps of the men. Women knelt only before the chief, and then just on the most sacred of the men's ritual nights. But Hamr knelt beside her, and the men laughed with relief.

The tribe's reprieve from defeat had been so unexpected and unprecedented that at first no one knew what to do. Then one of the elders called for the heads of the enemy to propitiate their fallen comrades.

The Blue Shell men paraded the heads of the Eyes of the Bear over the bodies of their own fallen. This was a rite the women were not to witness. Those mothers, wives, and daughters who had lost men in the battle gathered around Hamr and Blind Side, expecting to be escorted back to the camp to the joyful singing of the others. But this was a prerogative that belonged to the chief. Hamr looked to Gobniu. The chief met his proud stare unsteadily, and waved him off. "Our dead must be honored. Take the women away."

This was a concession to Hamr's greatness, for the chief belonged to the living and never tended the dead. Today, however, the chief had gone to the sea, believing the battle was lost. He had abandoned the women; they would not forgive him for that. He had no choice

now but to tend the dead like a common man, or to
return to the camp and be mocked by the women.

As the women marched off with Hamr and his
horse, their elated trills ringing off the seacliffs, Gobniu watched after them. Timov and the others observed
his face darkening. When he turned toward them, they
hastened to busy themselves with the dead.

"You," Gobniu's stern voice cracked the air over
Timov. "You're from the Great Man's family. You
wash the dead. That'll give them some honor."

Timov hurried to obey, though fear of the dead
rippled through him. The bodies had been stripped,
their wounds laid bare. Timov's breath tightened in
him at sight of the punctured flesh clotted with gore,
and the skulls bashed in, bonechips and bluewhite
brains frothy with blood. Gobniu signed for the other
men to move aside, and Timov was left alone to wash
out the wounds and pack them with seaweed.

Even in his glory, Hamr was causing trouble for
Timov. As a braggart fool whom his sister loved, he had
made Timov the butt of endless mockery. Then as a
horseman, he had favored Duru as much as himself,
and retarded his initiation as a Panther man. And now
this, a job that normally all the men would share,
spreading the possibility of spirit attack among them.
Surely, he would be possessed now, and he whimpered.

Gobniu barked at him to take more care, to accord
due respect to each of the corpses. Hurriedly, the other
men gathered driftwood to build deathrafts, hoping to
avert the chief's wrath. But Gobniu ignored them. It
was Hamr he hated and Timov was as close as he could
get to him—for now.

◆   ◆   ◆

A scream, shrill with evil, pierced the night.

A child had died. The ululating wail of the Mothers announced that to the tribe. By the wail's length and tone, everyone knew that the dead child was a daughter of the Panther cult. The wail repeated, slicing the night with its horror, until the elder women, the guardians of the Great Mother's mysteries, arrived. It was a long climb for the two women the Tortoise clan sent: Their gourd lanterns winked like fireflies on the clifftrails a long time before they reached the high camp. Before dawn, their sparklights flickered back down the trails, bearing the news of what they had witnessed to the other Mothers.

The dead girl had fevered the day that the Eyes of the Bear attacked, and she had died two nights later. None of the Panther Mothers' herb infusions or root broths had been able to quell the fire in her frail body. Hardened lumps had appeared under her arms and jaw that did not respond to the leafmash plasters strapped to her.

By the morning after her death, two more children and three adults among the Panther clan had also fallen ill. One of them was Duru, another Biklo.

Timov crouched over the old slave, where he lay under an acacia bush near the kindling pile. He had thought he would still be able to do his chores during his illness. He had been ill before and had worked. But this time was different. His body felt like a winter tree, empty of ambition, rattling in a wind reaching down from the cold heavens. Timov tried to soothe him with a twigfire and a wad of gum from the poplar, to dull the pain in his joints. But the fire's warmth gave no more strength than moonlight to Biklo, and his jaw ached too sharply to chew the medicinal gum.

When Biklo struggled to rise, to gather the day's

kindling and string the water-gourds, Timov laid him back down. The boy sorted the firewood in sight of the slave, so he could correct Timov's blunders, keeping the sweetwood for the braising, the slowburning hardwoods for the nightfires, the various barks with their differing scents separated to grace the unique stations of the day.

With palsied fingers, Biklo showed Timov the correct way to string the water-gourds, and Timov's eyes clouded with tears to see the slave's eagerness still to serve. While Timov was hauling water from the rill, Biklo stopped resisting the snow-wind churning in him; he convulsed violently, shaking new budded leaves from the acacia. When Timov returned, Biklo was dead.

None of the women wailed for the slave. Only Timov wept, remembering how often he had relied on the old man's spirited willingness. He wanted to go to the cliffedge and shout the man's death to the tribe. But Duru was dying. She needed the water he had hauled.

Had the spirits of the war dead, whom he alone had washed, come back to kill those he loved? Then why was he not ill? And why had the girl he did not know that well died? Clearly, something evil was happening.

In the summer Timov slept outdoors like the rest of the men. When the old women wanted him to pleasure them, they made a place for him in the bushes. He never entered the thatched huts in which the women dwelled during the warm months. But now he was needed to fulfill Biklo's chores, and one of those was carrying water into the huts.

Soon as he entered the hut where Duru lay, he smelled death, like scorched feathers or charred insects. He put the water-gourd down, wanting to back out right away. But the sight of his sister fixed him. She gleamed like a spring toad, her naked body glossed with sweat, shivering though the hut sweltered from a spitting fire.

Mother handed him a wad of poplar bark, and he noticed, with a flicker of alarm, that her hands shivered. With her chin, she pointed to the stone mortar beside the fire. For a moment, Timov could not move. The squalid heat, the child's slick thrashing, the illness already in Mother—

Cyndell, Duru's nurse and Mother's friend, stopped swabbing the sweat from the girl's wrung hair. "Biklo is dead," she said, softly. "We need your help."

The quiet words penetrated him as sharply as the death wail, and he jolted forward and knelt before the mortar. Biklo was dead now. A Mother had announced his death. Mechanically, efficiently, Timov arranged the fibrous bark in the mortar, picked up the pestle and mashed the poplar with the strength of his grief.

The amber color of nightfall still glowed in the west when the next death wail echoed from the cliffs. Two Panther men had died.

Immediately, the Pantherfolk built a bonfire on the edge of the seacliff and sacrificed all the pelts, feathers, and shells that had been distributed to them of the offering retrieved from the Eyes of the Bear. Everyone believed that the Eyes of the Bear had cursed them.

The men heaved Biklo's body into the flames, thinking he would explain the offering in the afterworld if he arrived with it. As the fire ate him, he twisted, as he had in dying, and sat up, arms extended, embracing what no one could see.

Before dawn, a Panther woman died, convulsing and vomiting blood. Mother, who had tended Duru without sleep since she fevered the previous day, suc-

cumbed to the illness herself. Soon thereafter, several
of the Tortoise clan fevered, among them Gobniu's two
wives and his eldest boy-child. For them, the drums
throbbed, and, hour by hour, everyone in the tribe
knew what they were enduring. Bonfires blazed on the
beach that night, and the heads of the slain Forest men
were burned along with all the seal-fur and mussels
that the Blue Shell possessed.

Hamr and Aradia built a lean-to behind Mother's
hut and helped Timov gather water and kindling, mash
the bark and steep the brews. When more of the Mothers fevered, Aradia took over the cooking and Timov
and Hamr foraged. Happily, mice and hares abounded,
and there was no dearth of meat for the cooking pot.

Cyndell tended both Mother and Duru, and when
she nodded with exhaustion, Aradia took her place. The
drum throbs from the Tortoise camp matched the pulse
of the sick, and by that they knew that the same evil
spirits were attacking both camps. More sacrifices had
to be made. Hamr burned his boarskin vest, Timov his
feather-cape.

The sacrifices proved futile. Mother died in the
night, delirious, not recognizing her own children.
Aradia wept and worked harder to make Duru drink the
bitter root broths. Timov sat on his heels in Mother's
hut, sobbing in big gasps like someone who had run a
long way, staring numb-eyed at Mother's torqued
body.

The death wail for Mother blended with the echoes
of other death wails. Many of both clans had fevered
and curled up by the fires, shivering as if winter blew
through their bodies. Spretnak lay among them and
died the first night of his fever.

That same night, the drum throbbing stopped.
Gobniu's eldest son was dead.

Hamr returned to the Tortoise camp for the burial of his sponsor. Six other bodies were laid out on the beach, to be carried to the seacaves for burial. Hamr draped them two at a time on the back of Blind Side of Life and carried them to the cliffs. The Tortoise Man himself, the tribe's spirit guide, was among those dead, and now there was no one to sing sacred songs over the corpses and lure their spirits out of their corrupting bodies.

The Tortoise Man's two disciples did their best. But, though they had learned all the words, they lacked the power of their teacher. The people knew, there would be many ghosts wandering the beaches as their spirits struggled to free themselves from their decaying bodies. Fire would only damage the spirits and impair their journey to the afterworld. Only slaves were burned. And as none had died in battle, they did not merit the deathraft journey over the sea. The ghosts would have to be left to wander—and that meant they would lure many more to their deaths.

"This is all Hamr's fault," Gobniu declared at the emergency council meeting called after the Tortoise Man's death. The council's three circles had been reduced to two by the many deaths, and quite a few among those who attended were ill. "He defied the Eyes of the Bear. He has brought evil spirits upon us."

"Killing our enemy would never call evil upon us," one of the Tortoise Man's disciples spoke up.

Gobniu glowered at him. "I did not say that," he quickly replied, making the mental adjustments in his argument to meet this challenge. "It was *how* he killed our enemy that has drawn this evil to us. The Boastmaker is enraged with us for using one of His beasts to kill our enemy."

"What do you know of the Beastmaker?" Hamr shouted from his place outside the circle.

Angry voices shushed him.

Gobniu smiled grimly to himself. At last, Hamr was trapped by his own greatness. "The Beastmaker favored you with a horse for the hunt—not for battle. To the Beastmaker all tribes are one. You affronted the Beastmaker by using his animal to kill men. Are not all tribes one to the Beastmaker, Tortoise Man?" Gobniu looked to the disciple who had not challenged him, conferring the coveted title on him with a solicitous nod.

"Men are simply men to the Beastmaker," the new Tortoise Man replied.

"That is why we are being punished," Gobniu continued, conviction compressing his voice to a near whisper, "why so many of our own are dying. Don't you see? So long as this one"—he pointed to Hamr—"is among us, our people will die."

Hamr's insides fisted. He had lost Spretnak. Aradia's mother was dead. Duru lay fevered. Certainly the Beastmaker, who had inspired his bravery, would not do this to him. He closed his eyes, seeking a sign. But there was only darkness and anger in him.

"Hamr is a Great Man," one of the Panther men said. "He saved our women and children. They would be slaves now had he not killed the Eyes of the Bear. The Beastmaker would not punish us for saving ourselves."

"Not for saving ourselves, surely," Gobniu conceded, "but for misusing his beast."

"Then what is to be done?" one of the fisherfolk asked.

Gobniu gazed steadfastly into the fire-painted faces. "Hamr and his horse must leave us," he said loudly. "Let him leave the Blue Shell at once and not return."

Fear floated through Hamr, but his face showed only defiance. "So be it."

Timov followed Hamr as far as the sedgegrass, where Hamr had killed the boar. The whole way he pleaded with him to stay. "Gobniu's afraid of you," Timov told him.

Hamr rode Blind Side of Life slowly, as if wanting the boy to keep up with him. Actually, the sightless horse could go no faster on this uneven terrain.

"You were born into the Tortoise clan," Timov went on. "You could be a chief. That's why he's afraid of you. I saw that the day you killed the Eyes of the Bear. He made me wash the bodies. He was angry. I saw it in his face. But as Biklo said, anger is never itself—it always hides in something else, hurt or fear. For Gobniu it's fear."

"I'm a Panther man now," Hamr said, without looking at Timov. "The Panther men can't be chiefs."

"*You* could."

Hamr ignored the flattery. He was tired from his several sleepless days, from grief for Spretnak and dying Duru, and the shared grief of his wife for her mother. He was tired and just wanted to go back to the fern holt where he had been happy with Aradia and sleep. When he woke up, the world would be different.

"You're running away," Timov said to Hamr's back, trying a new tactic. "You're afraid of Gobniu. You're afraid you're not a Great Man and he'll prove it."

Hamr stopped his horse and cast a weary look over his shoulder. "If I stay, Gobniu will come with his men to kill me and with me, Aradia—and you. Go back to camp and help Aradia. She's alone with Cyndell in that hut trying to save Duru. Help them.''

''Duru is going to die,'' Timov said. ''Don't leave us.''

Hamr turned and continued on his way. Timov walked after him. Where was the Hamr who ate spiders, who defied the omen-casters and smiled at death? He began again: ''Gobniu's afraid of you, don't you see? If you stay, you can sway the men. You're still a Tortoise man. The Panther men haven't initiated you yet. The tribe will follow you. You're the first Great Man in memory.''

At the sedgegrass, Timov stopped. To go any farther was dangerous. Boar, Snake, and Panther haunted these tall grasses.

''Don't go,'' Timov called after Hamr. ''Don't leave us.''

Hamr hurried Blind Side as fast as he would go through the switching grass with its wild blend of odors. From behind, the seawind luffed, salty and aromatic. Ahead, the pungent stink of the bog carried the sweet fragrance of blossoms and grassheads. Mouse scents flourished and hare, as usual. But no dangerous beasts, not yet, anyway. Blind Side obeyed Hamr and trotted forward, testing each step just enough to keep balance, his ears and nose constantly running errands for his absent eyes. What strength had grown around that absence.

Once Timov's angry cries dimmed away in the plangent breeze from the bog, Hamr slowed. He was in no hurry. His heart was too heavy to hurry. He tried to forget his grief by stroking the horse under him, threading sounds and smells to where the horse's eyes should have been.

Hamr remembered the old emptiness in his young life, the absence of a father, the fullness of dreams, which is no fullness at all, and how that emptiness had become the hole at the center of his life, around which his whole destiny had turned. And that was why he rode now, as no man in memory had ridden. But to what was he riding?

Sleep was the only answer he could understand. He rode on without thinking, watching the horse, watching the world. At the fern holt on the far side of the bog, the bower still stood. Vines speckled with tiny white flowers shrouded most of it and a patch of mushrooms gleamed like bones in the shade at its north side, but no animal had taken up residence within. The air there smelled damp and sweet. In moments after tethering Blind Side where there was clover to graze, and lying down on the white moss mat inside, he slumbered.

Hamr woke at night. The sky across the bog shone faintly red with the fever fires from the Blue Shell. Bats squeaked and tumbled in the black air. Huge stars shimmered with insomnia. The wind carried the exhausted smells of the bog and a dangerous scent of cat. But the rumbling of the night frogs told him that the cat was far away, and he got up and lumbered to the edge of the bog to empty his bladder.

Blind Side whinnied a greeting, and Hamr went over and stroked his neck. He had hoped that a dream would have come to him while he slept, but he remembered nothing. The faraway glow of the fires inspired fear in him. Of what? Not death, not his own, at least. The boar had killed him; and he had died again before the Eyes of the Bear. He knew with chilled certainty that he was not afraid to die.

Yet he was afraid. Of what?

Staring at the fire-glow beyond the bog, where the tribe was dying, the outline of his fear came clear, and he stepped back from Blind Side of Life and sat down in the wet grass. He was alone. Forever. Spretnak was dead. The old man was no longer there to define what was great, to guide him to greatness. Aradia was gone with the rest of the Blue Shell. They had sent him away—forever. The truth of that frightened him. At first, his anger had been enough to cover his fear. If the Blue Shell exiled him, so be it: He would live on the fringes of the tribe until they needed him again and called him back. Then Timov's pleading for him to return had been enough for him to believe he might return. But now, alone in the night, the truth bore down on him.

Maybe Timov was right. He was afraid of Gobniu and had run away. He was afraid of how the chief had made Hamr's greatness seem evil. And so he had run away, here, to figure it out—no, more than figure—to confront the Beastmaker Himself and find out for sure if he was the bane of the Blue Shell.

He returned to the bower and sat in the darkness. He would sit here until sleep or the Beastmaker came for him. He began a chant, a soft dirge for the dead and the dying, those he had left behind. As he chanted, he heard the night frogs splash, a snake slide through the debris of last season, and an owl talking nearby and no one talking back.

Timov returned to the camp to find the water low and the kindling gone. Without Biklo or Mother and so many ill, there were too many chores for those who could still work. Cyndell wanted water for Duru right away, and Timov grabbed the gourds, which no one had bothered to unstring from the last time, and hurried out to the rill.

Scooping clear water in the narrow-necked gourds went slowly, and Timov had time to grieve. He missed Mother and Biklo and could not imagine life's routines without them, yet mostly he just felt anger that Hamr had abandoned Aradia and him. Not for a moment did he believe that Hamr had caused the killing illness. He had seen the rage in Gobniu's face, and he knew the truth of Hamr's exile. How could that oaf think otherwise?

With the filled water-gourds strung over his shoulders, Timov paused to pluck sticks of kindling from the edge of the alder grove on his way back to camp. Most of the sizable kindling knocked down by the winter winds had long ago been cleared from the beaten path to the rill, so he detoured through the thornbramble, through a gap the deer had nibbled out in the winter, and found a jumble of fallen twigs and branches. He picked up two large branches and was deciding whether to take more or come back later when he spied through the bramble the figures of men.

A dozen Tortoise men clung precariously to the goat steps of a narrow clifftrail. Pebbles snicked into the void from around their handholds and toegrips. Timov knew at once that something bad was happening. Grown Tortoise men, spears and axes strapped to their backs, would not be climbing a dangerous goat path unless they wanted to reach the Panther camp without being seen. Then Timov spotted the square head and eagle-fan crest-feathers of the chief. Gobniu, royal red fishing spear at his back, huffed and wheezed as he clambered among the rocks.

Crouching backwards through the thornbramble, Timov retreated to the rill. He dropped the kindling but clutched the water-gourds tightly as he ran along the path to the camp. Several women chaffing oat grass and one whom he had often pleasured stopped to wail some grief toward him. He ignored them and ran on, looking for men. Most were out on the day's hunt. Among the huts were the boys, a few his own age, catching mice. The only men in the camp were the three who were fevered. He ran up to one, who lay curled on his side in the shade of a hedge.

"The chief and his men are coming up a goat trail by the rill," he said and had to repeat it while the man rocked out of his doze. When the man blinked into the sunlight, his pale, cracked lips trembling in that frightening unfelt ice-wind, Timov recognized him; he felt his muscles stiffen throughout his body. This was one of the great spearmen of the cult, the best of the hunters, though now he looked aged, emaciated, yellow crystals crusting his nostrils and eyelids.

"Hide . . . Aradia," he gasped.

Timov stepped back, horrified to see what was now this mere husk of greatness, too shocked at first to comprehend the warning. Then he understood: Not satisfied with Hamr's exile, Gobniu was coming to destroy all that was Hamr's.

He whirled about and dashed for his hut. Aradia and Cyndell were there, sitting beside stretched-out Duru, who looked dead, eyes shut, unmoving. "Men are coming!" he gasped.

"Hush," Cyndell frowned. "She sleeps. Give me the water."

"No—listen. Gobniu and his men are coming up the goat trails with spears, axes. They're going to kill us."

Cyndell shrieked, but Aradia rose calmly, brushed past her brother, and looked out the door.

"We must hide," Timov said.

"They are here," Aradia answered, quietly. "And we can't hide Duru."

"They don't want Duru," Cyndell shrilled, hurrying to Aradia and clasping her shoulders from behind, pulling her back from the doorway. "They want you, and the child you bear. Hurry, we must hide."

Mention of her child sent fear through Aradia. She let Cyndell guide her to the back of the hut, where the old yellow dog slept. "Timov—quickly," Cyndell beckoned at the thatched wall.

Timov fell to his knees and tore at the withes and dried grass until there was a hole large enough for Aradia to crawl through.

"Hide—hide—wherever you can," Cyndell urged as Aradia and then Timov squirmed through the torn hole.

But even as she spoke, Gobniu's square shadow fell through the doorway, and the men behind him hurried to the back of the hut. Cyndell screamed and screamed again as the Tortoise men dragged a struggling Aradia past the doorway.

Timov had ducked between the men's legs, and he sprinted among the huts until he was certain he was not being pursued. Crouching around a corner, staring past the Mothers and children, who had come to their doorways at Cyndell's screaming, he watched the men tear the rabbitskin wrap from Aradia and stand her up naked in the noon brightness. Two other men went into the hut. One pushed Cyndell into the clearing, the other dragged little Duru out by her ankles and stood over her in the dust.

The Mothers began to trill, the high, piercing cry of danger, calling their men back from the hunt. But Gobniu waved, and the Tortoise men unstrapped their axes and rushed at the Mothers, who ducked into their huts and fell silent. The men returned to Aradia's hut. One flint-struck a flame at the side, then another, and another.

Aradia hung limply in the arms of her captors. Timov could see her face clearly in the daylight. She was frightened—lips trembling, eyes fluttering—but she did not struggle or make a sound. Cyndell clutched at Gobniu's knees, howling and sobbing, until he kicked her aside. Then she spat curses at him, flew to her feet with a vile epithet, and would have flung herself at him to rip out his eyes, when two men grabbed her. One smote her over the head with his ax, and she went down like a bundle of kindling, arms and legs twisted, and lay still.

The flames leaped like red mice among the sheaves of grass, and a python shape of white smoke coiled straight up into the still sky. At Gobniu's sign, the Tortoise men pulled Aradia toward the blazing hut. She struggled, kicking up dust and straining against the men, so that it took another man, hoisting her from behind, to carry her to the flames.

Timov's heart burst in him, and he could not breathe. The men heaved Aradia into the burning hut and danced back from the heat. When she came flying out, one of them struck her between the eyes with the flat of his ax. She collapsed, and they flung her back through the sheet of fire that veiled the doorway.

The Mothers stood again before their huts, now trilling their slow, dirge wails. The boys had gathered in fidgety groups, their faces blank with fright. The conflagration settled a haze over the camp and with it a terrible, greasy stink of burned flesh.

The hut collapsed, the fire withered, and Gobniu and his men left, taking the most convenient clifftrail down to the beach. The Mothers hurried to the charred hut, but there was nothing to do for Aradia. She was a black, steamy bundle among the flattened ashes and the wispy sparks. The Mothers picked up Duru, whose mouth was open, gagging on a silent cry, and they carried her off. Several of the Mothers bent over Cyndell, and soon she wobbled to her feet.

Timov noticed then that the boys had turned from the fire and had gathered around him, sitting staring at him where he crouched in the dust. He met their peculiar stares, their frightened and mockingly relieved expressions—relieved it was not they crouching in the dust, or their sister smoking in the ashes, mocking him for crouching under the weight of his fear, for shedding tears when he should have been angry, for living when he should have been dead.

With a defiant cry no louder than a whimper, Timov sprang to his feet and ran at the mocking boys. They leaped aside as he flew past. Even as he kicked dust through the length of the camp and into the outlying hedges, they watched after him.

Timov ran with lunatic strength, racing his horror into the radiant green fields. The noise from the fire echoed like the roar of the blood in his head, and he cried his thin whimper. At the far end of his strength, everything flung out of him, he crashed through the blowsy grassheads and flung himself into the dirt, gasping, twisting his breath into sobs.

The smell of the earth, the labor of rotting and rising plants, was the first thing he noticed when full awareness came back to him. He sat up, weak, his head full of bright gnats.

He put his head on his knees and waited for the churning nausea to go away. After a while, a chill fluted through him, and he felt able to stand. The sky above unfurled its frayed clouds. Larks floated overhead. A new urgency occurred to him. He had to find Hamr. No matter the bushsnakes or panthers, tusked boars or dog packs, he had to find Hamr and tell him what had happened. Only then would his pain find its home.

Throughout the night, Hamr searched for the Beastmaker. But there was no sign of Him. Hamr felt abandoned, and that, more than his exile or the death of Spretnak, convinced him that there was some truth to Gobniu's accusation. Hamr thought that maybe he had been wrong to ride Blind Side of Life against the Eyes of the Bear. His own sacrifice might have fulfilled his destiny but taking the lives of the Forest men with the power of the horse had been wicked.

Adept, cunning, and fearless as he had once thought himself, he had blundered, he realized now. He had abused his divine privilege and had misused the Beastmaker's gift. Now there was nothing for him to do but accept the truth of his error and find within himself the strength to propitiate the Beastmaker.

At dawn, Hamr confronted Blind Side of Life. During the night only one sacrifice, apart from his own death, came clear as being meaningful. He would return to the Blue Shell, and he would announce that he would redeem the wrongful deaths of the Forest men by delivering to the Eyes of the Bear his horse. Probably, the Forest people would kill him as well as his horse. But if that turned the evil spirits away from the Blue Shell, his death would be great and he would live on in memory as a Great Man.

Resolved to this sacrifice, Hamr stood for a long time before his horse, admiring the creature's beauty. The heavy lids over the sightless eyes winked away flies, and he pressed his wet muzzle against Hamr's comforting hands. How wrong he had been to seek greatness. This horse could have lived among its herd; the Blue Shell could have been spared the agony of so many deaths.

Cold with anger at himself, Hamr mounted his horse and began the slow ride back to the Blue Shell. The willows and oak and hazel bushes were happy. Leaves jangled with sunlight and burst-open blossoms sparkled with dew. Hornets left amber tracks in the air. Small birds plunged in the wind. Grass billowed like clouds. Everywhere, the world shone with life.

Hamr had no desire to die or to turn his mighty horse over to men who would club him and cut him down to meat. But worse, he reminded himself, was exile from the Beastmaker, loss of his greatness, and the doom of the Blue Shell. Far better to say farewell to the trees full of agile birds, the noisy hives, bouncing butterflies, and the lonely blue of the sky.

A groan snatched Hamr's attention from his reverie, and he saw a figure slogging among the reeds in the bog. He recognized Timov, mud caked, dazed, arms outstretched, fingers wavering for something to hold. Quickly, he dismounted, grabbed a willow branch and leaned his weight against it so that it fell within the boy's grasp.

Timov had lost himself in the sedgegrass and had spent the night wandering through the bog. Most of the time, he had crept along the shaggy boughs of the marsh trees, thinking he was finding his way across the bog. But when the old moon had come up after midnight, he saw that he had gone the wrong way, toward the deeper wallows, where the hippopotamus herds lolled like boulders.

"Have you been following me this whole time?"

Hamr asked after the boy had struggled to firmer ground and lay hugging the earth.

"No, I went back." He sucked for air, not wanting to announce his news in a hurried breath. When he could speak clearly, he told Hamr all that he had witnessed.

Hamr stood impassively, his face quiet, eyes slimmed as if he had not fathomed what he had been told. Yet the veins at the side of his thick neck pulsed. Soon his eyes seemed to draw closer together as he understood the depths of his error. The Beastmaker had not abandoned him. He had forsaken his own destiny. He had forgotten what Spretnak had told him— the very last thing the old man had told him. He remembered those words now with a clarity that hurt his brain: "Whoever speaks of the Beastmaker, speaks lies. Only silence carries His power."

A look came over Hamr that Timov had never seen before. All the blood drained from Hamr's face, and the holes in the center of his eyes tightened to prickpoints. The nostrils of his hawk-bent nose flared and set wide, and his mouth clamped tight as a rockseam. He rose stiffly, mounted Blind Side and turned the animal toward the tall grass, which led back to the Blue Shell camp.

Timov, though wearied from his harrowing night in the bog, followed, hurrying alongside. Hamr suddenly remembered he was there and pulled him up so that he rode behind him.

"What will you do?" Timov asked.

Hamr said nothing. The boy persisted for a while, yammering incoherently about the Tortoise men, the fire, and his sister's soundless death. "What're you going to do? You've been exiled. They'll kill you when they see you."

Hamr listened. The boy mimicked almost exactly the frightened voice inside of him. But he said nothing. What was there to say? He knew just two things now for sure. The Beastmaker had not abandoned him: "Only silence carries His power."

Soon Timov fell silent, too. Death lay ahead, only that. Biklo was dead. Mother was dead. And now Aradia was dead. Soon they would all be dead. The feel of the bog-mud caking on his legs and arms seemed to confirm this. Life had hardened around him, and with every move something more crumbled away. Now, certainly, it would be their lives. Gobniu and the Tortoise men would kill them both on sight.

When the Panther camp appeared through the clumps of hazel shrubs and twisted thornapples, Hamr turned Blind Side of Life away from the huts. They rode through a stand of elm to another rill than the one the people used for water. Here the boys sometimes came to catch frogs. The frogs liked it, because the rill had worn away the land from around the treeroots and there were lots of webby places for them to hide. This was not ideal for drawing water, but it was an adequate place to wash the mud from Timov's body.

While Timov cleansed himself, Hamr strode to the top of a knoll and climbed a robust pine that had shot up among the elm. From a bristly branch halfway up the tree, he could see the Panther huts—the charred heap that had been Aradia's house—and beyond the seacliffs, the Tortoise camp. The people were too small to identify, but he was sure that Gobniu was there. The dugouts were beached. No one was fishing with so many ill and dead to tend and to stow in the caves.

Hamr checked the long, sloping trail that glided down to the beach through the giant cleft in the cliff. No one was there. Everyone was in their camp. If he rode Blind Side close to the clumps of shrubbery sprouting from the rockcrevices, only the Panther people would see him until he reached the beach. Then, if he slipped the right way among the dunes, he could reach the Tortoise huts without Gobniu ever knowing he was coming. Normally, boys playing among the dunes or the girls and Mothers foraging the cliffplants would see him, but now they were too busy dying or comforting the dying. The evil spirits would be his allies.

Confident of his approach, Hamr came down from the pine and returned to his horse. Timov had washed the bog mud from himself and stood in a slash of sunlight, drying. He shivered involuntarily at the sight of Hamr. The man looked bloodless. Was he frightened, too? There was no tremor on his pale face. His nostrils looked frozen in mid-gasp, his jaw locked, eyes unseeing, seeing across a span of light to what would happen soon.

Hamr mounted and Timov offered his hand to be pulled up, but Hamr did not take it. He looked down at the boy with his grim stare, then rode off. Timov hurried beside him, asking again what he was going to do, reminding him of the death that lay ahead. Hamr did not look at him again. As he turned the horse around the base of the knoll and moved over the sloping sward toward the wide course that dipped into the cleft of the cliff, Timov stopped. He knew that way led to the Tortoise men.

The Panther camp seemed asleep. The surrounding fields and groves were empty. No children played or shouted. No old women sorted grains under the big trees; no old men sat by the drying racks flensing hides or carving wood. Timov walked through the camp as in a weird dream. Through doorways, he glimpsed the people lying down or crouching. The dogs, too, seemed strange, wandering in and out of the tall grass at the far end of the camp, not chasing the mice that flitted there in swift shadows, just coming and going, as if they were afraid to approach the huts too closely and were yet unwilling to drift out of sight of them.

At the hut where Aradia had been killed, her body was gone. The Mothers had scattered over the ashes the plaited grass dolls they wove by moonlight and hung on the dead. Timov did not stare too long. He hurried by, peeking into each hut he passed, until he found Cyndell. She was among the old women whom Timov had spent the last three winters pleasuring in the chill of the night. Duru sat in her lap, clear-eyed, her flesh pink but no longer glossed with sweat.

"Duru, you're not sick." He took her hand, which was small and weak but no longer hot or slick. "The Mothers cured you."

Cyndell, who wore a weary smile, shook her gray head. "No, the Mothers had nothing to do with this. The spirits spared her for their own reasons. But others are still dying. The evil is not through with us yet. Where have you been, boy?"

He told her about Hamr, and the tired smile fled from her careworn face. Alarm tightened through her, and she looked side to side for the older women to take Duru. "I must stop him. He'll kill us all."

Duru rolled from Cyndell's lap, and one of the old women embraced the girl. Cyndell jolted to her feet and pulled herself through the door. Timov followed. She waved him back, but he would not be stopped. He read her urgency accurately. Since he had crawled out of the bog, he himself had seen and felt the murderous look on Hamr's face. But what could Cyndell do? He had no notion of her but that she was one of the Mothers. Her children were dead—they had died years before, one in childbirth, others in a tree-breaking storm, and one more at sea. It was true, the tribe respected her for her quiet strength and her uncomplaining grief. If anyone from the Panther people could intervene with the Tortoise clan, she was the one. But in such matters of killing—clansman against clansman—what could one Mother do?

Timov bounded ahead of her and picked out the fastest clifftrail that he felt a woman her age could manage. With her leaning on his arm, they skidded and hopped down the trail. She was far stronger and more agile than he had guessed, and they completed their descent as Hamr appeared among the dunes. He had not seen them yet, nor had the Tortoise clan spotted him.

Cyndell brushed away furies of sandflies that clouded up from the salt grass as they hurried through the sand to intercept Hamr. Blind Side had clopped ahead and disappeared among the dunes. When he reappeared, Hamr had already dismounted and was hurrying, spear in hand, across the open space toward the huts. The Tortoise women, sitting in the shade of a dune shucking clams, spied him and began their danger trill. Men appeared in doorways, axes in hand.

By then, Hamr had reached the central hut of the chief, outside which stood Gobniu's coup, two large fishingspears decked with silver seal-fur and garlands of rainbow-shot mussel. He knocked over the spears, kicked sand onto the fur, and crunched the shells under his sandals. Then he bellowed for Gobniu.

The chief charged from his hut, spear lowered. Hamr had hoped for that. He had feared only that Gobniu would have cowered and made the killing less noble. Standing firm on the fallen coup, he invited the chief's attack and turned swiftly only at the last moment. Gobniu's spear ripped Hamr's antelope-hide vest and snagged. With his own spear, he banged down hard on the chief's weapon, and the two spears clacked to the ground. His hands found Gobniu's thick throat as the chief dug his fingers into Hamr's. But Hamr was clearly the stronger, and Gobniu fell to his knees.

Other Tortoise men scurried toward the struggling men, spears raised. But Hamr sensed them and heaved around so that the chief's back faced the spearmen. The men balked, drew their knives. In the same instant, Hamr shoved Gobniu into the sand, drew his own wooden blade, and poised its tip at the chief's throat.

"Hamr—stop!" Cyndell shouted and came running through the salt grass between the dunes. "Don't kill him! If you ever loved your Aradia, don't kill him."

Hamr had wrestled the chief flat on his back, with his arms pinned. In one stroke, Gobniu's lifeblood would spill out of him. The Tortoise men danced from side to side, between fear for their chief, and eagerness to lunge at Hamr.

Cyndell pushed her way between the Tortoise men. "Hamr! If you kill him, you will die here—and all the Panther people will die. The Tortoise clan will want their blood. If you ever loved your Aradia, do not do this to her people."

"He'll kill you anyway—won't you? Coward! Killer of your own people!" Hamr's face shivered with fury as he pressed the blade harder against the chief's throat. Gobniu's grimace froze, aware that even too deep a breath would cut him.

"If you kill the chief," a voice spoke from the hut at Hamr's back, "the Panther people will indeed be slaughtered. The ancestors would expect nothing less.''

Hamr recognized the voice of the new Tortoise Man, the tribe's spiritual leader. His word was more deadly than the chief's, for he spoke with the authority of all who had gone before.

''But if you spare him,'' the Tortoise Man continued, ''you will be spared and the Panther people as well.''

''I've come back, broken my exile,'' Hamr gasped past his rage. ''For that alone, you'll kill me. And all the Panther people as well. You've already slain my Aradia.''

''The death of Aradia propitiated the evil spirits,'' the Tortoise Man claimed.

''Duru is healed,'' Cyndell confirmed. ''Do not forsake her life and that of her people now. Relent, Hamr.''

''The evil will pass,'' the Tortoise Man announced. ''In time it will pass entirely away. And so, your exile is lifted. Put aside your knife. Release the chief.''

''You will spare the Panther people?'' Hamr asked Gobniu.

The chief's eyes swore he would.

''Speak it,'' Hamr commanded. ''Tell everyone. Tell the ancestors. And if you lie, the evil spirits will destroy you and all the people. Speak it!''

''I will spare the Panther people,'' Gobniu said through his grimace. ''None will be killed.''

Hamr gazed hard into Gobniu's wrung face, imagined his throat slashed and his hot blood spurting. Then he stood up and sheathed his knife, picked up his spear. He nodded to the Tortoise Man, and turned to go.

''But—'' Gobniu shouted, up again, his hand at his

throat, "the Tortoise people will not have the Panther people among them any longer."

Hamr spun about, face hard. The spearmen at the sides of the chief raised their weapons.

"By morning," the chief said, "all the Panther people are to leave. Any who are found among our dunes, within our groves or our fields will no longer be our people but strangers—and they will be killed."

"You lied!" Hamr shouted.

"The chief has not lied," the Tortoise Man declared. "He has spared the Panther people slaughter. He has spared you and lifted your exile. And now he imposes a new exile, upon the whole of the Panther cult. What he does is just and good in the eyes of the ancestors. Now go. Tell your people to leave."

Timov, who had been watching from the edge of the camp, not daring to enter the space of the Tortoise people, reeled with sudden nausea. Exile for the Mothers and children meant almost certain death in the wilderness. The terrified look on Cyndell's face and the throbbing fury on Hamr's confirmed his fear.

Hamr slouched toward his horse. Instead of mounting, he placed his arm on the steed's neck and walked him between the dunes. Timov wanted to go after him, to query him about what would happen next. But Cyndell clucked for him. He followed her up the trail, wanting from her the comfort of something said, even in anger. But she only clicked her tongue disconsolately when he tried to question her.

At the top of the trail, Cyndell began her danger trill, modulated with mournful, wailing tones. The Mothers appeared and clustered. The men stood in doorways, the children behind them. Timov had never seen the likes of this, and his insides frosted. He went with Cyndell to the center of the camp and stood to the side as she related to the Mothers what had transpired. Then the dirgeful trilling began in unison.

Timov turned away, saw Hamr leading Blind Side of Life up from the cleft. Alongside the scarp of the cliff's edge, the horse found a patch of broad-blade grass to his liking and began to nibble at it. Hamr dropped his hand from his animal's neck and walked on, past Timov, past the wailing Mothers to the charred site of Aradia's hut. He recognized the stone ring, where the daily fire had burned, the slumped shapes of moss matting, where they had slept, and the ashen nest that must have been the drying racks for his wife's plants. In one corner, not completely burned, was her bride's wallet. He stepped through the ash and kicked it over. The flap opened, and he stared down at the Mother's Hair, the bundles of medicinal herbs that could not bring her back.

Among the crisped plants Hamr noticed a disk of tortoise shell. He bent over and picked it out. It was one of Spretnak's wheels. It still had the stick pushed through the hole in its center. What was she doing with this? He spun the wheel on its axle and watched the markings of the shell blur. Had Spretnak told her the significance of this device, this master symbol of Hamr's life—or was it simply given as a toy for the children they would have had?

The Panther men gathered behind him, a respectful distance from the ash heap. They made disgruntled noises but did not dare address him directly while he mourned, fearing the spirit of his wife, who was certainly still in the house and who would not want to be interrupted.

Presently, the presence of the unhappy men became less bearable than his grief. Hamr turned to face them. "Gobniu has exiled the Panther people," he announced.

"Because you returned," one of the men shouted. "Why did you leave if you were going to return?"

"Why should we suffer for what you've done?" another asked.

"Gobniu lied to me," Hamr muttered. "He said I brought the evil spirits upon us by using my horse to kill our enemy. I believed him. I was wrong—but I didn't see that until he killed Aradia. I returned only to kill him."

"Then why does he live? Why are we driven from the Land?"

"If I had killed him, the Tortoise men would kill you."

Angry noises blew among the men as they loudly discussed their options. Some wanted to attack the Tortoise clan immediately, others wanted to wait in ambush for them to come, a few wanted the eldoro to go to Gobniu and petition him for mercy, and one wanted Hamr killed and sent down as a peace offering.

The discussion blustered into an argument, and the Mothers stopped their wailing. The eldest among them approached the men, her arms raised, face scowling. The men fell silent at her shout.

"The Blue Shell are doomed," the crone told them. "Have you no sight in your heads? Have you not seen the war tokens that the Eyes of the Bear have nailed to the trees at the edge of the Forest? Have you no hearing in your heads? Have you not heard their drumsongs, noisy with wrath? The evil spirits have not built fires in their blood. Their strong men have not died. Their wise women have not died. Their hearts are not broken with grief, for their children have not died. The fires

burn in our blood. Too many of us have died. We are
weak—and the Eyes of the Bear know it. They have
seen our sacrifice fires. They have heard our funeral
songs. They have watched us from the Forest, and soon
they'll be coming down here to destroy all of us.''

"What can we do?" a man wailed.

"Gobniu has driven us out," the crone said. "We
cannot flee. Where would we go? Into the bog to live
with the swamp creatures? Into the mountains, to be
hunted by the Eyes of the Bear? We have no choice. We
must go to the Eyes of the Bear and live with them—as
their slaves.''

Shouts burst from the gathered men but soon subsided. The women were not protesting. The crone
spoke for them.

"There is another way," Hamr said to the stricken
men. "We can follow the sea past the bog. Eventually,
the beach turns north. If we journey far enough north,
we will find the other Panther people, the ones you
remember in your firesongs, in your histories. What do
they call themselves?"

"The Thundertree," Timov piped.

The men moaned with disapproval. North, the direction of darkness, source of the cold, and home of the
evil wolf spirit, was the wrong way to go. "The journey
is too difficult," one explained. "We're too weak from
our losses. And, besides, even if we were strong, even
if the Eyes of the Bear were not eager to kill us, would
we find the Thundertree? The last time we heard of
them was in the time of the Grandfathers, long ago.
What if they have moved on? What if their enemies
have destroyed them? We'll wander with nowhere to
go.''

"Is slavery better?"

"As slaves, we will live, our children will live,"
the crone answered. "North lies the wind of winter and
death. Which, then, is better? Life—or death?"

Hamr left the men to debate their future. For him,
there was no choice. After what he had done to the Eyes
of the Bear, they would kill him on sight. He pushed
past the wrangling men and met their glowering stares
without flinching. The crone was right: Whether he had
returned or not, the Blue Shell were doomed. Their
enemy would know of their terrible sickness and would
eagerly use it to crush them. His return, if anything,
had helped them to look up from their grief long enough
to realize the danger they were in. Now, if they wanted,
they could go with him or become slaves. They did not
have to die.

Blind Side of Life had wandered away from the
camp, following the patches of broad-blade grass he
favored, and Hamr went after him. The horse whick-
ered a greeting at the familiar scent of him. Hamr sat
down on a flat rock nearby and twirled the wheel he
still carried, watching the Panther people arguing
among themselves. Overhead, clouds toiled from the
sea toward the mountains, and in a short while there
would be rain. A crow jeered from the walnut tree.

The smell of the approaching rain, the racket of the
crow, and the wheel spinning in his hands helped Hamr
to sort out his feelings. The anger that had driven him
back from the bog had dissipated, replaced by a weary
futility. Aradia was gone. The raw path through the
blackberry brambles and hazelnut shrubs still led toward the sedgefields, and the fields still led to the
bower, where they had made their first child, and the
bower still squatted at the edge of the bog. But she and
the child who would have been were gone now. He had

not even seen her dead. His mourning felt all the more empty for that. And in the emptiness, around its own emptiness, the wheel spun, and a jay-crow squawked at the sweet smell of the coming rain.

3
Taiga

Dawn looked frayed the morning of the exile. Rain had pattered throughout the night and by morning still hung in gray veils over the mountains to the north. The sunlight filtering through tattered clouds looked brown and made the placid sea appear muddy. On the beach, the Tortoise clan had gathered to witness the dispersal of the Panther people. The Tortoise women stood silently atop the dunes, a few waving, though the heights of the giant seacliffs were already empty. Their men had posted themselves before dawn at the top of the clifftrails, axes in hand, faces smudged for battle.

The Panther people put up no resistance. Many had died from the fever, many were still ill. In the night, they had gathered up their possessions and with first light had begun dragging their bundles of hides and carved bone toward the cedar forest. As soon as they had trudged out of the camp, the Tortoise men advanced and set fire to the abandoned huts.

Only Timov, his sister Duru, and their nurse, Cyndell, had elected to journey north with Hamr. Timov was scared to go into the wilds with only grief-struck Hamr, a girl too weak to walk, and an old woman to fend off beasts and gather food, but neither did he want to live as Biklo had, ordered about by children and women, doing drudge work the rest of his days. Better to follow the Great Man into the wilderness and face death there, he bravely thought—or, he more fervidly hoped, find the Thundertree, the Panther cult to the north with whom the Grandfathers had once traded.

For Duru, still drained from the fires that had blazed in her blood and the shock of her sister's death, the journey was another fateful change she could not avoid. By custom, when a Mother died, her husband passed to her sisters. Hamr was now Duru's. Cyndell challenged this custom, for Duru had yet to reach womanhood. But Duru had shuffled through the night rains to the eldest of the Mothers and had the crone confirm that with Aradia's death, Hamr had become hers. Now she was determined to stay at his side and endure their journey as she had endured her fever and the horror of Aradia's murder.

Cyndell would have preferred to go to the Eyes of the Bear and serve them by the comfort of their fires. But she had known Duru's mother too well to abandon to the wilderness the child she had nursed. She packed her medicinal herbs, what dried meat she had, and her bone needles and scrapers in a satchel of sewn rabbit hides, and she stood with Duru and Timov as they bade farewell to their clan.

Hamr waited impatiently at the cleft in the rock-wall. He had thought that more of the Panther men would accompany him to find their totem brothers in the north; he was disappointed when only Timov came to meet him at the cliff's edge, to announce that Duru claimed Hamr for her own. How would they defend themselves in the wilds, just he, this boy, and two women?

He had spent the night among the knolls, under the locked branches of alders whose broad leaves offered some protection from the rain. With the strength of his anxiety and a flint knife, he had occupied his grief in the wakeful darkness by whittling a pliant sapling to a spear-shaft. He tipped it with a quartz blade given to him by Spretnak years ago, before his first hunt.

After midnight the glint of distant fires could be seen among the cedars on the high hills. The Eyes of the Bear had camped closer to the forest fringe, perhaps anticipating the arrival of their new slaves or preparing for a further raid on the disease-weakened Blue Shell.

Hamr wanted to be on his way long before the Panther people reached their new masters and could tell them of his decision to seek the Thundertree. Maybe the Eyes of the Bear wanted revenge enough to track him. Certainly, he and those with him were in danger as long as they were within sight of the cedar hills.

To help them move more quickly, Hamr had loaded their satchels onto Blind Side of Life, who was skittish because of the smells of pyre smoke and eager to be going. There was little for the horse to carry, mostly the hides that the Panther clan had gifted Cyndell and Duru so that they could make clothes to keep them warm in the north. If the child grew tired, she could ride. Her survival amazed Hamr, and he had not the heart to turn her away to a life of slavery. Who was he to say that the hardships of the journey ahead would outweigh the pain of serving the Eyes of the Bear?

As for her claim on him, he would not strengthen her conviction with his acknowledgment until they had found their way to the Thundertree. If she were still alive then and still wanted him, he would serve her to honor her sister. Aradia was yet his bride, though now she slept with the Mudman. He envied the Mudman, and would not release her entirely to him, yet. Her body was gone, but she lived on in him, unsmutched in his memory by pain or illness—in his mind as he had last seen her, dark-eyed, her face shining with health in the cove of her black hair.

On the walk down the wide sloping path in the cleft of the rockwall, Hamr stared boldly at the Tortoise men on their way to torch the Panther huts. The younger Tortoise men, who thought him a hero for taming a horse and killing the Eyes of the Bear, looked away, but the older ones, who remembered him as a braggart, leered to see him exiled with a boy, a girl, and an old woman to care for.

Among the dunes, the chief, the elders, the Tortoise Man, and their guards, whom he had thwarted the previous day, mocked loudly. The women hooted derisively. Why did a Great Man need a blind horse to kill the enemy? If the Beastmaker loved him so, where were the animal omens? Why did the gulls fly at his approach? Were the pigs and deer going to offer him their throats in the wilderness? And what a noble entourage for a Great Man! Why did the Panther people not see that the Beastmaker favored him? Why did they prefer to live as slaves to the Eyes of the Bear? Maybe the Beastmaker would send him animal guides to lead him to the Thundertree.

Hamr stayed calm by clutching his spear with one hand and resting his other on the back of Blind Side of Life, where the satchel lay that carried his wheel. Sooner or later, even this would turn around. He refused to panic at his freedom of exile, and, to prove that to himself, he stopped and looked back when he reached the firm sand before the sea. In the sunmist, the giant cliffs were red, and above them, smoke rose from the burning huts. The women and children standing on the dunes watched him, pouring out a song of hatred at him, as if he were the enemy.

Not he, he had to remind himself to ease the pain of their song, not he but his greatness was their enemy. It had always set him apart—had made him compete and win against their boys—had made him spurn their girls—had carried him above the ground they trod onto the back of a beast—and had lifted him out of their clan to another life. Of course they would hate him. He had eluded them. He had given himself to greatness.

Without a sound or a wave, Hamr turned away. He patted Blind Side's neck, and his horse resumed his gait. Ahead, the beach curved about the promontory of the cliffs and widened into pebbly flats. Hamr kept his eyes on the morning-light simmering on the wave-crests, with occasional glances ahead, into the baffling distances.

In Timov's chest fear rattled him. The mocking cries of the Tortoise people made him doubt his decision to enter the wilds. He kept looking back, wondering if it was too late to return, to run back through the dunes and up the clifftrail. Surely he could catch up with the Panther people, the boys he knew, the men who would initiate him.

"They're gone," Cyndell said in a muffled breath behind Timov's ear. "You can't go back."

He frowned at her, as though he had no idea what she meant.

Duru smiled at Cyndell. At one point during her fever, she felt she could have let go and her life would have melted away like ice at the first spring thaw. But she had wanted to come back. She had been hungry for everything in the world, nut gruel and honey, a song in her throat, fireside stories, even pain, the dull ache of hard work, but mostly laughter. She came back to laugh again, to experience once more the charm of life with fun. But then they killed Aradia. And Mother too was gone. And all the Mothers she loved were gone except Cyndell. And there was nothing to laugh about. So she smiled at her brother's false bravery and his yearning to go back. And the crushed smile that Cyndell returned said she understood.

Once the familiar terrain fell behind them, the travelers turned inland. Hamr sought the migratory trails, the ditches cut into the earth by the herds' seasonal movements. Blind Side of Life recognized the horse trail, which the travelers identified by the droppings that had hardened there. Blind Side, stimulated by the familiar smell of the herd, trotted north more quickly than the others could keep up. Hamr at first restrained him by riding him. Only after one end of a rope had been looped about the horse's neck and the other around Hamr's waist did Blind Side reluctantly slow down.

Traveling was slow, since they had food only for the first day and spent much time leaving the migratory trail to forage and hunt. The hunting went even slower. Neither Hamr nor Timov could manage to stalk an animal close enough to use the spears, and all attempts to rush deer and antelope toward coverts where the others waited in ambush ended pitifully. Other than rodents and an occasional hare and squirrel, the men caught nothing.

Duru had lost weight but was stronger than anyone's prayers had hoped, and she and Cyndell provided most of the food and kept up the daycount. The woods teemed with berries, nuts, edible grasses, and tubers. While Blind Side of Life grazed, tethered to a tree, the women foraged around him and prepared vegetable broths and mashes. When it rained, they knew which slick fronds to weave into makeshift lean-tos. And, with Cyndell's bone-needle kit, they kept their sandals in good repair, using bark and squirrel-hide to protect their soles.

At day's end, after the night fire was built, they counted the days on Cyndell's ivory bracelet. A meander had been carved into the ivory, a square spiral whose zigzag pattern outlined the thirteen chambers of the moon. Each chamber contained twenty-eight days; six chambers spiraled inward to the seventh at the hot, solar center of the year, and six more spun outward toward the darkness of winter. They were well into the dark turning now, and though the Forest looked robust, the calendar warned that the sap was already seeping inward.

Hamr and Timov snickered at the ritual daycount and the women's compulsive marking of time. For them, time was all around them, as weather and the directions. To the west, beyond the thistly tussocks, lay the sea, and to the east, the dense Forest, where night seemed to lie in perpetual residence.

The ravine country of the migratory trails boxed in the travelers but allowed them to move faster and farther north than they could have done either in the marsh or the Forest. At night, the culverts blocked the brisk sea wind that buffeted the great trees and sighed overhead dolorously in tandem with the night cries of the Forest animals.

One night Hamr took out his wheel and spun it in

the firelight. The others stared in fascination at the spinning brightness. "What is it?" Timov asked.

"A wheel."

"What's it for?"

"For nothing," Hamr answered. "You see, there's nothing in the middle." He stopped it and removed the stick, revealing the empty hole at the center. Then he replaced the stick and set the tortoise disk spinning again. "It spins around nothing."

"It spins around the stick," Duru said.

"No," Hamr replied. "An ax-head is joined to a stick, too, but it does not spin. It is fixed by the stick. But the wheel has a hole, and it is the emptiness of the hole that lets it turn. It's like our lives."

The others squinted, their perplexed faces gleaming in the fireglow.

"At the center of our lives is an emptiness, as well," Hamr explained. "Do we remember where we come from?" He parted the antelope-skin he wore as a wrap about his torso and revealed his navel. "There's our hole—the emptiness cut from the Mother."

Cyndell put a hand on Hamr's and stopped the spinning wheel. "We shouldn't speak of these things."

Hamr stared at her flatly, though inside him, the fog of his grief for Aradia deepened, glowed like a smoke-filled hut. "Why not?"

"These are mysteries for the tribe," Cyndell replied. "We have no tribe."

"We have each other," Hamr said, resolutely. "And someday we will have the Thundertree."

Cyndell nodded. "Then perhaps we can speak of these things. But now, we four are too small, and these thoughts are as big as everything around us. We could be crushed."

Hamr nodded once, remembering Aradia's admonition and tucked the wheel back in his satchel. He had spoken without forethought, simply wanting to fill his own emptiness from the mighty fullness of stars, wind, darkness, and the hulks of trees holding the many secret lives of the Forest.

Duru and Timov groaned with disappointment but Cyndell hushed them with a song. Her voice, strained with love, faltered briefly with the fear Hamr had evoked in her. Then her bright song lifted with the fire and wavered against the dark, offering the warmth of memories and the brightness of hope. Soon the children were asleep.

Hamr lay staring at her with a quiet, chill, and sober stare, Duru asleep with her head in his lap. Cyndell placed her hand on his and whispered, "The shadows heard you. I saw them closing in to hear more. I was afraid. But my song has pleased them. Now we can sleep."

Cyndell cowered with fear. Sometimes at night, even her own breathing frightened her. They were alone in the wilderness, with only the Great Mother to watch after them—and She, without the enwombing strength of the tribe, could do little for them but watch. From the faces of Her animals, what did She see but an old woman wandering the wilds with two children and a crazy man?

Hamr had to be crazy. Only a crazy man would drive a blind horse down a beach against men with spears. That he had returned triumphant frightened her even more. What spirit possessed this man who could ride a horse, who could face down three spearmen, who could speak blithely before the fire about the emptiness at the center of everything? It was not the spirit of the Horse, which loved the herd; this man defied his tribe and now wandered alone. Neither was it a tree spirit, which would have rooted him to one place. What crazy spirit owned Hamr?

Cyndell could not see what some of the truly old Mothers had seen from years of fire-watching; she could not see what type of spirit empowered Hamr. All she knew was that his spirit had had the strength to prevail against the Eyes of the Bear and to challenge the dark spirits of the north. Now they would continue on, ever deeper into the Mother's unpredictable body, farther from the well-known foraging terrain which was Her left teat, and ever farther from the warmth of the tribe which was Her right teat.

Timov recognized Cyndell's fear of Hamr. When they left Cyndell and Duru to set up camp and went out to hunt, he joked grimly with Hamr about it: "Mama Cyndell would rather rut with a cave bear than look you in the eye."

Hamr shrugged. "At least the Bear has a den. Every Mother wants a home. But for a man, there's only distance."

They walked along the doorways of the Forest, leading Blind Side of Life. The horse disliked the mushy ground, the whispering underfoot, the poking and scratching of undergrowth on every side, and especially the smell of rotting leaves overlaying a darker stink of Bear and Cat.

"Do you think we'll find the Thundertree?"

"Not if you keep talking instead of looking for their sign."

"But what am I looking for?"

Hamr frowned. "You're a Panther man. Don't you know?"

"I'm not sure. When the Panther men took me

hunting, I'd see them reading each other's sign in the grass and on the trees, and I'd look, but I didn't see anything."

"Then maybe they'll find us when we trespass in their domain."

"The Tortoise men initiated you. What did you learn to see?"

"I can read the sign the Tortoise men leave in the tide litter. You know, where the fish are running, what tidepools belong to what family, where the seals will beach with the tide. But the Forest tells me nothing."

As if to confirm that, a quail burst from a hackleberry bush an arm's length from Hamr and flapped into the canopy of the Forest. Her alarmed voice clanged back from out of sight, eerie as an unwrapped soul.

"We've got to catch something," Timov whined. "I'm tired of eating berry mash and tuber broth with lion-tooth grass."

Hamr peered up through the branches, saw the day's heat piling the clouds atop each other. "It'll rain tonight. Tomorrow we'll be slogging through mud. Even catching mice'll be hard. I say we get out of here and try to take one of the elk we saw in the fields above the ravines."

"Elk? That's a dream for the fireside."

"Look at the sky, Timov. The wind has banked and is blowing down through the Forest for the first time since we began. If the elk are still grazing on those fields above the ravines, we can get very close by crawling along the nearest gully. They won't see us or smell us."

Small lightnings flashed in Timov's eyes as he imagined the approach. "We'll have to leave Blind Side behind. They'll see him in the gully."

"That'll just convince them they're safe. Elk don't think of men when they see Horse."

Timov excitedly agreed, and Hamr arranged some stones and gravel into the shape of an elk and lanced its heart with a straw. After a quick petition to the Beastmaker for sustenance in the wilderness, Hamr and Timov led Blind Side of Life through the feathery grass at the Forest's edge. Their eyes watched the needlework of the wind among the clouds, and expectation buoyed them, though they were buffeted by the wind in their faces.

On a sloping field of tasseled grass between the dark wall of the Forest and the crooked seams of the migratory trails, a herd of elks browsed. They glowed almost red in the heavy sunlight. The wind glinted in the antlers of the big males, and the horns of the bucks appeared blue with velvet. A nervous joy thrummed in the men as they slid down into the ravine and crept closer, bent over, leading Blind Side by a rope about his neck.

The occasional lowing of the females became audible as the hunters edged near enough to smell the musk of the herd. Neither man dared to peek over the edge of the gully for fear of being spotted; they crawled to the end of the gully, to where the rains had dumped the silt of the Forest and the grass grew in tufts majestic as headdresses. There they poked their heads up.

The elk grazed very close. The men could see the bristly white hair in the clefts of their hooves, the stiff lashes of their eyes, their blue lips rippling as they pulled the grass into their mouths. A giddy muscularity tensed the men, seeing their own excitement shining back from each other's faces.

Hamr signed for Timov to stay while he went back along the gully to a vantage where they could attack from two sides. But suddenly the herd shifted briskly. Hamr thought he had startled them, but when he peered through the brittle weeds, he saw that the herd had sensed another threatening presence. From the Forest, a pack of hyenas loped.

Back at the clogged end of the gully, the branches of a dead tree jutted from the silt. Hamr tethered Blind Side there, then dashed up the rocky slope, carrying two spears and calling behind to Timov, "Follow me!"

On the field, the elk had bunched, the females and young moving to the center of the encircling males. Hamr rushed the herd, as soon as he was within throwing distance heaving his familiar spear. It wobbled through the air and disappeared in the grass. The herd, aware now of the attacking men, stampeded toward the Forest, scattering the hyenas.

Hamr and Timov dashed after them, Hamr hurling his new spear. It arced cleanly and stabbed into the earth, its haft waving above the limp grass. When Timov handed him the first spear that he had retrieved, the two sprinted again. Now the herd swerved away from the hyenas, and ran obliquely toward the Forest. One of the young stumbled and fell under the leaping panicky feet.

"Forget the herd," Hamr ordered. "Take the fallen one."

Timov balked at sight of the half dozen hyenas tearing at the small elk. But when Hamr charged, he mustered his courage and followed.

The hyenas snapped viciously as the men approached, crouched, growling and barking, dashing forward and circling back to protect their prey.

Hamr threw his newest spear at the most aggressive of the hyenas. It easily dodged the missile, but it retreated. Timov, hurling rocks, remained several paces behind Hamr as he advanced, waving and thrusting his spear while both men shouted.

The hyenas withdrew, but still they stood glowering only a spear's thrust away, fangs bared in their black faces. When Hamr stooped to pull away the fawn, two of the beasts lunged forward. Timov leaped back, and Hamr swung his spear.

"Get over here and help me!" Hamr yelled.

Timov nudged closer, spear warily thrust out before him.

"Grab its hind legs," Hamr commanded. "I'll hold them off."

Timov obeyed. As he dragged away the animal, Hamr charged and scattered the hyenas. Most of them had already realized their prey was lost and had skulked away. Only three remained, gazing sullenly. Hamr picked up the new spear and backed off. With the spears tucked under his arm, he bent and lifted the small elk's front legs.

At the edge of the gully, they dropped the heavy animal. Hamr took out his flint knife and cut back the hide before the haunches, so that he could unstring several tendons from the back legs. Timov stood, spear in hand, standing off the three hyenas that paced angrily in the grass. They were close enough so he could smell their hot stink, though the air was bossed with the aroma of elk's blood.

"Get Blind Side," Hamr said. He punched holes in the flaps of skin at the elk's torn belly and strung the tendons through, tying back the hide to keep the viscera from spilling out. When Timov brought Blind Side along the gully, Hamr picked up the hind legs, Timov the front, and they slung the animal over the horse's back.

They marched off with their prize, Timov hooting

a triumphant song, laughing at the hyenas—foolish night creatures daring to hunt by day and catching a meal for men instead of for themselves.

Hamr let him sing, glad for his help. But inside he felt a measureless silence. That was the quietude of his awe, which no song could dispel. They had failed today; if not for the hyenas, who usually prowled alone at night, there would be no meat again at the fire. Certainly this was the doing of the Beastmaker, providing for his chosen.

A mountain of clouds cast a shadow over the land, the hyenas' threatening cries grew long and lonely, and the syrupy smell of blood twisted like mischief in the wet wind.

Well fed and exhausted from dressing the fawn after a long day's work, Cyndell and Duru curled up together beside the fire while the sun still smoldered among the trees. When they were asleep and the fire burning vigorously, Timov climbed the knoll that blocked the rivering chill and found Hamr gazing into the nomadic fires westward.

"Why did you smile when Father was laid out?"

"Did I?" Hamr asked, distracted by the constellations hardening in the darkness. He pondered what he had done wrong during the hunt today, and saw the herd-patterns in the stars.

Timov sat down beside him, emboldened by their success at the hunt. Large emotions moiled in his chest: the joy of achievement and the fear of the next hunt seething above the constant sorrow of having lost everything—family, clan, and tribe. Kinship blazed in him for this man he had once feared. Now he was all that remained of the male mysteries. Timov stared hard at his bold profile, wondering at the malice he had learned from that face. He saw only the carved silhouette of the Tortoise clan, the features set wide apart from generations of facing out to sea. "You always smiled whenever the dead were laid out. Why?"

Hamr turned, his rapt gaze filled with shadow. "I will always laugh at death."

"But why?" Awe and fear clashed in Timov, and he had to look away, at the purple ethers in the sky, to keep the largeness of his feelings from breaking into tears. So much had been lost. Had Hamr felt none of that? "Death is terrible."

"To return to the Beastmaker is terrible?" Hamr put a firm hand on Timov's arm and squeezed till it hurt. A smile glinted in the dark. "You've got it backwards. Dying is all right. It's living that's terrible."

Timov flinched. Hamr saw the fear in the boy and let his arm go. He looked back into the dark wind and calmed himself. Timov's questions had reminded him of his grief, and he did not want to feel that anymore. Out here, grief was as dangerous as the Wolf. The boy had been good today, and Hamr would need him to be good again tomorrow. When he faced Timov, his voice had fallen almost to rustling silence, "Death makes it okay to laugh."

Duru beamed with pride for Hamr for days after he had brought back an elk from the hunt. Aradia had chosen him, so she knew he was good. Aradia would not have wanted him otherwise. She had always had the best of what the Blue Shell could offer—the best of Mother's love, the choicest cuts of meat at the feasts, for her renowned beauty, the best shells and pelts from her suitors, and, surely, the best of all men for her husband. And now he was Duru's, and she was proud of him, no matter that Mother Cyndell feared him and thought him spirit-possessed.

"You know why I've come, don't you?" Cyndell had told her several times since they had lost their chance to go to the Eyes of the Bear. "Your mother was my friend. Among the Mothers, death does not loosen any bonds. Her spirit would torment me if I left you to the men. You don't feel the difference yet, but someday, if we live that long, you will, and then you will be glad for the mysteries I will teach you."

Cyndell told her nothing more. They foraged together every day, sought fresh water and edible plants for hours, but the older woman told her nothing new. They reminisced about the Mothers and children they remembered. They sang the old songs, repeated many of the old stories, and discussed the various ways of preparing the plants they found.

At first, Duru thought Cyndell was withholding, waiting until she was older. Then she noticed that the older woman was far more intent on finding each day's food than in discussing the Great Mother and their place in the world with Her. And that was because the land was changing.

Less and less of the world was familiar. The farther north they journeyed, the stranger the plants became. Cyndell said nothing, but it was clear that her knowledge was of little use in a realm whose vegetation she did not recognize. The wide-branching trees of the south became rare, replaced by pines, enormous cedars, and goliath evergreens whose cones stood straight up on their branches. Firs. She had heard of these green monarchs, these grand, silvergreen giants, from an ancient song remembered by the Grandmothers. Those old dames had sung of their Grandmothers, whose Grandmothers had come from a place in the north where the pinecones stood tall on the trees and rivers of ice nestled between the mountains even at the height of summer. They had called that domain *taiga*.

Cyndell became yet more frightened of their fate when she remembered those songs from her faraway childhood. The Grandmothers of the Grandmothers had remembered a land of tusked panthers, voracious lions, and ghostly fires in the night sky. There was no point in terrifying Duru and Timov. They were proud to be traveling with Hamr. The elk he had scavenged had fed them well for many days, and they still had cords of its dried thews and had used its hide to replace the sandals they had worn out in their wandering. And though he had yet to kill any further creature in the hunt, even a hare or a squirrel, he was their strength.

What would become of them in this unknown land, where the trees stood like spears, where each leaf was sharp as a needle? Every day, at dawn's first sting of color, Cyndell made an offering to the Great Mother, thanking Her for sparing them from the hungers of the night beasts and begging Her to take them back to Her bosom, to nourish them again from the tribal warmth of her right teat.

Duru helped with the offerings. She was quickest to find a moss-bellied rock, a pregnant root bole, or a vulval tree cleft that had the correct shape to suggest the Mother's ubiquitous presence. There in the precarious light, they would fashion an offering of leaves or chaff-wings to suggest an animal or insect favored by the Mother.

For Duru, this was play. But Cyndell believed their survival depended on these prayers, that she had to focus her will strongly or death would gain on them. So, the rain-threaded morning when she crouched before the sacral shape of a hollowed stump and the wind broke the acorn doll she had meticulously crafted, she knew her trespass in the wilderness was endangered.

Hamr and Timov slouched past as she knelt to retrieve the broken acorn puppet. "Get out of the rain, Mama Cyndell," Timov said. "It doesn't look like it's going to clear anytime soon. You'll be damp all day if you get soaked now."

Cyndell knew Timov was right, and she stood up. What would be, she could not change. She looked for Duru. After finding the pelvic-shaped stump, the girl had gone back to the shelter of the hawthorn covert. Under the wall and overhang of the spiny shrub, she sat plaiting hemp and feeding twigs to a small fire. The remnants of the acorn and berry mash that she had prepared for the men to take on their hunt lay beside her on the sheet of bark, where she had crushed them with a rock.

Under the arbor, the ground was dry though the rain pattered brightly among the glossy leaves. Cyndell sat beside Duru. "I've seen signs," she said to the girl.

"Panther signs?"

"No. Mother signs. Bark scratchings, leaf folds. Tiny marks. Nothing a man would notice. I've been seeing them for two days now. Other women have foraged here during this last lunar quarter."

"You've told Hamr?"

"Not yet. I can tell they're not Panther women. They're some other clan—I don't know what totem. But I think they live in the fir forest. Hamr won't want to go there until he finds Panther signs. It's too difficult for his horse."

"But maybe these people can help us find the Panther."

"Hamr will fear that they'll make us slaves. A worthy fear. Every tribe wants new hands."

"We should tell him, though."

"First, I wanted to tell you. We should decide what we need to do before we tell Hamr, or he will decide for us."

"He is leading us, Mother Cyndell. He must decide."

"He is just a man, Duru. He can lead men, if others, like Timov, will follow. But we are women. Only we know our needs. We must lead ourselves. You're still a girl, but as you get older you will see that what I'm saying is true."

"What are our needs as women?"

"Above all else, the Mother. She sustains the whole world. Look about you. The land is Her body. See how strange Her body has become?"

"We are far from home. This is the taiga that you said the Grandmothers of the Grandmothers sang about."

"Yes, this is the taiga, but only its beginning. The land gets stranger yet, farther north. See this hawthorn arbor?" Cyndell opened her arms to the enclosure of tangled thorn boughs. "Why did we camp here and not over there, where it is just as dry?" She pointed across a thicket of birch to a dark den of fir trees.

"The plants there are less familiar."

"Exactly. Here, we know these pink blossoms, the mushrooms that grow nearby, and the animals that favor this shrub. There, we know nothing. It's the same with our wandering. With the Mothers—of any tribe—we will recognize the ways. But out here in the taiga, less and less is familiar, more and more we are in jeopardy of eating a deadly plant, disturbing a hungry beast. We need the protection of the Mother. As women we need Her, so that what children we bear will have protection and provision.''

Duru laid a small hand on Cyndell's knee, wanting the older women to feel her understanding. ''Everything you say is true, Mother Cyndell. But, for now, I'm too young to bear children. This is a good time for me to follow my husband, wherever he may lead me.''

''But why, Duru?'' Cyndell felt a burst of anger but restrained herself. ''Hamr is not your choice. Why let the dead choose for you?''

The child's face flinched with pain at the memory of Aradia. She had seen her die through the heat of her fever, and the image of her sister in the delirium of the flames always shimmered in her blood, an inch behind her eyes. ''Hamr is all I have left of Aradia. He's the best of the men. That's why she chose him. She always had the best.''

''Still, he's just a man. Just a man, Duru. You must think of the Mother. He won't.''

The rain had faded to a soft mist. Duru dropped the rope she had been twisting nervously and stepped out into the chill fragrant air. Nimbus clouds streaked scarlet with dawnlight promised more rain. She headed down toward the thicket, to gather mushrooms.

Mother, Aradia, Biklo, all dead—the Mothers she knew, gone. Why should she live as a slave? Why should she live at all? The fever should have killed her, as it had killed the others. Why was she alive and the others gone? Even now, a moon after those cruel days, the wildness of the fever and the grief still spun inside her like Hamr's wheel. It was far inside her—the chills were gone, the tears no longer burned her eyes and cheeks when she remembered those dear ones she had lost—but the grief still churned in her, the pain of dying churned far inside, where she only went in her fright dreams.

With Hamr, everything was different, new, unlike all that had gone before. Duru did not want to be with the Mothers of any tribe—ever again. She did not want to be reminded of the good way life had once been, and could nevermore be. She loved Hamr, not just because Aradia had, but because he had led her here to the taiga, to where summer had an unfamiliar shape and where there were new memories to be made.

Even Timov, idle and coddled, had become stronger, more alert and useful than he had ever been in the clan. Duru glimpsed in him the creative power of their suffering.

Mist dewed in her long hair, and her locks garlanded her neck as she bent to pluck white mushrooms from the turf among the skinny birch. She put the mushrooms in the woven-grass sack she carried at her hip. When she had enough, she looked up and marveled at this strange land that so disturbed Mother Cyndell. Indeed, it looked as though it had fallen from the sky; giant boulders scrabbled with vines teetered above the ravines, and along the bluffs and hillocks, among smaller boulders and shattered slabs of rock, fir trees glowed with an inner darkness. Blind Side would be having a hard time picking his way through this jumbled land.

Suddenly jays swirled around a blue spruce, then burst through the birch thicket with rowdy screams. Something had frightened them from the berry shrubs, where they had been loitering.

Duru pulled the draw-cord on her foraging sack and backed away, peering among the slender trees for what had startled the jays. She hoped to see a civet cat, though she was afraid to find a panther slinking through the narrow spaces of the grove. Instead, just coming clear in the dark rain-glinting shadows of the shrubs, she faced the grinning fangs and blackened visages of hyenas.

Shouting to frighten them, Duru looked about for a stick, a rock. Her noise made their grins wider; their thick shoulders, powerful striped legs, and leering muzzles pushed into the light. There were six of them. She recognized the pangs of hunger in their tiny eyes, their ribbed gutsacks.

With a howl, she swooped and snatched a fallen branch, used both hands to bring it up before her.

But the beasts growled shrilly, advancing. This was a creature their size, prey that would not thwart their hunger. Carefully they approached, each waiting for the other to initiate the attack, eager to follow through and get down to the urgent necessity of feeding.

Cyndell, who was busy filling gourds with rainwater, heard Duru's cries, dropped the gourds, and rushed down the slope toward the thicket. The girl backed into view as Cyndell reached the hawthorn arbor, and the older woman could see her fending off something. On the run, she snatched as big a rock as she could lift in one hand.

The hyenas, assured of their prey's vulnerability, converged with sudden swiftness. Duru thrust the branch at them, turned, and ran. The branch slowed the beasts, kept them from a lunging run, but sharpened the rage of their attack. With tails streaming, in full voice, they pursued.

Cyndell paused in her rush when she saw the hyenas shoot out of the thicket. Their enraged barks iced through her. Here was the doom the Mother had foretold. The pack, open mouths and grinning fangs, was gaining swiftly on the child and would momentarily pounce on her.

Crazed with terror, Cyndell screamed and threw herself forward. The slant of the land flung her faster than her feet could move, and she fell, rolled in a flail of arms and hair, cursing herself for failing the child, then leaped to her feet.

The hyenas fanned out and narrowed in from the sides, to keep Duru from fleeing left or right. As the land rose, her dash slowed, and they were following closer, ready to pounce, two paces behind their prey, black faces frenzied with chase-ferocity. At that moment Cyndell flew screaming down the slope of the bluff.

The rock she threw thudded off one hyena's back and elicited a hurt yelp that briefly slowed the charge of the others. Cyndell seized Duru's arm and hauled her past, pushed her up the bluff.

"Run! Run! Don't look back! Run!"

The next instant the beasts were upon Cyndell. One carnivorous jaw clamped on her arm and, in a stab of twisting pain, she was thrown off balance. Another jaw fastened on her leg. She went down in a tangle of sharp, gasping hurts. Immediately the others jumped her, sinking their fangs into her face and throat, tearing at the skin of her torso with their hind claws. Her blood sprayed; the steamy feel of it, the sweet smell of it, heightened their voracity. They were looped in salty entrails, burrowing their putrid muzzles under ribs for the glisteny liver and the quivering heart.

Screaming her terror, Duru flew up the bluff, past the indifferent boulders where the jays had perched already anticipating what carrion would be left to them. The snarling and snapping from below drove Duru harder than she ever thought she could run. Her breath had left her with her screaming, and she staggered uphill, toward the silver firs, taking in air with wrenching sobs.

Hamr and Timov had heard Duru's first cries from the high ledge, where they had gone in the hope of spearing one of the goats they had seen the day before. Hamr paused only long enough to loosen the rope that tethered his horse, so Blind Side could pull free if a big cat came. Then he and Timov, spears held low for balance, scurried down the broken landscape.

Before they found Duru, they saw from their high vantage what had happened. Timov howled his rage. But the hyenas did not bother to look up, though they recognized his voice from the day they had lost their elk to him. He was too far away. They would eat well before he came close enough to despoil them again.

Duru had collapsed among pinestraw and rock-clutching roots on the steep grade at the skirt of the Forest. Panting and blind with tears, she clutched at her brother when he lifted her. Hamr stood over them, a spear in each fist. The silence of awe in his heart that he had experienced when they had taken the elk had turned to horror.

Timov rose, left Duru sitting in the pinestraw and started down the slope.

"Where are you going?" Hamr asked.

Timov looked back, perplexed that Hamr would have to ask. "To drive them off. Kill one if I can."

"Leave them be."

Timov's perplexity narrowed to anger. "That's Mother Cyndell down there. We can't leave her to them."

"Let them have her meat. She's with the Great Mother now, not with them."

"Her meat?" Anger flexed in his voice. "You talk

of the body that nursed me and Duru. She should be buried.''

"Let the beasts have her,'' Hamr insisted. "Someday it'll be you and me.''

"No,'' Timov spat back. "That's Mama Cyndell.'' He turned and hastened down the hillside.

Hamr shook his head, but let him go. He felt a weak grip on his calf and looked down at Duru.

"Help him,'' she said. When he did not move, she added, "If I am truly your wife, then you must obey me. A woman of my clan is dead. Bury her.''

Hamr sighed and helped Duru to her feet. "You'll wait by the fire, where I can see you?''

After leaving the girl in the hawthorn covert, Hamr continued down the slope, shouting for Timov to wait. The youth was already at the top of the bluff, throwing rocks at the pack. The beasts moved off reluctantly but circled back, heads low, tails tucked.

"We'll bury her where she fell,'' Hamr said, coming alongside Timov. "You'll dig. I'll drive off the beasts.''

Timov thanked Hamr with a nod, not daring to meet his gaze, knowing the somber indifference he would face there. Shouting, the men advanced on the feeding hyenas. From the weedstalks and long grass, crows waiting their turn flapped up into the misty rain like black, answering cries.

Duru chanted while the men worked. The rhythmic words came from the inner place in her the Mothers had opened, where they now lived with their teachings. She was the last. But she could not imagine going on alone. Who would teach her all she had yet to learn?

As if in answer, when the men returned they brought her Cyndell's calendar bracelet. She wept over it while they cleaned up. Then she revived the small fire under the hawthorn trellis; if she did not make herself do something, she would turn into a rock. As she crumbled dried leaves to powder and struck sparks from her fire-pebble, the enormity of her aloneness crouched over her mind.

Hamr and Timov sat before the fire, soaked with sweat and rain, while Duru told them about the signs Mother Cyndell said she had seen in the Forest.

"Mother signs. There's a tribe living not far from here."

"Panther?" Timov asked, hopefully.

Duru pouted indifferently. "Someone is in the Forest. I'm sure if we look, we'll find them."

Hamr broke a pine bough over his thigh and fed the fire with the resinous wood. "So long as it's not raining, we're safer in the ravines."

"Not safe enough for Mama Cyndell," Timov said harshly, and stoked the kindling.

A sob broke through Duru. When her brother put his arm around her, she said, "She gave herself to save me. It should have been me."

"She's happier now, with the Mother," Timov soothed. "She didn't want to wander like this. She only came to be with you."

Duru wept quietly, eyes squeezed shut, face glistening in the orange blaze. "It should have been me."

Hamr poked at the fire. What do you tell a child? The truth would be: "It was you—that's why you're suffering. Cyndell feels no more pain." But those words would not quite fit his breath, nor would platitudes about Cyndell returning to the Great Mother, or the peace of lying with the Mudman. Silence was all that offered itself in him, and that made him angry. There had to be something with which he could face her tearful anguish. He looked at her. Her child-face buckled with hurt, and the tears flowed freely. Timov, too, wept, leaning against his sister, shoulders jerking.

Hamr's anger softened. He wished he could cry. Long ago, shortly after his father had died, that power had weakened in him. He had put all his will and energy into making himself strong on the outside, to make up for the loss of his father's power—and to fend off the mockery of others, who thought him a fool for wanting to be great. His body had become strong—his will had become strong—but he had lost that deepest strength that comes only from grief.

When he thought of Aradia, the softness in his life, who might have made him strong again in his deepest self, he felt rage at those who had killed her—and he felt emptiness. No tears rose in him. Yet, certainly, she deserved his tears if anyone in his life did. Spretnak, too, who had taught him to dare for greatness. The relief of tears had never flared in him for those he loved the most. Something darker moved inside when he felt grief. Somehow he knew: The dead did not need his tears. They were free. What he felt in himself when he thought of them, what he allowed himself, was the hurt of living on.

Once Duru and Timov had calmed, Hamr said in his softest voice, "Cyndell came with us this far. To turn aside now would be to waste her death. We must go on. We must find the Panther people."

"But they may be here," Timov said, "in the Forest."

"Perhaps," Hamr said to the fire, then looked up at the two across from him, "and perhaps not. We dare not gamble with our lives."

"How far will we go?" Duru asked in a thin voice.

"As far north as the herds have gone," Hamr answered. "Surely there we will find the great hunters—and among them, the Panther people."

That afternoon, though the sky continued to lower veils of rain, the travelers set out again. Blind Side of Life, happy to be back on the herd trail, accepted Duru's weight. She sat easily on the beast, clutching Cyndell's satchel to her chest.

Ahead, where a stream ran beside the trail, softer trees than the fir and spruce arched over the ravine and made a green tunnel. When evening fell, they camped in the gully. Timov started the fire, Hamr led Blind Side to the streambank, where he could graze, and Duru set about foraging nearby as she had with her nurse every evening till now.

She followed the contour of the land upstream, to where a pond had silted in, choked with mint grass, poplars, willows, and become a meadow. There, she knew she would find the tenderest shoots, the purple-tipped tubers that made the best broths, the soft-cored reeds whose hearts were sweet, and the chive grass and garlic bulbs that fortified with pungency the meal she was gathering.

Her hands expertly parted the turf to find the bulbs she sought, lifted rocks, always toward herself so they opened away and would not expose her to snake or scorpion, and plucked delicate blades from among poisonous creepers. She reached into her forage sack for twine and brought out a thin braid of silvery strands, hair Cyndell had plaited from her own head. Suddenly, the girl's wise hands, that long ago stopped needing supervision, forgot what to do.

The meal that night was silent. There were no songs or stories to fill Cyndell's absence. Each ate without speaking, staring into the fire, and when done, they lay with their backs turned to each other and slept. The next seven nights were the same. But then, the land began to change more drastically yet, and their evening meals gradually became more animated with the strange news of what they had seen.

The ravine country thinned out as the migratory trails opened northward into vast sweet-smelling grasslands. Ponds and kettle lakes shone in the distance like pearls. While to the south and east the Forest loomed larger than ever with giant green vaults. Among the brindled shadows, a white elk with immense antlers appeared and watched them. The wind carried new, peculiar smells. Silk tufts of unknown plants flurried by. Vast herds shifted in the north like dark clouds, too distant and too dangerous to approach. At the edge of creeks, the travelers knelt and did not recognize the swift stabs of fish that went by or the black toads squatting in the mud or the flickers of gray lizards among pebbles, big and speckled as eggs.

None of them could any longer explain the weather. Rain fell from invisible lakes, sometimes far away, leaning like lavender shadows over the blue firs, dropping out of a clear sky, and once in a while boiling overhead in clouds filled with silver light, then falling as steamy sheets and disappearing before reaching the ground.

At night, wolf voices cried from the Forest with supernatural sorrow, and blue and green fire reeled across the stars in aquatic ripples. The three travelers fell asleep every night with that radiant smoke in their eyes, trying to figure what it was, trying to read the unfelt wind blowing through it from between the stars.

Glaciers appeared in the north. They burned with sunlight under the enormous sky. Arrows of birds came and went from there each day. The sun was hot, but the wind, when it turned from those glares of ice, blew cool and delivered, with the witchy fragrance of the grass, the sadder, lonelier smell of winter.

No longer was food simply found. Hunting was nearly impossible in the open land, and only one rabbit fell under Timov's slingshot, none under Hamr's spears. Duru puzzled over wisps of mysterious grasses and nibbled at narrow, bitter roots, afraid to try them in her broths. She watched what Blind Side ate and cooked that. Gone were the sweet marrow of the cane-brakes, the fat tubers from the silted meadows, the friendly mushrooms, the well-known berries. Each day, all three had to forage to find enough edible plants to make one meal.

At last Hamr admitted the migratory trail was good only for Blind Side, who enjoyed grazing on the abundant grasses. For them to survive, they would have to leave the trail to forage in the Forest. They led the horse away from the path grooved by his ancestors, and made their way through the woeful terrain of scattered boulders and scraggly, twisted lone-pines toward the immense blue doors of the Forest.

Flowers burst wherever sunlight lanced the Forest. Purple mallows glowed in the shadows among clouds of mushrooms, and red and orange gills of fungus ledged tree trunks. Here was the forbidden realm of the travelers' past—the domain of the Eyes of the Bear. Here, everything was strange to the people who had lived among the seacliffs and the grasslands.

Yet, after long wandering among gullies and ravines, the plenitude of the Forest comforted the Blue Shell. The rank, sweet smell of burdock mingled with

resinous breezes slipping down the dark corridors
from the mysterious interior. And every turn of the
wind smudged the air with odors of blossoms, water-
plants, and a tumult of animals.

Duru stared up at the high peaks of trees burning
with morninglight and was glad Hamr had led them
here. Above the branches, the day opened like a sliced
melon. Another beautiful day, like the other eight glorious days they had enjoyed since entering the Forest.
She felt sure this day would be as bountiful as the
others. The skins of the squirrels Hamr and Timov had
killed stood taut on the drying rack they had fashioned
from branches. A dozen skins of tawny fur, ready in
another day or so to be stitched into clothing.

The remnants of last night's stew lay in the firepit,
furry with ants. Duru had wanted to dry the meat, but
Hamr had laughed at her efforts to do so over the fire.
"We need salt to do it right," he had said as though she
did not already know that. She had shrugged when he
dropped her meat skewers into the flames and doused
them with broth. "Let the Forest eat, too—She feeds us
well enough." Duru had shrugged, because she had
enough work to do curing the numerous skins and
strings of gut and sharpening their wooden knives for
that day's certain kill.

There was so much to hunt. Not only squirrels,
though they were the easiest to kill, but dwarf pigs,
thick black snakes more like eels for their lack of fangs
and poison, and weasels, ferrets, sloths, and porcu-
pines. So much to hunt that hunting had become more
like foraging. Hamr and Timov no longer bothered to
rise with first light. They slept on the soft leaf litter in
root coves until sunlight rays appeared like spears
among the trees. Then they leisurely nibbled the berries Duru had gathered the previous day, while Hamr

sat under a tree and plucked hairs from his chin with the clam shells he carried in his satchel.

Timov liked to explore the sunstruck corners of the Forest, startling mouse deer and tree foxes and once braining a surprised ptarmigan with a shot from his sling. He wore its feathers in his hair and believed he was now better endowed to ascend toward the Sky World. He climbed the tall trees, looking for bee hives. With smoking bundles of leaves prepared by Duru and lifted up by rope, he drowsed the bees, then broke open the hives for the amber combs and sweet larvae.

From the treetops, Timov stared out over the spires of the Forest, marveling at the green vastness rolling with the hills toward the snow mountains in the far purple of the east. North, the Forest ended, and he could see the seas of grasslands, the drifting herds, and the bluewhite curve of the world's icy edge. West, the land opened to the flat, torn terrain of the herd trails, and south, the trees ranged forever. The vantage always left him giddy, even when there was no honey to loot, and he came down into the gloom of the Forest with the wind shining in his eyes and ran among the trees on springy legs, yawping like a bird.

At nightfall, all three of them sang out the day-count and watched on Cyndell's bracelet their approach to the cold chambers of the moon. They had to find a strong, friendly tribe before winter, and they hoped that their fire-chant would alert others to their intelligence and worthiness. After the chant, when no answering call came, Hamr told proud adventure tales to bolster the courage of his young companions and keep his mind off their plight. Duru and Timov participated, embellishing the fantasies, until sleep compelled and they drifted into their dreams without the hurt of remembering where they really were, or why.

Only Blind Side of Life was overtly unhappy in the Forest. He missed the herd scent of the migratory trail and the prairie grass he preferred to the bitter tangled weeds that sprouted from the treerot in these tight spaces. The cluttered smells here sometimes confused him, and he always had to be led, for fear of breaking a leg among the numerous roots and fallen branches. While the men hunted, he moved among the trees, nibbling here and there, mostly sulking. Occasionally, the wind shifted from the north and delivered memories of the minty grass and the stale but comforting odors of the herd, which he sorely missed. Then he would lift his nostrils and turn his body into the wind and stand, head high, like a sighted horse, until the wind slipped away.

The morning of their ninth day in the maze of trees, Blind Side whinnied nervously. A harsh stench of decay spoiled the blossom fragrances. He tried to turn away, but Hamr took him by the rope tied about his neck and led him closer. Since entering the Forest, he and Timov had been finding bent blades of grass and nicks in the treebark that might have been tribal messages. Perhaps Blind Side sensed other people—or, if he was nervous about a beast, it was best to move anyway. They walked over a small rise and through a thicket of alders before they began to smell what the horse had smelled—the feculence of dead bodies. Hamr mounted his horse and Timov and Duru fell behind.

The thicket opened to a grove of blue-shadowed fir, where a woman in a plaited grass robe stood with her back to them, arms raised, a skull-sized rock gripped in both hands. Before her, hanging by their hair from the low limbs of the fir, were three human heads. Their eyes had been gouged by crows, and from their tattered necks hung juts of bone and blackened cords of flesh.

Duru gasped, and Blind Side of Life whinnied and stamped nervously.

The woman started, turned to face them, and they saw that she was pregnant—at least four moons. Long locks of yellow hair fell to her shoulders and were twined into the grass of her robe, which parted to expose large breasts circled in red and black paint. She held the rock toward them and backed off. "Get away!" she shouted. "This is tainted ground."

She spoke in words more roughly hewn than the speech they used, yet the wanderers understood her. Hamr lowered his spear and opened his arms in greeting. "No harm," he promised. "We're Panther people, looking for the Thundertree."

Duru put her hand on his thigh, wanting him to turn around and retreat from the horror. Instead, he walked Blind Side closer, and Duru and Timov followed reluctantly. Now they could see the entire grove and noticed, under a haze of flies, the beheaded corpses slumped under the trees, torsos ripped open and limbs mangled by scavengers. Beside them lay the carcasses of two panthers reduced to heaps of torn fur and exposed bone. In the trees, the birds that had been feasting fretted angrily at these additional intruders.

"Leave here or be cursed!" the pregnant woman yelled as she backed between the firs.

Hamr dismounted to pursue her, but Duru grabbed his arm and pointed to where a small wooden bowl wisped a burnt offering. "She's a priestess," the girl said. "She's burning resins to free the spirits of the dead. Let her go or she'll curse you."

Timov took Duru's hand and pulled her behind Blind Side and back into the alder thicket. The priestess was gone, and Hamr hurried to where she had been, to see which way she had run. Blind Side whinnied a warning, and Hamr pulled up short before a sudden rustling in the brush.

Ahead, a barberry shrub parted, and a black stump of a head emerged, ears laid back, green eyes glaring, fangs opened around a sizzling hiss.

Hamr shouted and thrust his spear. The panther jumped from its cover, a living shadow, and moved noiselessly among the trees, circling toward where Timov and Duru cowered. Blind Side cried out and kicked his front hooves. Hamr dashed to him and quickly pulled him back into the thicket. Duru clasped Hamr, while Timov, his back toward the horse, held his spear with both hands ready for attack.

The panther was nowhere to be seen. But Blind Side's jittery pacing indicated it was nearby. With Timov watching in the rear, and Duru close to the horse, Hamr led them back the way they had come. Warily, they edged through the Forest until they came to a brook, where they paused to orient themselves.

"Who were those dead men?" Timov asked.

"You saw the big cats that died with them," Hamr answered. "They must've been Panther men."

"That was a stalking panther stopped you from chasing the priestess," Duru observed. "Its tail was bobbed."

"But who killed the men?" Timov searched the shadowy chambers of the Forest for movement. "Their enemy must be near here. They were dead less than a day."

"If it's war," Hamr said, "everyone will think we're enemy—both the Panther people and their foes."

"What do we do?" Timov whined.

"We should make an offering to show we're outsiders," Hamr answered.

"The priestess would be near her people," Duru said. "The Thundertree will know about us soon."

"We're getting out of the woods," Hamr decided, playing his alert stare across the nearby branches, looking for spearmen in the treetops. Suddenly, the bountiful, sunshot woodland menaced them with every wind-blur and bird squawk.

Shadowy streams crisscrossed the Forest, swollen with glacial melt and the thunderstorms of summer, and the noise of their tumult charged the air. Before, the sound had been comforting, reminiscent of the sea, but now Timov's and Duru's ears ached, trying to listen past the water sounds for threatening noises. Hamr watched Blind Side, but could not entirely trust the stallion's more acute ears, since the horse was still unfamiliar with the Forest. They followed the brook north and did not stop to pick up the cured squirrel-pelts at their last camp even though Duru pleaded. By afternoon, they stepped into the brazen light of the open plains.

Blind Side was delighted, and waded eagerly into the sighing grasses. While he frisked and grazed, the others lay in the open, staring at clouds toppling across the enormous sky. Yet even with the sunlight hot on their faces, fright still chilled them. They listened hard and often raised their heads to scan. The darkness of the Forest had soaked into their senses, and as they sat on the boulders that rose above the tasseled rye, they heard the lowing of the Great Bear in the wind, the cough of the Panther in the soft clop of Blind Side's hooves, and the dead-leaf slither of the Serpent in the hiss of wind through the grass.

"A rival tribe would've taken the heads," Timov said, around the stick of grass he nervously chewed.

"No beast tied their heads to the branch," Hamr responded; he lay on his side atop a lichen-splotched boulder, watching his horse drifting slow as a cloud through the rye. "Had to be a tribe did it."

Duru grunted agreement from behind Hamr's sandal, tugging on a stitch with her teeth. "At least we should've gathered the pelts."

"We were scared," Timov said.

"Careful," Hamr corrected. He accepted his sandal from Duru and put it on.

"At least the priestess honors the dead," Duru said. "They must have some respect for the living, too. Maybe they'll come for us when the priestess tells them we're Panther people."

"Unless," Hamr suggested, "she was the enemy's priestess, catching her adversaries' souls."

"Then why did the Panther stop you from chasing her?" Timov asked.

They fretted the rest of the day. At night, they retreated to the edge of the Forest, to forage and to shelter from the soft rains. With Blind Side of Life to warn of beasts, they succumbed to their weariness and slept deeply, huddled in the embrace of root ledges, blanketed with leaves and branches. Usually on this wearying journey, sleep was dreamless or illuminated with radiant memories of that day's foraging and hunting or the persistent undertow of fleeing perilous shadows among the trees. But that night, still thrumming with fear after seeing the severed heads, Timov suffered a unique dream.

A thunderstorm, racked with lightning, burned in the night. Hot rain fell in sheets. Thunder squashed him, and he lay pressed against a tree, watching the torn rain part around a man, a hideously huge man with a square head and hair like hackles, beard short and stiff as pine needles. Long eyes stared from under a shelf of brow, above flared nostrils and a sinewy mouth. Rain streamed from naked, solid shoulders that in the gray light looked hammered from rock. A hard pulse beat in a neck swollen as a puff-adder's.

Sudden strong hands reached for Timov, and the blunt fingers pulled him close enough so he could see the fish-skin scar parting the beard of the giant's right jaw, to feel the velvet breath, musty as new earth, and to hear words, gruff as two stones clacking, "Go back!"

Timov lurched awake, the long eyes still visible in a flash of dream-lightning—wolfish, ice-green eyes, nailing him with cold rage. He sat up into a whispering rain, saw pink twigs of dawn among the trees, and hugged himself.

Hamr laughed at Timov's dream. "The ancestors are taunting you."

Duru rubbed her brother's hunched shoulders. Her sleep had been restless, too, for she had been too frightened to let herself sleep deeply. Every owl hoot and wind-rubbed branch defeated her fatigue, and she had lain awake with trepidation in the watched dark.

"Hamr," she said to his broad back as he urinated against a pine, "all night I felt we were prey."

"That's why Timov needed that dream," Hamr explained through a yawn, tightening the antelope-hide about his waist. He squeezed the back of the boy's neck. "We are prey for whatever can catch us, aren't we? Come on. Let's see if we can find a meal without getting eaten."

A short while later on the grasslands, while trying to run down a black snake for a meal, they found the site where the ghost dancer had killed the tribesmen earlier in the spring. Their bones had been scattered by scavengers and glowed white as pieces of cloud in the emerald shadows of the tundra rye. Hamr picked up a skull, smashed at one side like a piece of pottery. He examined the broken cranium, held it out to Timov, who shrank from it.

"It's just bone," Hamr said.

"Human bone, Hamr. They died violently. Their spirits—"

"Put it down!" Duru yelled.

"Spirits can't hurt us anymore than your dream can." Hamr dropped the skull, smiled at the others' diffidence, and waded through the rye. "Better to be afraid of what's living." In a lush patch he found a few charred twigs the rains had half buried and, nested among them, a black knife. The bone grip, though scorched, was intact. The leather bindings had burned away, and the seared handle opened its white interior like a pod to release the volcanic-glass haft of the knife.

"Duru," Hamr called from where he knelt. "Look at this." He pointed with the blade to a wavy line etched in the handle. "This is a Mother sign, isn't it?"

It was the Moon Serpent, who molted her two skins, of light and of darkness, each month. It was the birth knife, used to cut the umbilical. At midnight, it etched the protective circle in the magic ashes around the last tooth of fire, freeing the Sun from the womb-maw of the Earth. It was the only knife that could wound spirits. "It's Snake," she whispered. From her satchel, she withdrew a length of chewed tendon. "Will you bind it?"

Hamr fitted the bone halves together over the knife's haft, and wound the string about the grooved throat and butt of the handle. With his teeth, he tightened the bindings, then cut the tendon cleanly at the knots. It was a beautiful, mirror-black blade, he saw as he buffed it with his antelope-hide, far sharper than wood or flint but brittle, impractical for the hunt. He handed the knife to Duru. "Use it well."

Duru took the Moon Serpent in both hands, touched the tip to the charred spot in the grass where the fire had stained it. The knife's omen signified the cutting away of their old life and a new life promised. Giving Hamr a pleased smile she put the Moon Serpent in her satchel, carefully sheathed between leaf-packets of dried plants. Someday this knife would gleam before the fire of their own home, among new people, and she would tell their grandchildren how Grandfather Hamr retrieved the Moon Serpent from the Land of the Dead.

Timov called from a nearby gully. More bones lay there, with a spear hollowed by termites. They studied the spear and noted the Thundertree markings. But the wind shifted, and Blind Side whinnied. They climbed the scarp of the gully, searched upwind. Duru cried out, pointed into the glare of the rising sun where a shadow moved in the rye, larger than a panther, big as a deer but low, slinking under the grassheads. A moaning cry rose with the wind, reboant as a bull.

Timov clutched his sister, and they backed away along the edge of the gully. Duru flicked nervous looks toward the Forest, wondering if they could make it to the trees before whatever it was attacked.

But Hamr had lifted his spear and approached the shadow. Blind Side had backed off; there was no way to reach him without crossing before the thing in the grass. Hamr waved for Timov to back him up, and Timov left Duru behind a rock half her height and loaded his sling. He followed several paces behind Hamr, leaning back, ready for flight.

The moaning darkened to a bellow, and a figure rose from the grass, a black-furred shape, as big as two men, ox-shouldered, with a gruesome head and a cankerous craw of fangs. Ghoul eyes glared from a visage of pale, fungoid flesh.

Duru screamed; Timov whipped his slingshot, sending a rock whizzing wildly past Hamr's ear and into the grass. Hamr had ducked, expecting the creature to pounce. His spear left his hand of its own will, and gouged out earth beside the monster. It shambled forward with a mighty roar, and the two hunters ran.

Hooting cries assailed them as they sprinted for Duru, snatching her, each by one arm, and bolting for the Forest. Hamr glanced back once, to see the monster's head fall away and reveal a scowling man in panther-skin sitting atop another man's shoulders. A third man stood up in the grass and whirled the bullroarer he had devised from a vine and a thick piece of bark. Then they were off, bounding like pronghorns.

Stupefied at first, Hamr stalked to where the Panther men had duped him, and kicked the crude mask of birch bark and moss and shabby furs. The tribe of the Forest had just tested his courage, and found him wanting. He grabbed his spear, shook it over his head, and shouted furiously at the fleeing men. Laughter and jeers trickled back on the wind as the men disappeared among the ravines and gullies.

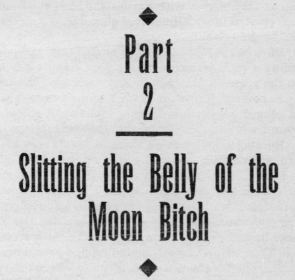

Part
2

Slitting the Belly of the Moon Bitch

For the Electrical fire is the spiritual substance, which God sends from heaven to sustain the bodies both of man and beast.

—Christopher Smart, JUBILATE AGNO

4

Ghost Dancing

Baat lay on his back, staring up through the branches of the Forest, watching the sun's light dapple with each breeze. He wanted to sleep, but dared not during the day, when the smallheads were about.

Since the spring, after he had killed that smallhead band on the tundra and raped their sorceress, he had slept fitfully by night, and never by day. Under the sun, the smallhead men stalked through the Forest in silent gangs, with poison-tipped spears and knives. Baat hid from them in the gloomiest enclaves of the Forest, among the tangled briars and snake-infested meres, where the smallheads were reluctant to follow. Yet here, too, in the darkest hollows, he was afraid to sleep. He blinked up at the sun, listening for the sounds of their narrow bodies slithering through the bramble.

At night, when the ul udi came down from the sky and fitted themselves into his body, Baat could see with their ghostly vision. The Forest shimmered like clear water then, and he could stare through the trees and the brush as if he were peering through the crystal clarity of a glacial lake. That was when he saw them dotting the terrain around him, each hunkered under a bush or beside a log, asleep or playing with their small fires, hugging their spears, waiting out the night to continue their hunt. Then, at dawn, the ul udi vapored away and left him blunt-sighted as any smallhead, knowing his enemy were out there but not sure exactly where.

But even so, Baat would not retreat to the eastern mountains, where he had lived before, free of the smallheads. He chose stubbornly to remain here, no matter his suffering, tied to these meres and briar patches by memories of a time long lost.

He fitted the bone-spout of his water-bladder to his lips, and washed the dryness of fear from his mouth. Though a creek ambled nearby, he never drank water from his hands. He collected his drink from pools where he could see the fish circling above their shadows. The smallheads poured their flavorless poisons in the streams and still pools and had killed most of the unwary People that way. Even at night, when these puny creatures huddled about their fires, they were a danger because they left deep pits in the Forest covered with branches and leaves and with sharp stakes pointing up from below. Sometimes they hid boulders in the treetops lashed to trip-vines. Once, as a child, he had found a clansman nailed to a tree with an antelope's prong weighted with rocks and slung from a vine.

Those dark memories convinced Baat that the smallheads were more deadly than the Dark Ones. The ul udi killed with Baat's hands and with fire from the sky, pressing their alertness into each moment of their victims' anguish, seeing and feeling death up close. But the smallheads killed from afar. To survive their killing wiles these several moons, he'd had to move about rarely and then only at night and with steadfast attentiveness. That had made it impossible for him to follow the north trails to the herds and the icefields of summer. Whenever he showed himself on the grasslands, they came after him. And now, despite all his precautions, they were closing in here in the Forest. Just yesterday three smallhead hunters had spotted him hiding in the bramble of a river isle and had used their drums to contact the others. He had been forced to kill them during the day, without the strength of the Dark Ones.

After that, Baat had run eastward until exhaustion had dropped him in this dark dell. But nightmares denied him rest, and now he felt sick with weariness and fear. He squinted into the sun, paring his attention to the fierce light above the branches, listening for the voices that sometimes came from there, when there was no wickedness in his heart.

Distantly, he heard a quiet voice: *Why do you stay here, where you are in danger? Nostalgia for these woodlands of your childhood is empty, Hollow Bone. If you die here, the Dark Ones will capture your light and torment you for many generations.*

"Bright Ones!" Baat called and immediately regretted his cry. He lay still, his ears straining to hear past the hum of his startled blood and the burble of the creek for the tiny sounds of encroaching smallheads.

Your days are almost over, the gentle voice opened again in him. *Soon, you can join us here in the sky, and we can listen to the wind of the sun as it sings through the heavens—and in that music, you will hear everything there is to know about peace and rest—and love. Come north, to the cairn of your ancestors, to the door of the mountain that leads to the sky.*

North—across the tundra, over the grasslands, where the smallheads could easily track him—was that his destiny? From the earliest days, long before there were smallheads to fear, the great ones of his tribe had gone there to die. How he yearned to follow them, to dance among the dolmen altar that the earliest ancestors had built. There, the Bright Ones had the power to lift his spirit out of the worn animal of his body and carry him to heaven. Yet it was this very hope of joining his ancestors that trapped him in these haunted woods.

As a child, these had been his groves and dells. He had grown up following the herds in the summer and wintering among these great firs. In his twentieth summer, without warning, the smallheads poisoned the streams and killed his two children, his wife and his parents. Grief-stricken, he left, and for many years lived with another tribe to the east. Now as an old man, he had come back to dance with the ghosts of his youth—at least, so he had thought when he first returned here, seven years ago.

During those years, Baat had visited the sky often: The Bright Ones came to dance in the meres and bogs far from the evil eyes of the smallheads, and with them he had soared up from the hungers of the earth, high into the star-studded void and had known the glorious raptures of the ul udi, while far below his body slept. Among those raptures was memory so vivid it was relived. He danced with the ghosts of his young family and lived a summer of happiness with them so sharp and intense that he wearied of the anguish he had endured in the years since their deaths. In autumn— scrawny from dreaming when he should have been hunting—he would return serenely to the eastern mountains, to the tribe of People, where his second family flourished, far from the smallheads.

In many ways, life in the mountains had been good to Baat. The children he had fathered there had grown to have children of their own, and he was revered as wise with years. Yet always he felt incomplete in their quiet realm, for this tribe of the People did not have or even want ghost dancers. In this tribe, the ul udi were met only in dreams and actively suppressed by day. At first, Baat had been glad for that. He had wanted to forget, simply by living each of the first twenty years of his life again without ul udi or smallheads.

Only as old age made its claims did Baat yearn to call the cold fire down into his flesh once more. He went out to find others of his kind. He did find them, childhood chums, who had lingered around the Forest despite the danger of the smallheads. Sharing their woe, though it fed Baat's hopelessness, nonetheless made him feel stronger because he was not alone. Then suddenly he stopped finding them; there were only smallheads left in the Forest where the People had once lived freely.

Most of the summer that Baat skulked about the ancient woods, he believed he would return to the mountains. But the season's longest day came and went before he admitted to himself that something *more* held him here. He had not relived the memories of his first family at all, had not even floated with the ul udi in their heaven. All he had done since arriving was watch for the smallheads.

Come north, to the cairn of your ancestors, to the door of the mountain that leads to the sky.

All Baat's instincts wanted to obey the ul udi and go there, where he could dance in the cold fire with all the ghost dancers who had ever lived. There he could make arrangements for his own death, for the time when he would make his last trek across the tundra a handful of summers ahead. Then, with his sons helping him, he would dance around his own corpse. Only in the north, where heaven came down to earth, where the holy cairn rocks anchored the sky to the ground, where the ul udi could walk the land in their bodies of light like creatures of flesh, only there could he leave behind his body like a shucked garment and journey to heaven with the Bright Ones, never to return.

But now, he realized forlornly, there could be no journey north without the certainty of being tracked by the smallheads. They populated the Forest fringe and roved the tundra in fierce bands. Besides, he was alone; there was no one to warn him as he slept in the day, exhausted from his nights of traveling. The closer he approached the north, the deeper his trances would become and the more vulnerable he would be, not only to smallheads but to ravenous beasts. If even one of his People had remained to travel with him, as the journey north required, perhaps the crossing would be possible. But—he was alone. Several months ago he had still hoped to find one of his own people to share the journey with him. That was why he had come north so early in the season to seek out the old places where the tribe once lived. Perhaps one of the others would have returned here too—though that hope now seemed foolish. The old places were overrun with smallheads. How could he ever have thought that any of the People would return to these woods of death?

The thought occurred to him: There was one small, desperate chance he might take, if all else failed. Not far from this shadowy tarn of vipers and humpbacked boars lived an old smallhead woman. Sly-eyed as a marmoset, she was a witch who had learned from the witches before her how to catch ul udi in crystal rocks. Using certain crystals to trance the People, these small-head witches could hold them enthralled for days while they spoke through them with the ul udi. And from the ul udi, the witches got their power and learned the secrets of heaven and earth.

If there was no other way, Baat decided, he would go to the witch and seek her help in eluding the small-head hunters and reaching the cairn of his ancestors in the north. He reasoned that she could use him at night, to converse with the ul udi, and by day she could watch over him while he slept.

Baat sat up from where he lay on a log, his vision branded with bright shadows from staring at the broken shafts of sunlight in the branches. He must be very tired to even consider trusting a smallhead witch. He rubbed his face with his hands. He listened to the summer, where birds clattered, insects droned, leaves whispered with wind.

Last night, after he had killed those three small-head drummers with his hands, the Bright Ones had not come. The Dark Ones had driven them away and had circled in on him, inflamed by the approach of more smallheads. Hunters were tracking the fringe of the Forest, looking for his spoor. The Dark Ones had haunted him with a nightmare vision of them: In storm-light, in the hot roaring of lightning cutting the dark-ness, he had seen them sleeping—two men, one white-haired and scar-faced propped in the branches of a tree like a drowsy ape; the other nearby, but apart, somewhere out there, beardless as a snake, slumbering on the ground with a rope in his hand tied to a horse, his shoulders as packed with strength as that animal's.

The third was a boy of no more than fifteen summers and the fourth a girl, younger still. She was awake, and he could not see her as clearly. For some reason he had not yet fathomed, the ul udi wanted him to look closely at the boy and the girl, the frail things with knobby elbows and ankles, their hairs so black they had raven-glints of blue.

As he had stared at that boy, he saw inside him the girl. *Sister,* a gentle voice had spoken to him from someplace deeper than the nightmare. That had been a Bright One's voice! They were showing him the girl for a reason, making him see her through the boy, though she was awake and he could not bring her to focus as clearly as her sleeping brother.

And when he looked harder at the girl-child within the drowsing boy, the vision had dilated to reveal a landscape he knew well: the giant, tree-crowned boulder of the Thundertree, where the People had once lived. Then the land folded into the girl, the girl collapsed into the boy, and he had been left standing there, staring at the smallhead asleep in the stormlight. Why had the Dark Ones shown him this? Why had a Bright One shown him the girl-smallhead and the camp of the Thundertree?

Then the smallhead-boy had somehow sensed him watching and had startled awake, seeing him, though he had stood there only in dream. He had warned the boy. What else was he to do? He did not want to kill any more smallheads, let alone children. But the Dark Ones *would* kill, even children—and he could not resist the ul udi when the time came. He only wanted to go north, like the great ones of the past. He would not let the smallheads stop him. He wanted to find the door of the mountain and meet the Bright Ones in their bodies of light, where they could free him at last from this murderous world, where life must eat life.

◆　　◆　　◆

"We need something more," Hamr said, holding up the two rabbits they had stoned. "The Thundertree are laughing at us. We ran from their mask, and now they're laughing at us. We can't go to them with two rabbits and ask for a place among them. We have to go back into the Forest and kill something larger."

Timov leaned against a boulder, tightening the straps of his sandal. Duru watched the wind ripple across the grass range. Neither of them wanted to look at Hamr.

"Sure, it's going to be fearful," Hamr said. "But we can't stay here. The days are getting shorter, the wind sharper. Winter's coming, don't you realize? *Winter.* We need the Thundertree. So now we've got to show them that they need us."

"The herds'll be coming south soon," Timov spoke, plucking at his sandal. "We can take a big animal when it comes down the trails."

Hamr blew a sigh of exasperation, threw the dead rabbits to the ground, and turned away. These were indeed children, he reminded himself and walked to where his two spears were stuck in the ground, crossing each other. What did they know of destiny? Their lives pivoted about their fear. They would stay here so long as there was no danger in view. But anger seethed in him at the thought that the Thundertree were laughing at them.

He put a hand on the speartip from his childhood, and the weapon gave him back an instant of strength. With calm regard, he faced his companions again. "All right," he said, quietly, "you can stay here. I'll go into the Forest with Blind Side and get our offering. If the Thundertree accept it, I'll come for you."

"No," Duru said, looking to her brother. "We must stay together."

Timov passed his sister a weary frown. He wanted to wait, but he knew she would be going with or without him. "We'll go."

"Not with that spirit. I need your help, not your reluctance."

"Then stay here," Duru urged. "Winter is coming and with it the herds, as Timov says. Let the Thundertree laugh at us. At least, they know we're not to be feared. In time, we'll earn their respect and our place among them."

"Maybe they'll come out to us," Timov offered.

"I'm going," Hamr said and went for his spears.

Duru picked up her satchel and the two rabbits and looked to her brother. Unhappy—but he pushed away from the rock he leaned against and pulled his spear from where it stood. She smiled at him and held up the rabbits. "At least we'll eat well tonight."

"Yeah, if we're not eaten first."

Hamr led Blind Side of Life by his rope and did not look back. He knew they were following. Their unwillingness made him feel more responsible for them, and he approached the Forest warily. While pretending to let Blind Side loiter in the bunch grass he liked best, Hamr studied the treeline. The Panther men, who had spooked them, presumably to test the newcomers' courage and worthiness for inclusion in their tribe, were not to be seen. Nor were there any obvious signs of dangerous animals. Yet even so he advanced slowly and stopped at the fringe, at their usual night shelter under the awning of the big trees.

They built a fire early, while the sun still dazzled in the branches, and they ate facing away from each other, the better to watch for the Panther men or an enemy. Before night fell they sang the daycount on the calendar bracelet, doused the fire, and lay down with their backs to a tree. Fear spoiled Timov's rest, and Hamr too dozed restlessly, anxious for the day so he could begin the hunt.

But Duru, exhausted from her uneasy slumber of the night before, slept deeply and dreamed she was awake and lying on her back, her mouth open and filled with nut oil. Her tongue was a wick. A yellow taper of flame stood on her tongue and illuminated the cope of a forest grotto feathery with ferns. Suddenly, she could hold her breath no longer; she gasped and swallowed the nut oil and the flame—and her whole body ignited. Blazing, she twirled and flapped upward like a burning leaf. Her sight flashed brighter, while memory blackened in the place above her eyes.

Quiet as a star she burned, silver, cool, shining through the darkness of distance, sliding across the night with a river's leisurely flow. All at once she was beyond the trees and saw them from above, ghostly clouds of treeheads shimmering with moonlight. Then tundra, lonely and silver in the night, stretched below. Boulders and stray shrubs swung past. Ahead, a tiny figure appeared, a snowflake, a glistening star, a man rushing closer.

The surge of her flow stopped sharply at ground level, an arm's reach away from a giant with a face chipped from a boulder, hair like short quills, and a lichenous beard cut by a scar across his jaw and right cheek.

Above him, the northern lights rippled under the stars, a luminous green smoke visible through the transparency of the giant's head and wide-slung shoulders. He is a ghost, she thought. Through his chest, wide as a treetrunk, sleek as the sharks she had seen beached after a storm, she watched two men approaching. She recognized the moon-limned silhouettes of Timov and Hamr.

The hunters hurled their spears, but the weapons flew harmlessly through the ghost. Movement turned her attention toward a graben fenced by shrubs as jagged as antlers. The ghost's twin climbed out of that ditch, but this time he was not transparent—not a ghost. His solid form loped smoothly as a wolf behind the hunters. They stood baffled, looking ahead, where their spears had penetrated the wraith.

Duru wanted to rush to them, to warn them of the giant behind them. But before she could move, she saw another figure, a serpent the moonlight had split to legs and arms, creeping up behind the giant, spear poised. As he neared, she noticed his white hair streaming like fog from a scarred face twisted tight up to the skull.

"I see you there, Yaqut!" the giant shouted to the reptilian man, and the white-haired hunter came running toward him, spear raised, face squeezed into a grimace of rage.

She willed herself closer to Timov, who had turned with Hamr at the sound of the giant's voice. But as she approached her brother, he retreated but without moving his legs, as if he was falling backwards and she after him. Their fall accelerated, then slammed to a stop—and she woke.

Or thought she had—but she could not move. Though her eyes had snapped open, her body lay paralyzed against the tree where she had fallen asleep. She saw Timov slumbering under a blanket of leaves between tentacles of treeroots. Hamr sat beside him, head leaning back against the trunk, eyes closed, hands in his lap gripping the rope tied to his horse. In the dark, Blind Side rubbed against the trees like rivermist moving.

Duru, bursting with fear, willed herself with all her might to stir. But she lay there like a dead thing, her terror still mounting. Then she twisted herself awake so vehemently that Hamr jumped to his feet, spear swung to block an attack. Blind Side of Life snorted fretfully, stepped to Hamr for a reassuring pat.

"I'm alive!" Duru said in a gasp.

Hamr blew a sigh of relief. "The ancestors are taunting you, little sister." He stroked Blind Side between the eyes and sat down.

Timov, rubbing the sleep from his eyes with one hand, put his arm around the sobbing Duru. When she could talk, she related what she had seen. Hamr huffed a skeptical laugh through his nose and closed his eyes. "A dream, a nightmare," he told her reassuringly.

"It wasn't a dream," she insisted. "I flew, far from my body. I had trouble getting back in."

"Uh-huh."

"I saw it all clearly. There's another hunter around here. The ghost man called him Yaqut."

Timov sat up, alert now, his eyes opening wider with fear. "The ghost man sounds like the giant I dreamed about last night," he said, slowly, with dawning realization. "There's an evil spirit in these woods."

The three sat in silence, letting that possibility sink in. Then Hamr got up and stoked the fire. "All the more reason to find the Thundertree then," he said resolutely. "We need a home, safe from spirits and beasts. Rest now, the both of you. Tomorrow we'll get our offering."

"Hamr's right," Timov agreed finally. "The spirits taunt us out here. Go to sleep now. A better dream will soothe you."

Duru closed her eyes, saw loose stars jiggling there. Her brother was fidgeting with his own anxieties. She stared out into the dark woods, wondering what had really happened. By dawn, she had convinced herself that her dream was real. As they resumed their search for food and the spoor of some large animal, for the offering, she looked about for signs that another hunter was nearby. With her brother, she climbed into a tree and scanned for smoke in the Forest or a human form on the northern plains but found neither. As the morning wore on, she began to believe that the ancestors were indeed toying with her.

At midday, Timov spotted a roe deer that stood immobile in a thicket of ash trees, the dark berries of its eyes watching to see if they had noticed it. The Blue Shell backed away and crouched out of sight. Hamr tethered Blind Side to a sapling, signed for Duru to stay with the horse, and indicated that Timov should crawl with him. Hunched over like apes, they scurried downwind among the trees until the deer's white rump came into sight through a screen of sunstruck foliage. It was sipping at a brook, apparently mindless of them.

Hamr crept forward, slow enough not to rustle the branches. Timov followed, froze when he saw the deer's head come up. Hamr had to edge forward another pace to throw his spear free of the bush. He waited with aching stillness. The deer's head lowered to sip again, and the hunters nudged forward. Hamr lifted his spear.

A neigh fluted from Blind Side, and the roe deer perked up its head and leaped the brook in one bound. Hamr dashed after it, Timov directly behind him. They splashed across the brook and barged through the bosk of slender ash on the far side and into a maze of thorn-bramble. Thrashing blindly, they pursued the fleeing white rump among the wends of the bramble, shouting and cursing at the sharp, lashing branches.

Hamr pulled up short, Timov slamming into him. Ahead stood a lanky, sinewy man, narrow as a shadow, with a mask-like face that peered at them from between long shocks of white hair and a stringy beard. It was a face that had long understood pain: The slash of mouth and lump of nose were twisted to the left around a raw, jagged splash of purple skin. The left eye slanted almost closed under the purple, while the right eye glared vindictively. At his thonged feet, the roe deer lay still twitching, a short lance piercing its arched-back throat. The stranger yanked the lance from the deer, and brilliant blood gurgled out.

Timov pulled at Hamr, wanting to run to the clearing, where there was room to dart and hide. But Hamr stopped, turned his spear aside, and raised his left hand in greeting. "I am Hamr of the Blue Shell," he said in a bold voice. "This is my companion Timov."

The stranger, content that the two facing him were no threat, knelt and plugged the deer's wound with a wad of grass, and held it there until the animal lay still. Then he looked up with a fierce squint. "Get away from here or I'll kill you."

Timov tugged at Hamr's arm. Hamr, stunned by the hatred in that crooked face, backed off. They crossed the brook and returned to Blind Side, looking over their shoulders to make sure that the burn-faced man did not pounce on them.

When Timov told Duru what had happened, she said, "That's Yaqut, I know it."

Hamr mounted his horse, and scowled at her. "We'll follow the brook and go around him."

Blind Side waded slowly upstream, while Timov and Duru followed, hopping among the cobbles, occasionally glancing behind. At the first bend in the stream, the narrow man waited, his short lance held in both hands across his wiry thighs, blocking their way.

"I told you to get away from here," he said in a voice thick with menace.

Hamr stopped Blind Side and leaned forward, eyes narrowed. "We are leaving."

"You're going the wrong way. Turn around and take your runts out of here. If I find you anywhere east of this stream, I'll cut your limbs off and leave you for the wolves."

Hamr's nostrils flared. "We're going east of here," he said through his teeth. "Get out of our way."

The twisted half of the stranger's mouth bent in a rictus smile. Hamr drove Blind Side of Life forward, spear raised. But the gaunt hunter did not move. As soon as Hamr was close enough to see the veins twisted at the stranger's bony temples, he pulled Blind Side up to strike with his hooves.

But in that instant, the spindly man had neatly sidestepped close to the horse. With one hand, he grabbed Hamr's knee and shoved, sending the horseman toppling from his steed.

Hamr splashed onto his back, thunking his head on a cobble. Through scattering pinpoints of hot light, he saw the stranger's grimacing face loom over him. Sharp flint pressed hard under his jaw and despair forced a whimper from him.

"Don't kill him, Yaqut!" Duru shouted from the bank.

The stranger held the tip of his lance firmly against Hamr's throat while he looked hard at the girl, then at Timov, whose spear was raised tentatively. "Put your spear down, boy. Come over here."

Timov dropped his weapon and swashed into the brook.

"Sit down."

Timov obeyed.

The hunter gazed down at Hamr's anguished face, and his rictus-grin returned. He looked again at Timov, then Duru, while his grin slipped away. "How do you know my name?"

"I heard it in a dream." Duru held her breath. The sight of this scrawny old man atop big-boned, muscle-shouldered Hamr terrified the girl. "Please, don't kill him."

"Why shouldn't I?"

"We're hunters like you," Timov blurted. "We mean no harm."

"You attacked me."

Hamr struggled briefly, but the point of the flint pressed sharper against his jugular until he lay still. "I attacked you," he rasped.

"You did—and you'd be dead now but that you know my name. Who are you?"

Yaqut looked to Timov, whose eyes, circled by white, could not hide his horror. "We're the last of the Blue Shell, from the south."

When the boy finished their story, Yaqut pressed his face closer to Hamr's. "With one stroke, your life's blood will run with this stream. No man attacks me and lives. Do you want to live?"

Hamr nodded, and the blade bit him under the jaw.

"Say it," the man insisted.

"I want to live," Hamr muttered.

Yaqut smiled his distorted grin, exposing teeth worn to brown stumps. "Now you owe your life to me. For the sake of these children, I will spare you, Hamr

the Arrogant. But if you raise your hand to me again—"
His good eye hardened with the promise of death.

Then he stood up, sheathed his knife. "So you're
Panther people." He spat into the water. "I hate Panther people. They're weak and hide in the Forest like
squirrels." He put his hands on his hips, playing out
the moment, and studied the strays before him. He was
surprised himself that he had thrown such a large man,
had actually dominated him—and he was even more
amazed that he had not killed such a dangerous one
when he had the chance. But the girl *had* known his
name, had heard it in a dream. What manner of child
was she? He had heard of sibyl-children who possessed
such powers of knowing from their dreams. But he had
never met any before. Could she be one?

This was an opportunity not to be squandered. For
four moons, Yaqut had crawled among brambles and
slept in trees, stalking the monster who had killed his
clansmen, and he had yet to see more of the creature
than the thing's day-old droppings.

Maybe these simpletons from the south were just
what he needed to flush out his prey. If the girl was
indeed a sibyl, then the priestess among the Panther
people could very probably use her to track the ghost
dancer. He looked the trio over shrewdly, then he said,
"The Thundertree are not far from here. I'll take you to
them. They need hunters—and they'll be proud to
show off their skills to men who are weaker than they
are."

Hamr sat up, rubbing his throat, and Yaqut waved
him and Timov to the mudbank. "Get out of the water,
you dolts." He picked up their spears, walked over to
Blind Side and led him to where Hamr and Timov stood
dripping on the bank. "You're the saddest horseman
I've ever seen," he told Hamr, handing him the rope

and his spear. He shook his head with scorn. "And you—" He turned his disdain on Timov. "You with the spear in your hand—why were you just standing there?"

"If . . . if I'd attacked, you'd have killed him," Timov ventured nervously.

"If you would have bothered to attack, maybe I wouldn't have gotten to him," Yaqut derided. He heaved the spear's haft into Timov's hands so hard the young man almost collapsed. "Your fear will kill you, boy."

Yaqut stepped close enough to Duru to peer down into the small holes of her eyes. "Now, tell me the dream that showed you my name."

Duru, staring back frightened but unflinching, observing the whipstroke of purpled flesh that seared the man's face, told him her nightmare.

With an amazed laugh, Yaqut blessed himself for his restraint in not killing them. "Aye me—you saw the ghost dancer. You actually saw him. Few people have seen one and lived, you know. You're lucky he visited you only in a dream."

"Ghost dancer?" Duru repeated.

Yaqut paused to see if she was pretending, saw the sincerity in her open stare, and felt his wonder kindle. These were certainly far-traveled strays not to have heard of ghost dancers. "He happens to be your salvation." He waded across the brook and came back with the pack of stitched pelts he had dropped. "He knows my name, and that knowing saved you. He knows my name well, because I'm hunting him." He pointed upstream, and swept his arm toward the marshy terrain downstream. "I've tracked him from the mountains where this stream began and through the bog where it ends, and I haven't seen him once. The Forest is big, and he knows how to hide. But before winter, I will have his head." From the pack, he lifted a large skull and regarded it smugly. "Here's one I took last year. Behold the size of it."

It was a human skull, yet it was far bigger than any human skull they had seen, the blockbrow thick above wide apart orbits, the cranium longer, capped at the back with a knob of bone, the molars broad as thumb knuckles and the incisors truly fangs.

"Imagine the flesh this skull wore," Yaqut said. "Imagine the strength that strapped these jaws." He laid the skull down and lifted from his pack a long bone, the radius bone of the arm. It looked like a club. "Can you see the power this bone held in life?"

"He must have been a giant," Timov marveled.

"This was a female." Yaqut put the bone aside. "She belonged to a tribe of giants, whose smallest stands a head taller than our biggest. They're enormous and powerful. But their strength—their real threat—is not size or strength but that they carry fire. Not the earthly fire we spark from flint and rub from wood but the sky fire that spears down from the storm and splits the oak."

Yaqut grinned at the shades of incomprehension in the Blue Shell's faces. "You don't believe me. Yes, how can people carry lightning? Understand—these are not people; they're beasts that do not fit our imagination. And this one whom you've seen in your dream—he's old and cunning, eager to murder and defile and too wily to get caught."

He put the skull and arm bone in the sack, then nodded to Hamr. "Go get the roe deer. And you—" He pointed to Timov. "Make a fire. We'll prepare enough meat for the next few days. The ghost dancer already knows we're here. Pointless to hide now."

Duru went with her brother to gather kindling, but Yaqut stopped her. "Have you had other dreams?" he asked, after Timov and Hamr had gone off.

"No, but my brother did. He saw the ghost man in a dream, too."

Yaqut nodded to himself, turned away, dismissed her with a backhanded wave. These young ones were more than sibyl-children. Elation flared up in him. Their dreams, so precise and vivid, were not dreams at all. Surely they were seeing this ghost dancer, exactly as the priestess had described him. Surely they were linked with him in the unique way that only blood could bind. Though they did not realize it—though they had not even heard of ghost dancers—yet he was certain that one of their ancestors, perhaps not so long ago, was kin to this breed of monster.

Hamr stood over the dead deer, noticing the precision of the puncture that had killed it. His own neck still ached where the flint had nearly severed his pulse, and he rubbed his throat absently while he stared down at the dead animal, considering the expertise required to kill so efficiently.

At first he had seethed inside with the indignity of being bested by such a scrawny and aged man. For a while he had considered betraying his life-debt to the stranger and goring him while he showed them the giant's bones. But the Beastmaker had not led him this far simply for him to kill vengefully. That was not the way of a Great Man. And now that he contemplated what had happened, his humiliation faded, he realized that this was indeed the work of the Beastmaker.

Hamr examined the clean wound at the exact point of the animal's jugular and remembered how swiftly the deer had been running when it was stabbed. Here, obviously, was a master hunter and a fearless warrior, whose spirit defied his advanced age and small body. There was no shame in being bested by him. The ferocious degree of the man's burned face only heightened Hamr's regard for him.

Yaqut was surely a guide sent by the Beastmaker to lead them to the Thundertree, after they had come so close and could go no farther. What more signs did he need of the Beastmaker's presence?

Swans whistled in the sky, confirming this truth. With a silent prayer of gratitude, he bent to tie Blind Side's rope to the deer's hind hooves.

Yaqut touched the tip of his lance to the space between the deer's eyes, intoned: "The Beastmaker gave us your flesh and your bones to sustain us that our flesh and our bones may fulfill the Ways of Wandering. Great is the Beastmaker."

Hamr shared a look of pleased surprise with Timov and Duru: This strange hunter recognized the Beastmaker. He closed his eyes and thanked the inward darkness for finding them this leader whose bond to the hidden world they could trust.

After the deer had been butchered, his marrow devoured, his heart and brains seared and divided among them, and the haunches skewered to be braised, Yaqut mixed the blood with brookwater in the ghost dancer's skull and passed it around. How primitive these Blue Shell looked to him, with their faces and limbs smudged with crude bodypaint, more like greasy ash than pigment. They seemed as likely to dash off senselessly into the woods as to eat the food he offered them. He decided then to hold them with stories, beginning with his own. That was the easiest way to keep them close until he could figure out their usefulness in the hunt. While they sipped and ate and braised the legs of deer, he told his story.

"I'm of the Longtooth. Unlike the Blue Shell and the Thundertree, we've not forgotten the Ways of Wandering. We follow the herds across the tundra in the summer, and we winter in the taiga, falling back to the Forest only when the big storms roar from the north.

"Many summers ago, when I was a boy younger than Timov, my tribe was attacked by a band of ghost dancers among the rocky fields to the far north. There the glaciers had piled boulders atop each other taller than trees, had strewn them across the land like shattered mountains. The ghost dancers knew the land better than we, and they trapped us in there. By day, many were killed by thrown rocks. At night—" He paused, his crooked lip trembling. "Do you know what happens to ghost dancers at night?"

The Blue Shell shook their heads, staring at the livid ugliness of the skeletal hunter squatting beside the fire, the flesh around his slanted eye hot as an ulcer.

"At night, they carry fire from the sky." Yaqut lowered his head like a bull, paused a moment to control the ancient rage impacted within him. "More! They become that fire. The spirits that rage in the night put on the bodies of the ghost dancers and walk the land. Can you grasp what I'm saying?"

Timov had stopped turning the spit over the fire, and Hamr reached over and rotated the haunch. "What are these spirits of the night? The Blue Shell have never seen them."

"No one sees them. I tell you, the spirits wear the bodies of the ghost dancers. Otherwise, they cannot be seen, anymore than the deaf can hear sounds, yet the sounds are there." He nodded knowingly. "The Long-tooth have a saying, 'Beyond the shadow *is* the ghost.' The spirits are like ghosts—less than shadows, yet real."

"And these spirits inflame the ghost dancers as barley-sours inflame us?" Hamr queried, fascinated.

"Far worse. Barley-sours inflame us with the passions of the blood. But these night spirits inflame the ghost dancers with a murderous lust more wild than the yearnings of the blood. They kill simply to kill. And so they killed us that night." Yaqut closed his good eye with grief, stared sideways at the Blue Shell wanderers through his scar-hooded eye. "I hid when they came down from the rocks. I found a cranny, and I hid. But I saw them. Fire speared from their arms like lightning. Lightning! Can you see that?" His good eye snapped open, and he looked fiercely at them, daring them to doubt him. "The lightning blasted our hunters into smoking corpses before they could throw their spears. And worse—far worse for some of them—the lightning did not blast them but lifted them into the air and burned them slowly, while their suffering howled out like the wolves."

Timov and Duru turned their amazement on Hamr who sat unstirred and reached over to turn the spit again. "How is it that the ghost dancers are not burned themselves?" Hamr asked.

Yaqut jutted his lower lip, shook his head. "That I don't know. But they were wearied by each bolt they flung. I remembered that, and it saved my life years later. But on that terrible night, the last night of my childhood, I was ignorant. There were many ghost dancers, almost a dozen of them, males and females. When some fell back exhausted from throwing light-

ning, others attacked, and with their bare hands tore
off the heads and limbs of the remaining men. And then
they danced with the corpses. Mired in blood, they
danced.'' He whispered the last words, stared into the
flames, and fell silent.

After a while he peered up from under his one
silver-flared eyebrow joined to a crust of scar where
the other had been, and forced out a dark, one-sided
grin. ''You don't believe me. How could you? This is
more evil than anything you've known. And there's
more to tell. They didn't kill all the women—some became sacrifices to the evil spirits' lust. That's right.
They didn't kill us all. By dawn, when they were gone,
a handful of women remained, and myself and a few
other children who had also hidden. We wandered
south till we found the other bands of the Longtooth.''
He stopped, rubbed the pain of remembering from the
skull-gleam at his temples. ''Ach, you've heard enough.
Now tend that meat before it's all ash.''

Timov obediently turned the haunch and Hamr fed
the fire. ''You said the ghost dancers are wearied by
throwing lightning,'' Hamr spoke, ''and that saved
your life years later. What did you mean?''

''Just that.'' Yaqut drained off the last of the blood
from the skull. ''You see my face, don't you? What do
you think did this to me? I've been hunting ghost dancers since I became old enough to know what revenge is.
I know all their wiles. But I paid a dear price to learn
them.'' He ran a brown thumbnail along the purpled
side of his face. ''Ghost dancers not only throw lightning, they throw dreams. They appear to be where they
are not. And when you attack them, they're behind
you.'' He passed a ghastly smile to Duru. ''Like your
dream, child. That happened to my first hunting party,
after we had tracked down one of those bonesuckers by

moonlight. We fell on her ghost—and she blasted us from behind, killed the other three and burned me as I was turning. Other men would have fled, half their face on fire, fearing more flames. But I knew she couldn't throw lightning again right away, so I dared to attack.''

Yaqut turned the leather straps he wore across his chest and revealed a row of thick fangs. ''Ghost dancer teeth. One from each kill.'' He flipped the straps so the teeth were hidden again, then tapped the gut-bindings, where the straps criss-crossed over his chest and a white circle showed. He parted the bindings and exposed another fang embedded there. ''I wear this one closest to my heart. It's hers. She made me wear my pain outside for all to see. So I keep hers in sight.''

Timov mechanically tested the roasting haunch by pressing his thumb against it and gave it another turn. ''We saw three dead Panther men yesterday. Their heads were torn off. Was it the ghost dancer who killed them?''

Yaqut hissed through his teeth. ''The Thundertree aren't real hunters. They're trackers. They follow their cats, who hunt best at night.'' He clicked a fingernail against the fang over his heart. ''She taught me never to hunt them at night. And it's even better not to confront them by day. Those corpses you saw stood against him by day. He killed them with his hands.''

Yaqut removed a hide sash from his waist and opened it on the ground. Inside were a dozen wax leaf packets. He peeled apart several, disclosing yellow powders, amber resins, and gummy black oil. ''Poisons,'' he said, quietly, as if the venoms were sleeping and should not be woken. ''I've learned them all. The powders for tainting drinking pools and the resins and oils for tipping spears and knives.'' He meticulously closed the packets, folded the sash, and tied it about his waist. "The best way to kill bonesuckers is without ever seeing them until they're dead. Even in daylight, they can reach into your spirit and make you see and feel things that aren't there."

"Why do you call them bonesuckers?" Duru asked.

"Because if they get you," Yaqut answered, with malevolent amusement, "they'll do to your bones what we did to this deer's."

This was the end of the twelfth moon, the Pine-Shouldered Moon, the first moon of the cold season, riding lower in the sky than the moons of summer and spring. Each day the sun rolled farther south. Already the small changes of autumn had begun: Days shortened; the smell of snow opened in the mouth of the wind; the hard nuts had formed, and the seed-strewn floor of the Forest crunched underfoot. Watching the watery birches swell with the first chill, hearing the drone of the bees lower as they moved their hives into the deeper hollows of trees, anticipating the next moon, the Frost Moon, Baat squirmed. If he were to reach the cairn of his ancestors in the north before winter, he would have to leave the Forest and cross the tundra immediately.

The thought of trekking the grasslands alone stopped his breath. He had done it before, eight times. He knew well the dangers, but he had never dared to cross the thunder of the herds while being hunted by the smallheads. Out there alone, he was sure they would find him, and then his headless body would feed the dog packs and the crows, the ants would hollow his bones, and the Dark Ones would trap his body of light in the groaning wind and give him pain forever.

Don't be afraid, a dulcet voice spoke from inside him.

"Bright One!" Baat whispered with surprise. The red disk of the sun, though low among the trees, had not yet set. The ul udi only rarely came to him before dark.

We came soon as we could to tell you: There is a way to go north, to the door of the mountain, the sweet voice said.

Baat stepped through a windfall scattering of tiny brown apples and peered around a stout fir, looking for smallheads among the shallow stream-waters sliding by. Mists welled in the ditches of the older rivulets, spilled over among the trees. The hulking silhouette of a bear lumbered by, smelling him and moving away. Otherwise, the twilit woods were still and empty. He could speak aloud without fear of betraying himself to the smallheads, and he said, softly, "Bright One, the smallheads hunt me everywhere. I must hide."

Winter is coming, Hollow Bone. You must not tarry any longer.

"I've been thinking of going east, Bright One, and wintering in the valleys, where the mountains break the big storms. I could come back here next summer and try again. By then, the smallheads may have forgotten me."

You are too old to wait another season. Winter is harsh. If you die where we cannot help you, you know what will happen: The Dark Ones will take your body of light for their own. You must not wait. The smallheads will not forget. They will be searching for you till the end of your days. You must make the northward journey now, tomorrow—no later.

A goldfinch sparked overhead. Baat clambered into a sprawling hickory and surveyed the surrounding land. The smallheads would be settling in for the night, he told himself. He need not be afraid. Wren-song rode a breath of rain from the northeast, and the bear he had spotted rummaged among the leaves looking for mice. "I'm afraid to walk the tundra alone. The smallheads will see me and track me down."

No. Travel at night; we will guide you.

"But in the day, when I sleep, their stalking animals will track me down, and they will pounce on me. You won't be there to warn me."

You will not travel alone. Your companion will watch over you while you sleep. And when your companion sleeps, you will hunt. You will travel together at night.

Baat raised his empty hands to the lavender sky. "Bright One, I have no companion. I am alone."

You are not alone. We have shown you that you are not alone. Don't you remember? Go—and take your companion.

Baat sat on the tree limb, listened to the swifts creaking in the higher branches on their way to sleep, and tried to remember. Looking down at his thighs, he watched the afterglow of sunset shining there. The darkling gloom brightened as a blue light came on around his body. The ul udi were climbing down the sky toward him.

Out of the sunset blur, the old ones appeared, faceless human shapes, the color of moonlight, standing in a circle around him. He bowed to them. They opened their arms, linked hands, and began to dance, silent as the rising mist.

The diaphanous shapes of the old ones danced like flames, like underwater shadows. They closed in. He held his arms out to them, saw the cold fire bristling green from the tips of his fingers, sparking blue at his

elbows. A whirling laugh spun him around, and sparkles unfurled from his body, fluttering through the
leaves, high into the brown air and clicking among the
first stars.

He became the still point of the reeling earth, the
old ones spinning around him and effervescing to cold
light. When he stamped his feet, neon snakes slithered
away in all directions. When he clapped his hands,
fireworks splashed in front of his face. Electricity
veined his limbs, sent thin, hot wires shimmering
through his hair and beard. Joy arced from his testicles
to his brain, and he convulsed in a stagger-step dance
to the sizzling, crackling music of pure energy pulsing
in him.

Suddenly, he no longer danced but soared above
the woods. The fog under the trees shone through the
branches, a phosphorous mist fleshing the black veins
of creeks, brooks, and streams. Where were the Bright
Ones taking him so swiftly? To the companion they had
promised him, yes, of course. And when, in the next
instant, his flight stopped, he stood in the night haze
before a horse tied by a rope around his neck to a
thick-shouldered man asleep under a craggy butternut
tree.

Baat remembered the beardless man and those
around him—the white-haired scar-face, Yaqut, who
had been stalking him all summer, and the young
brother and sister. The Bright Ones had brought him to
these children the last two nights, when the ghosts of
the old ones had come down from the sky to dance with
him. *Timov* and *Duru*—he had heard their names, as
alien to him as their swarthy looks. Both times he had
been eager to return to the dancing rapture, and he had
pulled away quickly, though not without the boy and
the girl both seeing him clearly. That was strange. Ex-

cept the witches with their crystals, smallheads never
before were able to see his body of light.

Now Baat looked more closely at these smallheads.
They seemed typical, except for the one with the broken face, who was far more sinister than any hunter
Baat had seen before. Even in sleep, hostility snarled
his mouth. Baat had been careful to keep his distance
from this one. The girl whimpered, already sensing
him, somehow fitting him into whatever she was
dreaming. The boy stiffened. An alarmed tremor startled the eyes under his lids, and Baat realized that
these two young ones were already seeing him.

Dance, a Bright One commanded.

Baat stepped back, felt the rhythm of his dancing
body far back in the woods, and moved with it. He
swayed, gently at first, afraid to lose sight of these
smallheads in the bright smoke that streaked around
him as he stirred. But he noticed that his movements
calmed the children. They lay still as he veered about,
and he knew that, as they watched him in their dreaming, they were less frightened to see him dancing than
when he simply stared at them. Of course, he thought
to himself; he must look terrifying to these small
things. So he gave himself to the music in the cold fire
that fell from the sky. And, as ever, the fire carried him.

Slippery green light swung him in circles, looped
him into the air and back. Bodiless, he danced as he
never could anchored to his bones. Twirling in radiant
motion, he rode the rapture of the ul udi, the hawk-
rush, falcon-tilting pleasure of the Bright Ones, the
meteor-stab, comet-feather, aurora dance of the star-
whirling night. He danced until he reeled, as with
drunkenness, and collapsed.

He was alone, back in his body, lying face up and
staring through the leaf-rustle at the borealis painting

the sky chill green. His breath pumped hard, and his ears rang with cricket-noise. He sat up, clutching his head. The ghosts of the old ones were gone. Only a faint glimmer shone on his skin, where he had worn the ul udi's cold fire.

What had happened? Why had the Bright Ones made him dance for the smallheads? "Bright Ones—" he moaned.

Hush. Sleep now. Tomorrow you must begin the journey north.

"With those smallheads?"

The Bright One was silent. An owl's hoot floated through the trees. The crickets trilled. And a lithe rain began. Baat lay back and let the fog ruffle over him as the truth of what he had seen began to come clear.

At dawn Duru and Timov sat huddled under the big fir where they had slept, chattering like the loud sparrows hidden in the branches above. "It *was* the ghost man," Duru asserted.

"It didn't look like a man at all," Timov said. "It was spirits. It looked like the sky's night fire come down with the wind."

"No, Timov," Duru said, with petulant certainty. "I saw him before he started dancing. It was the ghost man."

"What happened?" Hamr asked, stepping out of the bushes.

Timov and Duru looked at each other, and he saw that she would not speak about it. That frightened him. Maybe this was some bizarre Mother mystery. Stricken, he turned to Hamr: "We had the same dream last night."

Hamr repressed a sudden shiver. The night before,

Duru had learned Yaqut's name in a dream, and that had saved his life. What was this long sight she had? A spirit—and was it invading Timov as well? He turned a narrow eye on the girl.

Under Hamr's gaze, Duru wilted, said quietly, "The ghost man came to me—to us. He stood where you're kneeling now. But he didn't say anything."

"I didn't see any ghost man," Timov asserted. "Just ghost fire, like in the sky at night, whirling like a waterspout."

"Let her finish, Timov."

"The giant was the ghost fire," Duru piped, reclaiming her annoyance at Timov's distortion of her vision. "I saw him standing here, under these trees. When he started to move, to dance, his body melted almost, became liquid flames that swirled round and round. Then he rose into the air and was gone, like that. I couldn't see where he went."

"He went where the rain lives," Yaqut said from the bushes. He stepped out, his hands still tightening the leather straps of his loin-pelt. "That was the ghost dancer. So both of you saw him again?"

"You did, too?" Duru asked, staring up at him with trepidation.

"No, child. I dream only of what's past. But you—and your brother, too, it seems—have something of the sibyl's gift. When we reach the Thundertree, that may prove useful. There is a priestess there from my tribe. She will know how to use your power."

"When will we reach the Thundertree?" Hamr asked, standing up. He was a head taller than Yaqut and looked almost twice as wide, but his voice had a hush of respect when he addressed the wiry man.

"If we leave now, before nightfall—before the ghost dancer arrives in the flesh."

The Blue Shell quickly gathered their satchels and strung them from their horse's back. In moments they were ready to go. Yaqut needed to get these strays to the Thundertree before another night fell. There, with the help of the priestess, he could use them to track down the ghost dancer. But here their deaths would be wasted.

By midday, the travelers had left the flat river-forest and climbed into a confused and beautiful land of tree-crested ridges overlooking a necklace of lakes. Blind Side moved falteringly through the undulant terrain, feeling his way cautiously among the cobbles and boulders under the trees and across the traps of glacial sand in the sudden glades.

At the summit of a winding hill, Yaqut paused and pointed down at a somnolent hollow of giant oak and maple beside a kettle lake. From the center of the hollow towered an immense boulder, a glacial erratic, gigantic as a mountain's flank, with trees sprouting from its top like hair. Smoke threaded into the sky from among those trees.

"Thundertree," Yaqut announced.

Hamr shielded his eyes against the westering sun and gauged the distance across the tumbled landscape to the splinter of mountain. "We'll not make it before dark."

Yaqut agreed with a nod, held up a disk of polished abalone, and flashed a sun-signal to the camp. A few moments later an answering gleam sparked from the top of the massive boulder. "The Panther men and the priestess will meet us in an elm glade midway from here. We'll be safe among them."

Timov and Duru smiled at each other. Duru took Hamr's hand; their long journey was nearly over, and for the first time since their exile began, something akin to a song rose up in Duru. She began to hum. Hamr's hand tightened on hers—proud to feel her ease, to know that, at last, his faith in the Beastmaker and in himself was rewarded by the joy of those in his care.

They marched down the grassy hill, among hot-colored rhododendron and the brilliant green grass that furred the slopes, and Timov sang the words to the tune Duru hummed—a song Mother had often sung to calm them when the dark came:

> Now that the sun is setting
> Panther walks like smoke
> sleek as the muscled rain
> where the night wind woke.

In a clearing made from a toppled giant elm, the priestess waited with a band of Panther men. The sun, low among the trees, pierced the glen with shafts of crimson light, and the hunters loitered nervously under the uplifted roots of the fallen tree, building a fire and making torches from their long spears. Their cats floated like pieces of night at the perimeter of the clearing, restlessly waiting for the command to stalk.

The priestess, with her rock of fertility pressed against her naked, swollen belly, sat on a convenient limb of the prone elm. She stared down at the red and yellow circles painted on her bloated breasts and widening around her puffed-out omphalo, and she muttered to herself, "Yaqut—where are you? It's getting late."

Since the ghost dancer had filled her with his child on the tundra five moons ago, she had resided with the Thundertree. Her clan in the Longtooth had sent her here with the rock of fertility to win the favor of the

Panther people, to lure great souls into the wombs of their women. The Longtooth desired the indebtedness of the Thundertree so that they might shelter in the Forest with them when the terrible storms of winter raged.

Power, the priestess said to herself with disgust. She had been sent to earn a privilege among these primitive people, and now, because of the ghost dancer, she was doomed to bear a child among them. She had expected to return to the Longtooth, be called to the chief's hut as reward for her troubles, and bear his children. Never could she have guessed a ghost dancer would take her. There had been no ghost dancers in these woods for years.

The priestess knew which berries to eat to abort the child, but then she would have to return to her clan to recover and lose her chance to convey her chief's power to the primitive Thundertree. Instead, she grew larger and lived like a chieftess.

The priestess gnashed her teeth and silently cursed Yaqut's tardiness. His flash-signal had promised strays—ghost-dancer half-breeds. Well, if that were true, she could use them with the crystal to hunt down the ghost dancer who had done this to her. She wanted that creature's head, not just for her own revenge, though that grew in her with the weird child growing in her womb—but she also wanted the giant's head to present as a trophy to the Longtooth chief, to assure that she would indeed have other children, noble children.

The witches would hate her for this, for they used the ghost dancers to speak with the spirits, and hated those who killed them. But they could have her weird child for their trance-work, so long as they left her

alone to live out her life as a chief's woman and a noble
Mother.

One of the cats sounded a cry, and a Panther man
broke from the group and hurried to the edge of the
clearing with a torch. "Someone comes," he called.

The priestess did not bother to rise. These fools
had often been wrong. They relied almost entirely on
their animals, beasts that growled and snapped at
every hare. With disdain, she regarded the hunters in
their mangy pelts, their lax limbs sheened with animal
fat to ward off biting flies and mosquitoes, their beards
braided about bits of bone. As soon as she dropped this
weird child, she would take the ghost dancer's head
and leave these smelly louts behind.

From among the trees, Yaqut appeared leading the
two darkhaired youths and the girl she had seen three
days before, when she had been sent to free the spirits
of the latest Panther men killed by the ghost dancer.
The bigger of the youths, a beardless man strapped
with muscle, held a rope looped about the neck of a
horse that shuffled nervously before the panthers.
Only the youth's constant reassurance kept the beast
from rearing. The Thundertree men gasped and muttered at the sight of the regal animal, and their cats
walked tight circles, fighting the urge to pounce, looking to their masters for the word to attack.

The priestess rose and lifted the rock of fertility in
greeting to Yaqut. He was the most famous of the Longtooth hunters. She was proud to see him again, though
always before, among the wandering camps of her
clan, she had feared his marred and deathly stare. No
mangled pelts hung from his taut frame, only well-
chewed leather and the chamois of the tundra gazelle.
Among the shabby Panther people, here in the gloomy

and treacherous Forest, he looked divine, like the wrath of her ancestors sent to avenge her.

Yaqut accepted her greeting by touching the rock of fertility with the tip of his short lance. "The young ones have weird blood," he said, soft enough for her ears alone. "They've seen the ghost dancer in their dreams. He told them my name."

The priestess' eyebrows flicked up. "Oh, they will be very useful then. But we must get them up into the Thundertree soon, where the crystal is hidden. I thought you'd be here earlier."

"But for that blind horse, which slowed us down."

The branches on the fringes of the clearing rattled in a sudden wind, and then went silent. The panthers pacing before Blind Side of Life cringed. Their bellies pressed the ground, and the horse, who had been wagging his head with fear of the big cats, lifted quivering nostrils, smelling something new.

A throb of thunder lifted everyone's gaze to the purpling sky. Stars glinted in a cloudless twilight.

Yaqut and the priestess exchanged a knowing glance. "Quick," Yaqut ordered, "into the woods. Leave the strays here."

A cold wind blew through the clearing, fluttering the spearflames and the fire under the crown of roots and making everyone's small hairs bristle.

"It's too late," the priestess gasped. "Look!"

Overhead, against the last red streaks of day, a ball of blue fire swirled. Moans of fright escaped the Panther men, and they bunched, their burning spears raised against the celestial fire.

Hamr pulled Duru and Timov closer, wedged them between himself and Blind Side. He looked to Yaqut, but the old hunter had backed against the fallen elm, lance poised, his mad face turning its fury to all sides, seeking his prey.

Horrified shouts cut through the knot of Panther men, as they spread out into a line and pointed their flame-tipped spears to one side. There, a fiery being raced among the trees, arms whirling, head shooting sparks and clots of flame.

The hot silhouette flashed closer, and Hamr pulled Blind Side forward to block the approach. A spear in each hand, he leaped to the side of his horse and widened his stance, ready to heave his weapons at the advancing fire-creature.

Timov, his face drained of blood, pushed Duru behind the horse, rushing around the steed to join Hamr. His legs quavered at the sight of the blazing apparition rushing closer, flashing among the trees, and he had to use his spear as a staff to lean against.

The Panther men had formed a line facing the burning demon, spears held high. Only Yaqut looked the other way and was shouting for them to turn. But he was blocked by the fallen elm, where the crouching priestess clutched his legs, and his cries were lost in the fearful shouts of the Panther men screaming for their cats to attack. The panthers crawled on the ground, hissing and raising their claws at the radiant shape hurtling toward them.

Only Duru, peering out from behind Blind Side, glimpsed Yaqut as he broke free of the priestess and clambered atop the log. He pointed his spear the other way. Before she could turn to see what he gestured at, a marshy odor whelmed up. Gruff hands grabbed her. She screamed but she was hoisted up.

Blind Side startled and sprang aside, and Duru saw the faces of those nearest her falling away. Hamr and Timov, following her with their eyes, gasped and shouted. And then they were gone, blocked by the trees that abruptly converged as she was hauled off into the darkness. She twisted in the grip of what had seized her and arched her neck to see a big horrific face above her: the cruel visage from her nightmares, the beast-man, whose bone-hooded eyes stared down at her with vast clarity.

◆ 5 ◆
The Invisibles

Baat ran hard, with the small girl tucked under his right arm. Though she kicked and flailed, she could do nothing to slow his flight into the Forest. He leaped over fallen trees and splashed across creeks, crouching over the girl to protect her from thorns as he crashed through walls of bramble and vetch. She was light, and he had no trouble carrying her. But her screaming bothered him. The smallheads would not pursue him now that night had fallen, but they could hear from her piercing screams the direction he was fleeing. Not wanting them to know he intended to go north, he hurried south, deeper into the Forest. Later, when he had somehow calmed her, he planned to backtrack.

But how to calm her? Or even yet, how to calm himself? His raid of the smallheads' camp had drawn the Dark Ones down on him. Aroused by the fear and fury of the smallheads, the ul udi swarmed through him, expecting violence, needing bloodsmoke.

Kill the smallhead runt!

"No!" he barked. "She is my companion."

She is a smallhead! She is the runt of those who killed your children! Spill her blood! Break her bones! Rip out her entrails! Leave her carcass for the smallheads to find! Make the smallheads weep—as you wept!

Baat could not ignore the Dark Ones. They inhabited his flesh. Their voices reverberated in his skull with such insistence that he lost his concentration and ran hard into a tree. He fell on his back, sharp points of light spinning before him.

Duru twisted free, scrambled to her feet, and burst away. She ran hard through the darkness, pulling herself past the trees in her way, squeezing through the tangled branches of a hedge, and skidding down the embankment of a brook into utter blackness and a chill of mist. She wanted to scream, but there was only enough breath in her to run. Groping blindly, she splashed among the rocks, found her way to the other side and crawled furiously up the muddy slope. Behind her, she heard the monster's roar after her, bellowing like a bear as he crashed through the hedge above the brook and lunged into the descending darkness.

Baat yelled, "Come back! I will not hurt you! I will not let the Dark Ones hurt you!"

To Duru, he sounded like a ferocious beast. When she reached the top of the bank, she heaved herself forward, grateful for the dim illumination of the auroras surging above the trees. Terror clotted her chest, her breath pounding so loud she could no longer hear the monster's chase. Yet she felt him gaining on her.

Her foot snagged on a root and sent her sprawling. As she staggered back to her feet, she cast a fearful glance over her shoulder and saw him, huge against a gap in the leafy branches, spike-haired and swollen-shouldered under the fiery fog of the borealis.

Duru screamed, but Baat lunged for her, snagging her by her arm, and jerked her off her feet as she bucked and kicked.

Smash her head! Rip off her arms! Kill the small-head runt!

"No!" he shouted at the ul udi. "Go away! Leave me alone!"

Kill her! The smallheads killed your children! Kill her!

"No!"

They're coming for you! Kill her now! Look! The smallhead comes! Kill the runt!

Baat held Duru above his head, to see past her, but she thought he was going to dash her to the ground, and her screams doubled. Then she saw what the monster had already noticed: Something moved directly ahead. A shadow broke from the darkness. A human figure approached.

"Duru!" Hamr's voice called.

Baat gaped in amazement. The smallheads never hunted by night. Who was this one? He tucked the girl securely under his arm and squinted. It was the beardless one, this time without his horse. He came through the trees with his spear raised, uncertainly aiming the weapon, forward and back, afraid to throw, afraid of hitting the girl.

The Dark Ones' wrath swelled up in Baat from his core as they rallied for the kill, and the air brightened with the cold fire that suddenly limned his body.

Hamr fell back a step at the sight of blue flames crawling over the giant, sparkling green from every pore of his body.

Duru had stopped squirming when the fire swept

over her. Vision suddenly widened, and a chill pervaded and soothed her. With perfect clarity, as though the full moon had broken through the clouds and she were suspended in the air with it, she gazed down at the giant, saw herself under his arm and Hamr standing there, gawking.

Burn the smallhead! Quickly—quickly! His spear is tipped with poison! One cut and you will die! We will eat your soul! We will eat you, Baat! Kill the smallhead!

Hamr edged closer, spear poised.

Baat could feel the lightning taking shape, burning, but he would not throw it. The Dark Ones would not master him: If he killed this one before the girl, she would never be his companion. The Dark Ones would defeat the Bright Ones, who had led him to her.

Burn him! Burn him now—before he strikes!

"No!" Baat yelled and, with an effort, painfully pulled the blue lightning back, deeper into himself.

Hamr's whole body was shaking. Meeting the ghost dancer's blockbrow stare, he was not sure what he saw there—rage, and yet something else. "Let her go!" he shouted back.

Though Baat did not understand what the smallhead was saying, he knew what he meant. He swung the girl around so she was in front of him, shielding him from the spear. He looked deeply into the smallhead hunter before him, recognizing the fear in his tight face, and felt a glimmer of wonder at the courage it took for this one to have run through the night Forest to stand here at the brink of his death.

"Let her go," Hamr pleaded, and lowered his spear.

Baat hugged Duru to his chest with one arm. He raised his other arm, palm forward, no killing fire in his hand now. "I will not hurt her," he said. "I will die before I allow her to be hurt." He backed away, turned, and sprinted into the trees.

"Wait!" Hamr bawled and ran after them. But the ghost dancer moved too swiftly, somehow seeing his way in the dark. What had he said? The gruff voice had sounded almost gentle. Despair mounted in Hamr as he realized the ghost dancer had taken Duru for his own. "Come back, you bonesucker! Damn your blood! Come back! She's my wife!"

Duru heard Hamr's cries dimming away. Fear skirled again in her. What had happened? For a while she had been stunned, somehow freed of her fright, even of her body. Now, she was again firmly locked in the grip of the monster. His swamp-stench sickened her, his outbursts of grunting speach filled her with animal dread.

Was he carrying her off to kill her, to shuck her brain and suck on her marrow as Yaqut had warned? She remembered the beheaded bodies she had seen in the Forest, and struggled to break free, but he only tightened his grip until she could barely breathe.

Now Baat fled more cautiously through the woods, ignoring the commands of the ul udi. Since he had pulled back their killing fire, they had somehow become less frantic. His insides cramped around the knot of resistance lodged somewhere near his heart, but he did not care. Let the Dark Ones hurt him. Let them rend him inside out with their anger.

He had not killed to take the girl. The Bright Ones would be pleased. "Oh, but where are you, Bright Ones?"

But the Dark Ones answered him.

You belong to us, Baat. You are bones of the earth, flesh risen from the mud. You will die for what you

*have done this night. The smallheads will hunt you
down and kill you with their poisons—and we will
eat your soul—oh, yes, Baat, we will eat your pain in
a darkness where the light never comes.*

There was no ignoring those voices.

Kill the runt! Kill her!

He might endure them until they faded away. And
they would fade if he could get far enough away from
the smallheads. With each creek that he splashed
across, with each black wall of undergrowth he shouldered through, with each rocky ridge he mounted and
crested, the smallhead hunters fell farther behind him.
The dark took him in. The cold fire lit the night flam-
boyantly—and the lichen on the trees glowed for his
eyes, mushrooms gleamed, rocks breathed with the
last heat of day. Owl eyes sparked from a high branch,
fireflies flickered. Like a piece of ice hung in the sky,
the evening star flashed, low among the trees.

Once Baat was sure that he had traversed a greater
distance than any smallhead could track in the dark, he
stopped. He stamped the ground to clear off snakes,
and lowered the girl to a mound of leaf debris. She
twisted off on all fours, and he had to scramble to catch
her.

Smash her head!

''No!'' he screamed. But the girl thought he yelled
at her, and hung perfectly still in his grasp. He placed
her on the leaf mound again though he could see, even
in the dark, the skittish look in her eyes. She would bolt
as soon as he stepped back.

Break her legs!

''Good idea,'' he muttered. He reached up and
snagged a fistful of crawling ivy. He wound the vines
about her ankles and tied the other end to his wrist. He
squatted over her and scrutinized his catch. She was

older than the girl-child he had fathered and lost—so long ago. In her seventh winter, his child had convulsed to death in his arms, banging her head against his chest.

Kill this runt! Kill her for the young you lost!

"Bright Ones—help me!"

The girl cringed under his loud voice, not hearing words, only gruff animal noise. Tears channeled her cheeks. He pulled away from her but could not stop looking. Was this truly his companion? Had he evilly deceived himself? This was a child. But of course: If she had been a woman, the Dark Ones would want to wreak their lust on her. He had wanted to take the boy, but the girl had been easier to grab. And now? She would be hungry, thirsty.

Baat rubbed his face, looked up through the branches at the vaporous fire. What had he done? How could he hope to feed her, to gentle the terror that owned her now that he had ripped her from her own people? He moaned; and she curled up into a ball and shivered with her sobs.

Kill her and be done with it. Do it for your dead children.

Hands to his head, Baat rose to his toetips and screamed at the sky: "I will not kill! I will not! Not now! Never again! Go away!"

Duru peered through her fingers at the ranting monster, his incomprehensible noise battering at her, his hulking shape glowing like the sky above. The gloom had darkened, and a scatter of rain raked the treetops. The ghost dancer stamped furiously, luminous arms upheld, face wracked with grief, grunting and gnashing, slapping his head. Sparks flew. Then he turned and looked at her again, his huge face sorrow-

ful, angry, tormented, gazing down at her through unfathomable suffering.

Hamr returned to the clearing, where the Panther
men had built a raging bonfire. Timov waited for him
beside Blind Side of Life, and rushed over when he
came through the trees. "Did you see her?" he asked
frantically, but Hamr strode past him. He ignored the
spitting panthers and went directly to where Yaqut
squatted before the flames, gnawing at the deer haunch
they had cooked the day before.

"Why didn't you come with me?" Hamr asked.

Yaqut looked up, nonchalantly, and placed a
thumb against the scalded side of his face. "It's night.
The bonesuckers will burn you at night."

"He didn't burn me."

"You found him?"

Hamr threw his spear down in disgust. "Duru
broke away. He had just caught her again when I found
them. If you'd been there, we could have saved her."

Yaqut cocked his head with surprise. "He saw you
and he didn't burn you?"

"She's alive then?" Timov blurted. "He could have
killed her on the spot—but she's alive?"

"The girl," the priestess said, looking up at Hamr.
"He spared you for her sake."

"What do you mean?" Hamr's face still showed
the exhilaration of his confrontation with the ghost
dancer, but his eyes now darted from the priestess to
the hunters hunched about the fire, angry at their cow-
ardice, angrier yet at his own ignorance.

"She means her dreams." Yaqut nodded wisely.
"Yes, how she knew my name. She said that the ghost
dancer told her in a dream. She and the boy saw him

dancing last night. Those weren't dreams. Her spirit was already with the bonesucker.''

''Aye, she has the spirit of a ghost dancer herself,'' the priestess added. Timov exchanged alarmed glances with Hamr. ''He didn't kill you for the sake of the girl. She is one of his own.''

Hamr scowled incredulously. ''Are you two crazy? She's no monster. She's a girl from my tribe. There are no ghost dancers in my tribe. We'd never even heard of them until yesterday.''

''Look at me.'' The priestess put her hands to her enlarged belly. ''There are no monsters in my tribe, either. Yet I carry one. The ghost dancer raped me at winter's end. Now our bloods are forever mixed.''

Timov crept closer. ''But what does that say about me? You mean—one of my ancestors is a . . . a . . .''

''Maybe.'' The priestess smiled ironically. ''Remember—we are the intruders. The ghost dancers have lived in these woods, and all these lands, from long before our first ancestors came here. When the Ways of Wandering led the Grandfathers out of the grasslands, the ghost dancers were already ancient in these places. What has happened to me has happened before to other women.''

Timov sat down under the weight of all that had been said. ''But why? What does he want with her?''

The priestess' haughty face spoke to the fire, ''A wife.''

''She's a child!'' Hamr snapped.

''For now.'' The priestess sighed. ''Almost all the ghost dancers have been killed in the Forest. I was surprised when this one attacked us on the tundra. Clearly, he is alone. He has no tribe, no clan, no one. Now he has the child.''

Hamr squatted beside Yaqut. "You hunt these monsters. Why is this one here?"

Yaqut threw the gnawed haunch-bone to one of the attendant panthers, wiped his fingers on a dried leaf. "It's been eight winters since I killed a bonesucker in these woods. And even then I'd been called here by clansmen, who'd traded here for years and never seen one before. On the tundra and in the mountains to the east, I've led the Longtooth on many a poison foray. But the mountains always seem to hide more than we can kill. Maybe this one drifted down from there. Last winter was harsher than most. Big storms from the south clashed with the cold of the north and many of the red deer died. I've seen packs of wolves and hyenas prowling rib-shrunk through the summer woods. Why should it be different for a bonesucker?"

"I want Duru back," Hamr stated. Timov nodded, wild-eyed.

Yaqut showed his worn, brown teeth in a smile that was a grimace. "If you can take her, she's yours. I've been stalking this bonesucker all summer, and only saw him for the first time tonight. The Beastmaker made him a sly one."

"Duru will slow him down," Hamr said.

"Maybe not." Yaqut picked at his teeth with a splinter. "He'll bind her and carry her like a satchel. Soon, it'll be winter. He'll disappear into the mountains, and the blizzards will make pursuit impossible. By thaw, he will be long, long gone. I think you'd best accept it: You'll never see your Duru again."

Timov groaned and hung his head. Why had he tried to safeguard her behind the horse? Her dream had warned them of the ghost dancer's feint. And Yaqut himself had told them the same. Why had he not remembered? He pressed his fists against his eyes; his

despair must not wrench uncontrollable sobs from him
in front of the staring Thundertree hunters.

"The crystal," the priestess spoke, her eyes
brightening. "Maybe the boy can track with the crystal."

"What is that?" Hamr asked impatiently.

"The fire from the sky is a spirit," the priestess
said.

"Many spirits," Yaqut corrected.

"Yes," she agreed, "there are many spirits in that
strange fire that the ghost dancers wear. They live high
in the sky. You can see them there." She gestured to the
auroras wavering among the stars beyond the shreds of
cloud. "They come down to live in the bodies of the
ghost dancers. The witches catch those spirits in special rocks, the clear stone of crystal and amber. I have
such a rock. When the moon is full, one can see shapes
in it. If the boy has the long sight, he may be able to see
the ghost dancer who took his sister."

"The moon's dark," Hamr despaired. "We're a
dozen days from full."

"Take my crystal, anyway," the priestess offered.
"Come with us to the Thundertree, and I will give it to
you."

Hamr shook his head. "That's another day's trail
and another after that to come back here. By then the
bonesucker's tracks will be cold. And maybe the crystal won't work." He looked to Yaqut. "At dawn, I'll be
going after him."

Yaqut snorted. "You can't even hunt a roe deer."
He spat his toothpick into the fire. "You've lost the girl.
Accept that and make a new life for yourself, here,
among your Panther people." With a nod of his grizzled
head, he indicated the sullen Thundertree men, who
clustered on the far side of the fire, away from the

strange priestess, the scar-faced hunter, and the Blue Shell with ghost dancers' blood.

"I'm going," Hamr rasped.

Yaqut peered deep into Hamr's dark eyes, gauged the cold certitude there. Then he turned to the Thundertree men and said across the fire, "Here's a Panther man. He traveled a long way to be with the Thundertree. Who among you will join him in the hunt?"

The pale-bearded men muttered uneasily and shrank back.

The Longtooth hunter smiled wolfishly. "None of them will face the ghost dancer with you, Hamr. Not one." His smile withered, and he glowered contemptuously at the huddled men. "They hide like squirrels."

"Duru is my clanswoman," Hamr said, as much to the Thundertree as to Yaqut. Somewhere in the huddle were the ones who had frightened and mocked him and Timov in the tall grass, with their mask and bullroarer. Now they would see, he was a great man after all. Real pain revealed itself in his voice, "I won't abandon her."

Yaqut heard his determination; he acknowledged it by gripping the youth's shoulder. "We will hunt the ghost dancer together. But you must obey me. If you want your Duru back, you must do as I say!"

Hamr nodded.

"I'm coming, too," Timov's small voice piped up.

Hamr gave him a cold stare. "You'll just be in the way. Stay here, make a place for us among these new people."

"She's my sister—I can't just wait here. I want to help."

"You can help by staying out of the way," Hamr said.

"Maybe my dreams will help," Timov contended.

He was afraid: He had seen the hulking creature snatch his sister, had seen by fire-glow the horrid face hackled with stiff hairs, the bison-humped shoulders and the limbs like tree boughs. But he had also seen the terror on Duru's face, had heard her shrill screams. Afraid as he was of the bonesucker, he was more frightened of doing nothing for his sister, of hearing her cries every time the wind caught in the branches, of knowing she was alive somewhere out there in the hands of that spirit-possessed beast. "I won't be in the way," he promised. "I'll do whatever you say! But let me come with you."

Hamr looked to Yaqut. The aged hunter scratched his scar-riven beard. "Your dreams may help," he admitted. "I've had no success tracking this one. Too bad we don't have the crystal in hand."

"What about the witches who make the crystals?" Timov asked, feeling suddenly expansive and useful. "Maybe they can help us."

Yaqut barked a laugh. "They'd as soon cut off their thumbs. Witches love their bonesuckers. They won't help us kill one."

"The boy has an idea," the priestess argued. "There is a witch not far from here, Neoll Nant Caw by name. A Longtooth woman. I promised her the weird child, when I drop it. She may want to help if you tell her your purpose is to get the girl back."

"No witches on this hunt." Yaqut shook his head vehemently. "Their magic will baffle us. We've troubles enough with winter on our heels."

The priestess clucked. "You've had all summer to catch your prey, Yaqut, and what can you show? Neoll Nant Caw is east of here, the direction you're heading anyway." She fixed him with a shrewd stare. "If you're afraid, send these two in to ask for help."

Yaqut rose and shivered with disgust. "We'll talk no more about it tonight." He walked off into the dark to make his bed.

The priestess turned her proud face to the fire. "He'll go to her. I taunt him, but fear has never stopped a man like Yaqut."

Fear filled Timov, however. He imagined Duru smothering in the huge locked arms of the ghost dancer, her despairing spirit hanging in the black branches, the bonesucker circling back through the tattered fog for him—and he tossed with fright before he slipped into a dreamless sleep. In the chill of dawn he woke, surprised there had been no nightmares. He had slept at the edge of the clearing alongside Hamr, both of them tolerating the fresh stink of Blind Side's manure, wanting to be near the horse in case he warned of another attack. No attack came and no nightmares. Timov blinked away the grogginess of his deep sleep to see the Panther men already moving about in the clearing.

Eager to return to the safety of their abode atop their towering rock, the Thundertree men gathered around the stretcher they used to carry the priestess. But she had them wait, while she held out the rock of fertility for the Blue Shell to touch. When Hamr and Timov put their hands on it, she whispered, "Bold hunters—beware. Every hunter of the Old People is himself hunted." Then she lay down in her litter, and the Panther men sent their cats running ahead into the Forest and carried her off.

"She's right, of course," Yaqut told them, climbing down from the tree where he had lain all night between sleep and watchfulness. "Once he knows we're after him, he'll come for us. We must stay hidden long as we can.''

''But won't the spirits warn him?'' Timov asked.

''The witch may help us with that, if you're brave enough to face her. But no magic will avail if we go blundering through the woods. You must learn the ways of traveling like true hunters.''

In the first shadowy hours of morning, Yaqut taught Hamr and Timov to move silently through the Forest, walking on the root bridges between trees, varying their pace through the leaf litter to mime the wind, reading the birds' signals in the branches for what the birds saw of other animals, especially the large ones like Bear, Sloth, and Elk, whose movements could mask the hunters'.

''The horse we leave behind,'' Yaqut declared. ''It belongs on the grasslands and draws too much attention in the Forest.''

They were sitting on the fallen elm before the last embers of the fire, and Hamr had been staring up at the fast clouds, keeping his mind free of distraction so he could absorb all that Yaqut had to teach. He glared at the hunter. ''Blind Side of Life stays with me.''

Yaqut's mouth opened around a silent laugh, like a skull's. ''In the Forest, it's Bright Side of Life, blundering through the shrub. The ghost dancer will hear us a day away. We leave it behind.''

''No.'' Hamr said this without expression, though a vein ticked at his throat. ''The horse stays with me.'' He read the sudden grim intensity of Yaqut's stare. ''And if you're thinking of killing it, kill me first.''

Hamr had already placed his hand in the satchel at his hip, and Yaqut knew he was holding a knife. He sighed, disappointed that so much strength had joined to such a childish mind. ''I've had my chance to kill

you, Hamr the Arrogant," Yaqut said. "I won't kill you
now unless you betray me." When Hamr's hand did not
come away from inside his satchel, he added, "Keep
the horse. But you will ride ahead of us. We'll let the
ghost dancer see you. The boy and I shadow as I direct.
Understood?"

Hamr nodded. He stepped out of Yaqut's striking
range before relaxing his grip on the obsidian blade in
his satchel. Timov had watched apprehensively, and
shrugged. Now the boy visibly relaxed, and when
Yaqut told him to bury the fire site, he stooped to the
job eagerly.

"That horse is your death," Yaqut warned Hamr.

Hamr brushed away the insects buzzing around
his head and ambled toward where Blind Side stood
fetlock-deep in the thick grass of the clearing, grazing
contentedly. Hamr's body felt sweaty with fear, and
the bump at the back of his head from his fall two days
before still itched. Maybe Yaqut was right—but he
knew the Beastmaker did not want him to leave his
horse behind. "Death is certain," he whispered in the
animal's ear. "So how a man gives himself to his life
should be decided as surely."

Hamr rode Blind Side of Life ready for death, if
that was what the Beastmaker wanted of him. Yet he
remained keenly alert. The late-bearing summer trees,
laden with nuts and fruit, hung their boughs low in the
dells, and the horse chose the more open ways along
the knolly ridges of pine and fir. Up here Hamr could
see the entire broken landscape, from the flat outwash
plain of the tundra, through the stream-webbed woodlands, to the lakes among the lumpy hills, where they
journeyed now. Looking down, he occasionally caught

a glimpse of Timov among the dense trees. Yaqut was nowhere in sight.

The startled cries of crows announced the horse and his rider as Blind Side clopped along, the birds' echoes flapping back and forth above the dark valleys. The crows clamored so persistently that in the afternoon, when a tribal site came into view, Hamr made no effort to hide. He sat high on Blind Side's back, surveying the gloomy dale below, where stone fences crisscrossed among enormous firs and bunkers of cobbles and boulders. Between steep hillocks, a black pool glittered with swans, and on the near slopes of the approach from the ridge, sunlight gleamed off totems of animal and human skulls.

"The glen of the witch," Yaqut announced, appearing suddenly behind Hamr.

Blind Side started, and Hamr had to hug his neck. Timov waved from below; hunched among a cluster of alders, he pointed through the yellow dappled leaves at two men on the hillside above the swans, kindling piled high in their arms. They were staring up at Hamr and his horse. One of them yelled, and from a cobbled bunker, two women emerged.

Yaqut signed for Timov to wait. "You go down. Take the boy with you. But mind you—don't eat or drink anything in this place."

"Aren't you coming with us?"

The flesh between Yaqut's eyes flinched. "I hate witches. They love the bonesuckers. You and the boy go. It's your clanswoman he's taken."

Hamr peered apprehensively at the two women, who had stepped into a clearing among the sombrous firs. Sunlight glowed like snow from the head of one and like fire from the other's. "Will they help us?"

"That's for you to find out." Yaqut kept the horse

between himself and the view of the witches, and backed off into the underbrush. "I'll wait up here. Don't tell them about me. Get out before dark if you can. And *most important*—don't eat or drink anything they give you!"

Hamr nudged Blind Side of Life forward. "Where's Yaqut?" Timov asked as the horse picked his way down the hill toward him.

"We're going in alone. Stay beside me. We may be leaving fast."

Hamr wanted to carry his two spears like lances but thought that seemed too threatening. He left them crossed in his lap. When they came to the first stone fence, he opened his empty arms in greeting. The fence was a natural configuration of rocks and boulders that had been shoved into a long line by an icesheet long ago. Numerous breaks opened to the fir grove, where the witches waited. But only one was large enough for the horse. As Hamr led Blind Side through it, a fierce growling and howling assailed them from among the clustered trees. In the shadows, a pack of wolves crouched.

The white-haired witch pointed her longstaff first at the pack and then at the strangers, and one of the wolves broke from the pack and charged.

Blind Side of Life, already anxious because of the howling of the wolves, panicked at the sound and smell of one hurtling toward him. He jerked his body upright with a startled whinny, and Hamr flew from his back and crashed among the rocks. Timov rushed to him but was brushed aside as the frightened horse clattered past, swerving blindly among the rocks until he found the gap and bolted through it.

The attacking wolf was now close enough for Timov to see the foam threading its fangs as it snarled.

He swung his spear up in time to block it, and it bit the haft, the force throwing him off his feet. Its ferocious face pressed close, its claws were tearing at the hide over his stomach.

A shout shrilled out from the old witch, and the wolf curled away, tail tucked under, and dashed back to where the others milled among the trees. Timov sat up, slick with sweat and shuddering. "Let's get out of here!"

Hamr ignored the ache in his bruised back, staggering upright. He helped the boy to his feet, saw that he was unhurt. "Did you see that? The witch called the wolf off. Look."

The white-haired woman waved for them to approach.

"Hamr, let's go!"

Hamr picked up his second spear. He wished he had his satchel with the obsidian knife in it, but was grateful for at least the wood blade sheathed at his hip. "Go to Blind Sido and wait for me there."

Timov watched Hamr walk toward the witches. He wanted to flee but could not. Yaqut was watching, and the boy didn't want to face that stiff visage alone. He scampered after Hamr. But as the witches came more clearly into view, his run slowed; he kept well behind the larger man.

Before the darkness of the firs, the women stood like apparitions risen up in the sunlight, their bodies draped like ancient tribes' in plaited grass and moss, their faces white as moth-wings. The old woman, with her lichenous hair and flesh as cracked every-which-way as bark, seemed a part of the fir gloom, more tree than hag. The younger one looked keen as a fox, the sun's flame in her tangle of red tresses that fell past a throat as long as a water bird's—but there was something secret and dark in her gaze. The two stood like the very reflections of time that the old Mothers were fond of sketching in the warm ash: youth and crone, beauty and age, the cresting fullness and the drained end of life.

Beyond them, the men who had been carrying kindling dropped the wood into a fire-pit between soot-blackened pines, and were busy as they arranged the branches for that night's fire. They ignored the strangers. Only the witches watched them approach. The old one seemed to be staring through them, but the young one's eyes, green and slow, were piercing, like a cat's. She flicked a glance at Timov, then steadied her stare on Hamr. A smile shadowed her pale lips.

As the hag's eyes sharpened suddenly, the travelers stopped. Hamr leaned both of his spears in the crook of one arm, and raised his hand in salutation. "I am Hamr—this, Timov. We're the last of the Blue Shell and have traveled far to be here. Are you Neoll Nant Caw?"

The crone's taut gaze did not flicker. The young witch looked amused.

"The priestess of the Longtooth sent us here," Hamr went on. "She said you could help us. Our clans-woman—"

"Where is the third?" the aged witch interrupted.

Hamr said nothing, and Timov looked to him, waiting for his reply. "We're alone," Hamr said, finally.

"You lie!" The crone raised her longstaff, and the wolves howled from among the trees. "You'll speak the truth or not speak at all."

Timov cowered, both hands on his spear, staring toward the fir darkness, where the wolves paced. Hamr leaned forward on his spears, and Timov's chest constricted to see anger throb in his jaw. He reached out to tug at his arm—to urge him away, back to the horse and their journey. But then Hamr spoke and surprised Timov with the composure of his voice, "Old Mother, you mistake me. We've come here, to you, alone. Our companion waits for us in the hills."

The crone nodded, eyes a-glare. "Yes, he waits. Who is he?"

"Yaqut," Timov quickly said, before Hamr angered them with an ambiguous answer. "A hunter of the Longtooth, who—"

The old witch cawed like a crow. "Yaqut of the Evil Face! I know that devil. So he is here in the Forest." She cocked a glance at her companion. "How unlike him. Much easier to kill his prey in the open grasslands, where he can see them drinking from afar and can poison their water."

Casually, Hamr glanced past the witches to where the men had finished arranging the kindling and were now busy dragging lugs of nut shrubs from the treeline to the clearing of the unlit fire-pit. They seemed oblivious to him and Timov, and he decided they would pose no obstacle if he chose to use his spears on the witches. He shifted his weight so that he could more easily hoist his weapons.

"Are the Blue Shell a horse clan?" the red-haired witch asked.

"No," Hamr answered, noticing the softness of her voice, unlike the crone's harsh tone. The crone noticed it, too, and stared at the young woman as Hamr explained, "Before sickness destroyed our tribe, we were fisherfolk, Tortoise clan, with a few who worshiped the Panther. We've come north to find the Thundertree, to—"

"Enough banter," the crone groused. "You ride a horse. That has not been seen here before. It drew us out of our burrow. If you'd come on foot, the wolves would have dealt with you as they do all strays—which, I can see now, would have been best.''

''Your wolf attacked us,'' Hamr said.

''Only because you passed our fence bearing weapons,'' the crone replied. ''You still bear weapons. Did Yaqut not tell you? This is witch ground. No men tread here but as our guests or our slaves, and neither bears weapons.''

''I think the Evil Face would be just as pleased if the wolves had killed them,'' the young witch said.

The aged one concurred with a nod. ''Yaqut despises strays as much as he hates the Old People. Why has he let you live this long?''

''He would have killed us,'' Timov answered, ''but my sister knew his name from a dream.''

The wisps of the old woman's eyebrows raised, and she looked to the younger one, then turned an owl's stare on Timov. ''A dream?''

As Timov told the witches the dreams of the ghost dancer, the women listened, their eyes bright with surprise and understanding. When he was done, she regarded him carefully for several long moments.

''Leave your weapons here,'' the crone said finally, ''and come with us.''

''Wait,'' Hamr said. ''You sent a wolf against us. You were ready to turn us away because we don't know your customs. Now you order us to part with our weapons. We have yet to know who you are.''

The crone smiled, her mouth pegged with yellow teeth worn almost to the gums. She rested her longstaff against her shoulder, and put a gnarled hand on Hamr's spears. ''We are witches, and we are more than you will ever know. If you want our help, leave your spears and your knives behind.'' Her smile thinned away. "The Invisibles are astride you. Given the chance, they would gut us hollow. Leave your weapons."

Hamr saw no alternative. He stabbed his spears into the earth and flicked his knife point-first into the ground. Timov did likewise and dropped his sling and rocks. Then they followed the witches between two tall staves mounted with the skulls of Bear, Wolf, and humans. Femur bones hanging beneath the skulls clacked in the wind soughing down from the hills.

Past small stacks of cobbles and heaps of gravel arranged in symmetrical patterns, the clearing ended. The bunker from where the women had emerged rose like a stone outpost out of the weed-matted hillside. Dark trees screened its cave-hole entrance, yet as they passed, Hamr and Timov peeked in, saw beyond parted curtains of braided vines to the cavern-depths, where nut-oil lamps glimmered far inside the hillside.

The men, who had gathered kindling and large gourds from the Forest, squatted now beside the fire-pit, mashing acorns with pestle-rocks. Like the witches, they wore garments of plant-fiber: breech-thongs of woven grass, tree-bark sandals. They did not look up as the witches and their guests walked by. Hamr stooped in mid-stride to look into the eyes of these strongboned, blond-bearded men, so busy doing woman's work, and met stares blue and empty as the sky. He tapped Timov's shoulder and jerked a thumb at the tranced workers.

Timov was already aware that those men were not themselves, that this was a place of danger. He pleaded with a silent look for Hamr to stay close and not challenge the strange women. But Hamr frowned, wished he had questioned Yaqut more thoroughly about the powers of these witches and their weaknesses.

They stopped before a black and highly reflective pool under an overhang of rock banded with red jasper. Swans, perched like butterflies on their mirrored images, glided away.

"Kneel," the crone commanded.

Hamr and Timov knelt on the muddy lip of the pool. Waterbugs skittered across the slick surface.

From within the pleats of her grass robe, the old witch withdrew a clear glass dagger. Hamr pulled back, ready to rise, but the witch put the claw of her hand on his shoulder and steadied him. What she held, he saw, was not a dagger but a large, oblong crystal with sharp facets. She pressed it against his brow—between his eyes. It felt warm from her body and pinched but did not cut his flesh though he felt foolish.

The crone removed the crystal and stepped to Timov. He could see from Hamr's derisive frown that there was nothing to fear, yet apprehension stirred in him. The long crystal touched his brow—and a pang of icy pain pierced inside his skull. His vision grew black though his eyes stared wide. A scream left his mouth and carried him with it, out of his body, into the sky.

Sunlight was scorching his sight. Through the glare, he could see again, but what he saw set panic leaping where his chest should have been. He was rising and, below him, he saw the black pool with its swans and, on the slick bank, Hamr and the witches bending over him. He lay sprawled on his back, a thick foam oozing from his slack mouth. He cried out, and there was no sound. Yet there was noise. A massive droning vibrated across the sky, moaning through him like the groan of the bull-roarer that the Thundertree had used to terrify him days ago.

He was dead. The witch had killed him. His spirit had leaped out of his body, and now he soared away from the appalling sight of himself dead, eyes sightless. He lofted into the clouds, and the clouds shredded around him to mist, burst apart into sudden blue reaching a zenith of indigo.

He looked back, aghast at the abruptness of his departure, unready for the afterlife. He saw under him the vastness of the Forest shrunk to nubbly lichen, a sprawling splotch of mold, veined with silver rivers and streams, pocked with bright lakes beneath cloud plateaus and jagged, radiant peaks of snow. The sight mysteriously soothed his shock, and he lofted even higher, suddenly no longer afraid.

Mists swarmed in the mountain valleys and mighty rain clouds churned among the icy summits. The violet cumuli, stabbed with lightning, towered against the blue emptiness, casting enormous shadows across the rocky chasms. Sadness came to him as he realized that soon the rain would fall where his body lay. So quickly, so implacably, his life had ended—and now, he flew upward to the spirit realm, his whole being humming with the deep vibrancy of the sky. Yet he could not take his sight away from the earth. He strained to see through the shreds of clouds to where the dense forest gave way to chaparral—*taiga* Cyndell had called it—and he glimpsed, far off, across the taiga, the wide, brown plains of tundra. Glaciers glinted on the brink of the planet like stars fallen to earth.

The land began to tilt, to bend. On the distant, bellied horizon, the sea appeared, agate blue shattered by the sun's fierce reflection. The land was not flat after all but curved, just as the storytellers of the Blue Shell had said· The land curved like the back of a tortoise.

Amazement muted to awe as the bright sky fell

away, and Timov hurtled into the cave of the night. The sun had shrunk to a small white shell, and hard points of stars nicked the darkness. Underneath him, the earth's giant blue tortoise shell glowed with a silver haze.

The massive droning in the sky now sharpened to voices, frenzied voices sounding closer and louder, like a clashing of rocks: *A hole! A hole! A hole for an axle!*

Needle through the brain!

Chill! Shiver! Spasm!

Iciness penetrated Timov as the fleeting warmth of his life seemed to flee into the vast darkness. He looked to the sun, to feel again its warmth—but the sun was small, perfectly round, and with no heat at all to it. He quaked with cold.

A hole for an axle! Pierce him!

Pierce the needle through his brain!

Shuck the flesh! Shuck it!

Timov convulsed with cold, wanting to press his hands over his ears to shut out the harsh voices. But he had no hands, no ears. He had no brain to be pierced, no flesh to shuck. Unless—

The cold burned, wrenched him with the deep torment of a storm-twisted pine even as he realized he was not dead, not yet. He was dying! Somehow, his spirit still clung to his body far, far below.

He almost lives! Catch him!

Spasm! Convulse! Die!

Die, Timov! Die!

The battering voices were killing him. They were the cold, twisting hurt tearing him from his body. He had to get away from them. Down—down through the agony, back to the misty dew of the turtle's shell, down to earth and his body.

Catch him!

The evil voices darkened to thunder.

Catch him! the thunder boomed.

Laughter roared out. Thunder bellowed like bulls. Darkness glared. And Timov, clenched in spasm, screamed a fractured scream.

''Catch him!'' the old witch yelled. She squatted over Timov's chest, the crystal shaking violently in her hand, as if it was pushing itself away from the boy's skull. From out of his mouth a white ooze flowed, gathered into a reptilian shape beside his face, then slithered through the grass, away from the water's edge. ''Catch him, Kirchi!''

The red-haired witch stood aghast beside her elder, staring with unbelieving eyes at the white effluvia snaking through the grass.

''The crystal!'' the crone shrieked. ''Use your crystal!''

With a trembling hand, Kirchi drew a daggerlength of quartz from under her grass robe and pursued the wriggling coil of vapor. She jumped and stabbed at the earth with the crystal until, when she stood up, the milky white rock had become black.

The old witch's crystal pressed against Timov's forehead stopped vibrating, and the crone sat down heavily on his chest, forcing the air from his lungs. A loud gasp shook him, and his staring, sightless eyes relaxed, focused.

''Hamr!'' he called out when he saw the crone astride him.

Hamr knelt so the boy could see him. ''I'm here, Timov. You're all right now. The witches took an evil spirit out of you.''

Timov's pale face shivered. ''I heard them. I heard

the spirits. Voices like bulls. Hamr—I was with them! In the sky."

"Yes," the crone agreed, her wrinkle-webbed face flushed with her exertion. "In the sky. That's where they live. And they come down at night and feed on the pain of the dying. Lucky for you we put the crystals on you by day. At night, you'd never have come back."

"I thought you said the evil was invisible," Hamr blurted. "I saw it. It looked like a white snake."

"Not a snake, but a piece of the boy's life that the spirit took with it to escape. The Invisibles have no shape."

The witch got off Timov, and Hamr helped him sit up. "It was horrible," the boy said in a thin voice. "Cold. High up above the Turtle's back it's horribly cold."

"Gets colder yet when you die and the Dark Ones get you," the witch said knowingly. "Kirchi, show him the evil."

Kirchi snapped alert from where she had been standing, staring at the black crystal. This was the first one she had ever seen, and though the witch had prepared her with many stories and, in trance, she herself had heard the evil voices, never had she seen one. She held the black rock away from her body, glad to pass it to the old one.

The crone waved it before Hamr. "Listen." She held the rock to his brow, and a chill crawled across his scalp. A whisper sounded deep in his ears, *You will die!*

Hamr jerked away, and the crone snickered. "What did it tell you?"

"What I already know," he answered gruffly.

The witch showed her yellow tooth-stubs, and winked. "You understand this spirit." She hurled the black rock high into the air, and it splashed into the pool.

"Can it escape?" Timov asked anxiously.

"Water locks it away from the others. In time, the great ice will come again and bury it and the many more I've cast there before it. They will not return to the sky—not for a long, long time. But time means little to them. And there are many others up there, indeed many others."

Timov stood up heavily, as if rising out of water. His hands clasped his body; and he was grateful for the warmth of the sun and the lavish algal odors of the pool. Stunned by the events that had carried him to this strange moment, he stood silently with the old woman. His mind went back: He had truly soared above the Turtle's back and into the void. The spirits had actually spoken with him. Anything might happen now—and yet the world looked the same as before. He watched a swan unfold its wings and walk several paces across the water to a shadier feeding place.

"Now you are free of the Dark Ones," the old witch said. "But they will come for you again."

Timov's stare hardened into fear, and he squinted at the crone. "They will?"

"You have the blood of a ghost dancer in you."

Timov turned away abruptly, remembering what the priestess had told him last night. Though he had dismissed it at the time, he now found the truth of it hard to deny. He felt dizzy with the prospect of the evil spirits returning for him. He looked imploringly at Hamr, who shifted his weight uneasily, met his gaze with a sad shrug.

"What can I do about it?" Timov muttered bitterly. "This has never happened to me before."

The crone put one hand to the side of the boy's face

and gazed at him compassionately. "You can be proud. You have a gift. The Invisibles visit us all. But you are among the few who can visit them."

"I don't want to! I never wanted to." He grew silent, then added sullenly, "And my sister? What about her?"

"She is like you," the old woman replied. "That is why Baat took her. The spirits recognize her."

The crone stepped back from Timov and looked to Hamr. "You will never hunt down the ghost dancer."

"It's not the ghost dancer I want, old woman," Hamr replied. "Will you help us get Duru back?"

The witch sucked in her lips and considered this. Her tongue flicked, tasting the air like an asp. "Do you have something of hers?"

"I have her satchel."

"Then get it."

Timov and Hamr started toward the horse, where the satchel hung, but the crone hissed at Timov to stop.

"Little man—stay here." She clutched a twisted cord of bine about her neck strung through a chunk of crystal, and lifted the rock from under her robe. "You must stay near the crystal till your spirit sets back into your body—otherwise you'll fall out again and die."

Timov nodded. "Go ahead, Hamr. I'll be all right."

Hamr leveled a fierce stare on the hag. He had been watching the red-haired Kirchi covertly and had seen the apprehension in her fox-bright face. She was as fearful of the old witch as they were. "If any harm comes to this boy, your wolves will not stop me from spilling your blood," he warned.

The witch met his stare coolly. "You've come to me for help—and now you threaten me? Take the boy and go! Why would I want him?"

"To enslave him as you have those men," Hamr

said, inclining his head to where the two workers squatted, mashing acorns.

"You speak with an empty voice," the witch said. "Get the girl's satchel, or take the boy and go."

"Get Duru's things," Timov insisted. "I'm okay now. Just a little groggy."

Hamr had been trying to see the ghost dancer traits in Timov, incredulous that his Aradia's ancestors had been sired by monsters. He wanted to doubt, but he had seen the spirit drawn from the boy's body, had heard its wicked voice in the stone. So what? he defied himself. The Beastmaker had shaped them all from mud, ghost dancers and people alike.

Resolved that this fact was unimportant, he placed a reassuring hand on Timov's shoulder. He did not care if toads were his ancestors, this lad was still his clansman. After fixing a stern gaze of warning on the crone, he jogged off to where Blind Side of Life waited on a hillock beyond the stone fences.

"How did he come to master a horse?" Kirchi asked, watching him disappear.

Both women looked to Timov. His insides had unclenched in his gladness that the crone had not raised her longstaff to send her wolves after Hamr. Nervously he began the story of Blind Side, and as he told it, the old woman leaned closer, as if to hear better.

Suddenly, with the striking speed of a serpent, her hand shot out. The crystal chunk in her grasp, she gently touched her fist to the boy's brow.

Darkness surged over Timov, and he collapsed.

"Quickly now," the old woman commanded, "get him into the burrow. I will get rid of Hamr."

◆　　◆　　◆

Lashed to a fir all night, Duru had worked hard to loosen her bindings but to no avail. The ghost dancer had secured her with devilish knots that tightened the more as she fought them. At last she lost sensation in her hands and feet and hung there in the dark, pressed to the tree by the taut vines.

The monster had gone off, either to hunt or to circle back and see that no hunters followed them. No ordinary man would dare trespass the darkness of the Forest, she knew—except her Hamr. Over and over, she muttered prayers to the Great Mother to protect him. Mosquitoes raged in her ear, stinging her exposed flesh where her bodypaint had come off in her struggle with the giant. Owls talked to each other, and the frayed howl of a lone wolf curled on the wind, sharpening the ice-barb in her chest.

But Baat squatted in the darkness watching Duru. The harsh voices of the ul udi had worn down his determination to protect her from them. Now there was only silence in him. Even the chill fire from the sky had dulled on his flesh, leaving him dark as any beast of the night.

Slowly, he got up and gathered enough food to offer her a meal—yet he waited before he returned, listening to her muttered fear, watching her tears fall as she strained against her bonds.

You've done well, Hollow Bone, the gentle voice of a Bright One whispered.

Baat shook his head, incredulous. "How can such a frail and frightened smallhead help me?"

Someone must—and soon, no matter how frail. Have you not noticed the thinning streams? The ice appears in the north already. You must leave at once for the door of the mountain.

"The leaves have only begun to change," Baat said in a hush. "Surely, there is time."

No time. Already you may be too late.

"But what can I do? She is frightened of me. She will never consent to help me."

Loosen her bonds. The blood is cut off in her hands and feet.

Baat rose and moved toward her. At the sight of him, she stiffened and a cry burst from her. He placed before her the skin of nuts and berries that he had collected and opened his arms, showing her that the fire from above was gone. Then he walked around to the back of the fir and loosened the knots.

"Don't be afraid," he said to her soothingly as she knelt and rubbed her wrists and ankles. "I will not hurt you. I need your help for one journey—my last journey. Then you are free of me."

The ghost dancer's voice sounded to Duru like gravel sliding down a rockface. He pushed the pelt of nuts and berries closer, and she recoiled.

"Eat it," he said. "It's for you." He remembered the sound of her name from his first encounter with her in his body of light. It sounded strange to his ear, yet he tried to mouth it: "Doo-roo"—he pointed at her. "Baat," he said, putting his hand to his chest. "Doo-roo," and he pointed at her.

The sound of her name coming from this huge face startled her so that she uttered a small cry and curled up.

Leave her alone now. Secure her gently and leave her alone.

Baat re-tied the girl loosely to a fir and backed off into the trees.

Duru watched after him with speculative eyes. When he was out of sight, she tried tugging on her leash and fraying it with her fingernails and teeth. But it was a tightly reeved vine that resisted her efforts. Frustrated, she curled up tight, her back against the tree, and stared through her tears into the darkness.

Hamr ran hard across the dell of firs, past the glassy-eyed men mashing acorns, past where his spears and knife stood in the ground, all the while eyeing the wall of Forest where the wolves lurked. Not a howl lifted from the dark trees, but the ground near the totem of skulls and clacking bones displayed numerous wolf prints. Chanting under his breath to the Beastmaker for protection, he skirted the totem and penetrated the wall through a smaller gap. His mind reeled with dread. Timov and Duru were haunted. The spirits of the sky owned them as they owned the ghost dancers—even as they had owned Aradia. He felt lightheaded at the memory of her, and the anxiety in him was stilled momentarily. For a moment, he stood in the dry grass smelling her again. From far away, a drumbeat of thunder rolled.

Blind Side of Life, nuzzling among plush ferns, whinnied happily at the scent of Hamr and ambled toward him.

Hamr's back ached from his earlier fall among the rocks, but he felt no ire toward his steed. "The wolves obey the witch," he said, rubbing Blind Side's brow. "You were right to run."

"Where's Timov?"

Startled, Hamr turned and saw Yaqut's waxen face watching him from the bushes. "He stays with the witch. She drove an evil spirit out of him, and he's resting. I've come for Duru's satchel so the crone can find her."

Yaqut rose from the bushes with fury. "You dolt! You've lost him, don't you see?"

Hamr stepped back, expecting the hunter to strike him. "She . . . she drove a spirit from him. I saw the thing crawl out of his mouth!"

Yaqut shook his head, his face unreadable. "Where are your weapons?"

"The witch said—"

Yaqut hissed scornfully. "She wants something from you, or you'd be dead now. Quickly—make a brand. We're going in."

They searched around in the bushes until they found two arm-length branches. At one end of each, they bound dried bracts with twined creepers and resinous strips of pine bark. "These will burn long enough for what we have to do," Yaqut said.

Dread, anticipation, and anger at being duped knotted Hamr's stomach. He knew that the brands were meant to keep away the wolves, but he did not understand Yaqut's urgency until they had crossed through the stone fence. Then, from Blind Side's back, he could see that Timov was indeed nowhere in sight.

Yaqut ran ahead of the horse, burning torch in one hand, lance in the other. He retrieved Hamr's and Timov's weapons and prepared them for battle. "Stay mounted," he warned. "And be ready to make this horse kick for your life."

From the Forest, there was yapping but no wolves appeared. Ahead, the witch waited, standing before her burrow, still as the black pines beside her. She kept her longstaff tight at her side, the signal for the pack to stay away. They had never seen a man astride a horse before; she was afraid her wolves would disregard her signals and approach just to see what new manner of beast this was. But her fears proved unfounded. As the horse drew near, the wolves barked with mounting frenzy, but none defied her commands.

As the horseman and Yaqut neared her bunker, the witch reached in her pouch and took out an oblate rock smoothed to a glossy polish. Many ul udi had been trapped in this gray stone. They were the voracious Invisibles that the Old People called the Dark Ones. Their excitement when they sensed others of their kind made the stone grow colder. It was the chill of this stone that had alerted Neoll Nant Caw to the Dark One residing in the boy. She held the stone up for the approaching hunters to see.

"This is what you want from me," she called to them. "With this you can track the ghost dancer."

"Where's Timov?" Hamr shouted and poised one of his spears. Yaqut stopped with his back to a giant fir, but Hamr rode Blind Side to within a spear's thrust of the witch and stared down into her weathered face.

"I have the boy in safe keeping," she answered him and waved the stone.

"No," Hamr said flatly. "You can't have him. Where is he?"

"He is safe," the witch insisted. "He is far more safe with me than he would be hunting the ghost dancer."

"What've you done with him?" Hamr pointed a spear at the witch's heart.

"What I have told you is true," the crone said earnestly. "Your companion will succumb again to the Invisibles if he leaves this place. Let him rest with me while you hunt the ghost dancer. When you return to me this tracking stone that will guide you to your prey, you may have your friend back."

"I want Timov now," Hamr demanded.

"Yaqut," the witch called out. "Tell this one who I am."

"It is true—she is a witch with many tricks," Yaqut cautioned Hamr. "Neoll Nant Caw of the Longtooth. Watch what you say to her."

Neoll Nant Caw wagged the smooth stone. "This tracking stone will take you directly to the Old One, who has taken the girl. It is yours in exchange for custody of the boy." The witch stepped closer and nudged the spear-tip aside. "Listen: Truly I cannot lie to you before Yaqut of the Evil Face. If what I tell you is untrue, he will spread that lie among the Longtooth and my own people will become my enemy. Is that not so, Yaqut?"

Yaqut edged forward, stood behind and to the side of Hamr. "The truthfulness of a witch is her strength among the people. She dares not lie to us. But in her truths there may be deception. Old woman, you know I will kill the ghost dancer if I find him, and yet you are sworn to protect the Old People. Why then do you give us the means to find him?"

"Finding him does not assure that you will kill him," the witch replied with a sly smile. "If you die trying, the boy remains with me. He is better than a ghost dancer, for he is human, yet I have seen him carry the ul udi."

"What are these ul udi?" Hamr asked.

"Evil spirits," Yaqut replied.

"Not all are evil," the witch countered. "Some speak truths we can learn no other way. With the proper training, this boy can learn those truths."

"And if we succeed?" Yaqut asked. "If we kill the ghost dancer, will you return the boy to us?"

"Yes. If you return, you may take the boy back."

"I want to see Timov," Hamr said.

"He rests now."

"I will see him!"

The witch shrugged. "Kirchi! Bring up the boy."

The red-haired witch emerged from the burrow with a groggy Timov. At the sight of Hamr and Yaqut, he shook off his stupor. "I fell asleep," he said meekly, not remembering the witch's pressing the crystal to his head.

Hamr explained the offer Neoll Nant Caw had made. "Will you stay?"

Timov ran quickly to Hamr's side, fully alert. "No. I don't want to stay here. I want to go with you. I want to find Duru."

Hamr sat tall on his mount. "Timov has decided. He comes with us."

"Wait," Yaqut said. "We came for the tracking stone."

"The boy for the stone," Neoll Nant Caw said. "If you take the stone by force, you take my curse with you."

"The boy will be safer here," Yaqut said, hesitating.

"No," Timov bleated. "I want to come with you."

"We have the witch's promise he will not be harmed," Yaqut reasoned. "When we have Duru, we'll come back for him."

"Hamr!" Timov clutched Hamr's leg. "Don't leave me here."

"If he comes," Yaqut said, "we go without the tracking stone. We may never find Duru."

Hamr stared up at the fleet clouds and considered impaling the witch and taking the stone. Yaqut read his intent and said, "The stone is no good to us if it's cursed."

Hamr closed his eyes, looking for the Beastmaker.

Black clouds drifted in a white sky behind his lids. He had to decide. The witch wanted only to keep the boy in custody—but Duru was in far more danger. He looked down at Timov and handed him his knife and his spear. "I'll be back," he promised.

A reluctant Timov took his weapons.

Neoll Nant Caw nodded sagely, and handed the polished stone to Yaqut. "Turn, Evil Face, and feel the chill in the stone."

Yaqut walked a tight circle. Indeed, the stone frosted in his grip when he faced southeast. "How do I know that this is the ghost dancer we want?"

"This is Frost Moon," Neoll Nant Caw replied. "Whatever Old People came through here this season have long since retreated south. Baat is the Old One you want. He alone lingers in the Forest. Find him—and may he break your necks!"

"Harm this boy and I'll break yours." Hamr spoke through his teeth, though within his heart the words felt empty.

Timov moved back as Hamr turned Blind Side around. His eyes stung with tears, but he blinked them back and felt them drain into the hollow of his chest.

"I'll be back!" Hamr swore again and clacked his spear against Timov's.

He remembered the boy in the Blue Shell days, when Timov and his friends would laugh at him behind his back. Now there was only sadness between them. Like Aradia and then Duru, Timov had become a loss that mocked his greatness, the greatness that had become an emptiness when he lost Aradia and with her his tribe. Hamr swore to himself that he would come back for Timov; with the Beastmaker's blessing, he would reward the boy by initiating him himself. As a man, Timov could make his own destiny even without a tribe. That decided, Hamr joined Yaqut. They walked across the dell in the opposite direction from which they had come, toward where the icy feel of the stone led them. They did not look back.

Neoll Nant Caw took away Timov's weapons and put him to work at once. She had him sit with the dreamy-eyed men and sort wads of grass into piles of weaving fibers of varying kinds. The work was tedious, but Timov resigned himself to it, afraid to anger the witch. The men beside him breathed not a word nor gave him even a single glance to indicate that they acknowledged his presence.

The young witch had a less fierce mien than the crone, and when she passed by to oversee, he summoned the courage to ask her, "Who are these men?"

"They're Longtooth hunters," Kirchi whispered, "who broke the tabu of the Mothers and are here to be punished."

"Why don't they see me?"

Kirchi pointed to an inflamed sting-mark under the ear of one of the men, and Timov noticed that the other also bore that wound. "Neoll Nant Caw pricked them with a trance-thorn, and now they see only their work. Hush now and do what she says or she'll prick you."

Kirchi drifted away, and Timov bent more earnestly to his task, though the light dimmed. He flicked a glance to the sky, saw clouds the color of rocks tumbling out of the east. Here was the storm he had seen building over the mountains during his death-flight. Static thrummed in the air.

Timov worked without lifting his head until the light had darkened; then he peered up as if at the overcast and looked around for the witches. They were nowhere in sight. If he bolted now and ran hard he could easily outdistance the old woman. The storm would certainly slow Hamr and Yaqut, and he could probably find them before nightfall. His spear leaned against a larch beside the barrow, and he decided not to backtrack for it. The others would understand. And with that decision, he leaped to his feet and dashed around the heap of wood beside the fire-pit and across the dale.

The wet wind in his face pressed against him and slowed his flight. The run across the hilly vale seemed far longer now. Sharp yelps cut along the grain of the wind. Among the trees to his left, slinky shadows glided. He peeled to the right, though that sent him toward the stone fences.

Shouts flapped with the wind from behind, and he threw a look over his shoulder to see the two Longtooth men plodding after him. Their gait was like that of lame men. Timov felt confident he could elude him. But then the yelping broke into howls, as the wolf pack shot out of the woods toward him. He pumped his legs harder than he could run, and tumbled to the ground.

As Timov jumped to his feet, the first of the wolves was upon him. It clasped his loin-pelt in its jaws and spun him about. He bent over, held his arms to his torso and his hands across his face. The beasts swarmed around him, yawping and growling.

Hands grabbed Timov's shoulders and pulled him away from the snarling wolves. He looked up into the flat gazes of the Longtooth hunters. The wolves' cacophony had diminished; they loped back to the Forest as the tranced men dragged Timov back.

Neoll Nant Caw waited outside her bunker, her face squinting with her anger. "You broke your promise," she snarled, and her hand lifted.

Timov cringed and, from the unexpected side, the witch struck him with the flat of her hand. A sharp pain jabbed him in his neck, and he staggered backwards.

"Now you'll do no more running," the crone cackled and turned away.

Nausea mounted in Timov. He reeled into the arms of the tranced men. As they lowered him to the ground, he felt his strength bleeding from his legs. Emptiness hollowed his bones, and he sat dumbfounded before the stack of wadded grasses. Fear knocked at his heart for several minutes, then dulled away.

"I am becoming like they are," he said to himself. Moments later, even that thought had become too ponderous to hold in his mind. His hands moved automatically, unraveling the tangled grasses, sorting the threads by feel alone.

Rain pattered through the trees. Hands touched him, pulled him upright. The sky had turned green. Against it, Kirchi stood, her features softened with wry sorrow.

"You shouldn't have run," she said. "You should have waited for me. You can't get away without me." She led him out of the rain, into the burrow. Moss curtains parted, and the blue fragrance of burned pine resin greeted him. He sat where the other men already sat husking pine seeds. His hands fumbled with the cones, shook loose the white pellets.

Kirchi's hot whisper sounded behind him, the sweet spice of her breath close enough for him only to hear: "Evil Face and your friend are not coming back for you. The stone the witch gave them has wicked spirits in it—spirits that will attract the beasts. We must escape on our own."

Neoll Nant Caw's voice called from deeper in the burrow, and Kirchi scurried off. Alone with the others,

Timov worked steadily, mindlessly. His blood sucked in his ears. Had the red-haired witch truly spoken to him? He listened hard for his own memory and heard only the thunder cutting the rain into its endless parts.

At the center of a subterranean chamber with root-woven walls, Neoll Nant Caw sat in a circle of blue fire. A gopher-tunnel and several mouseholes overhead vented the smoke, yet the place still reeked with the acrid fumes from the burning tar-oil. Kirchi feared this chamber, for here was where the witch made her drink the bitter dreaming-potions. Many a night she had sat on the packed earth at the center of that circle, watching the slim blue flames twist inside the witch's crystals. With the help of the dreaming potions, she had seen deep inside those rocks, seen the moon-bright Forest under the mountains, watched her clan wander the grasslands with the herds, and once witnessed a ghost dancer possessed by the Dark Ones. That was early in the spring, when Baat defiled the Longtooth's priestess and slaughtered her escorts. Even now, eight moons later, she still felt that nightmare whenever she entered this chamber.

"The boy works?" the witch asked.

Kirchi nodded and was glad to see that none of the crystals were unsheathed. "But he should be watched. He might easily doze off."

"You watch him then. And steep him a brew of this." The crone held out a rolled leaf packed with root-tip pinchings. "It will give him strength to work. Study what I've mixed here. I'll ask you later to make some of your own."

Kirchi stepped closer to the ring of fire. Though the flames were low, no more than a skinny blue worm glowing in the dirt, she dreaded the circle. Inside was the trance, the way out of her body and into the misting gulfs, where the Forest and even the mountains were no more than ghosts. She snatched the leafroll and backed away.

"When he's finished with the pine seeds, have him shave some tinder." Neoll Nant Caw shooed Kirchi off with a hiss, and a frown crossed her face as the young woman disappeared. Four years they had worked together and still the child was afraid. Perhaps the old woman had been too strict, made Kirchi drink too many dreaming brews—but there was so much to learn, and with so little time left her, how else could she have trained this neophyte?

The crone despaired at what her life had come to. Since the day in her twelfth summer when a witch had touched a crystal to her forehead and she had heard a Bright One singing, Neoll Nant Caw had wanted to be a witch. The Bright One had been singing about trees and how they were lanterns of water that shone with the light of the sun. After hearing that song, nothing about the craft frightened her, not leaving her clan, not drinking the sour brews or losing herself in trances; all she yearned for was to hear the Bright Ones and to learn everything from them.

In those days, it seemed that from the ul udi everything could be learned. They knew not only how trees ate sunlight but also how the sunlight in the grass became the life in the herds. The men, who wanted only to kill the Old People and were afraid of the dire spirits they called down from the sky, did not care if it were true that sunlight had become grass and then beasts. They wanted only to know where the herds were beyond the horizon. So long as the witches could tell them that, they were left alone with their ghost dancers and their crystals to learn how sunlight broke into rainbows, which the plants ate, except for the green, the color of the middle, which they wore instead to signify their place between heaven and earth.

But that was long ago when there were many more of the Old People than there were now. In those times, a dozen witches lived together in the Forest, working with three or more ghost dancers at a time. The ul udi taught them how to store their energy in the crystal rocks and how to use those stones to speak with them and learn what they knew. Everyone was excited about speaking directly with the spirits of the sky and many secrets were revealed and stored in the stones.

The crone huffed a sigh at all that had been known and now lost. During her lifetime most of the Old People had disappeared from the Forest, and without them to call down the ul udi, the craft had withered. The tribes, busy with the hunt and the Ways of Wandering, thought it foolish to sit around sipping dreaming potions and gazing into crystals, so few women chose the craft. Now all that remained were a handful of stray ghost dancers like Baat, three or four aging witches, and these few crystals that had not yet been broken.

Neoll Nant Caw lifted the moss-plaited cover from the small heap before her and revealed a cluster of quartz chunks. The blue light from the burning circle scattered in bright grains and glassy shadows as she picked up one of the rocks. She searched its rough facets for a way in, found a radiant seam and gazed into its hot glare. After a lifetime of trancework, she no longer needed the dreaming potions to use the crystals. One deep breath opened her to the energy in the rock.

With dazzled eyes, the crone stared into the invisible kingdoms, and saw. Bare trees against a gray sky wreathed a vision of herself bundled in fur, walking among shifting paths of snow. She bowed before the wind, protecting something from the gusty cold. The wind lifted the fur from the crook of her arm, exposing the squinty face of a newborn child—and the shock of seeing its small body broke the trance.

With a trembling hand, Neoll Nant Caw lowered the crystal and shut her eyes, trying to reason through what she had glimpsed. She had intended to seek knowledge from the ul udi about the boy, and had not expected to see herself carrying an infant. The ul udi in these stones were not deceptive. What else could it mean but that, sometime in the icy months ahead, such a one would be in her care?

The crone touched her cool fingertips to her eyelids, and let her flesh hang heavy on her bones. She was far too old to rear a child. Her own children, three girls, she had given to the families of their fathers so as not to be distracted from the craft. Whose child could this be, come to trouble her last days?

The possibility grew in her suddenly that this could be the young wanderer's child, begat on Kirchi. The witch had come to the crystals to ask about Timov—perhaps this was their answer. The boy could attract ul udi like a ghost dancer. He was a rare being, and in fact should be bred so that his skill was not lost.

Neoll Nant Caw muttered a prayer of thanks to the Great Mother, wanting this to be true. If Kirchi were mated with Timov in the spring, after they had tested his usefulness and proven him worthy, then her vision would be fulfilled the following winter. She could not hope to survive much longer than that; yet that would be enough, for then there would be others to continue the craft.

The witch picked up the stone and squinted at it again. The trance did not work as deeply. She was tired, and saw only the usual fretwork of energies, the frozen lightning that was the ul udi in the stone. *You are made of light,* the soft voice spoke to her. *Everything is made of light. Each grain of sand is a world of light squeezed to a mote.*

Neoll Nant Caw had heard this story many times, and she put the rock down. Later, when she was rested, she would enter the crystal again and try to scry the future. The Great Mother had delivered to her a young man who could carry the ul udi. For the first time in seven years, she would once more have the chance to speak directly with the spirits and to make more crystals. Vital as the stories in her crystals were, she knew them too well, and her heart hummed with excitement that soon she would hear new stories and learn more about the invisibles.

◆ 6 ◆

Moon Bitch

_____

Dawnlight lit up the mists of the Forest to golden vapors, and Duru peered through them, looking for the ghost dancer. She had woken in the dark to find herself alone, yet still leashed to the fir. The nuts and berries that the monster had gathered still lay within grasp on a pelt of silvery mink. At first, she ignored the food and waited nervously for the giant to return. But as the Forest grew brighter, her hunger increased.

Duru had never seen mink before, and she let her fingers crawl over her bed of pine needles to the bright hairs of the pelt. The fur felt softer than she had guessed, and she was impressed by the many colors in the pelage. She wondered what manner of creature wore this skin, as her fingers walked among the hazelnuts and mulberries. The fur reminded her of the weasel pelts that the Mothers used for trimming mantles in the wet season. She remembered her own mother had once lined a tunic with weasel for her and she had worn it several winters before she outgrew it.

Sadly, lost in memory, she carried a mulberry to her lips and mashed it between her tongue and palate, sifting the tiny seeds with her teeth. The berry's sweet ripeness exploded in her mouth and reminded her she had not eaten all day. She helped herself to several more of the purple drupes. Then she sampled the nuts and noticed that they, too, were of perfect maturity, their husks peeling away easily. She found two rocks under the duff of fallen needles and used them to smash open the hard shells, exposing meats dark yellow and oily. She began eating avidly.

Baat watched with satisfaction from the covert of the dense undergrowth. With the rising sun, the voices of the ul udi had entirely vanished, leaving him weary but clear-headed. He was proud that he had not succumbed to the murderous insistence of the Dark Ones, prouder yet that he had offered her food she found appetizing.

He observed her nimble way of shucking the nuts with her fingers and cracking them with rocks, sparing her molars. Apparently the mouths of the smallheads were not as useful as those of the People, so they had to find ways to employ their hands for things he and his kin would do with their teeth. Intrigued, Baat studied the way his captive broke off the cap of each nut to expose the hard shell and then how she braced several nuts together on one rock and bashed them with the other. Among the People, only children whose teeth were immature did this, and for a brief moment Baat imagined it was his own daughter he was watching.

Strings of sunlight dangled through the branches, and several touched the girl, lighting the crow-black of her hair, the tawny hue of her flesh. All the smallheads Baat had seen before had hair red as his own or paler, their eyes, pooling the blue light of heaven, whence came the clearest light. This one's eyes seemed like chips of night, and her look puzzled him, as though she gazed with the mirror-depths of a still, dark pond. Looking at her, he experienced a tinge of fear. After all, wasn't she something more than a smallhead? She had seen him in his body of light, which no other smallhead had done—except her brother.

Who were these exotic smallheads? If he had the strength, he would dance with the ul udi this next night and ask the Bright Ones to tell him. But to do that, he would have to sleep now in the daylight. Certainly, the smallhead hunters were already tracking him, especially the beardless one, who had dared trespass the night Forest to pursue him. And the beardless one had allied with Yaqut, who had stalked him all summer in these woods and denied him his flight to the cairn of the ancestors in the north.

Baat rubbed the ache of fatigue around his eyes and tried to think clearly. If he fled now with the girl, he would be too tired at night to call down the cold fire of the sky. Then he would have to spend another day in ignorance, unsure of who this girl was and what he should do next. Besides, another run through the woods would only heighten the unwilling girl's fear. Perhaps if he stayed here for the day, she would come to see that he meant her no harm. Then travel would be easier, and she could help him. That was what the Bright Ones would want.

His decision felt just, even though it played into the vulnerability of his exhaustion. He sighed—a frustrated sigh. Let the smallheads come. Let them find him if they could. During his bolt last night, he had been careful to leave few tracks behind, running much of the way through the swift course of streams and on the boulder paths of extinct riverways. Finding him would not be easy, he assured himself.

But before he could let the weariness in his muscles claim him, Baat had to show himself to the girl. He stood up and stepped slowly through the shrubs. For a while, he just stood there and let the smallhead see him in the misty morninglight, his eyes lowered so he would not have to meet her dark stare.

Duru started back at the sight of the giant and hugged the fir. In daylight, he appeared even more gruesome than he had in the smudged boreal glow of night. His garish red hair stood up like bristles from the cube of his head, stubbled along the broad curve of his pike-thrust jaw and missing entirely in a crescent scar on his right cheek. Flame-flared tufts twisted above downsloped green eyes that, to her great relief, did not stare at her but looked away, inviting her to study him. But she had seen enough of his brutish features, the lump of his nose, the cruel slash of his mouth. She rested her gaze on the broad stoop of his bare shoulders, glinting with red hairs.

Unlike the hunters of her tribe, the giant did not wear fur but deer hide, like Yaqut. But where Yaqut wore his buckskin in straps across his waist and sinewy limbs, the ghost dancer had wrapped a complete skin about his body, tying the leg-strips off at his shoulder and hip. And, like the Tortoise people, like Hamr before he wed, he used no bodypaint.

The giant advanced, and a mossy odor came with him. He knelt before her, his hands open before him, huge against his wall of a chest. "Baat," he groaned. Then he lay down nearby, facing away from her, the long hackles of his ruddy hair streaked like a mane down the muscled curve of his back. In moments, his breath soughed with the rhythm of sleep.

Duru's fingers flitted among the nutshells she had cracked until she found the shards she wanted. While she ate, the idea had leaped up in her that the sharp hazel shells could cut her leash, and she had been about to test her idea when the giant appeared. Now that he had fallen asleep, she immediately set to picking at the reeved twine that bound her.

The shell shards proved too dull to slice the vine, but they were sharp enough to separate the fibers, which she could cut tediously between the two rocks she had used as a nutcracker. The morningmists burned away. Jays swirled among the trees. The wind turned and delivered the red leaf of a nearby maple and a shadowy hint of rain. Overhead, a woodpecker tapped persistently, and Duru used its noise to mask the sound of the gnashing rocks as she crushed the last fibers of the twisted vine between them.

The vine snapped. Duru sat still, waiting to see if the ghost dancer had heard. But his breath flowed deeply, and she crept away crabwise from his hulk. Once she had crawled past another fir, she leaped to her feet, running as silently as she could.

Where to run? Duru had no idea in which direction the giant had carried her during the night. She moved west, following a ridge-back above a snaky stream whose water swirled into foam among black rocks. Jay screams alerted the whole Forest to her flight. Finally, she slid and skidded her way down the embankment to the stream and the riffle of water that seemed to mute the noise of her downstream run.

She clambered over beech trees felled by erosion and, when the stream pooled to a mire of kelp-like grasses and bearded hemlocks, where the sunlight layered but did not reach, she decided to get out. She crossed the stream along the peak of a cluttered beaver dam, teetering on shaggy logs. Halfway across, she paused as the beaver, huge as a bear, slithered out of the black water and shambled ashore. It paid her no heed, and she hurried over the crookbacked dam and into a fern grove.

Burly oaks stood among rocks above the bracken, their interlocked branches sun-chinked and dark as the legendary rooftrees that held up the sky. Duru decided to wade through the fern holt to the giant oaks, hoping to find edible mushrooms in the damp dark there. But as she crossed through the sedge, a stupendous shadow rose from the field.

With a bellow that made Duru's teeth clack, a bear reared from the reed bank and the hackleberries on which it had been feeding. Duru scampered away, but the bear lumbered through the bushes after her. She headed for the oaks. As she struggled up the steep rise, the bear loping after her, she heard a whooping cry. Looking to the side, she saw the ghost dancer on the far shore of the stream.

Baat called again, "Doo-roo!" He waved her toward him. Knowing that bears ran faster uphill, he tried to signal her toward the stream.

Duru understood. And though she had been fleeing the ghost dancer, hope and desperation burst, together, in her at the sight of him, and she turned sharply and dashed down the hill.

The bear yowled and banked after her. She slogged through the rush grass, where the bear's pursuit slackened, slowed by the mud. When she heaved herself into the stream, the beast shambled two lengths behind, groaning with the effort to catch its prey. It splashed in after her.

Baat stood on the bank and threw rocks at the pursuing bear until it dove. "Doo-roo!" he cried once more, and signed for her to hurry. But he knew she could not outswim a bear. A rock in each fist, he sloshed in, and stood waist deep, shouting her on. The beast's air bubbles frothed just behind the girl's splashing legs. She scrambled upright in the water, a terrified look on her face, then sank again out of sight.

Baat ducked under but could discern nothing in the turgid stream. He bobbed upright and saw the surface churning, and Duru reappeared, gasping. Beside her, streaming water, fangs bared, the bear rose.

Baat hurled his two rocks and struck the beast's snout squarely, and it dove again, coming into view farther away, retreating to the distant bank.

Duru twisted onto her back and stroked to shore. Blood was ribboning behind her. Seizing her shoulders Baat carried her through the canes to the mossy slope. Her right sandal was gone, and her calf was split open like a gutted fish.

Swiftly, Baat unstrapped his clan belt and lashed it around her wounded leg. She clutched at his arm, gritting her teeth, gnashing back her pain. "Doo-roo," he said, softly, and put a broad hand to the side of her face. He took the leather sheath of his flint knife and placed it between her teeth. Then he set to work splitting canes to extract the soft punk, which he mixed with the bast from a nearby poplar. Removing his clan belt from Duru's leg, he plastered the gash with the mucilage. With long strands of sedge grass, he wrapped the calf securely, then gave the girl a chunk of the poplar bast to gnaw.

Duru struggled with unconsciousness. When Baat lifted her, she put her arms around his thick neck, glad for his strength, for his lonely smell of the sodden earth, and for the pain in her leg that hooked her precariously to life.

◆   ◆   ◆

"Wake up," Kirchi whispered in Timov's ear. She had come to collect the large pile of pine seeds he had shucked. The two other workers had already cleared away the empty cones and gone to their own burrow for the night.

Timov watched from far inside his head as Kirchi used a slice of smoothed bark to scoop the white seeds into a basket. The rhythms of the pine-husking continued to tremble in him, and he heard the young witch's voice weave in and out of the sizzling rain: "Wake up, Timov. Evil Face and your friend are lost. We must save ourselves." And the noise of the rain carried the words into the hissing blood in his ears.

Kirchi leaned close and gave Timov the juniper bough that Neoll Nant Caw wanted shaved for tinder. As she fitted it and the flint scraper to his dull hands, she said in chant-voice: "Timov, your body is equal to the sunlight. A star baked your bones. Your blood is red with dust from the center of that star. So are my bones, my blood. So is everything on the Earth, everything made from fire and ash. Wake up and look around you at all that's come from inside a star!"

Kirchi began Timov's new work rhythms by moving his hands through the actions of scraping off the bough's bark and shaving strips of green-white pith. Once the rhythm asserted itself and he began doing the work without her guidance, she picked up the basket of pine seeds and left her charm to do its work.

Everything made from fire and ash . . . your body has come from inside a star. The words disappeared into the seethe of his pulse, and the blood echoing in his ears, circling through its thick night.

◆   ◆   ◆

Thunderheads brooded over the Forest, piling high into the ether, blotting out the afternoon sun in malignant violet billows and casting everything below into eerie, luminous darkness. Lightning streaked, and the birds fluting in the treetops went silent, waiting for the thunder.

Yaqut had found shelter beneath the overhang of a terrace strewn with juniper. The stream that had cut the rock shelves meandered below, chortling loudly as it foamed among rocks fallen from above. Overhead, caverns gaped from the hollow faces of the worn-away land, but their refuge belonged to Bear and Lion. Yaqut built a lean-to among the dwarf trees clinging to the stone ledge, and Hamr gathered dried grass and branches of deadwood to spark a fire.

Thunder pealed, and Blind Side of Life shuffled nervously and tossed his head. He smelled the lightning on the wet wind and neighed with concern. Hamr stoked the fire to a blaze and watched Yaqut pace with the tracking stone in his hand, absorbed in feeling the direction of his prey.

"I'm taking Blind Side to a patch of milk grass I saw on our way up here," Hamr said. "It'll calm him."

Yaqut grunted, staring at the stone in his hand as though he could see the ghost dancer in it. "Hard rain's coming. Look out for washes or you'll be riding the river."

Hamr untethered his horse and led him back along the shelf the way they had come. Soon as they were out of sight, he mounted and drove his sightless horse harder. They had a long way to go, and the rain was already upon them. Pellets of water smacked among the rocks and fluttered the leaves of the claw-rooted junipers.

By the time sheets of rain swept through the Forest, Hamr and Blind Side had found their way off the terrace and into the big trees. Lightning crashed on all sides, and Blind Side jumped with each boom, forcing Hamr to ride hunched over, clutching his mount's neck.

Darkness fell swiftly, and Hamr guided Blind Side to a pigwalk he had noticed earlier in the day. The rutted path stretched through the wooded hollows and puzzled among the knolls, eventually leading back to the vicinity of the witches' dell. Crouched over his shivering animal, dripping rain and plastered with windcast leaves, Hamr kept Blind Side in the muddy rut until he heard the femur bones of the skull totems clacking in the storm.

A sprawling oak beside the farthest fence of the dell provided some protection for Blind Side, and Hamr tethered him there before crawling through a break among the piled rocks. He ran crouched over, though the night of driving rain was black, illumined only by glaring fits of lightning. In each hand he carried a spear. His footfalls sucked at the mud.

At the first bunker of moss-matted boulders, he crawled on top and listened hard but heard nothing. When he poked his head in, he smelled the human musk of sleep, barely discerning the reclining shapes of the two tranced workers. The drumming rain masked his movements, and he backed off into the night and resumed his search.

Woodsmoke tainted with an acrid whiff of incense guided Hamr through the dark to the next mound of grass-seamed rocks. Here vaporous light leaked from a vent hole, and the rain glittered around it. Hamr listened, heard scraping. Pressing his face to the narrow space between the rocks, he spied hands using a chipped rock to peel strips of green spunk from a thick branch. The hands were Timov's.

Hamr crept around to the front of the burrow, stood, and took a deep breath to steady himself. Then he charged through the moss curtain. The interior glowed amber with burning nut-oil cupped in root burls perched in the crannies of the burrow. A twigfire crackled in a small hearth, where curls of the green spunk wisped aromatically. Timov sat alone beside the hearth, working with the same tranceful rhythm of the Longtooth slaves. Seeing him thus, Hamr's heart constricted, and he knelt before the boy. "Timov!" he whispered sharply.

The youth looked up groggily and stared with glassy eyes a long moment before his mouth worked. "Hamr." His hands did not stop moving, his face remained slack. "Is it you?"

Before Hamr could reply, the bone-beaded grass curtain at the back of the burrow parted, showing the red-haired witch. Her green eyes widened—and Hamr was upon her. With the spear-tips crossed under her throat, he guided her away from the curtain and pressed her against the damp wall. "Scream and you die."

Kirchi gasped, shook her head.

"Where is the hag?"

"You came for the boy?" Kirchi was astonished.

Hamr pressed harder, making the witch gag. "Where is she?"

With startled eyes she looked to the grass curtain. "Inside—with her crystals."

"What happened to Timov?"

"Trance-thorn—she pricked him."

"Take me to the witch. She'll undo it or I'll kill her."

"No! It will wear off. Quick, we must get away from here before she hears us. Take me with you, I'll help you."

Hamr's scowl darkened. "You? You're a witch."

"Not by choice. Please, we must hurry."

"You're lying! You'll call the witch and her wolves down on us."

Kirchi's face pleaded, her glance darting to the bone-beaded curtain. "She'll be out here soon. Please, I tell you, you can't stand against her power. Take me with you. I swear, I can help you."

"How?"

"The tracking stone—it uses the Dark Ones. It will draw the Stabbing Cat and the Lion down on you before you ever get near the ghost dancer. I have a better tracking stone."

"Where?"

She looked to the hearth, and Hamr stepped back but kept his spears trained on her. With another nervous glance at the grass curtain, she ran to the fire and dislodged the central stone behind the flames. A web of light sparkled from a cache of crystals. Kirchi withdrew a dagger-shaped jewel similar to the one that had drawn the evil spirit from Timov.

Hamr leaned one of his spears against his shoulder and took the crystal. He turned with it—and felt a palpable chill come and go as he changed direction. He tucked the tracking stone in his loin-pelt, and pulled Timov to his feet.

"Take me with you," Kirchi begged. As Hamr shoved Timov into the rain, she clutched at him. "If you don't, she'll surely kill me for giving you the stone."

Trying to gauge her truthfulness, Hamr stared hard at her. She had given him the tracking stone, but that might have been a ploy to save her life. Yet if he left her behind, she could immediately alert the witch. He seized her arm, pulling her after him into the night.

"Wait," she whispered and lifted a bag of woven rush-grass from its niche beside the entrance. "My medicine bag—"

Outside, the rain thrashed. Hamr braced Timov with an arm around his shoulders, leading him toward the stone fences. But Kirchi blocked the way, waved them in a different direction, hurrying through the pummeling rain, past the flooded fire-pit and toward the black pool, where the evil spirit had been driven from Timov. In the flashes of stormfire, the pool glowed.

Kirchi led them on. Hamr hesitated only long enough to look back once: to see silhouetted in the flashes of thunderbolts the two tranced Longtooth men running across the field where he had headed until diverted by the young witch. He moved hurriedly after her, Timov shuffling under his arm.

The witch led them past the pool and up a rocky rise sluicing with runoff. The slope leveled to a copse of young fir bunched close enough to thin the downpour, a stab of lightning igniting numerous yellow sparks among the trees—the eyes of wolves.

Hamr raised the two spears in his right hand to use as a club. But Kirchi faced him, her arms spread. "Don't threaten them. They know me." She whispered to the eye-glints as she had often heard Neoll Nant Caw whisper, her insides icy, wondering if they would indeed recognize her, then reached into her medicine-bag and clutched the moonstones there, whispering the song-chant that soothed beasts. "Yes, they'll let us pass now."

Hamr walked backwards, one hand on Timov's shoulder, not taking his eyes off the humped shadows as Kirchi guided them through the thicket. The wolves did not stir, and soon disappeared in the darkness.

A flare of lightning revealed the stone fences at the edge of the dell. Hamr whistled, and the white shadow of his horse stepped from behind the distant oak. With the spears he pointed to Blind Side and with his other hand made Timov look. The boy's numbed face stared for what seemed a long while before his slack lips offered a tiny grin. Hamr cast a triumphant smile at Kirchi, who wiped the wet-strung hair from her face, casting a nervous glance back toward the burrow of the witch. She followed the hunters into the slick night.

Heavy rain flooded the rut that Hamr had followed to the dell, and he guided Blind Side of Life to higher ground. The stream that led back to Yaqut's camp roared invisibly in the darkness, and Hamr followed its sound. With the drumming rain, the horse weary from walking all day and into the night, and Timov trudging heavily but as one asleep, under the witch's poison, the trek went slowly.

Hamr wanted to stop under the trees and wait for dawn, but Kirchi insisted they keep moving. "Neoll Nant Caw already knows we've stolen her good tracking stone," she said urgently. "She'll be after us. The rain may protect us from her wolves, but only if we keep moving."

Following ridgebacks through the drumming rain above the stream, Hamr picked his way carefully. One misplaced step would send them plummeting into the engorged stream to be swept through the darkness and bashed among the rocks. With his spears he probed ahead, testing the footing on rocky ground and finding passages through the stubborn hedges.

When fire flickered in the distance—Yaqut's campfire—Blind Side would go no farther. Hamr had Kirchi and Timov wait with the horse, and he hastened ahead. The spark of light brightened into a blaze far larger than the campfire Hamr had built. Yaqut had stoked it into a bonfire. As Hamr darted among the trees, he understood why. The roars of beasts resounded above the tumult of the surging stream.

Hamr stopped, squinted into the wet wind. Then a bramble of lightning lit up the terrace where Yaqut had camped, and Hamr saw Yaqut standing before the bonfire waving a torch. On the ledge above, the slinky shadows of Stabbing Cats paced back and forth. They were big as lions, with incisors like long knives. Hamr had heard tales of these beasts, ferocious hunters of the Hippopotamus and the Rhinoceros, from the elders, but he had never seen them before.

Using his spears to brace himself, Hamr descended to the rushing stream to avoid the big cats. The soaked earth constantly slipped away from under him, and he slid through the darkness. Bramble and rocks slashed him as he went by. One of his spears snagged on a protruding root; the other fell from his grip into the churning torrent below as he used both hands to hang on. His feet kicked, found purchase among exposed roots, and he stood up and inched his way upward.

Now the frenzied roars of the Stabbing Cats battered the air louder than the thunder. Heaving himself onto a rock shelf, Hamr saw that he had crawled to a terrace level with Yaqut and could see the hunter silhouetted against the smoking flames of his big fire. The wind drove the rain under the overhang, wetting the burning wood and scattering swells of smoke. Yaqut slashed with his torch overhead to keep the Stabbing Cats from pouncing onto his ledge while he dragged more dry wood out from the crevices against the rock-wall. Soon the wind and the rain would defeat him, and the Stabbing Cats would close in.

"Yaqut!" Hamr yelled, but the wind snatched his cry. He pulled himself up with his spear and ran toward the fire, keeping close to the rockwall so the cats would not spot him. When he reached the dwarf trees in the shimmering glow of the fire, he shouted again, "Yaqut! Throw away the tracking stone!"

Yaqut glared at Hamr, his waxen face blurred with the strain of defending himself. He waved Hamr closer.

"Throw the stone away!" Hamr shouted, afraid to move nearer. Beyond the dwarf trees, he would step into range of the Stabbing Cats, where they could easily leap on him. Their roars rose in volume, infuriated as they were by the storm. "The witch duped us! The stone is calling the cats to you!"

Yaqut plucked at his waist-strap and held up the stone. "How do you know?" he cried.

"I went back—for Timov! The young witch told me! Throw it away!"

With an angry shout, Yaqut spun around and sent the stone flying into the blackness above the flooded stream. Immediately, the roaring of the Stabbing Cats died away. The lashing rain and the spitting fire drove them off.

Hamr climbed over to Yaqut and took his torch. "You were right about the crone. She would've killed us to save the ghost dancer."

Yaqut spat out a curse. "Why didn't you say you were going back?"

"You'd have tried to stop me."

He turned and scurried away, Yaqut's bitter words pelting him. When he returned with Blind Side, Timov, and the red-haired witch in his trail, Yaqut was still fuming.

"Have you lost your mind, man? Why'd you bring her?" He turned his twisted eye on her and blocked her way to the fire. "She's a witch!"

"She helped me." Hamr showed the long crystal. "This one won't draw the beasts down on us."

Yaqut eyed the crystal suspiciously, refusing to touch it. "It may not draw beasts, but it will draw Neoll Nant Caw."

Hamr looked to Kirchi. She nodded. "She will know where her crystal is."

"And she'll come after it, be sure." Yaqut waved the tracking stone away. "Beasts we can fight with fire. The witch—she's death itself to us."

"You'd have died tonight, Yaqut." Hamr tucked the crystal away.

"Maybe." Yaqut eyed Timov, where he stood beside Blind Side, staring blankly. "What happened to him?"

"Trance-thorn," Kirchi replied. "He will come around in time. But he needs to be warmed and fed."

Yaqut stood aside, let the witch and the boy approach the fire. As Hamr stepped past, he took his arm. "You abandoned me."

"I came back, for Timov and for you."

"We don't need Timov." The good side of Yaqut's face looked sour. "And we don't need Neoll Nant Caw after us."

Hamr said nothing. He took Blind Side's rope and walked stiffly to the fire.

Kirchi sat Timov close to the flames and blotted his

soaked hair and damp flesh with warm ash. Hamr led the horse to the far side of the fire, near the wall, where there was no chance of his slipping down the dark slope. Then he squatted beside the witch, and the chill that had penetrated him made him shiver and was lost in the flush of heat. He bowed his head, throwing his long hair forward, and squeezed the rain from it.

"I remember you from the Longtooth," Yaqut said to the witch, squatting with a puff of exhaustion. "Your mother is a sybil. Why have you left Neoll Nant Caw?"

"I never wanted to be with her." She stopped wringing the water from her hair and regarded the hunter with a steady but respectful gaze. "My teats were too small for the Mothers, so they gave me to Neoll Nant Caw. But I hate it with her. I swear it by the Mothers, I hate it with her."

"What do you hate?"

"The trances. The potions are bitter; they make me sick. I don't like leaving my body, seeing afar."

"You ever see a ghost dancer?"

"In trance only."

"Never in person?"

"No. There aren't many left around here. Neoll Nant Caw hasn't seen one herself in seven years."

Yaqut's stare made the witch look away, but he kept staring. "Where are you going? The Longtooth won't have you back."

"I . . . I don't know where I'm going. Just away."

"You think you can get away from Neoll Nant Caw?"

"I was with her four years. I remember everything she taught me." She patted her woven-grass sack, strung to her waist. "I have my medicines and my charms. Maybe I'll go south, find a tribe that needs me.''

Yaqut frowned. ''You'll go nowhere till we kill the ghost dancer. If Neoll Nant Caw comes for us, you'll stop her—or you'll die trying.''

Hamr glared from under his hair at Yaqut. ''Save your bluster and threats for the bonesucker, Yaqut. You'd be torn apart by those Stabbing Cats if not for her.''

Yaqut snorted. ''Maybe that would be better than letting the old witch get us.''

''What will the crone do? Send her wolves? We've got fire.''

''Fire won't stop her. You've stolen her crystal.'' Yaqut reached over and took Kirchi's chin in his bony fingers. ''You want to tell him what she can do?''

Kirchi stared at his deformed face with undisguised revulsion.

Yaqut released her and threw another branch on the fire. ''Tomorrow we split up,'' he announced. ''Can the boy travel?''

Kirchi shrugged doubtfully. ''He'll be very tired the next few days.''

''So long as he can walk. You—Hamr,'' he ordered, ''You take the witch and the crystal north, out of the Forest. I don't want Neoll Nant Caw stalking me. The boy and I will go east to the bluffs of the Big River. We'll move north this side of the river, and you come south. When we meet—if we meet—we'll be closer to the ghost dancer. If I don't find you among the bluffs, I'll take the boy to the Longtooth. He'll be a slave, but he'll have his life. By then, the bonesucker will be too far south to hunt.''

''You're more afraid of her than of the ghost dancer,'' Hamr realized slowly. ''If she's that dangerous, then Timov is safer with you. I will go north with the witch as you say.'' He added in a show of bravura: ''I went back for Timov. Now, if I must, I'll stand off Neoll Nant Caw.''

Yaqut sneered, shook his head dolefully.

Hamr flinched, chanted silently to the Beastmaker: *Help me out of this trouble.* He had left Timov with the crone and now the boy was locked in a spell. If he expected the Beastmaker to help, he had to confront the witch without exposing the boy to any further danger from her. He had to agree to Yaqut's plan and face the witch on his own. But what was her magic? ''She must be very powerful,'' he ventured.

Yaqut gazed into the fire, the scarred half of his face rigid as ice. ''You'll find out.''

Duru watched the flames of Baat's fire seizing twists of its dried wood as the Rain Master sent wet fingers of wind through the thicket to taunt the blaze. Baat was adjusting the tinder to catch the gusts and burn brighter. Earlier, when the thunderheads swelled, he had carried Duru here, high above the stream where the Bear had clawed her leg. Under an outcrop of granite and behind a thicket of young birch, the Rain Master could not touch them. Duru lay on a bed of pine needles and feathery sumac, her head propped on a rock padded with moss, so she could watch the storm raging over the Forest. Baat crouched beside her, offering her sips of rainwater he had caught in a burl of willow bark, the willow resins that would ease her pain.

There was not much pain now. The poplar plaster and the willow tinctures had soothed the wound. And she had slept. After Baat had prepared her bed, the afternoon sky had darkened with squall clouds, the air had gone still and warm, and she plunged into a dreamless sleep that endured the batterings of thunder and the crash of rain. She woke deep in the night to find Baat mashing pine nuts. She ate those and the hackleberries he had gathered outside their shelter, and watched the staggered lightning slashes over the Forest lifting the turtle-backed hills briefly out of the darkness.

Now rested, her hunger appeased and the hurt in her leg dulled, Duru scrutinized the giant who cared for her. His marsh scent filled the enclosure, the fetid exhalation of stirred mud, the undersoils of Turtle and Frog competing with the pine smoke of the fire. But she did not find the reek offensive anymore: It had the pungency of a slow kelpy river and brought to mind cattails and cress. Nor was his appearance as frightful to her now that she knew he did not intend to break her bones for her marrow. Large as he was, his thick body moved lightly upon his bones, and even in this tight space, he turned and rose as graceful as smoke. His harsh face, carved sharply around steep cheekbones, looked far more dolorous than dangerous, the long eyes slanting downward and lit green with the phosphors of sorrow.

"Baat," she said.

He startled when she spoke his name and stared at her curiously. When she said nothing, he offered her more water. She shook her head and began to talk, words spilling out of her in a gush of relief: "Why did you take me from my people? I thought you were going to kill me. But even when I ran away from you, you came after me—if not to eat me, then why? And why did you save me from the Bear?"

Baat understood not a word. But the cadence of

her speech was gentle though swift. Strangely, she no longer feared him, and he allowed a smile to lift the heavy muscles of his face.

A spasm of lightning lifted into view for a moment the large world beyond the thicket. Baat glanced at the writhing energy and thought of the ul udi. While the girl had slept, he had tried to reach them, to converse again with the Bright Ones, but the storm had interfered. He had heard nothing but his own confusion. What to do now?

He held up his left hand and willed some of the cold fire into it. The hand lit up with blue voltage, a wavery sheath of fire arcing between his fingers.

Duru gasped, pulled back.

"No—don't be afraid," Baat said. But he knew now that his voice was so much gruff noise to her. He could not explain that this was healing energy. Instead, with his right hand, he steadied her hurt leg and touched the wound with the blue energy.

Duru tightened to cry out. But there was no pain. The lightning in the ghost dancer's hand crackled over the bindings of her damaged leg, and pulsed coolly through her flesh. When he took his hands away, her leg hummed with strength.

Baat laughed at Duru's amazement, and she smiled, at first tentatively, then more broadly as the good feeling suffused her torn leg. Timov and Hamr would never believe this, she thought—and her joy dimmed. Where were they in this storm? Surely they believed she was in danger—or dead. Taking a twig from the fire, she drew two stick figures in the dirt, one of them astride a crude likeness of a horse. The ghost dancer watched, then turned away. The flesh he could heal, but for her fear and her sorrow there was little he could do.

In the fargone days of his childhood, Baat remembered the old ones gathering the clan together during the storms and singing. The ul udi could not come down through the tempest, so the People would send songs up to them. He hummed a tune he recalled from that time, a lullaby he had once sung to his own children. The stabbing hurt of those memories startling to life with that song astonished him, and his voice trailed off, leaving him bewildered.

But Duru picked up on the music with a different song, a rain chant of the Panther people:

> Let the lightning flash—
> Riding into the darkness—
> And the thunder crash—
> Riding into the darkness—
> I will not be afraid
> Riding into the darkness—
> In the world the rain made
> Riding into the darkness—

Baat smiled again. The girl smiled back. Outside, the Rain Master's lightning raged in surges, while behind the thicket, under the granite outcrop, the ghost dancer and the girl hummed the storm music together with the thunder.

As the horizons exploded with lightning, Hamr and Timov crouched near the battered fire, Blind Side behind them, his large body shivering with fear. Yaqut fed the fire with juniper branches and glanced about for the young witch. She had gone into the bushes some while back and had not returned. He motioned for Hamr to seek her out.

Hamr patted Timov reassuringly, though the boy's gaze had locked on the jumping flames and he seemed oblivious to all else. "Kirchi!" Hamr called, rising and stooping into the rain. Maybe she had fled, which would not be bad: one less to protect and feed.

Kirchi had not run away. On her way back to the campfire, lightning stabbed overhead so close that the air crackled and sent her sprawling. When she looked up, the after-glare of the bolt still lingered in the sky like mist. Out of that misty patch, translucent and shimmery, Neoll Nant Caw's spectral image came flying toward her.

"You betrayed me," the crone cried, her haggard face vindictive with rage. "Four years I fed and sheltered you. I taught you the wise ways. You cannot run away now."

Kirchi clutched her medicine-bag, felt the jangle of moonstones within. The power in those stones could dispel this wraith, she was sure. She had seen Neoll Nant Caw use crystals to drive off spectral ul udi—but she had never actually done it herself. "Go away," Kirchi warned.

Neoll Nant Caw's image swelled closer, her furious face a dense thicket of creases. "Come back now, Kirchi—or you will die with the others."

"Get away from me," Kirchi whimpered and curled up tighter. "You know I never wanted your food or your shelter. I never wanted to be a witch."

"You are a witch," the wraith spoke like soft thunder. "You can never be otherwise. Come back."

"No. I'm not a witch. I'm not—and I'm not coming back."

The wraith narrowed in, her clawed hands glittering with punishing barbs.

Kirchi clutched the charged moonstones in her bag and called the power into herself. To her surprise, the power came. A rich, amazing, flamboyance of strength puffed through her.

Neoll Nant Caw sneered. "You wouldn't dare! I taught you everything!"

With all the vehemence of her fright, Kirchi flung the energy at the wraith. Lightning clapped, and the crone shrieked and was gone.

In the glare Hamr's figure was silhouetted. "Are you all right?" He helped her to her feet, felt the fear loosening her muscles and took her weight, thinking she had been startled by the lightning.

Kirchi trembled in Hamr's grasp. She had driven off Neoll Nant Caw! She had actually dared—and had been strong enough to do it. She had defended herself with her own powers—and as a witch. For a brief moment, pride dazzled her against a black sky of fear.

Dawn broke in long rays of scarlet whose light blurred everything. Timov stared empty-eyed into the slashes of red clouds, while Hamr leaned close, trying to stare past the glaze to the boy inside. "You sure this'll wear off?"

"It will take several days," Kirchi answered again. She stood at the edge of the rimrock, staring in the direction of Neoll Nant Caw's camp. Her insides still felt the fright of last night's confrontation. She had told no one what had happened, for there was nothing they could do. The storm had protected them from the full brunt of the old witch's power. But how much longer before she came again for them? The moon was growing, and the crone would surely use that strength against them.

Yaqut kicked through the embers of the bonfire, stamping out the hot ashes that remained. Though they were on a rock shelf with nothing nearby to burn, he did this out of ritual habit, not ever wanting the fire to follow him. After the tremendous bolts of lightning during the night, he had expected dawn to reveal several forest blazes. He was pleased to see that the only flames in the Forest were the sun's rays probing through fog and mist.

"Don't leave me," Timov begged in a wilted voice.

Hamr looked to Yaqut. "Let me take him with me."

Yaqut shook his fierce face. "He goes with me. You have the tracking crystal. When the boy's head clears, I'll have his dreams." He lifted Timov under his shoulders and stood him up. "The bonesucker escaped me all summer, but with the boy I have a last chance to track him. That right, Timov? You going to find your sister for me?"

Timov blinked, worked his mouth, but no sound emerged.

Yaqut sucked a slow breath through his teeth, and nodded. "He'll do it. A few days of walking will clear his head." He faced Hamr, noting the concern in the big youth's face. He liked this oaf and wished the lad were as bright as he was brave. "You did right to go back for him. No matter what I said last night. But now you must contend with the witch"—the flesh between his eyes twitched at that thought—"the boy will be safer with me. If you survive the journey to the Big River, you'll see him again. I'll watch over him, be sure."

Hamr placed Cyndell's ivory calendar bracelet in Timov's hand. "I'll be back for you."

Timov's mouth worked again, and from far away,

he said: "I know." He looked down at the bracelet and his gaze lost itself in the swerves of its carvings.

Hamr turned for Kirchi and saw her with Blind Side, grooming him with a pine-needle branch. Yaqut, too, watched her, and he said out of the twisted side of his mouth, "Be wary of her. I want the bonesucker. You want Duru. What does she want? Mind that."

Taking Timov by the elbow, Yaqut led him away from the stamped-out fire, down the slope toward the stream. Hamr looked after them until they disappeared in the sun-shot mists. He felt Kirchi watching him and wondered if she had deceived him and was still loyal to the old witch. Would she be a nuisance? Or did she truly want to flee her past? Silently he asked the Beast-maker for a sign.

"You were brave to come back for him," Kirchi said from beside the horse. "Braver yet to take me with you. Most men would have been afraid to trust a witch. But then most men wouldn't have trespassed witch ground."

Hamr scanned the terraced slopes above them. "We better go before the Stabbing Cats return. They'll want the horse." He observed her sandals, noted they were plaited grass, already well frayed from last night's trek. "You'll need new footwear. Soon as we get away from these ledges, we'll cut some hide and fit you." He patted the pelts across Blind Side's back.

Kirchi smiled gratefully. She would be glad to get out of the grass robe. She wanted to leave behind every witch-thing she had. But after last night's visitation from Neoll Nant Caw she dared not abandon what protection she had. "I better not wear animal skin for a while," Kirchi said, and when she saw Hamr's puzzled expression, added, "I'm still a witch—until we get

away from Neoll Nant Caw. I may have to talk with the
animals. They won't talk if I'm wearing their skins."

"Talk to animals?"

"They could help us." She saw he did not understand. During the storm last night and again at first
light, she had heard him praying to the Beastmaker,
and she had expected him to be receptive to her talking
with animals. For now, though, he was more concerned
about the Stabbing Cats and eager to get away from the
ledges, where the big cats could pounce on them. But
she knew the cats had left before dawn, when the rain
stopped, moving up the slopes and west. Blind Side of
Life had heard them. When everyone else had been
sleeping, he had been listening with his deep ears, each
moving independently, separating the noises of the
stream and the wash of the rain from the stirring of
animals. Each ear was filled with delicate hairs that
could catch sounds no person could hear. At first, she
had felt sorry that the horse had no eyes, but once she
talked with him and realized how clearly he heard, how
fully and deeply he listened to everything, envy dis-
placed her pity.

The paths that the rain had washed into the rocky
slopes led down to the stream, glutted now with boulders, uprooted trees, and the carcasses of animals
drowned by floods. At a bend where the debris had
silted a gravel bar, they forded a stream to put water
between them and Neoll Nant Caw. On the other side
they stopped to gather some purple whortleberries for
their pouches.

"What do you want?" Hamr asked her bluntly at
last. "You don't want to hunt the ghost dancer. And
Yaqut says you can't go back to your tribe. You said
you want to go south, find another tribe. Why don't you
go?"

Kirchi regarded him curiously. "You'd let me go?"

Hamr shrugged. "You're a witch—how could I stop you?"

"I thought you'd try. Yaqut said I had to help until the ghost dancer is taken."

"Yaqut's not here. You can go."

Kirchi smiled, a white-toothed grin that softened the sharp angles of her face. "Maybe I will."

A warm feeling suffused Hamr's breast. He had hoped to get rid of her, despite Yaqut's command; at the least, he had expected her to be a nuisance. Yet now he felt inspired by the way she played the brightness of her eyes over him—green eyes. She was the strangest woman he had ever seen, with her orange hair and fox-slanted eyes. She lacked the ampleness men wanted in a woman, that Aradia had carried so well. She was boyish, but her expression was strong and direct, the look of someone used to facing challenge, who knew more than she would say, like an Old Mother. That was what warmed him, the realization that she was old in a young body. And he liked her looking at him with esteem, making him feel he was a great man.

She had returned to gathering berries.

"Maybe?" he asked.

"Now that I can go," she said, without looking at him, "maybe I'll stay."

"But why? The Frost Moon is growing. Now's the time to go south."

"I don't really want to go south. Strays are killed by other tribes or made slaves. Let me stay with you. You took me from Neoll Nant Caw when I'd thought I'd never get away. Let me help you."

Hamr doubted she could help him, but he was

pleased with the way she regarded him. He shrugged. "Which way do we go?"

Kirchi smiled with relief, then quickly marked the sun and pointed a way through the shrubs. "If we hurry, we can get out of the hills before dark. Tomorrow we'll reach the taiga." She took Blind Side's rope and guided him.

Glad that Kirchi knew her way, Hamr concentrated on looking for food. Among the tangles of alders, willows, and dwarf birch, small mammals flitted, and Hamr whipped rocks at them with his sling but missed each time. Kirchi giggled with amusement. Then she knelt in the deep moss hummocks beside a creek, snatched a rainbow fish from the purling water with one hand and tossed the trout to an amazed Hamr. They ate the roe as they walked and wrapped the fish in river kelp to keep it fresh for that night.

A shifting cloud of mosquitoes followed them along the hill slopes, swarming louder in the depressions, until Kirchi found a milty pod of milkweed, mixed the latex with bile from a trout's gut and dabbed it on their faces and limbs. Hamr recognized the repellent as a variant of the fish paste the Blue Shell used. Hers smelled less vile and worked as well. He admired her competence and her unhurrying way of doing things.

When she paused by a swollen stream, Hamr waited patiently, thinking she was preparing to snatch another fish. Then the waters separated and a large shadow lifted itself upright—a giant beaver, taller than a man. It bobbed back into the stream, with only its big-toothed head, thick as a stump, breaking the surface.

Kirchi held the moonstones in her medicine-bag tight to her chest, letting their energy stream through her and into the Beaver. In that way, the witch power

in the stone soothed the creature and opened its mind
to her. How quiet that mind felt, still as a snag pool—
Kirchi shared with him the black water, watching mosquitoes dimple the surface, pike poised like knives,
bolts of dragonflies flicking under basswood trees, and
a black-haired girl in a tattered hide hurrying beside
collapsed earth banks.

"Beaver has seen the girl," Kirchi said in a sleepy
voice, viewing Duru's small body crossing Beaver's
wicker dam and disappearing among the pale blades on
the shore. Then Bear reared out of the slick grass, and
Kirchi nearly lost her vision. She watched the girl flee,
saw her swim the stream, toward the far side where
Baat stood throwing stones at the Bear.

Kirchi pulled back, and Beaver slipped into the
amber water and vanished. "Duru was near here yesterday," she said quietly, her voice sounding loud even
in a whisper. "I think she surprised Bear."

Hamr, who had watched her communion with Beaver with an open mouth, snapped alert. "Bear would
kill her."

"Baat was there too. I think he saved her. I think
she's all right."

"You think—" Hamr looked with exasperation at
the ripples in the stream, where Beaver had floated
only a moment before. "What did Beaver tell you?"

Kirchi shrugged. "That's all. I'll ask other animals
as we go. Maybe we'll learn more."

Hamr followed the witch lightly, alertly, but he
felt suspicious and nervous. Had she really spoken
with Beaver? How? He watched her carefully as they
moved, but no other animals came to her.

Late that afternoon, at the end of their arduous
walk through the hills, Blind Side of Life was left to
nibble the last green shoots in the russet grass. Kirchi

cleaned the trout while Hamr used a big rock to fell spruce poles for a lean-to. He asked her, "Can that crone really come after us this far away?"

"Oh, yes." They had chosen a sandy bench above a creek that drained the hills they were leaving and opened into the grassy flat ahead. Low, broad rays of sunlight spread through the trees, brightening their leaves' autumnal colors: scarlet maples, yellow birches, silvery willows.

"What is her power?" Hamr asked, dragging the spruce poles from where he had felled them. "Is it the power to talk with animals, the way you did with Beaver?"

Kirchi laid the fish she was flaying with a sharp rock into the creek water. She held up her hand to stop Hamr's feet, cleared the damp leaves from under the fir, which he was trampling, and revealed a crop of mushrooms.

"Will she send the wolves after us?" Hamr asked.

"No. They guard the witch ground." She selected two handfuls of mushrooms and returned to the creek to wash them and continue scaling the trout. "Neoll Nant Caw's power is the moon. As the moon waxes, the witch's power grows."

"What kind of power?"

"The next few nights, she'll send wraiths."

"Spirits?"

"More like animal ghosts. I can't describe them. You'll see."

"After that?"

"The Moon Bitch. When the moon is strong enough, Neoll Nant Caw will come to us as the Moon Bitch."

"As a dog then?"

"Yes, a wolf-wraith—but it's her, her spirit. We'll be on the tundra by then. We'll see her coming."

"What can this Moon Bitch do to us?"

"Tear us apart if we give her the chance."

Hamr looked skeptical. "A ghost? The fire-songs say ghosts are mist. They drive people mad but they don't tear them apart."

"This is not a ghost. It's a power, a moon power. Neoll Nant Caw has trapped ul udi in her crystals. They've taught her how to shape the fire from the sky."

"Ul udi," Hamr tried the name. "Like the spirit you drove out of Timov."

"Yes. Now how about a fire for us? Or do you like your fish raw?"

While they ate, the sun set, and the needle of the Frost Moon gleamed in the lavender dusk. Kirchi asked about the Blue Shell, and Hamr told her about his life on the seacliffs, the wave that swept away his father and gave him his ambition to be a great man, how he captured Blind Side and won Aradia, and what he had learned of the gap between fate and destiny—before fire burned in the blood of the Blue Shell and changed everything.

From Duru's satchel, Hamr removed the tortoise wheel and spun it for Kirchi on a stem of cane. She listened intently to what he had to say about Spretnak's idea that life is a wheel and destiny the emptiness at its center. She questioned him about his destiny, and he talked about his visions of the Beastmaker, with His antlered head, man's body, and eyes like moons of blood.

"When did you see Him last?" she asked.

"The last time, Aradia watched. I rode Blind Side on the beach, the same beach I used to run on till I dropped from exhaustion and saw Him in the blood light pounding behind my eyes. Only this time with Blind Side, it was the horse that got tired, and when he stopped, I lay on his back and heard his breath rushing. And in the sound, I heard Him, the Beastmaker, calling my name. With my eyes closed, He was there. He never said anything more than my name. But that was enough. I knew He was pleased that I loved the Horse that He had sent me. I knew He wanted me for His own. And that's what makes a man great, isn't it? To belong to what is greater.''

Kirchi had lifted her head while he talked and was staring past him, a peculiar look on her face. ''There's one,'' she said.

He turned. The last light of day lay across the sky above the bluffs like green marrow. At the edge of the creek, where mists flowed among the cane and woodbine, yellow eyes blazed. Hamr started, then squinted to see what animal was there that had come to speak with the witch. But there was no animal—only eyes, floating bodiless, brighter than stars.

The day after the stormy night, Baat carried Duru north. She rode lightly on his shoulders, and though the gash in her leg throbbed dully, she ignored the pain. She felt no concern for herself anymore, only for Timov and Hamr who, she knew, feared for her. This she tried to tell Baat when he stopped on a shelf of hillside above a flooded stream.

But Baat had no idea what the girl was trying to say. At first he thought she anguished over her wound. He unwrapped it, while she chattered and gestured. The gash was lividly swollen and would be hurting more now and in the coming hours than any time since the bear claw ripped it open. But the healing had already done much to restore the ripped tissue. The pain would end soon.

Baat had chosen this site to stop because the plants he needed for a new dressing were here. As he set to work gathering them, he watched the black islands in the flooded stream and the pale sandbars for smallheads. The heavy rain would slow them today, but they would be out, stalking him. The muddy ground and the added weight of the girl would make tracking him that much easier.

Day travel was most dangerous, and he had hoped to move only by night. But tonight, he knew, he would dance with the ul udi, dance to win their wisdom for the girl. She would have to meet them for her to understand the journey. There would be no traveling this night; he hoped to make up for that by day.

Duru lay on her stomach, her gashed leg propped on a log, exposed to the styptic rays of the sun. The flawless blue of the sky seemed strange after last night's fury. Rusty stalks of burdock ranged the hillside, their feathery bolls perfectly still in the windless air. Bumblebees and wasps surged among the marigolds, their drones the only noise in the hollow above the flooded woods.

When Baat returned he gave her a wedge of poplar bast to gnaw while he dressed her wound. He talked to her as he worked, pausing frequently to listen, to smell the still air, and scan the brightly mottled terrain. Awe, sadness, and fear mingled in his voice, low and guttural as a river in its rocky bed.

"The herds are moving south now," he told her, though he knew she did not understand. "Soon you will see the woolly rhinos darkening the plains, immense as evening. And the mastodons, their giant thunder shaking not just the earth but the clouds in the sky. But

first, we must get out of these dangerous woods. The
smallheads are everywhere with their poisons. They
are so silent and deceptive; the shadows are their allies.''

Duru sat on Baat's thick shoulders, and he carried
her up the hill and down the other side into a confusion
of dales and knolls. This complex land gathered the
runoff from the far mountains into narrow lakes and a
scrawl of streams and rills. In the basins, only tree
crowns and the tops of giant boulders showed above
the sunny mist. The ridges, threaded by waterfalls,
mazed northward to where the giant icesheets had
flattened the land and tall grasses shimmered like fur.

Along the way Baat stopped often to watch for
smallheads and to gather food. Traveling was slow—
Baat figured that at their careful pace, they would need
ten days to reach the tundra, at least that long because
he had chosen a way that far skirted the Thundertree,
where Yaqut lurked. But the abundant land provided
much to eat and unless the smallheads found them,
they would not suffer.

By evening, when they made camp beside a kettle
lake under a long moon, they were exhausted, Baat
from walking, Duru from pain. Beside the windbreak of
a boulder, Baat meticulously prepared Duru's bed of
dried leaves with lit cattail punks on either side to keep
away the mosquitoes and, because the air was damp
with the mist of last night's rain, a blanket of cane
feathers.

He studied the bed with satisfaction. Such beds he
once had made for his own children. He decided that
soon he must fashion a spear and begin collecting pelts
for the cold nights to come. Then he gingerly changed
the dressing on the girl's hurt leg, while the red salmon

he had netted with a vine basket at a creek earlier in the day steamed under hot rocks.

Duru's eyes had glistened with tears all day as she thought of Timov and Hamr without her, fearing for her, perhaps thinking her dead. Baat, thinking she wept from the pain of her wound, had offered her more poplar and willow bark. Angrily, she brushed the medicinal woods aside. "I want to go back to my people," she said again as she had been telling the giant all day. "Don't you understand? I belong with them. I can't stay with you."

But Baat frowned with sorrow, comprehending her pain though not her words. She was a child and belonged with her people. If the Bright Ones had not chosen her for him he would never have thought she could help him. Let the Bright Ones explain themselves. He held up both of his big hands and showed her the blue glow between his fingers. That silenced her, and she lay back in her bed, eyes wide.

"Don't be afraid," he said softly, his large face gruesome in the gloaming. He pointed to the sky and gestured downward to himself. So long as she was not afraid, the Dark Ones would ignore her, and he could call on the Bright Ones to come down and dance with him. Still, Duru recalled her dreams of the ghost dancer, and wonder and fear quavered together in her.

Baat was gesturing for her to lie still. Then he stretched tall, reaching for the night sky, where the stars flecked brightly in the ghostly green mane of the borealis.

The air chilled—and a weird, clear light appeared around the giant's body. He turned his back to her, and his body-light intensified its blueness. Sparks flickered at his fingers and the tips of his ears. And when he came full around, his face was transfigured, the skin seeming to float like a hot haze on the pulsing glow of his skull, his eyes brittle as mirrors of ice shattering sunlight.

Duru gasped. A black wind rattled the trees, pressed the campfire down to crimson embers, and opened a luminous darkness around Baat, like the giant wings of a crow. In that black shine, figures stirred— faceless human shapes glittering like mica.

The wind lifted, and the old ones stood around Baat, their arms open at their sides, linking hands. They paced a circle around him, and he turned with them, obeying some unheard music, head bowed, arms winged. Blue fire crawled over his body, flurrying off him and spinning upward into the purple edge of night.

Slowly but with gathering speed, the ghost shapes narrowed closer, and the sparks capered hotter and higher into the sky. Baat blurred among the encroaching specters, a vortex of blue flames. The old ones swirled around him, compressed to a windy streak of smoke.

Abruptly, Baat stopped turning, and the smoky light whirling about him entered the cave of his chest. He stood before Duru dream-like, weighted with radiance, a meshing of starfire shaping around him. He reached out, his fingertips like pieces of the moon.

Without thought, Duru raised her hand to meet his. When they touched, the silence deepened; she could hear her heart's enormous footsteps. Beyond that, a far sound drew nearer: a voice like a glitter of rain, calling her out of herself, into the lighted depths of the night.

Neoll Nant Caw watched Baat dance until his blur sharpened to a star. Then she looked away, to keep from falling into the radiance. Beside her, the flame of an oil-lamp rose pale as a new tooth. With wet fingers she snuffed it and immersed herself in darkness.

Reassured that the child Duru was safe, the witch let the night penetrate her. She became a numb lump, a rock. All her heat seethed out and floated above her, leaving her dense with cold. The cold sank deeper, till all her heat was gone, given to the thermal swirlings trapped in the burrow. The mist of heat glowed infrared, churning and boiling into fiery clouds.

Shaped by her rage, gangrenous odd shapes appeared out of the roiling air: slithery body organs blotched with tufts of electric fire, ulcerous sparks, and arcs of tiny lightning. The mutilated forms breathed with the heat of her being. They milled around her—tattered entrails, flopped off claws, snarling dog-faces in blue jellies.

She was building the Moon Bitch, as she had before, building a fiery body of wrath to defend the ghost dancer. He was a source of the tribes' knowledge and represented all that she had loved in life. To defend him, she would use everything in her power. Already this Beast had devoured all the witch's memories, all her hungers, her very will, and even her wobbly bones. Each night, she grew stronger: Her parts healed their defects and shone brighter, her grim purpose burned keener.

She would kill the hunters of the ghost dancer. She would kill the thieves who stole the tracking crystal. Above all, she would kill the traitor, Kirchi, who would use the wise ways to kill Baat.

The Moon Bitch dreamed herself more real. Far away, Neoll Nant Caw watched, sitting under the skyhole of her burrow, a rock, patient and sure, as the starlight scratched at her cold surface.

◆ ◆ ◆

The stars were sharp, even through the gusty auroras. Hamr scanned the dark crests of the hills looking for movement, but only the whirr of bats disturbed the night. The yellow eyes that had stared from the creek had vanished hours ago. The mist still crawled there, lit up by the sky's glow.

Kirchi had said the eyes were the wraith of Neoll Nant Caw come to spy on them. Now the young witch lay curled beside the spent fire, snoring gently. Blind Side, too, snoozed calmly, twitching an ear occasionally against the whine of mosquitoes.

Hamr could not sleep. Knowing that Neoll Nant Caw had the power to pursue them stoked his alertness. But talking with Kirchi had stirred him more deeply than the sight of the wraith. She was the first woman who had wanted to hear what he had to say about the Beastmaker. And the peculiar thought occurred to him that perhaps the Beastmaker had led him to her. Without him, she would have remained a captive of the crone—and without her, he would have been alone, perhaps forever, in his secret knowledge.

Before she had fallen asleep, long after the demon eyes had blurred away, Kirchi had said to him: "Everything you've seen of the Beastmaker is true. I've seen so myself, at the ripped edge of sleep. That's where witches live, entranced by their potions, watching the dream that's living us. You see, that is why we need slaves. Most of each day, we are only half in this world, half a woman, half a dream. And what frightens me is knowing that the dream is far more real than the woman. Men and women, we're born and we die—but the dream goes on. It's the dream that makes us go on. For you, the dream is the Beastmaker, the Being made from animal jaw and human flesh. Isn't that what's dreaming you, the beast becoming a man?''

"And you?'' Hamr had asked. "What's dreaming you?''

"What dreams all women—the Mother. She births us and eats us. We are always in Her belly. We drop from our mothers and we fall into the earth. We're always with Her. She dreams me. That's why I can't be a witch. I'm just an ordinary woman. I want to be a Mother, a simple mother, not a witch.''

"What dreams the witches?''

"The Word.''

At that, Hamr had blinked like a rabbit. "What word?''

Kirchi had smiled at his befuddlement, not mockingly, but with understanding. "Sounds strange, I know. But before there were people or animals, before there was this huge, wild earth, or even the stars, sun and moon, there was the Word. Perhaps Thought is a better way to say It, but Thought sounds so quiet—and what happened wasn't quiet. What happened made everything that is. It began the dreaming. And the dreaming began the living—and the dying.''

"The witch told you all this?''

"No. She just showed me the potions. Everything I've told you, I saw for myself, the same way you saw the Beastmaker. He's real. He's more real than we are, because He's closer to the Word.''

Hamr now looked at Kirchi, asleep on her side, her eyelids fluttering. She was pretty in a strange way, and he thanked the Beastmaker for guiding him to her. For a long time, he had not thought much about the Beastmaker, not since the hyenas killed Cyndell and he had begun to doubt himself.

A silent, ironic laugh twisted around his heart, to

keep back the weeping that welled there: The Thunder-tree that he and the others had come so far to find, and that Cyndell had died for them to reach, these Forest-dwellers were cowards, who would not welcome strays with ghost dancers for ancestors! The strange pain of that thought was heavy in him, and he lay back beside Kirchi, holding his spear hard to his side. He would get Duru back and Timov, too. Kirchi would help. She already had, by returning him to the Beast-maker, Whose eyes like moons watched him relax into sleep.

Each day, as the sun dove behind the trees and the sky shone like water, the clouds like strands of red kelp, Baat danced. The blue fire dazzled out of his flesh and wove itself over his turning body, his swampy odor thinning away, replaced by the smell of thunder. And when the moon-tips of his fingers touched Duru, she felt herself fly out of her body and rise above the sea-weed clouds and the swarming auroras to the stars.

But when she woke, she remembered nothing. At dawn, she would find herself in a different place in the Forest, Baat asleep among the shrubs or under a blown-over beech tree. She had slept deeply and woken refreshed, her hair and pelts smelling like the air before a big storm. By day, there was food and water to gather, which in the abundant Forest took little time, even with her injured leg. With a sturdy spruce pole for a crutch, she hobbled through the lavish undergrowth, plucking berries and wedges of fungus from tree trunks. The rest of the morning, she ground the seeds and nuts she found on the ground, fashioned nets from creepers, and gathered the kindling at hand. In the afternoon, she cast her net into a bend of the nearest

creek and used Baat's flint knife to scale and gut the
fish she caught.

While Duru worked, she idly wondered what was
becoming of her. Since the first night that she had
witnessed Baat's dance, her apprehensions had almost
entirely vanished. She thought about her brother and
Hamr, but she no longer worried about them or about
rejoining them. That in itself inspired a detached concern, yet even more curious to her was the understanding that had come upon her entirely on its own, that she
should stay near Baat, gather food, listen for large animals and for others like her, the ones who were hunting
him.

Pondering these changes, smelling the lightning in
her hair, Duru began to recall snippets of her nights. A
huge listening stillness occupied the space in her memory where before there would have been dreams. In
that vast hush, swift images came and went of her
hanging in the night among tremors of blue and green
auroras, looking down, seeing herself slung over Baat's
shoulders and he blazing with spectral fire, a living
torch hurrying through the darkness.

Gradually, over several days of deep listening,
Duru remembered the voices in the trembling glare, far
away echoes, rippling closer. Finally, on the turfy bank
of a brook, waiting for her net to pull tight with that
night's meal, the heard before voices returned, pliant
with gentleness, speaking in mellifluous chorus: *Baat
needs your help, young Duru. He is on a journey to
visit us, at the door of the mountain, in the north.
There, we walk the land fleshed in fire. We would
walk with Baat. But he cannot reach us unless someone guards him by day from beast and man. Help
him, Duru. Go with him across the tundra to the
icefields. Watch over him while he sleeps.*

The voices disappeared, but their commands reached deep into Duru, to the deadness at the core of her being, where Mother, Aradia, and Cyndell had gone. These were spirit voices, from the other world, from where life came and went, and they spoke with the authority of those she loved. Even later, when the Bright Ones told her that her thoughts and feelings were electrical fields that they could shape the way she molded wet sand, she still believed that the Bright Ones were the guardian spirits she had first heard about from the Mothers.

That first time the ul udi spoke with her, Duru deeply accepted their commands. And that gave her joy, for until then she had simply been lost. Now she was on a journey to the north, an ally of spirits. Only Hamr and Timov had to be informed, and since Timov had already shared one dream with her of the ghost dancer, she was sure the spirits would find a way to tell him.

That evening while they ate Duru tried to talk with the ghost dancer. She signed herself asleep, eyes closed, head resting on the back of her hand, and indicated with her other hand her ear, listening. She pointed to the sky, then tapped her head. "I understand now," she said. "I heard the spirit that watches over you."

"Ul udi," Baat said, raising a finger to the sky and then to the violet shine already beginning to suffuse his skin.

"Is that her name? Ul udi?"

Baat nodded, then placed both hands over his heart and opened his palms to her with a bow of his head.

"You're thanking me," she grasped. She put her small hands in his. "I thank you. You led me to the guardian spirits. Baat, they spoke to me today! I heard their voices. They're so gentle. They told me about your journey. I want to help you.''

Baat's huge face bobbed, smiling, and he gently squeezed the girl's hands. The Bright Ones had found him his companion, this unlikely child, this daughter of the smallheads! She was all he needed now to reach his goal. Holding her hands, he looked up at the last light of day burning on the tips of the trees, and the fear that had harried him all season lifted away into the violet chill. He released her hands and lay down beside the fire. The smallheads would not kill him, the Dark Ones would not take his spirit. He closed his eyes, released a long sigh and, at last, slept deeply.

The next four days Hamr and Kirchi trekked through mossy spruce terrain under high ridges of aspen and birch. The dense, shaggy land made travel arduous and slow, and Blind Side of Life followed unhappily, even though Kirchi favored him with honey-bubbled roots only she knew how to find.

At night, the hot disembodied eyes of the wraith returned, gazing at them from the shadows of the moon-lustered fog. Each night, the moon grew brighter and higher in the sky, and the yellow eyes glittered sharper. A bestial shape began to take form around the burning stare, something like the matted face of a hog, with upcurved, evil tusks and gnashing fangs.

Blind Side noticed the wraith first, whinnying shrilly into the dusk where nothing was. Then, out of the smoldering remains of the wrecked sun, it shaped itself—serpent stare, hog snout, wolf fangs, and a squat torso muscled with the scaly integuments of an alligator.

Hamr shouted his battle cry and heaved his spear through the lizard frills of its throat. Its eyes flared before it floated off with the night mist, unwounded.

"No weapon can pierce it," Kirchi told him grimly. "The most we can hope to do is hold it off. Before each sunset, I'll build a circle."

Kirchi doubted she could actually stop Neoll Nant Caw, yet she showed Hamr her moonstones and warding powders as though they were powerful weapons. She had learned to use them to keep the ul udi from penetrating her trances and possessing her. But she had never tried or had reason to hold off a wraith before.

"What about this?" Hamr asked, taking out the tracking stone. During their trek he had used the stone to feel the direction of the ghost dancer and had always found that the stone chilled to the east, each day a little farther north. The bonesucker was not retreating to the mountains after all but heading for the tundra. And if Yaqut and Timov had not been deflected from their easterly course, they would intersect with the ghost dancer any day now.

"It's true, the stone is good for more than tracking," Kirchi said. "It's a scry crystal, too. In trance, one could use it to see afar. But it's not a weapon, not against the Moon Bitch." She pointed to Duru's satchel, which Hamr carried at his hip. "There's a knife in there that could kill a wraith. I saw it when you showed me Spretnak's wheel."

Hamr took out the obsidian blade he had found on the tundra and given to Duru. He had not used it because its glass edge easily chipped. "This is a flensing knife."

"No. It's more. Look at the haft." Kirchi took the knife in her freckled fingers and touched the viper-curves carved in the bone. "This is a Moon Serpent knife. It's a ritual implement. Only a priestess would have this." And with those words came the memory of the one trance where she had seen a ghost dancer— Baat on the tundra at night, attacking the priestess and her escort. She remembered the priestess taking this knife from her attendant and throwing it in the fire. Her fingers feeling suddenly brittle, she returned the knife. "The Moon Serpent can cut the Moon Bitch. And my moonstones can block her. We have our weapons, Hamr."

The moonstones, four chunks of pearly feldspar, had been polished to a glossy sheen that made them look as if they held trapped light. At sundown, Kirchi talked to them and rubbed them with her bright hair, waking their power. Then she used each one to etch a quarter arc in the ground, encircling their sleeping space. "The smaller the circle, the stronger its protection," she said when Hamr complained that Blind Side was not included.

Kirchi admired Hamr's solicitous care of his horse, and each night, after she groomed the animal, she sprinkled him with warding powders, the gem-dust of old crystals. Hamr was grateful for that, and also for the way she gentled Blind Side after the wraith came and went. This horse was the outside shape of his soul, and her care for the creature justified his showing his affection for her.

After Aradia died, Hamr had thought he would always live as though she were still in this world with him. But now this witch had begun to earn his caring— and his desire. While they traveled along the leaf-clogged creeks or struggled over boggy ground, he often found himself noticing how she took time to find footing for the horse, or the way she pulled aside bramble without hurrying or cursing when she snagged herself. Simple things, like reading the land, spotting the tiniest pawprints of mice and voles—that led to caches of winter grouse eggs hidden for the spring—impressed him. Despite all his losses and the great uncertainties ahead, he felt happy with her.

Hamr continued to remind himself that Kirchi was not as beautiful as Aradia, but each day he believed himself less. The day the Forest finally ended and the wide grasslands opened before them, his and Kirchi's joy was so strong they could no longer hide their passion. While Blind Side of Life romped through clouds of grass scents, Hamr and Kirchi clasped each other, tumbling to the ground.

With swift fingers, Hamr caressed the girl. Her breath was coming in a moan, and the hollows of her body swelled with pleasure. In a hot glut of desire, she tore the antelope-hide from his body and pressed her hands against him, his nakedness feeding her heat.

Hamr peeled off her wrap, and his long hair tented over them, hiding them from the bright day as they stared at each other, amazed and shining. Kirchi mewed softly as she received him, her eyes rolled up and closed, and her legs hugged him as they rocked and plunged.

Afraid to shut his eyes, afraid to see the ghost of his wife, Hamr watched her move under him. He wanted only this skinny, pale-eyed witch, he insisted to himself, only this moment and the flash of rapture he had won for them by losing everything. So he stared at her luminous face until their passion exploded and banished all his grief.

◆　◆　◆

Afterwards, Kirchi asked him to grow a beard. With snippets of grass and daubs of mud, she pasted haygold whiskers down the line of his jaw and over his chin and upper lip. He cleared away the brown algae of a rainpool and laughed at the sight of himself. That night, inside the magic circle, he used his clam shells to tweeze away only the hair of his cheeks and neck. Lying naked together in the fireglow, the lovers dropped resin chips on the embers to drive off the biting insects and rubbed the smudged ash on Hamr's stubble, darkening his beard.

When Blind Side of Life whinnied nervously, Hamr and Kirchi untangled themselves from their lovemaking. The moon was tilted like a cup, high in the blue depth of the night. Out over the tundra, in the darkness of the west, another moon had begun to rise—a swell of ghostly light. Blind Side whined as it rose higher, though there was no scent or sound.

Hamr quickly donned his antelope loin-wrap and deerskin sandals, crouched beside the fire, spear in hand. The moonshape took form as the lope of a huge beast rushing toward them with a howl of wintry wind. Hamr's hackles bristled. He had never heard the wraith before, nor seen it moving, its huge head hanging forward, fanged mouth brushing the ground. He looked to Kirchi, saw her wrapped in her grass robe and fumbling with her bag for her warding powder.

With a sudden lean-legged stride, the Moon Bitch hurtled itself at them, its bat-fanged face glaring, and as it neared, Hamr saw that its wrinkly eyes were indeed the crone's.

But when Hamr rose to meet it, Kirchi grabbed his leg. "Don't leave the circle!"

The storm-whistle of the Moon Bitch cracked the air. Ripped scams of green fire fell like a net over the area of the magic circle. Fangs drooling, the beast pounced.

Hamr and Kirchi cowered as the monster crashed into the invisible barrier, bounced off, and lay in a stunned crouch. The moonstones at the four points of the circle pulsed crimson. Howling, the Moon Bitch slashed her talons across the nearest power point, trying to dislodge the stone, but lightning met her at the edge of the circle, and her claws came away curled with pain.

Her head slung low, the Moon Bitch glared at the lovers, hissing so loudly that Hamr and Kirchi cried out as one and hid their faces.

Sudden silence made them look up. A slavering grin was distorting the Bitch's muzzle. With new purpose she strode to where the Blind Side of Life strained at his tether. The horse bucked and neighed in terror.

"No!" Hamr yelled, and leaped to his feet.

Kirchi threw her arms around him, and he staggered backwards.

The Moon Bitch leaped upon Blind Side's back, her powerful hind talons ripping the stallion's flanks, her fangs stabbing at his throat while he bucked and kicked wildly, his blood shooting out in black jets at his flanks.

Hamr threw off Kirchi's hold and leaped out of the circle. His spear held high, his war cry rattled in his throat.

Immediately, the Moon Bitch abandoned the horse. Hamr heaved his spear. The weapon sailed *harmless* through the apparition, and stabbed the tree where Blind Side was tied. The wraith smashed Hamr to the ground. Her powerful jaws pierced his chest, and blood sprayed over his face, surged up his nostrils and down his throat with the bitterness of death.

Hamr's hands fell away from the scaly body of the

Moon Bitch and seized the Moon Serpent at his hip. The fangs knifed deeper into him, and he heard his ribs crack. With a last flare of strength, he gripped the black-glass dagger in both hands and drove it up hard into the Moon Bitch's belly.

She roared with pain, and her hind legs worked frenziedly, tearing open Hamr's abdomen and kicking his bowels out behind her.

Hamr pulled down with all that remained of his life force, slitting the belly of the Moon Bitch. She reared, her mad visage twisted, and a cascade of live blood and sticky tangles of hot matter spilled out over him. With the last gasp of breath in him, Hamr wept aloud, for the bloody knots of tissue flowing from the Bitch's underbelly were alive.

Red-fleshed, raw foetal monsters slithered over him, glossy, big as rats, their lidless yolk eyes staring mindlessly as they whirled squealing on furious claws into the pitch darkness.

Ncoil Nant Caw jarred awake in her burrow and found herself flat on her back, every muscle throbbing with pain. Her face twitched and flinched with her effort to sit up, but all her energy had been depleted; her body lay there inert as a clod, her strength dead with the Moon Bitch. She tried to wail but could not. Where were her slaves? A muffled cry squeaked out of her gaping mouth, and the darkness ate it.

Her only illumination was a shaft of moonlight reflection that had pierced the gopher tunnel of her subterranean chamber. The blue tar-oil fire had burned out. The crystals she had used to build the Moon Bitch lay around her in the dark, lightless, thrumming with a pain only she could hear.

"Those lunks," she cursed her two slaves. They would look for her at dawn and find her like this, battered flat to the ground—but not dead. She felt as though she was dying—pain quilting her muscles to her bones, air barely seeping into her lungs. But she would not die. She would not let herself. She would lie here in the moon-glossed dark sucking in air through her mangled mouth, waiting for her lunks to find her. Waiting for her strength to return and with it vigor and malice of the invisibles.

Neoll Nant Caw's slaves found her at dawn sprawled unconscious on the floor of her burrow.

One slave plunged off into the woods, toward the Longtooth to get help. The other propped the witch's head on a reed pallet, then jerked back from her with a grunt of alarm. On the mat beside her, a tangled mass of gelatinous flesh throbbed and pulsed blue, breaking apart into a panic of tiny pieces. Each piece suddenly metamorphosed into a rabid bitch, a miniature beast shattering into smaller explosions of snapping jaws. In a moment, the break-away blue jellies dispersed and disappeared, tarring the air with a black stench.

The spiraling song of a thrush called Hamr back to life. He woke with a cry, his eyes snapping open and flinching before the sun's glare. Kirchi's shadow blocked out the radiance, and her lean face moved closer.

"I'm alive," he said, his voice raspy. His hands passed over his chest and his stomach—to his shock, finding himself whole. A giddy tremor shook him, and he would have laughed with joy but Kirchi laid her fingers over his lips. They smelled like grass, and he kissed them. "I dreamed—"

"It was no dream," she said glumly.

"The Moon Bitch . . ." he mumbled and sat bolt upright, pushing Kirchi aside. He saw Blind Side of Life nearby, grazing in his own shadow, not a mark on him. "I thought—I was killed?"

You were, Kirchi knew, but could not say. "You fought the Moon Bitch. You slit her belly open. She wounded you—and Blind Side. You worse. But your body lives."

"How long was I out?"

"The night and the morning. It's almost midday now."

Hamr looked down at himself, astounded. "The pain was so real."

Kirchi nodded. She had not been sure he would wake at all. Throughout the night and the morning, after the Moon Bitch's wraith had withered to fog, she had sat over him, listening to his breathing. She had seen everything. She knew his body of light was mortally wounded. No one could survive that. And though he was awake now, she knew the shadow of death lay darkly on him.

"The pain—" he repeated. "It was so real. Did you see?" He stared at her with large, astonished eyes, remembering but not believing.

"Oh, yes," she said, and pressed her cheek to his. "I saw."

Hunger Music

In the firelight, Yaqut's face looked like a burst blood blister. Timov did not like to face him while they ate or dressed the skins of the animals the hunter had killed during the day. Even after the sombrous effects of the trance-thorn wore off, Timov continued to shuffle along behind, head lowered, not meeting Yaqut's harsh gaze when addressed, and keeping his eyes on the fire when they sat together at night.

Eating was plentiful, and there was no lack of garments or bone-fashioned implements. Yaqut made hunting seem effortless, and the few times Timov looked at him directly were when the hunter whipped his sling or hurled his lance. Rarely did he throw in vain. He was deft at killing animals, skinning and gutting them swiftly, almost casually. But he was impatient with Timov's awkwardness, and as punishment for the boy's many missed shots, each night he made him chew hide to leather and stretch and stitch the pelts caught by the older hunter. The one kindness he showed was to replace Timov's hand-thrown rocks with a sling trimmed from a marten's belly—only afterward to snap at him for his incompetence with it.

Once, when the shot from Timov's sling struck an otter a glancing blow and laid it out squirming on a rock in midstream, Yaqut sent him to retrieve it. Timov waded through the cold rushing water and found the otter staring at him, his brown eyes bewildered and hurt. The boy reached for his knife.

"Put that away," Yaqut called. "I want this pelt whole, and I'll do the cutting. Strike it but don't crush the skull. I won't have bone-splinters in my tongue when we eat the brain. Knock him out with a blow across the nose—then grab him, break his neck. And hurry. We've a long way yet to go."

Timov picked up a blunt rock; the otter, still too stunned to get up, was alert enough to watch him. He had killed many small animals but always before with his sling and his knife, and he wished now that he could simply sever the animal's heart strings and be done. He struck the otter between the eyes, and the creature abruptly stiffened.

Quickly, Timov knelt and seized the unconscious otter's forepaws and pulled it under his arm. He could feel the small heart beating against his side. Any instant, the animal could revive. He grasped its muzzle firmly and twisted its head as far as he could. He felt the neckbone crack, and blood spurt from the nostrils. The small, furred body shivered and went still.

A great loneliness pervaded Timov as he sloshed back across the stream to give the limp body to Yaqut. The Forest seemed immense in its perpetual darkness, jammed with lives eating lives, and himself just another small life in the gloom. He felt sure he would never see his sister or Hamr again.

At night, with the fire leaping under the skinned body of the otter, Yaqut confirmed his fears, "The moon is filling out." He lifted his blurred face toward where the moon hung like a silver ax above the trees. "The witch is growing stronger. She will surely kill Hamr and the fool girl who ran away with him."

Timov stared hard into the tatters of flame that sputtered with each drip of the otter's fat, not wanting to see the malice in the hunter's crooked features.

"He was a dolt to go back for you," Yaqut continued. "A brave, arrogant dolt. If he had stayed with me, we would have held off those Stabbing Cats. The Beastmaker favored us. Soon enough we'd have figured out that the witch had duped us with the tracking stone. We'd have hunted down the ghost dancer on our own. But now—" His scarred face gleamed in the firelight like a painted mask. "He has brought Neoll Nant Caw down upon himself. He will die. You will never see him again. Look at me, boy."

Timov looked up and wished the trance poison were still in him, blocking off his fear.

Yaqut's ruined face nodded with satisfaction. "Hamr is dead. You are mine now. And you'd better do just as I say, or I'll skin you like this otter."

Timov had no appetite for the cooked meat. But he ate it because Yaqut ordered him to. And when he was done, he stripped the bones off the remaining flesh as Yaqut commanded, braided the flesh with vine, and hung it from a branch over the fire, out of reach of ants and scavengers, to dry for the next day's hike. Then he banked the fire, crawled between two forked roots, and covered himself with leaves. Yaqut climbed into the tree above him and disappeared in the darkness.

As soon as he was alone, Timov found the hard, round shape of Cyndell's bracelet in his sling-pouch. By feel, he followed the carved meander, chanting the day-count silently. They were deep into the Frost Moon, close to the meander's turn, where the First Snows began. Before then he should be with Hamr again and they would be closer to finding Duru—if she was still alive.

On the nights that the trance-thorn had possessed him, he had fallen asleep swiftly, and had slept dream-lessly. But this night he lay awake, worried about his sister and afraid for himself. Then, in the midst of his fretting, he saw the otter he had killed standing among blue cloverheads. His sleek body had a silver outline, and he smelled of honey. But the look in his stare was not animal; it was human and crazy.

Timov knew he was dreaming and tried to force himself awake. But the dream colors sharpened, and a frightful sound began—the thunder-like drone that he had last heard when the witch had flung him out of his body, far into the sky. A sense of impending calamity deepened in him.

With a ripping sound, the otter's dream skin tore away from its dream body, and the ragged pelt winged into the storm-green distance, leaving behind the crimson, raw-muscled body with its silvery tendons and small cage of teeth. *Life eats life*, an unseen voice said, and the human eyes in the otter's skull blinked. The humming thunder darkened and seemed to echo from inside his bones.

Before Timov's eyes, the skinned otter decomposed: The strings of muscle and the dangling fruits of viscera greened, fluttered, dissolved to blistery jellies; the skeleton broke apart, shattered to bone-chips. While storm-smoke closed in blackly, the melted flesh became plasma, and the bone-chips, stars. And suddenly, Timov hung in the incandescent night under the auroras.

You will die! a cruel voice said. *And when you die, we will eat you—like this!*

Pain jolted through Timov, many tiny, needle-fine teeth stabbing into his flesh. He cried out, but his noise vanished in a loud static humming from inside him. The pain rose toward a convulsion, and fear suffused him as he struggled to wrench himself out of his nightmare.

You will wake, the evil voice said. *But when you die, you will never wake, and we will eat you like this—forever.*

The fear became a fire consuming him—so suddenly that he actually felt his skin blacken and curl away. He screamed in terror, his cry bleeding into a long moan, dissolving into the lion roar of the stormwind.

Look at the stars, a quiet voice counseled in him.

Timov responded mindlessly to the benign command, and stared through his pain at the hard points of light in the darkness. The pain lessened, the thunderdrone softened. *Look at the stars, and the Dark Ones will lose their grip on you,* the gentle voice said.

The stars shifted, became glinting reflections in the eye-facets of a giant fly, its buzzing cutting loudly through space. *You will die—and we will eat you! the stark voice said again,* and the stabbing agony in him sharpened.

There is no giant fly, the gentle voice insisted. *The sky is the void that holds the stars. See the stars.*

Timov did—and the pain eased, the buzzing dulled. He concentrated on the stars, noticing their watery colors, their fiery barbs. The pain vanished entirely; and the loud drone condensed to the muffled drumbeat of his own heart.

The Dark Ones enter you when you are afraid,
the calm voice said. *Yaqut opens you to them. But you
needn't be afraid. Put your attention outside your
fear, outside your pain, and you will find us. We are
the happy dreams of animals. We live in the sky—
and we live in you.*

This night, after the eating was done and the fire
shrunken to embers, Baat danced with abandon. The
blue flames whipped from his whirling arms, scrib-
bling the dark spaces with glittering tracks, comet
tails, and meteor streaks. He approached Duru, and
this time, when his luminous fingers touched her, she
tried to stay awake, to hold on to her memory of the
frail voices—the ul udi—and soared into the tangles of
auroral radiance with her eyes open.

The whisper-light of the stars slipped through her.
In the boreal glow, she watched the moon watching her
as she pivoted in the emptiness, and looked back the
way she had come. There she was, draped over Baat's
shoulders like a dwarf deer, her hair bouncing as he
bounded north through the woods.

Duru stared ahead of him, across the canopy of the
trees, the herded hills, and the webwork of streams
shining silver in the moonlight. Mirror lakes glared.
Fog breathed in the teeming darkness. And beyond the
confusion of the many-faceted land, the tundra opened,
almost blue in the lunar haze. Somewhere out there,
Timov and Hamr wandered.

At that thought, Duru felt herself swooping, saw
the treetops skim by. She plummeted into the darkness
of the Forest. Timov was there, buried in leaves, only
his face visible, a soft moon in the shadows. Above him,
eye-level with Duru, Yaqut lay on a bough, a patchwork

of pelts warding off the Frost Moon's chill. His marred face looked as pocked as a gourd. His hair was as white as root-ends.

Duru dipped closer to her brother, saw small stars bobbing in the air above him. When she touched one of the stars, she entered his dream: A silver otter hung upside down from a branch, staring into a bloody puddle at a reflection of Timov. He floated in the sky. She looked up beyond the hung otter and spotted him there, limbs outstretched limply as if he were floating on his back in a clear pool. She rose toward him and called his name.

"Look at the stars," he said in his dream. "Look— or the Dark Ones will get you."

"Timov—it's me, Duru."

He looked at her, and a baffled shadow darkened his eyes. "Duru?"

"Yes—I'm with the ghost dancer—and the ul udi, the spirits that visit him from the sky. They carried me here, to see you. Are you all right?"

Timov's whole body trembled, and in his dream he reached for her. But he touched emptiness. He shrank away. "Are you a ghost?"

"No, I'm alive. I'm okay. The ghost dancer is not hurting me. He needs my help. We're on a journey." Concern came into her dream face. "Timov, where's Hamr?"

Timov reached for her again, but his agitated effort pulled him farther away. "Duru—come back!"

Duru willed herself closer. But an inexorable force drew her down, back to the blood puddle and the silver otter's dead stare. The next moment, she had lifted free of Timov's dream entirely. Caught in a celestial undertow, she flew back into the night sky.

◆ ◆ ◆

Timov wrenched himself awake. Through a gap in the branches, the lemur-face of the moon gazed down. Somewhere inside him he felt the dream continuing. But this was not a dream, he realized. With his eyes closed, he could still feel his sister's presence, farther away now and moving rapidly. To his left, to the south. She was still moving now but slower. His flesh jarred on his bones as he felt her flight end. She had returned to the ghost dancer.

"What is it?" a gruff voice broke over him.

Timov flinched, thinking it was the Dark Ones returning to torment him. When he opened his eyes, he saw Yaqut lowering himself from the branch above, soundless as a snake.

"The dreams have begun again, haven't they?" Yaqut's face gleamed in the moonlight, almost jovial. "What did you see?"

Timov told him and felt uneasy at the glint of cunning that edged the other's stare. "She's helping the ghost dancer," the boy said. "She's not in danger."

"You believe that—after what the ul udi did to you?" the old hunter sneered. "The Invisibles can put any words they want into your sister's mouth. For all we know, she may not even be alive anymore." He gazed in the direction Timov indicated his dream-sister had flown. "Sleep now, if you can. At first light, we're going to follow your dream."

Yaqut climbed back into the tree and squatted on the bough above Timov, contemplating killing the boy now. The ul udi were in him—that was reason enough to kill him. Both the priestess and the witch had recognized that his ancestors were bonesuckers. What stayed Yaqut from plunging his poison-tipped lance into the youth below was the same truth that urged Yaqut to kill him: The spirits in Timov knew how to find the ghost dancer.

At the first smudged signs of dawn, Yaqut roused Timov, and they moved quickly south through the loamy woods. More quickly than they had ever tramped before. The hunter made no pause for food, though they crossed the tracks of Fox and Marten and spotted Red Deer prodding a pine sapling, sharpening his antlers. Yaqut even broke his own rules of silence, rushing through leafdrifts, snapping tinder underfoot, startling coveys of Partridge.

At midday, Yaqut stopped on a turf-bank, where the land divided before a fault that humped fir-strewn knolls to one side and on the other dropped into an oak grove of sunk glacial rocks. He looked to Timov. "Which way?"

Timov shrugged.

"Look inside," Yaqut said sharply.

Timov squinted, bewildered

With the haft of his lance, Yaqut rapped the back of Timov's knees and toppled him. He bent close enough for the fallen boy to smell his sour breath, "Close your eyes. Think of your sister. Remember her carefully—and you'll feel where she is. She's still now. The bonesucker runs at night. Feel for Duru. And when you find her, point."

Timov closed his eyes, astonished by Yaqut's confidence that he had the power to find Duru. Only darkness greeted him, but he did as Yaqut had told him and thought of Duru, remembered her baby-round forehead, the dimple in her left cheek, her swollen upper lip that was Mother's, and her large eyes that had always narrowed so drastically when she called him Saphead. Then a quivering of shadows separated from the darkness behind his closed lids and began to glint with the bruised blood of a sunset.

"We have to catch him asleep," Yaqut mused. "Then the killing will be easy."

Timov grunted for silence. The tawny hues gathering in the dark behind his eyelids fitted themselves into his memory of Duru. She was there in him, as she had been last night. Only now she was not moving—she was still. Somewhere to his left. He turned his head that way, toward the image of Duru leaning on a spruce pole under a slope of ferns. He raised his hand toward her, and Yaqut pulled him upright.

"Come on," Yaqut crowed. "We've got to find them before dark."

Timov felt faint, almost collapsing under the heavy burden of his trance. As his head cleared, he began to realize that if his sister's visitation of last night was not a deception, he had betrayed her.

Yaqut did not wait for him. Unsteadily, the boy veered up the hillside. The moon hung overhead, milky in the day sky, when Yaqut found his prey's droppings. "Less than a day," he judged, scowling at the bloated sun in the treetops. He stabbed his lance into the leaf-matted stool. "We're this close. But we need a few more hours. That's all."

A strange, divided relief flooded Timov's chest at the sight of the reddening sun. Strange, because he too wanted to reach the ghost dancer—to get Duru back; and yet he was afraid of what Yaqut would do when they found their prey. What did Duru mean?—that she was helping the ghost dancer? What could a child do for a giant? That had to have been one of the ul udi's deceptions. A tremor prickled his flesh at the memory of what the evil spirits had done to him, and his anxiety mounted with the approach of night.

"We will track until darkness," Yaqut decided. He picked around the area with his lance until he found the ghost dancer's prints. Timov followed reluctantly, stopping only briefly to fit his foot to the giant's. It was nearly twice his size.

"Isn't it dangerous to get too close now—at nightfall?" he asked.

"Be quiet." Yaqut turned, his scar-hooded eye looking over his shoulder. "If your noise betrays me, boy, I'll kill you."

The giant's spoor led the hunters over a ledge of maple, whose crimson leaves mimed the sunset, and down toward a dank fen. Timov recognized the slope of ferns where he had visualized his sister. They were close now. But the mushy terrain slowed them, and the sun's last rays fanned out overhead while they were still knee-deep in the bog.

On the ridge across the fen, a blue light flared among the trees, and Yaqut cursed. "We've lost him now. The Invisibles will warn him about us. He'll stay ahead of us, try and lose us in the streams."

They climbed onto a hummock and struggled to flint-strike a fire with the few dry twigs they could find among the soggy sponge-wood. Over on the crest of the ridge, the spectral glow winked back and forth among the trees as the giant danced. Timov stared in wonder, until Yaqut barked, "Help with this fire or the mosquitoes will eat all our sleep tonight."

With dry duff that Yaqut carried in his satchel, they started a twigfire and used those flames to dry a small dead branch snapped from a scraggly larch. Once that limb ignited, they fed the fire damp chunks of wood. By then, the ghost dancer's eerie blue light had begun to move off quickly along the ridge.

"He's going north," Timov observed. "Hamr will meet him on his way toward us."

Yaqut spoke with crisp certainty, "Hamr is dead." He peered at the lad, who was gaping up at the ridge, watching the ghost fire spin away. Again he considered killing him at once and leaving his body in the fen as an offering to the Beastmaker for His help with the hunt.

"Why is he running north?" Timov asked. "Why doesn't he run south or east into the mountains, where he can find shelter from winter?"

"He knows we're watching," Yaqut surmised and reached for his lance. "He thinks he can baffle us. Later, he'll break east."

"But he was moving north last night, when Duru visited me and he didn't know I was watching." Timov looked at Yaqut, his dark eyes suddenly bird-bright. "He's heading for the tundra. He'll run right into Hamr."

Yaqut's good eye half-lidded. His hand moved away from his lance and reached instead for his satchel. He broke out the last shreds of otter meat and a handful of acorns and hazelnuts he had collected along the way. Maybe the boy was right. Yaqut looked at the meager food supply, then offered the boy half. "Tomorrow we'll get food and more pelts. We're going north."

He leaned nearer, placing the food in Timov's hands and staring with stony command into his eyes. "Watch your dreams. Tell me everything you see."

The sheldrake soared ahead of the flock. Hamr stopped Blind Side of Life and followed the arrowheads of ducks with his gaze. Since the attack of the Moon Bitch, the air had felt heavier, the chill never quite leaving it even at noon, when sunlight slanted amber across the tundra. This was the shadow of winter, Hamr wanted to believe. But Kirchi's avid care of him, her eagerness to please him—even pretending to ignore the menace in the air—assured him she thought he was doomed, already killed by Neoll Nant Caw.

Hamr watched the lines of birds waver into the turquoise light of the southern sky. For a while he stared at the distant dark firs, feeling as strong in his body as any of those sober trees and as pure in his mind as the deep sky. Then he turned his horse the other way, toward the clump of wiry shrub, where Kirchi had already set camp for the night.

Though Kirchi had not wanted to think of herself as a witch, the Moon Bitch had forced her to use what she had learned. Every night since then she had placed her moonstones on the ground, each of them touching, forming a small circle. In the tiny opening they made, she gathered up the moonlight into smoke. The smoke quivered as radiantly as the auroras.

"Sky-fire," Kirchi called it the first night she showed Hamr. "Lightning caught in the air." She chattered on about tapping the ghost dancer's power, the way a tree could be tapped for syrup. But Hamr paid little attention to how this magic worked. He simply wanted to see.

Each night Kirchi and Hamr searched for Baat and Duru in the moonstones' plasma window. The tracking stone indicated they were southeast, in the Forest; but Kirchi never found them with her magic. Most nights, they saw only the windy trees and animals drifting among the silver paths of moonlight. She knew it was her incompetence with the plasma window, and kept trying. But the view lasted only as long as the moon shone, and it rose later each night.

One night, as Hamr drowsed—dreaming of an up-side-down tree hung in the sky, its naked roots tangled with stars—Kirchi woke him. "Look! I've found Timov!"

Visible in the smoky light, Yaqut and Timov were crouched in the watery glow of the moon, both asleep, the hunter in the crotch of a furry marsh tree, the boy among its thick roots, Cyndell's white bracelet in his hand.

The vulnerability of Timov, asleep where any panther could pounce on him, frightened Hamr, with anger at Yaqut for separating them. He sat back from the misty peekhole, and faced the darkness to the south. "The Moon Bitch is dead," he muttered. "We've gone enough nights without seeing any trace of her. Tomorrow we go back for Timov."

Baat gazed down below, on the meanders of all the brooks and creeks he had crossed to reach this crest of gooseberry bushes and twisted conifers. The People had names for the larger streams and for the big rocks, the giant slabs and immense tree-spired boulders the water sluiced around or disappeared under. He deliberately kept those names at a dim distance. Whom would he speak them to?

Northward, the land fell to flat stretches of nut-hatch groves and firs grown huge in the loam that silted down from these high rocks. Through weird-shaped trees, he peeked at the tawny depths of autumn, blowsy clumps of fire colors among the blue pinnacles of evergreen. One more night's march would cross that flat fringe of the Forest, and then the taiga's stunted pines, the wolfsbane brushlands, and the viper grass would lead them at last to the tundra.

Baat looked down at Duru, standing in the seam of the rock sheets that had mated to form this crest. She leaned on her crutch and plucked the gooseberries dangling from overhead, occasionally glancing up at him—probably wondering why he was still awake. The morning sun, high in the spiky trees, glinted brilliantly in the dew that beaded everything. But soon enough that dew would be frost. Maybe even tonight (though, seeing the clear atmosphere to the north and the puffs of warm clouds flocking from the south, he doubted that). Soon, anyway, the frost would set. In the night, as he had run through the cold vapors of fog, he had felt the girl's body chill, and he had lifted her from his shoulders and carried her against his chest, even though that slowed him down. Today he had decided not to sleep but to get the hides they would need to face the frigid nights ahead.

Baat signed for Duru to wait for him where she was, then picked his way nimbly along the rock spine to a vantage that looked down on a narrow gorge. It was choked with scree and thornapple whose glossy, lobed rose-madder leaves were favored by Red Deer. A dozen of the deer grazed in the ravine as Baat silently crawled across the ridge to a cairn of sharp rocks.

The cairn, a tall heap of stones piled here by the People, was for killing animals who entered the gorge. In the years since it was stacked no one had come to use it until now, and Baat was glad to find that the trigger stone at the base of the pile still had a sturdy vine-rope attached to it. He gave it a mighty tug, and the stack of rocks tumbled down the steep slope.

Most of the deer bounded agilely to safety. But three of them stumbled among the scree and were struck by Baat's avalanche. He drew his knife and swiftly scrambled down the incline to where the deer lay stunned among the thornapples. In moments, three big deer carcasses lay before him.

A jubilant cry came from above. Baat looked up to see Duru clapping her hands over her head. She crawled down into the gorge, favoring her good leg, and together they skinned the beasts and disjointed several haunches. Duru was glad for the bounty the Great Mother had given them. But she felt another joy that they two were together—this great being and she, laughing together, empty of regard for tomorrow. If only the Great Mother would unite her with Hamr and Timov all would be truly well.

But that was more than she dared ask. Mother had taught her never to pray for kindness to happen, only for strength of purpose. In the simplicity of her joy, she believed that getting the ghost dancer north, where he could commune with the Bright Ones, would be enough. She laughed away her doubts and fears, and Baat laughed with her.

After cutting free the hearts and the livers, breaking off the antlers, smashing the skulls for the sweet and tender brains, they left the rest for scavenger birds and animals. At the place where the cairn had stood, Baat left the antlers for the Old Ones, who had thought to make the cairn in the first place. There was no need to pile the rocks again. And no time. Already the sun peaked.

Baat built a large fire on the ridge. He knew the smoke would alert the trackers, but the meat had to be cooked, the hides seasoned. After eating his fill of brains and liver, he left Duru to tend the fire, and walked the ridge. Scanning the convoluted land of the south and opposite that—the expansive plains where the mountain-high ice had once rested—he searched for danger.

He had planned a vigil of watchfulness, hoping to locate his trackers. But what he looked for he found almost immediately: They were closer than he had imagined. Down a wrinkled granite incline, flashing in and out of the pine shadows, a human spark scrabbled—Duru's brother. Yaqut would be nearby, though he was nowhere to be seen.

Facing the other way, Baat spotted another dot of motion among the yews of the taiga. Squinting, he saw that the distant point of color was a lone horse. *The beardless one.* He was traveling with someone, a youth, maybe a woman—they were too far for him to tell. The trackers had locked him in—unless he tried to skirt them. But that would use up precious time, and increase the likelihood that the first winter storm would catch them on the tundra. No—he would have to face them.

Baat looked south again, watching the tiny jig of movement that was Timov zig-zagging among clumps of pine. He shifted his gaze and let the broken landscape float before him, searching for Yaqut. In a cluster of cedar, deer glittered like red stars, and on a far hillside he recognized the slouching motions of Bear. Jays swirled above the folded and twisted hills, and flicks of dragonflies, too. His attentive mind was clear and cold as any of the rockpools glinting below in the noonlight—and then he saw him, a tiny blur among the tortured trees on a high ledge above where Timov ambled. He disappeared into the juniper shadows and did not reappear.

A shiver shook Baat. He did not want to face Yaqut. Throughout the summer the Dark Ones had taunted him with nightmare images of that ruined face. Facing the other way, looking down into the Forest, he saw clusters of granite monoliths that the ice of long ago had bunched and stacked. That place was famous to the People for its caves and for the lions that dwelled in them.

An evil idea offered itself, and he sweated, feeling as damp in his bones as though the Dark Ones themselves had suggested the idea to him. But the ul udi were asleep now, far up in the blue. The idea was his own. But to fulfill its evil, he would need the help of the Dark Ones. He was not sure they would obey him, yet if he chose he could talk to them. They would not answer him now. They were asleep, but in their sleeping they would hear him. Maybe, when they woke tonight, if the evil of his prayer pleased them, they would heed him.

As a young man, the elders had taught him how to pray to the Dark Ones. Only rarely—and not in many years—had he availed himself of that grim knowledge, and he wondered if he still could. With his eyes fixed on the distant stacks of granite rubble, he began to hum the hunger music that the old ones had first wept for him. The sound he made was more a gasp—soft, a beast in pain with too little life left to cry out, calling the crows to take his eyes, strangling on his own breath. To hear it would not be to call it music but suffering, suffering that was music to Raven and Hyena, and to the Dark Ones, who relished evil.

Now that Baat had bade for the ul udi's attention, he hoped to impress on them his prayer: *Be lion's flesh—and the hunger that lives in that flesh.* He lifted his gaze slightly and fixed on the moving motes of the horseman and his companion. *Be lion's flesh that stalks the horse. Be lion's hunger that devours the horse. Rage with the hunger of the lion. Come down through me and be lion's flesh and lion's hunger. Come down through me.*

Duru found Baat squatting on the chine of the ridge, eyes half-closed, arms hanging limply between his legs. His breath came out of him in muttering and faltering, and he did not respond when she called his name. How could he sleep in so uncomfortable a position? Since last night, when the blue blaze of his touch had sent her flying out of her body, alert for the first time, she had been afraid for him. Her flight had taken her to Timov, and she had clearly seen the fear in her brother. Hamr and Blind Side had been nowhere near Timov, yet Yaqut was there—and now Duru was afraid that the Longtooth hunter was nearby. Tonight, if Baat danced and touched her with his celestial fire, she would concentrate harder, and try to see exactly where Timov and Yaqut were.

While waiting for Baat, Duru had fashioned a poppet from a pinecone. It had grass stem limbs and acorn caps for breasts—the kind of image that she and Cyndell used to offer the Great Mother. She had made no offerings since—each day of survival had been its own deeply thankful offering—but now she wanted to leave a sign for Timov that she was all right. After crafting the poppet, she had propped it beside the fire and come looking for Baat.

She called his name several more times, but he did not stir, and she reached out. At her touch, he sagged forward, so heavily she feared he would fall over the precipice, and she seized his arm. He rolled backwards and lay blinking at the amber sun.

Baat roused slowly, then flashed into alertness when he saw the girl beside him. Quickly he looked north and south but there was no sign of the trackers. Afraid that if she saw them she would not go on with him, grimacing against the cramps in his legs, he stood and they limped back to the fire.

The skins that had been stretched on birch poles to dry close to the flames were still damp, but there would be no time to finish curing them today. The moon hung like a half-blown ball of dandelion seed in the blue sky, and the clouds cluttering up the horizon in the west already shone orange. Duru lashed the cooked deer haunches together with strips of tendon, and Baat unstrung the hides and rolled them up.

Satisfied that her leg was strong enough to walk on until she was ready to sleep, Duru leaned on her staff and shambled after Baat. He carried the pelts across his shoulders and later, when Duru was sleepy, he would roll her up in them. By then night would have descended; with the chill darkness, the ul udi would bring their living fire and their deepening hungers.

Yaqut and Timov found the ghost dancer's fire-site on the spine of the ridge early in the morning, before the sun cleared the treetops. During the night, they had camped on a hillside so close by that, until dawn, they had listened to the scavengers fighting over and devouring the deer carcasses Baat had left in the gorge. The fierce noises had kept Timov from sleeping deeply, and he had experienced no further dreams of the ul udi or Duru.

Yaqut held up a pinecone braided with grass, and Timov snatched it from his hand. "That's Duru's!" He turned it around, recognizing his sister's handiwork, saw how the arms of the poppet were crooked at the elbows, touching the acorn-cap breasts, to signify child or caring. "She's all right!" A smile flickered, lingered, over his smudged and scratched face. "My dream was true, she's helping the ghost dancer. Somehow, she's caring for him."

"Bah!" Yaqut knocked the poppet from Timov's grip, and smashed it into the ashes with the blunt end of his spear.

When Timov sprang forward, to strike the hunter, Yaqut did not flinch, and the boy shrank back. "You don't know the devilish powers of the bonesucker or the Invisibles. Don't believe what you see—that's how we lost your sister in the first place."

Timov stared angrily after Yaqut as the bony man turned away and strode across the crest of the ridge, looking for signs of the ghost dancer's new camp. Timov knew that with a running push he could send the old man careening down the rockface into the green tapers of fir below. That would redeem the humiliations Timov had suffered since being left alone with Yaqut—the menial work of chewing hides for Yaqut's winter garments, eating gristle while Yaqut took his fill of the best meats and left the rest in the ashes for the Beastmaker, and, worst of all, running ahead through the woods alerting Bear and every other beast, just to disguise Yaqut's secret moves in the shadows.

One shove now, and the Beastmaker could share his beloved hunter with the Mudman.

"Timov—look!"

Timov stepped behind Yaqut and stared along the extended length of his lance, expecting to see the plume of the ghost dancer's new camp. Instead, what he saw brought a joyful cry from him. Tiny figures moved among the trees, specks of pollen glinting in the violet morning haze—barely recognizable as Hamr, Kirchi, and Blind Side of Life.

Not waiting for Yaqut's order, Timov scurried ahead along the ridge's downward slope, using his spear to keep his haste from tumbling him among the rocks. Yaqut let him run ahead and watched the surrounding tree-shagged hills carefully, feeling for the threat he knew was there.

Down in the sapphire mist, Blind Side of Life moved warily, and Hamr was not impatient with him. The tracking stone was very cold in his grasp when he pointed it toward the fog-hung hills. Kirchi, too, held tight to Hamr's arm. The land had become rough since they had turned south at the bend in the Big River. Among the numerous clumps of boulders and half-buried rock slabs, large animals could appear from anywhere.

With her moonstones held close to her mouth, Kirchi had already talked Wolf and Panther into leaving them alone. Both times, Hamr had infuriated the beasts by trying to drive them off with thrown rocks. He had been amazed that Kirchi's soft mutterings had made the snarling creatures back away. "What do you say to them?"

"That there's easier prey in the Forest."

After the attack of the Moon Bitch, Hamr was disposed to believe anything Kirchi told him. Neoll Nant Caw had not appeared again since that evil night, but as the moon grew, so did Kirchi's fear. "You wounded her terribly," she told Hamr that first day after the confrontation, when he started at every colorful tree and dew-baubled bush as if seeing it for the first time. "Those half-formed monsters you spilled from her were all her rages—monstrous angers that have been growing in her a long time. She's furious that the Old People are dying out, and that the men of our tribe, of all the tribes, are devoting more of themselves to politics than to the Mother. She sees ahead, far, far ahead. The Invisibles give her that power to see what will happen to our furthest children, high in the tree of generations. And what she sees maddens her."

"And so now we are the target of that fury," Hamr said. "To what end is all her knowledge if she uses it to do us evil?"

Kirchi sighed. "She will not let us escape. She rests now, rebuilding the strength of the Moon Bitch. At the full of the moon, she will attack again. I'm sure of it."

But Blind Side of Life was balking, and would go no farther. "Get your moonstones out," Hamr said, surveying the airy open woods and fixing on the black granite platforms inset among the trees. "There are beasts ahead."

A small group of antelope emerging from the maple grove, where they had spent the night, walked sedately onto the pale grass. Then a growl vibrated loudly from the rocks, and the antelope bounded away, disappearing into a beech thicket. Blind Side of Life trembled and backed away.

"What was that?" Hamr asked, his heart pounding with the nearness of the roar. "Panther?"

"No, the cry was too deep. Lion."

"I've never seen a Lion. Can you talk to it?"

Kirchi already had her moonstones out, cupped in both hands, and began chanting to them in a persuasive voice. Another resonant roar shook the air, and Blind Side whinnied with fear and pulled away, his hind quarters hitting Kirchi. She dropped her stones. As she stooped to retrieve them, she froze. Hamr too staggered backwards and reached blindly for her, his gaze locked on a massive silhouette rising from the mist around the granite outcropping.

A red-furred lioness, her black mouth hung open with the breadth and weight of her fangs, slumped closer. Now other huge silhouettes appeared. Three more lionesses, muscle-shouldered, heads slung forward, prowled out of the shadows, followed by a male the size of a horse, his mane a blaze of black.

Blind Side reared up in a panic, and Hamr, holding his rope, was jerked backwards. Kirchi fumbled with her moonstones—but she could already tell something was wickedly different. The brutes lumbered forward steadily, haze steaming off their rippled backs, eyes tight as embers.

"Get behind me," Hamr whispered. He gripped Blind Side's rope fiercely in both hands, not even bothering to go for the spear lashed to the satchels and pelts on the horse's back. He judged the distance to the nearest heap of boulders; it would be a hard, desperate run.

The lioness roared again, battering the air with the mightiness of her signal. Blind Side bucked, eager to flee, and Hamr took advantage of his fright to lead him in a dash toward the granite blocks. "Hurry!" he called after Kirchi as she lagged, trying to make her moonstones work.

Suddenly the pride shot forward, roaring together, and in an instant, they were upon their prey. A lioness sprang on Blind Side's back. In a writhing panic the horse threw off the giant creature. Hamr and Kirchi fell back, but Hamr swiftly leaped for his steed, grabbed his spear and pulled it free. The lioness had lunged and was atop Blind Side again and, with a helpless cry, the horse fell.

Yaqut and Timov had climbed down to the grassy verges, but halted at the sight of the lions. When the horse went down, Yaqut seized Timov's elbow. "Up into the rocks, quickly, before they spot us."

Timov stood transfixed. Blind Side of Life was down, his legs kicking, his entrails tugged free in the black mouths of the lions.

"Quickly," Yaqut hissed in his ear and scampered toward the birchwood that led to higher ground.

But one of the lionesses—which the others had shouldered away from the kill—had spotted Timov and now loped toward him.

Timov darted across the clearing, away from Yaqut and toward the rockpile, where Blind Side had been headed. Glancing behind, he saw the big cat gather itself for a run and knew there was no chance of making the rocks. Thrashing through a brace of skinny hemlock pines, he bolted for a yew whose roots had pulled from the ground at one side and tilted against a rocky hillock.

Breathless with terror, Timov clawed his way up the trunk, heard the lioness scratching after him. The dense branches slowed him down but also stopped the giant feline, and at last he hung among the top boughs gasping with relief.

Below, he saw Hamr and Kirchi dashing for the rocks. Behind them, he heard tearing sounds and frenzied growls. Ahead, the wall of rocks lifted its jagged affliction. They vaulted the first low stones and drove their sandals hard into footholds choked with nettles. Hamr threw his spear onto a higher shelf, and helped Kirchi pull herself up the skewed steps.

From atop the ponderous rocks, sucking deep breaths as Timov watched, they looked back, saw the lioness huddled over Blind Side, his stiff legs sticking out from among their jammed shoulders. But there was no time for anguish. The enormous male had followed them; with furious agility it was finding its way up toward them.

The lion, too big to rush vertically up the jutting rocks, swerved among the staggered shelves, and they had a long second to marvel at its muscled forelegs, thick paws, and fierce open jaws beneath eyes blind as fire. Then they hugged the rocks and climbed. Hamr cast his spear up to the next ledge, hoisted himself to it, and reached back for Kirchi.

Timov, who had followed their retreat, saw no hope: The rocks bunched to a tumblestone pinnacle inaccessible from where they stood. In moments, the predator would reach them. Swiftly, Timov edged out to the creaking limit of the bough where he perched, and leaped out onto the rock-strewn hillock alongside. Stones spun away under his feet, but he plugged his feet into the earth, and dragged himself upward. At the nape of the hill, he was one bound away from a rockledge that overhung the lion and his prey. Before he leaped for the ledge, he removed the sling that Yaqut had made for him from the underbelly of a marten, and grasped two sharp rocks.

With a violent growl—that almost toppled Timov from the edge—the lion found a shorter route among the granite blocks and scampered onto the ledge where Hamr and Kirchi cowered. Hamr swung his spear and thrust. The creature pulled back, coiling to lunge. Teeth set, Hamr braced his spear against the wall, and made himself small.

But before the lion could leap, a rock struck its brow. Its roar bruised hearing.

Hamr glanced back at Kirchi, saw her despair, and realized she had not thrown the rock. Above, in the trees of an overhanging ledge, Timov whirled his sling, and let fly another stone. Again, this one cracked against the crouching lion's head.

Bellowing raw pain and anger, the lion pounced, claws splayed. Hamr pressed back against Kirchi, and with an alacrity and deftness inspired by terror drove his spear hard into the beast's eye. The lion thundered rage for a black instant as it rose in fury. Then, front paws grasping the spear, it sagged to its belly before spinning off the ledge in a shower of rubble.

Timov whooped from above, but Hamr was gazing numbly down at the scope of the disaster, the price of his own safety—staring beyond the dead lion to where the pride continued to devour Blind Side of Life.

Timov shouted again from above. When Kirchi turned her attention to him, she saw that he was leaning against a pliant juniper so that its branches hung down to the rockpile: They could climb to the hillock. Gently, she tried to make Hamr understand, but he brushed off her grip, transfixed by the horror of the feeding lions.

Emotionless, almost as if dreaming, Hamr drew his knife and leaped down the staggered rocks to where the dead lion lay. Slashing at it with vengeful strength, he worked down from the tail and the back legs, peeling the skin from the hot, pliant muscles. While he worked, he changed to the Beastmaker in almost incoherent gasps: "Blind Side of Life is dead. My animal is dead—my soul is fed to the Lion. Now the Lion feeds me." But before he could slit the belly of the beast—and reclaim his soul by eating its heart—he had to skin the creature whole. That was the way the great men of old did it when they wanted to take an animal's power with them. The Beastmaker would expect him to do no less for Blind Side of Life.

Tears hampered Hamr's vision, and before he made the delicate cuts at the front toes and the head, he had to wipe his eyes, leaving bloody streaks on his cheeks. Since Neoll Nant Caw's attack he had begun carrying the Moon Serpent. The obsidian blade could cut tissue as his wooden blade, now lost with his satchel, never could.

The nose and lips came free. Harm stood up and stretched the wet skin of the face above his head, and shouted down at the two lionesses that still lingered over the broken body of Blind Side. They ignored him, and continued to pull the meat from the horse's underside and tear at what remained of his haunch. Half-hidden among the twiggy growth of birches, a pack of hyenas waited, where crows gathered. Hamr knelt again and cut the mastoid tendons, severing the lower jaw. Then he set to work lopping the paws before he cut open the belly for the heart and liver.

Finally, the heavy lion-skin pulled around him, the teeth, claws, heart and liver wrapped inside, and his spear in one hand, Hamr slowly made his way up the stack of rocks. Watching in mournful silence, Kirchi and Timov pushed down a juniper branch with their weight, and he passed his spear and the lion-skin to them. Then he pulled himself up to the rockledge, and looked back.

Jubilation and grief mixed convulsively in Hamr. Throughout the walk across the stony back of the hill, he moved hunched over and shuddering, like a poisoned man. The riotous clash of emotions felt like a sexual contact that peaked but could not release. The animal soul that had saved him from the Boar, that had brought death to his tribe's ancient enemies, that had led them north to this land of the auroras, it was gone now—and in place of the strong, melancholy, and loyal horse, a dead Lion's skin hung heavily on his back, gummy with drying blood. Where the Horse had been life to him, and alive, the Lion's soul was death.

Though he implored all through the night, Hamr did not see the Beastmaker in the darkness that clamped tightly to the tearless grief behind his eyes—

yet he knew the Maker was there as the darkness itself, black as every beginning and every end.

Baat lay shivering in a ditch beneath heavy pines. Water had once run through here before a rockslide clogged the flow upstream and left only the egg-smooth rocks in the grooved earth, where the ghost dancer had curled up to sleep. Duru watched him anxiously. Always before, he had slept silently. But since yesterday, when she had found him squatting on the ridgerock, entranced in his own muttering, he had not been as before. During their night run, the light around his body had glowed dully and red, the deep, dark red of drying blood.

No voices had come to Duru when she had slept wrapped in the deer hide carried in Baat's arms and no flight outside herself. She had slept deeply and woken to find Baat here in the ditch, shivering. After covering him with the deerskins, she had built a small fire upwind of him, though she well knew that would signal the others where they were. But if he was dying, what did it matter if the others found them? Let them come. She thought that maybe, if they knew his need, they would help.

From inside his sleep, Baat heard Duru's concern. The hunger music he had used to reach the ul udi had worked: The Dark Ones had used him to house themselves at daybreak, instead of returning to the sky and going forth from him, as he had directed, into the lions. But when Timov and Hamr had killed the lion that the Dark Ones rode, the ul udi had suffered the death of the beast, and they had made Baat suffer with them.

Knives of pain had stabbed Baat, had flayed the skin from his muscles as he writhed in the ditch. From without, it had appeared as though he were shivering, but within, he had thrashed and howled with the agony of being skinned alive. The Dark Ones had exulted, feeding off his suffering. Now, gorged, they slept, waiting for night to return them to wakefulness.

Baat floated in the afterpain, the wearied anguish that was almost bliss now that the torture had ended. Partaking of the ul udi's telepathy, he could feel all the small lives around him: mice avid with hunger after the chilly night, red fleas torpidly fat with the blood of the mice, ready for their winter sleep, and a hawk circling above, searching for mice and seeing the smaller birds flitting on the fog paths among the trees in their endless tumult of feeding.

And there was Duru sitting under a pine, where the small birds rested from flight, chattering about the hawk they had glimpsed in another corner of the morning. She was not listening to them. She was afraid for him. He could feel her fearful caring, and that calmed the hurt in his big body. He had found his companion. The Bright Ones had truly led him to the one who would watch over him. But tonight, when the Dark Ones woke inside him, would he be able to protect her from their evil?

A memory returned to Baat with the pulsing of a fever, a memory of the Dark Ones and their usefulness to the People. He saw himself again as a child during the summer wanderings. That summer he had been confused by the hurried pace across the tundra, the wild wailings of the women, the sudden absences of some of the best hunters, their bodies not laid out with their spears, not blanketed in flowers as men who had died on the hunt. They were simply gone.

Looking back, Baat realized that had been the terrible summer when the People had fled before the smallheads, and not escaped. He saw now that the People had been falling back from the smallheads since before his grandfathers were children, but always before, there had been room on the tundra to hide. This mournful summer, the smallheads had encroached to the last possible border: to the door of the mountain, the sacred burial site of the People.

But back then, Baat had been too young to understand. He remembered being carried among the giant stones of the icefield and the People shouting with anger and pain. And he remembered the hunger music that the old ones sang. That had been the first time he had heard it—the numb voices of the singers chanting to Crow and Hyena with the languor of the dying, inviting the Dark Ones down into their flesh.

From high on the tall rocks, held firmly in his mother's arms, he watched as the men, possessed with the Dark Ones, lured the smallheads among the boulders and hurled stones at them. His mother did not hide his eyes or turn him away when the killing began. She let him see the men leap among the wounded smallheads, rip the limbs from their bodies, smash their skulls to bloody bonemeal. She let him see the Dark Ones do their frenzied killing, for she knew that someday he would have to sing the hunger music himself.

What his mother had not foreseen was that he would have to sing it alone, without the others to call down the Bright Ones when the killing was over. He, alone, would have to carry the Dark Ones tonight and, at the same time, protect the child Duru from their bloodlust.

And if he and Duru did survive the madness that would rise out of him tonight, what lay ahead? the journey north to the door of the mountain, to the ancient cairn of the old ones, the journey that walked straight into winter. He could hear the birds talking about winter coming, when insects were fewer and the seeds less plentiful. Soon, they were saying, soon they would find their own way south.

The immense sadness of the approaching cold rode on the wind, and he could feel its disconsolate energy in his bones, which were certainly too old now to survive another winter. The wind blew through his bones as through the stark trees, carrying a darkness in which stars and snow were both hidden, carrying a whole new season that could not yet have been seen, yet sharing its secrets with him and with all the animals.

Eating Darkness

In the poor glow of the waning moon, Neoll Nant Caw sat on the ground outside her burrow. Three other witches circled her, raven-beings, all silent and preternaturally alert, pacing swiftly back and forth. Each held a chunk of crystal, the facet-seams shining violet as they passed before her.

Neoll Nant Caw stared flatly at the running witches and the cold energies in their hands. The death of the Moon Bitch had nearly been her own death, and she was too weak to participate in the building of another. These women had come from their lairs in the Forest to help preserve a ghost dancer from hunters— or, if they failed, to bury the crone in her burrow and take her crystals for their own.

The old witch, proud that the others had come so eagerly for these rocks, waited passively for death. Her real life was in those crystals, mixed with the power of the ul udi. Many of the stones, several generations old, carried light from the first witches, the outcasts and strays of the Forest's early tribes. She had long feared that when she died the ignorant might discard her crystals among the wild rocks, and she was glad to see they would be taken up in able hands.

A thermal mist red-black in color, made a shadow between Neoll Nant Caw and the circling witches. A smear of face appeared in the dark mist: an eye-glisten, fang tremor, saliva thread of a ravening strength.

"When I left you with Neoll Nant Caw," Hamr said to Timov, "I promised the Beastmaker I would initiate you myself when I came back." They sat by a rainpool in sight of the feeding pride. At their feet, the lion-skin soaked in mud and leaf-mash. Hamr, still grimed with the Lion's blood, leaned forward with his elbows on his knees, red hands tangled in his hair. He was tired, yet smiling, eyes bright with jubilation, not tears. Glad he had come back for the boy. Glad even to sacrifice Blind Side to the Beastmaker, he thanked his guardian power for sparing Kirchi and Timov. They lived, to hear the roars and masticating of the ravenous beasts. They were alive, as he was, because they had struggled together.

"This skin is yours," Hamr declared. "It is the sign from the Beastmaker I knew would come when you were ready."

Timov squinted at Hamr, baffled that he was not mourning his animal, yet pleased to receive praise. "You killed the Lion."

"No, Timov. You've earned your initiation. When the skin is dressed, I'll present you to the Beastmaker myself." He reached over and put his hands on Timov's shoulders. "Young brother, the Blue Shell will not be separated again."

Timov nodded, his heart suddenly big in his chest, squeezing against his ribs. "We'll get Duru back," he asserted and felt his clansman's grip tighten with certainty. "We'll be a tribe."

At midmorning, the lionesses decided they were done with the horse and sauntered back to their caves among the rocks. A few cubs lingered but when the hyena pack began closing in, they scurried off.

Hamr, who had spent the time stretching his lionskin on a rack of pine boughs and scraping the inside clean with an edged rock, stood up, took his spear, and walked out of the thicket into the clearing. Timov and Kirchi followed.

"Where are you going?" Yaqut yelled from his place under a crookbacked pine. "Hyenas will jump you."

No one had spoken to Yaqut since they found him waiting in the thicket, watching the lionesses devour Blind Side of Life. Feeling their withdrawal from him, he had wanted to explain: He was not a coward, but neither was he willing to die for either a horse or another man. He was hunting the ghost dancer, and the Beastmaker did not want him vainly sacrificing himself. But no one had asked; so he sat in silence while Hamr dressed his lion-skin.

To show his respect for what Hamr had done, Yaqut had collected oak leaves and soaked them in a nearby rainpool. After he boiled away the water with hot rocks, the tannin-rich sludge that remained was ideal for toughening the skin and keeping it from rotting. Hamr had used it, but with not a word of thanks. The boy and the witch, too, had offered him only skulking glances—as though he should be ashamed for saving himself for the one hunt that mattered.

Now, Yaqut sat under his pine and watched the others driving off the hyenas with shouts and thrown rocks. What did they want? To bury the dead beast? To weep and chant over its red bones? Let them. The ghost dancer was nearby. In a day, two at the most, they would find him, and then they would need all the courage that had been tempered in them today.

But it was not the lamentation for his horse that Hamr wanted. The Beastmaker had given him the animal and now had taken it away. So be it, Hamr thought to himself. Rather, it was his and Duru's satchels, and the pelts that Blind Side of Life had carried since they left the Blue Shell, that he wanted. Kirchi followed him, looking for her moonstones.

Timov alone stood over the torn carcass of the horse and wept. Alone in the woods with Yaqut, he had missed Blind Side's big, snorting presence, and now would never know again the companionship of Horse. His grief for the animal made his chest heavy with melancholy music.

"Cut it out," Hamr called coldly over his shoulder. "Blind Side's returned to the Beastmaker—and he's weeping for us. We're the ones got left behind."

Timov wiped away his tears, saw the back of his hand come away with the Lion's blood, and smiled. Blind Side was dead, but he had also been changed, made into the Lion's skin. Now any tribe would proudly make a place for them. Except, perhaps, the Thundertree, who knew he had ghost dancer ancestors.

Looking back at Yaqut, where he sat under the dark green shade of the pine, Timov remembered the poppet Duru had left for him on the ridge. He told Hamr about it and Yaqut smashing it.

"Maybe Yaqut's right," Hamr said. "It's possible Duru's possessed. The poppet could have been left to make you think she's all right and caring for the bone-sucker when, more likely, she's his slave. The spirits—these ul udi—are more powerful than anyone from our tribe could ever have known." He found his satchels and most of the pelts unmolested and pulled them free of the dead horse. As he scanned the ground for Kirchi's moonstones, he related the attack of the Moon Bitch.

Timov listened in dismay. "What if she comes back?"

"She will," Kirchi said. "Very likely, soon. She'll know we're together again, and will want to stop us from going after the ghost dancer. We must find the moonstones. They're the one thing that might stop her attack."

Timov joined the search, pausing only to throw rocks at the hungry hyenas. Soon all four stones were found, though one had been fractured. Kirchi fingered the spalled moonstone nervously. "There will be no circle to protect us now."

"But three are intact," Timov noted hopefully.

"Three are not enough." Kirchi's eyes despaired. "Neoll Nant Caw will know it instantly. Tonight she will attack."

"What can we do?" Timov whined.

Kirchi shook her head. "Nothing." Then she looked at the two men with a desperate new hope. "Unless we simply give up the hunt."

Hamr glared disapprovingly. "I don't care about the ghost dancer, but I won't abandon Duru."

"What if the poppet she left is not a ruse?" Kirchi pressed. "What if she *wants* to be with the ghost dancer?"

Hamr frowned with disbelief. "Why would she want that?"

"To care for him, as her poppet said," the witch answered. "Baat's among the last of his tribe. And he's old. All summer, Yaqut and the Thundertree have stalked him. Why hasn't he fled? Why has he stayed in these woods? Because this Forest is his ancestral home. This *must* be the reason."

"Perhaps he's come home to die?" Timov wondered.

"Yes, yes," Kirchi said. "Of course. He's dying!"

"Then why hide?" Hamr asked. "He should let the hunters finish it for him."

Yaqut, who had been watching and saw them conferring, walked over. "What are you three gibbering about? Let the hyenas eat in peace and let's move on with the hunt."

Kirchi held up the broken moonstone and explained about the Moon Bitch.

Yaqut scowled at Hamr. "You stole the damn crystal. *You* face down the Moon Bitch!"

Coldly disregarding Yaqut, Hamr turned to Kirchi. "I want to find Duru. If she's helping the ghost dancer, I want to hear that from her."

"If she is helping the ghost dancer," Timov said, "maybe we shouldn't be hunting him."

"Helping the bonesucker?" Yaqut hissed with anger. "You damn fools—the poppet is a ruse. The ul udi squat in Duru right now. She's *their* poppet."

Facing Yaqut, his stare flat, Hamr looked at the sinewy old man. He reached out, took the straps that crossed the hunter's narrow chest and roughly reversed them to show the rows of teeth stitched there. "This is all you want, old man. More teeth. Another dead bonesucker."

Without warning, Yaqut swung his short lance up hard between Hamr's legs. But Hamr was faster, blocked the blow with a downward swat, and with one hand grabbed the straps and lifted Yaqut off his feet. His other hand seized the hunter's lance and twisted the weapon free. He threw Yaqut to the ground and pressed the length of the lance across the man's throat.

"We're not hunting the ghost dancer anymore," Hamr said and forced a gagged cry from the mutilated face. "We're going to find Duru. You can either come with us—or you can die here."

He rose and held the short lance over the felled hunter.

"Kill him!" Timov said in a hot whisper. "If you don't, he'll kill you!"

But Yaqut sat up, and returned Hamr's steady stare. "We will find Duru," he said flatly.

"Swear it by the Beastmaker," Hamr said. "Swear you will harm none of us."

"No, Hamr," Timov warned. "He's too dangerous!"

Hamr ignored Timov. He did not want to kill Yaqut. The hunter's skills might save their lives if evil spirits had possessed Duru and the ghost dancer was indeed their enemy. And with winter approaching and no tribe to shelter them, he needed the old hunter.

Yaqut sensed this, and relief pervaded him. "I was wrong to strike at you, Hamr," he muttered. "I swear by the Beastmaker, Whose vision path we call life, that I will do you and the others no harm." But the bone-sucker, he thought, I'm going to kill him. My life is his death.

Hamr threw the lance into the ground beside

Yaqut. "So be it. Let's leave this hateful place. If we must face the Moon Bitch again, let's not do it here."

Without the horse, the satchels and pelts had to be carried among them, in four packs. Hamr was also burdened with the lion-skin, which had to be rolled up still damp and half-cured. Following the chill in the tracking stone, the hunters and the witch climbed into the hills of big pines. By nightfall, they had come to the ditch of withered creek. The crystal pointed south along the stony streambed and was colder than ever to the touch. Not far ahead, perhaps around the next bend, the ghost dancer lurked—close, yet too far to pursue in the gloom.

The sun hung briefly among the trees, and the hazy air became milky as fog lapped the hillsides. On a fragrant carpet of marjoram, among sprinkles of blue asters and red buttons of amanita, Yaqut built a fire. While Hamr stretched his lion-skin, Kirchi and Timov prepared the berries and nuts they had gathered during their trek, and skinned Yaqut's fox.

Wolves howled far away, owls hooted, insects chirped from the sourgrass. Wrapped in warm pelts before the fire, the wanderers ate in silence. The gibbous moon shone through the trees in hazy shafts and lit the knee-deep shallows of the fog.

And then the night noises stopped; an iridescent silence suffused the woods. Fog spilled out of the creek bed and rose like a dustdevil. Hamr stood up. In his hand, he held his spear, the Moon Serpent lashed to its tip.

Wild, white-rimmed eyes snapped open in the rising fog. Timov squealed weakly and instantly regretted it. He crouched behind the fire, commanding himself to be brave. Yaqut rolled backwards into the darkness.

Kirchi stood behind Hamr, and snatched two flaming brands from the fire.

The Moon Bitch emerged from the haze with a bull-heavy roar, and the fire fluttered green, then charred black. Kirchi threw the burning brands at the apparition. They flared emerald through its empty shape and out again, and landed in the creek bed.

With a show of sharp fangs, the Moon Bitch lunged. Hamr stabbed at her with his glass-tipped spear, but the Bitch batted it aside, heaving him to the ground. Kirchi fell back under the baleful gaze of the monster. The Moon Bitch's horrid mouth grinned like a lizard's.

Timov, who had pressed himself flat to the earth beside the fire and peeked out from under his arms, saw the abomination rise above Kirchi, claws splayed to wipe out the life of the witch who had betrayed her. Instinctively he leaped at the red-haired witch, meaning to tackle her and sweep her out of the path of the slashing claws. But as he struck her and she fell, the talons ripped through his own flesh and stabbed into his heart.

Hamr had grabbed his spear, now hurled it into the wraith's eye, the glaring, vindictive eye of Neoll Nant Caw. Pain stabbed through the wraith and echoed across the Forest in a thousand screams. Collapsing under her own cries, the Moon Bitch's massive body withered until it was a puddled mess of luminous syrups.

Amidst the shrinking slime, Hamr's spear stood straight up, its glass tip poised above the ground. When it collapsed, the glowing steam shriveled to a splat of fire and, at its center, the crone's glaring eye.

Hamr snatched the spear before it hit the ground

and drove its tip into the eye. A green flash clouted the darkness, and a greasy smell whooshed upward and dangled in the breeze, until the wind forked and carried the vileness away.

Neoll Nant Caw shrieked and heaved backwards to the ground under a blast of cold air. Wind-fall leaves gushed through the tunnels of the Forest and flooded into the clearing. In a gale of leaf litter, the cry of the Moon Bitch resounded across the clearing. The three witches, who had mounted the power for the wraith, dropped their crystals and ducked into the burrow. When the scream died away, they peeked out and saw the crone's hand and part of her leg, where she lay buried in brown mulch.

"Is she alive?"

"I feel her. Her light is weak, but she lives."

"Don't touch her. Get the crystals."

"My ears ache."

"My every bone aches. Had we grasped the crystals a moment longer, we'd have died with the Moon Bitch for sure."

"We must get the crystals away before we move her. She could yet fall into the sky."

Neoll Nant Caw heard the witches' voices tightly bundled, bobbing in a sea of silence. Their voices and the world around her seemed a mirage—the leaves piled on her face, the hard earth under her, were all transparent, part of the emptiness. She floated at the brink of her body, a lazy ghost, knowing that the void before her was her death.

The old woman might have plunged headlong into that peaceful silence, except that she had collided with another soul. As the Moon Bitch, she had tried to slay Kirchi for betraying her and instead had caught Timov in her claws. His body of light hung above her now, a twitching star at the purple cope of the sky. If she let herself fade into the silence, he would fall into the emptiness with her. But he was too valuable to lose; the ul udi could come down to earth through him and make new crystals. Even now, the Bright Ones were communicating with him. Far away, she could hear their eerie music coursing through the blue air and could see the youth's star trembling to its rhythms.

Over the years Neoll Nant Caw had learned enough from the ul udi of the lightning in her own flesh to be able to pull back from the void. She concentrated on the voices of her sister witches, ignored the lightness expanding in her bones.

"One of us should go get her slaves. They will tend to her."

"Leave her be. She must bind her light first. Come away and bring the crystals."

"But what about Baat? She gathered us here to save him from the hunters."

"Forget him, sisters. He's old. He'll die soon anyway."

"And the wanderers from the south—the girl and the boy who carry ul udi?"

"So Sister Caw says. But she, too, is old and may have seen what she wanted to see at the end of a long, bitter life. People can't carry ul udi. Only the Old People could do that and they are almost gone."

"Then we should take the crystals to our dells and use them for teaching the people instead of attacking our own hunters."

"Yes, Sister Caw is old. We must prepare for her loss."

Neoll Nant Caw drew her attention away from the witches. She was not going to die yet. She focused on the mirage itself, the heat shivers of pain that were her muscles, the comforting grip of the earth under her, and the bisque of decayed leaves filling her sinuses with their odor. This was the dream that held her life in place.

Kirchi placed her three undamaged moonstones on Timov's chest so that they touched and formed a triangle. Their power was weak with out the fourth, and she had to lean close to find the mica-glints of energy that formed images.

"What do you see?" Hamr pressed close behind her.

Sapphire gleams gathered briefly to an image of Timov in a void. He had been knocked out of his body and had fallen into the purplish luminosity that was the auroral sea above their heads. Firepoints flickered around him, and then he was gone.

"The ul udi have him," she said.

"Then he's dead." Yaqut spoke matter-of-factly from where he crouched beside a tree, searching the darkness for wraiths.

Kirchi held her breath and steadied her gaze. She pushed her will into the plasma-field of the peephole, trying to see deeper into the sky, to where the Bright Ones had taken him. But the window was too small. Her attention fell back to earth, and she glimpsed the ragged firs and crooked shadows of the Forest. A young girl appeared, sitting at the edge of a trench, her eyes and hair as dark as Timov's and Hamr's.

"Duru!" Hamr shouted, and the image was gone.

Kirchi hastily arranged the stones and breathed on them again, but the plasma was gone.

"That was Duru!" Hamr said in amazement and bent closer over Timov's body to stare at the moonstones. The vision had vanished. In its absence Hamr felt his need: If he lost Timov and Duru, nothing of his past would be left. A moan escaped him.

"Timov's not dead," Kirchi whispered, peering into Timov's tranced eyes.

"Then what is he?" Yaqut asked, gruffly. "He's not sleeping."

Kirchi ignored him and looked at Hamr. "Timov has fallen into the sky."

The sun set among mountainous purple clouds, and wind bursts carrying the smell of rain whooshed through the trees. On a sheet of birch bark Duru collected the chestnuts she had baked among the embers and set them steaming at the edge of the ditch, where Baat lay. She hoped their toothsome smell would ease him awake, but he did not move. His large body lay curled on itself.

"Baat," Duru called in a voice heavy with concern. Was he ill? Was he dying? Anxiety prickled through her as she tried to figure out what to do: Stoke the fire, heat rocks, drop them in a hollowed burl filled with water, saxifrage, and lupine seeds. That was what Cyndell or Mother would have done—make a medicinal broth. But would that help a ghost dancer? Surely it would, she decided, for he had known how to heal her gashed leg. Their medicines were the same. But she had no hollowed root burl, and finding herbs in the thin moonlight would not be easy. She called again, ''Baat. It's night. You've slept all day.''

Baat heard her but he was afraid to move. His mind was maggoty with the Dark Ones he had called with his hunger music. The lion's death had defeated their evil intent, and now they writhed inside him, wanting carnal satisfaction, demanding the bloodlust he had promised.

Rage with the hunger of the lion, the Dark Ones echoed his prayer. *Come down through me. Be lion's flesh. Be lion's hunger.*

If he lay perfectly still long enough, they would grow bored and go away. He had invited them with his hunger music. He had called them into himself. They were one flesh now, until they chose to leave. Among the People, there were means of driving them off; but alone, he was helpless.

''Baat,'' Duru called again and lowered herself into the ditch. As she neared, the amethyst light encasing him streaked red, and she hesitated. ''Are you all right?'' she whispered. ''Can I help you?'' She remembered seeing oak galls not far away and thought she could find them again in the dark. With the saxifrage and lupine seeds, they would make a strong medicine. But before making the broth, she must know if it would help him.

Timidly Duru extended her hand and touched the glassy glow around Baat. It felt hot, like glue, like blood, and she snatched her hand back. The red glow came with her and began to burn her fingers.

You will die! a voice out of the glow opened in her head.

Duru eked a small cry. At the sound of her fear, maniacal laughter exploded around her. She scurried to climb out of the ditch. In her haste she grasped a dead branch that looked like a root in the dark, but it gave way and she fell backwards and landed on Baat.

The giant reared up, powerful teeth bared around a ferocious roar.

Duru leaped away. Her fright propelled her swiftly up the slope of the ditch, and she sprawled over the brink, the ghost dancer's glowing hand clawing the space behind her. Her foot landed on the chestnuts she had placed at the edge, and sent her flying back into the ditch.

Baat watched from inside his horror as the Dark Ones powered his body with the Lion's hunger. Every effort he made to stop himself rebounded with the mocking singsong, *Come down through me! Be lion's hunger!*

Duru rolled to her back and saw Baat burning, red clots of fire crawling off his enraged face and spinning out into the dark. She wriggled backwards, felt a rock under her hand, and heaved it. With a quick swipe, he deflected the missile. Bellowing, flames spluttering around him like blood spray, he lurched toward her.

Sobbing with fright, Duru shielded herself with her arms—and saw blue fire gleaming from her own hands. The ghost dancer's eyes saw it too. Baat recognized the power of the Bright Ones streaming through the young smallhead; and called the serene energy into himself to counter the fury of the Dark Ones. His face still fixed with rage, he stopped; slowly, his expression dulled. He sat down. Jaw slack, eyes suddenly drowsy, massive arms resting limp at his sides, he hunkered in a shrinking aura of red light.

Duru put her hands on his; and the blue radiance condensed to a shining window in his chest. In the azure glow, shadows materialized into a close-up image of gravel. The field of stones shimmered with movement, Duru saw that the gravel units were people, a large crowd milling on the tundra, seen from above. They flowed in one direction, then turned in unison to stream the other way—dancing. The crowd danced, and as she looked closer, she saw that they were a teeming throng of red- and gold-haired people like Baat.

Music poured out from bone flutes, drums, and clappers, and the People moved in a frenzy, bobbing to the rhythm. Duru moved with them, caught up in the urgent power of the dance. When the crowd shifted to the left, the music jangled out of tune, and the dancers gyrated faster, afraid and angry; right, and the music brightened, and fear and wrath changed to a twirling ecstasy. The People were dancing the ul udi down to Earth. The Bright Ones and the Dark Ones merged into the passion of the dancers. A flinty smell charged the sweaty air, rose with the heat of the packed bodies.

In the blue fire, Duru rose with their heat and met the cold of space above the churning People. The music dulled away; and another tuneful energy took up, eerie with longing and beauty, synchronized with the beat of the dancers but trembling with silences and long, strange notes.

Fear gripped Duru as she experienced the alien presence of the ul udi. She moved back to the dancers, down from the cold and into the heat of the People. But the crowd had dispersed, scattered like pollen across the suddenly hushed brightness of the sky. She was alone under the blue heavens, listening down all the length of the wind for the music of the People.

With a jolt, Duru realized she was not alone. She

was with Baat, listening in his memory for the music of his tribe—music he would never hear again. All at once, the death of his people meshed with Duru's own great losses, and she felt a kinship of suffering with him. Far away but getting closer, she heard the whimpers of his children as they died, heard Baat's answering cries, and her own sobs for Mother, Aradia, and Cyndell.

The pain was lifting the edges of the trance, and she sat again in the night before Baat's thick body. His chest still glowed with the radiance that the Bright Ones had sent through her to calm him. In the blue fire, Duru glimpsed the webby fire of the auroras and the vaulting gleam of stars. Cold curled around her again, and she trembled at the sound of that wind beating her upward, full of wailing voices.

But then the sun appeared, a wingspread of orange fire perched on the blue edge of the Tortoise shell. She floated into its enfolding bright silence, and a joyful warmth suffused her; out of the solar glare a shadow swelled and became Timov floating in the watery distance, gempoints of light glinting around him.

Duru called out to him, and instantly found herself back in her body, staring into the misty shine in the hollow of Baat's chest. Timov vanished, and the blue luminosity darkened to violet night. Drowsiness attacked her, and Duru struggled to stay alert. She leaned backwards and looked away from the ghost dancer, until the chill wind rattling down through the treetops refreshed her, and she could focus her eyes.

A slender figure had congealed out of the shimmerings of moonlight—an old woman with ragged lengths of hair. The wraith of Neoll Nant Caw drifted closer, her face bright as milk, the crinkles of her age like veins in marble.

The last, violet gleam of the Bright Ones' energy blinked out, and the ghost dancer sagged in sleep. Now the pressures of the darkness at last overwhelmed Duru, and she swooned to the ground. The last thing she saw was the crone shredding to vapors, leaving only her head floating briefly in the darkness, flame lighting up her face, her mouth gaping wide, rayed with needle-fine teeth.

Hamr labored over Timov until dawn showed among the trees. He sat on the boy's chest, the way he had for those who had drowned, pushing the wind out of his lungs and then breathing it back into him. For a while Timov survived, sucking shallowly at the air. Then he stopped breathing and by first light it could be seen that, though there was not a mark on his body from the Moon Bitch's attack, he was dead.

Yaqut, who had crept back into the camp after the battle, took a pinch from his poison pouch and burned a puff of acrid smoke under Timov's nose. Timov did not flinch; his cold face glowed blue in the dawnlight. Kirchi pressed her moonstones to his temples and shouted, but could not startle his eyeballs into movement; her fingertips came away chilled.

With a flat rock, Hamr dug a hole in the carpet of marjoram. He cut at the sweet decay under it, hacked at roots and tugged free rocks, all with a locked-jaw strength and fierce frown, as if attacking the Mudman himself. But when he laid Timov in the hole, he did so gently.

Kirchi gathered asters and placed their humid blue heads on his chest, so their fragrance would please him in the afterlife. Yaqut took the sling he had cut for

Timov, fitted a stone to its strap, and wrapped the throwing strings about the boy's icy hand. Then Hamr chanted greetings to the Mudman and acknowledgment to the Beastmaker, but midway a silent sob supplanted his voice, and Yaqut finished for him.

Hamr waved the others aside after they had thrown their handfuls of dirt, and he covered Timov with the earth. He tamped it solidly, and tucked the minty carpet of marjoram back into place so the animals would not dig him up. Done, he sat on the grave and felt all the sorrows of his shared journey with Timov fill him to the rims of his eyes. But the grief would go no further. Life was too hard to be softened by tears.

Timov woke up and saw the black turtleshell of the world drifting under him. He saw it there only because the auroras outlined its shape against the star-hung darkness. Bluegreen veils shimmered over the carapace of the Great Turtle, outlining a black circle to the north, where Its head must be. East and west, the ghostly lights condensed to fiery green fringes at the edge of the Turtle's shell.

He floated downward in the night, returning to where he had begun. Since the Moon Bitch's attack he had been drifting in a wondrous trance, full of voices and visions. When he closed his eyes he saw the sun blazing among thousands of suns, a majestic whirlwind in a maelstrom of fire.

But that trance was already dissolving like a dream. He soared toward the azure apex of the earth, gliding over the dayside of the planet. Sight opened for him wide as the dawn. He saw land far below, clouds and color patches of autumn, where life carried on as he remembered: herds and flocks threading south, weather tugging its freights from the sparkling sea to the aloof mountains, and lives invisible in their tininess thriving in the valleys and forests.

He looked back to where he had been—to the highest reaches of the atmosphere, where plasma rolled like fog in the black of space, veiling a disarray of stars. Up there, he had dreamed something wonderful, about all of creation. Though he had already forgotten almost everything, he grasped tightly what was left: *Our bones were baked in the stars so they would be strong enough to lift us from the mud and yet delicate enough to hold the light of the mind.*

He was afraid to go back down, sensing that everything he had found out here would shrink to a kind of puny wonder down there, reduced by the necessities of eating and killing to eat, sleeping and forgetting. Somewhere below were Duru, Hamr, and Kirchi—and the ghost dancer. Yaqut, too, was down there—all the predators weaning the herds of their sick and aged. So many lives wandering the Earth, regal with alertness, destitute with hunger. How many lifted their faces to the sky? How often had he looked up himself and wondered about the stars and the ruffling auroras, only a moment later to turn his attention to a fiercesome growl among the trees or a wisp of meat crisping over a fire?

Far away, the thunderous fugues of the solar wind boomed against the sky. Inside that perpetual music was other music—voices sang, beckoning him into the spirit stillness of the dark.

But he was falling. The magical voices, calling with

the beauty of sadness, thinned to a rapt memory. The nameless stars disappeared, leaving behind only the luminaries and the constellations. Then they, too, vanished behind the blue abundance of the sky. He passed through clouds, the color-patches of autumn, and crashed headlong into the Forest.

Suddenly, pain sank its venoms into him once again. Earth clogged his nostrils, and he was blind. His eyes flew open and were stung shut. Mud gagged him and in a panic he struggled to catch his breath, to move. The earth held him down, pressing him hard to her cold bosom.

With a huge effort, Timov tore his hand free of the packed ground, ripped at the matted grasses smothering him, and wrenched himself upright in his grave.

The ceremonies were over. Eager to close in on the ghost dancer, Yaqut led the way along the dry creek bed until the tracking stone in Hamr's hand pointed them east. The land sank to blueberry-laden woods whose trees looked like wild dancers waving red rags. The clear sky above swerved with birds, but ahead, over the mountains, weather clouded and rain feathered the wind that swooped from there.

Under a haze of midges, Yaqut knelt, read the tracks in the soft earth, and hurried on. The tracking stone was no longer necessary, but Hamr held it anyway, his heart trotting faster with their quickening pace, afraid the ghost dancer might double back faster than the old hunter could read the land. He knew that was absurd; but it was how he felt after losing so much so quickly—Blind Side and Timov gone to the Mudman in one day. The wet wind seemed to be slapping at his heart, the sky crying for him, and he was afraid of what the world in its grief might do.

The tracks vanished among groundsel and bracken. While Yaqut scrutinized the earth and Hamr swayed back and forth with the tracking stone, feeling the chill of its direction, Kirchi looked around her. This place was the broken end of summer, cluttered with harebells and red mushrooms, tangles of ivy over a fallen tree, drifts of brittle leaves among bush ferns. Beside a creek no wider than her wrist, a falcon's nest had fallen, scattering animal bones, tiny fishskulls, shells, bleached twigs and haywire, bright as pieces of the moon.

She hoped they would find the ghost dancer today, that he would drop the girl, and flee from them into the mountains. But she knew that he would not. He had come back to die, she was certain of that now; he needed Duru to accomplish it. During the summer, when Neoll Nant Caw had made her drink the trance brew every day and sit looking in the crystals for the whereabouts of Baat—hoping to find him before the hunters did—the crone had told her, "The Old People cross the tundra when they're ready to die. Baat wants to do the same. That's why he's come back. We must find him and help him."

But they had never found him. Unless he let the Dark Ones use his body, the scry crystals, which only tracked the evil ul udi, could not see him. And all summer he had hidden in the Forest and not called down the Dark Ones. Kirchi had been glad not to have to look at him again. She remembered watching him in the spring, when the Dark Ones last used him, seeing how swiftly he had killed the Longtooth and Thundertree men before pumping his lust into the priestess.

An upright shadow was moving among the twisted

bilberry shrubs, and Kirchi shuddered, a cry escaped her. Hamr and Yaqut, spears ready, pressed past her, then fell back. Out of the shrubs, scabrous with mud and peeling leaves, Timov lurched.

Hamr dropped his spear and slashed the tracking stone into a knife.

"Pierce his heart!" Yaqut yelled. "That's a dead-walker's only weakness—the heart!"

"Hamr!" Timov shouted.

Hamr lunged forward, pressed the crystal dagger to Timov's chest.

"Hamr! I'm alive! I'm not—what he says . . . a deadwalker! I'm alive!"

Hamr stared into Timov's face, recognized the fearfulness of life in his wide eyes, and lowered the crystal. "I buried you, Timov."

Kirchi put a hand to Timov's slimed neck and felt the bloodbeat. "He was in a trance," she said with awe. "By the Power of the Mother, he lives. The Moon Bitch didn't kill him after all."

"See if he bleeds," Yaqut yelled.

Hamr shot him a dark look. "How'd you get out?" he asked Timov.

The boy shook his head. "I don't remember. I was choking, couldn't breathe. I got out."

"Build a fire," Kirchi ordered. "We should warm and feed him."

"No," Yaqut insisted. "The ghost dancer is too near, and there isn't time left in the day. At night, we'll be *his* prey."

"We're building a fire," Hamr declared and held the gaze of Yaqut's bent face until the hunter turned. "Where are you going?"

Yaqut said nothing, stalked off, and disappeared among the shrubs. Hamr sang a thankful song to the

Beastmaker while he sparked a fire in the fallen falcon's nest and piled on dead branches. Timov's return
was the Beastmaker's sign that they were meant to be
a tribe and that Duru would be returned to them. Kirchi
had won his heart with her caring wisdom and would
always have a place at his side, but Duru, as Aradia's
sister and the last female of the Blue Shell, owned his
soul. She was truly his wife, and when she grew to
womanhood, they would have children and begin a new
clan.

In the warm flush from the crackling wood,
Timov discarded his antelope-hide and rubbed himself with warm ash. Water from the rill and wads of
wet grass and moss cleansed the ash-softened mud.
Kirchi gave him soapwort from her plant pouch, and
he sudsed his hair, lay down, and let the creek wash
over his scalp.

When their elation over Timov's miraculous return from the dead had subsided to a happy content-
ment, Timov told the story of his journey into the sky.
Hamr listened as he awled holes in the Lion's skin with
his knife and threaded thongs to secure the hide to the
boy's body. So glad the youth was alive, Hamr was
happy to let him prattle on, honored even to give him
the Lion pelt and speak his praise to the Beastmaker.
He cut the skin with the black-glass knife, trimming the
hide so that the front paws would cross over Timov's
chest and the mane would collar his neck and block the
wind at his back.

Kirchi's hands worked absently, cracking nuts
with a rock. Timov, his face clean and shining, told her
raptly, "Everything you said is true. I met the ul udi.
The Bright Ones. It's just as you say, Kirchi. Our bodies
are equal to the sunlight."

Hamr looked up from his cutting with a quizzical frown.

Kirchi squeezed Timov's hand, reassuring him. "That's the chant I gave you after Neoll Nant Caw pricked you with her dreaming thorn."

"It's true. I was light. My body had become light."

"Your body was buried," Hamr said through his teeth, using them to tighten a knot.

Timov chewed his lower lip, trying to remember. His journey to the sky was now no more than a dream, most of which he had forgotten. The wonder remained, a secret feeling no words could hold. But he could recall only a few of the astounding things the Bright Ones had actually told him. *Your body is equal to the sunlight. A star baked your bones.* He remembered Kirchi whispering that into his ear, while he sat in the witch's burrow, enslaved by the dreaming thorn. But he also remembered floating above the world's curve, the luminous blue crescent fleeced with clouds. And the ul udi had told him the same things, only up there they spoke with music—and the music had made him see the truth of what they said.

"Our bones were baked in stars," Timov asserted. "The ul udi showed me." Distantly, he recalled staring up at the huge stars above the blue haze of the world, and he had felt as though the stars were emptying their light into him—that the stargleam had sown bright ideas inside him, as part of him, as though he had always known that the earth was round, not a tortoiseshell after all, but an egg with an eggshell crust of granite, albumen of melted rock, and a yolk core of the hardest rock of all— He could not bring forth its name now. But he had known then, floating up there under the seething starlight.

Kirchi put both of her hands on his, said excitedly, "I know something of what you saw. In trance, I've seen as much. That's why I gave you the chant. It's what the witch gave me. It's a place to start with the ul udi, a way of remembering their music."

Timov's face shone. "That's what they are. Music."

"They're light," Kirchi corrected. "We hear them as music."

"What're you two talking about?" Hamr asked, not diverting his attention from his work.

"We're made of lightning," Timov said, squinting to remember. "All of us—Horse, Lion, Bear, the People, Falcon, and Trout—even the trees and the rocks. All lightning."

Hamr had been humoring Timov, but now looked up slowly, the thought suddenly occurring to him that something more had happened to the boy than simply being knocked out. "Flesh and blood don't look like lightning to me," he said and watched his companion closely to see if his near-death experience had addled him.

"The lightning is inside. It's what makes the tiniest pieces of our flesh and blood and bones stick together."

"Lightning?"

"Yes. It's incredible. But it's no weirder than the Beastmaker, who cuts our bones down from antlers and squeezes our blood from rocks."

Hamr sat up straighter. "The Beastmaker is greater than lightning," he replied testily and motioned for Timov to stand. Trying not to show his mounting irritation over the boy's talk, he placed the bulky mane on Timov's shoulders and pulled the tail between his legs, tucking up the rest of the large pelt to form a breech-wrap. He cinched the tail around the waist. "Lightning might hold the Lion together, but the Beast-maker put the lightning in the Lion."

"I've heard Neoll Nant Caw talk about lightning," Kirchi interrupted softly. "There's an ocean of lightning in the sky, and that's where the ul udi live."

Timov nodded, packing the nuts he chewed into his cheek so he could keep talking. "It's true. Even our thoughts are lightning. And many of those thoughts come down from the sky and into our heads, where we think them."

"Nonsense!" Hamr said, slapping his chest. "We think in our hearts."

"That's what we imagine," Timov insisted, "but, really, we think in our heads, in our brains."

"That's crazy," Hamr derided. "The heart moves. And it moves with our thoughts, faster when our thoughts are excited, slower when we're bored. It's obvious. The brains are head marrow, they fill the hollows of the head bones. That's all. And I know for a fact there's no feeling there. When they drilled a hole into Gobniu's father's head, to let the head pain out, I was there; I saw the Tortoise Man stabbing his living brain with a sharp fishbone. The old man didn't feel a thing."

Kirchi laced the waist-thongs on Timov's lion-leather wrap, stood back and nodded with satisfaction. "You won't be cold this winter."

"If we see the winter," Timov remarked and sat down with Hamr. The memory of his journey to the sky continue to dim away, but one truth had come clear to him that he could not forget: The ul udi were real—as real as the Beastmaker—and he had to make Hamr understand that. "If we keep after the ghost dancer, we may all die. His brain is shaped differently than ours. Somehow it can hold the lightning of the ul udi in ways we can't. Not just their thoughts, but their strength. When the Dark Ones enter him, they run his body."

"I don't understand any of this . . . whatever you're talking about. But even if it is so, then all the more reason to go after him." Hamr clenched his fists resolutely. "If the Dark Ones are in him, what will they do to your sister?"

Timov pondered this for a moment. "She didn't seem afraid. You know, I think she's even happy with the ghost dancer. Maybe it's a trance-thorn. Maybe he's protecting her from the Dark Ones. Maybe we shouldn't try to get her back right away. We could follow from a distance for a while, see if I can reach her in dreams again."

"Timov is right," Kirchi chimed in. "We've seen for ourselves, what Neoll Nant Caw says is true: Baat is old, ready to die. He's the last of his tribe, and he needs Duru to watch over him."

"So he simply kidnaps her from us? No, he's nothing like us. We don't dare trust him." Hamr scratched at his new whiskers and shook his head at Timov. "You could be as wrong about his protecting Duru as you are about us thinking with our brains. Neoll Nant Caw attacked us." He cocked a glance at Kirchi. "The Moon Bitch would have killed you if Timov hadn't taken her blow. You can't trust the witch." He returned his stern attention to Timov. "And we can't trust the sky spirits, either—not with all their befuddling trances and visions of lightning in our bodies. Can't you see? They're trying to distract us. They obey the witch and the ghost dancers, because that's how they get their blood sacrifices. If we listen to them, they'll control us. I say we track down the ghost dancer and get Duru back, find out from her what she wants: us or the bonesucker."

"The ul udi are powerful, Hamr," Kirchi said. Timov was alive, the Moon Bitch was dead, and Kirchi wanted Hamr to take her away from these woods before the Dark Ones could use Baat again to do their violence. "I saw how they can inflame Baat—and how terrible his slaughtering can be."

"Let me try to reach Duru in trance again," Timov offered.

"I'm telling you, we can't trust what happens in a trance," Hamr contended. "What if that bonesucker's raping her but these evil spirits are sending you visions of her happiness? She's your sister. And she came with us because she thinks she's my wife. I have to *know* she's all right—not dream about it."

The sound of a twig cracking among the nettles interrupted them. Out of the purple light Yaqut emerged and crouched beside the fire, the mottled shine of his scars glinting with sweat. While they had been talking, he had sat on a tree limb listening to the wind. His voice was low with fear of what he had heard. "He's coming for us."

Timov perked up his head like a rabbit. "You saw him?"

"Listen. It's too quiet. He's coming."

Hamr held up the tracking stone, felt its scalding cold. He jumped up and swung around, and the cold level deepened in every direction.

Kirchi read the alarm in his stare and whispered, "He's here."

Duru woke from the witch's trance and found herself once more lashed to a tree. Baat squatted in the morning steam staring at her with a heavy expression. She looked for the crone she had seen last night, but the tatters of dawn mist showed only emptiness among the crooked trees.

"Why am I tied?" she asked, sitting up with the rope of creepers in her hand.

Baat stared silently, his pale eyes watchful, alert, hard as stars. The simple caring she had seen there before was gone, the dumbstruck look gone, replaced by an unflinching stare. Cold touched her spine.

"I saw the ul udi, Baat," she said, trying to evoke some emotion in his stony face. "I heard their music. And I saw the People dancing—thousands dancing."

Baat stood up, and Duru's piping voice, even with its few recognizable syllables, fell mute. He no longer stared at her, but was looking up into his head, his eyeballs rolled up under the rock of his brow. Fear grew in Duru; she pressed her back against the tree and pulled her knees to her chest. The demons were still in him, the Dark Ones who had tried to kill her last night. The Bright Ones did not get rid of them.

When Baat's eyes swung down back into place, they glinted with tears. But there was no warmth. They were the tears of someone who had gazed into the wind. He pushed a rock closer with his toe and she saw that it had been smashed to an edge. He was giving her a tool to cut herself loose from the tree. As she reached for it, he turned away and loped into the morning's rags of mist.

The spicy scent of a river rose with the haze, thinning to the sweet char of dead leaves and a twang of deer musk. No evil woodsmoke odors tainted the day. The smallheads had slowed in their pursuit. Yet they were near. Even if he was not yet close enough to smell their fire, he knew they were closing in. The Dark Ones told him so.

After his hunger music had called the ul udi into his body—after they had gone from him into the Lion to kill his enemies but the Lion body was killed instead—they had sunk their menace deeper into him. He could not shrug them off. Last night, they had tried to kill the girl. The Bright Ones the girl had carried down had stopped them, but could not drive them off.

When he had woken in a sprawl with the girl asleep on his chest, the Dark Ones had woken with him. He had been afraid they would make him kill her. But the Bright Ones' influence had muted the killing madness in him, and he had had enough clarity to twine a leash from creepers and tie Duru to a tree. Then he had chipped an edge in a small rock so she could eventually cut herself free after he had gone, because he did not expect to come back.

A grandmotherly fragrance crossed Baat's path, and he paused. A gnarly hawk-nut tree dangled its aromatic burrs, its boughs coiled like giant serpents. He husked several of the yellow nuts, popped the juicy meats into his mouth, and rubbed the oily insides of the burrs against his beard, perfuming himself with the odor of autumn. This had been a favorite pastime of the People. The nuts yielded lamp oil, too, whose incense had flavored all his childhood winters. Smelling this again, he remembered the People and how every day had its own ritual, every rock and all its pocks their names. How much he had forgotten.

Shame weakened his knees, and he sagged under the hawk-nut tree and leaned his brow against his knees. What anger would spit from the old ones if they could meet him in the flesh and see how he had abused the hunger music. Every dark calling had to be countered by a bright calling. How could he have forgotten that? He had thought only of killing his enemies. If the Lion had succeeded, he would have left the Dark Ones there and gone on his way free of them and the smallheads. But the Lion's death had turned the ul udi back on him, and now there was no one to perform the bright calling that could free him. At night, the Dark Ones would wake in his body and use him. Eventually, they would kill him, and his soul would become the plaything for their horrors.

Baat wrenched his head back, and his mouth opened around an inaudible cry. The door of the mountain was farther than he could walk in a dozen days. He knew he could never reach there on his own. And the girl was doomed if she went with him. Why not just die here?

The sweet smell of the hawk-nuts cloyed him with their memories of a painfully lost time. He jumped to his feet and barged, heedless, through the tortuous undergrowth. If the Dark Ones were going to rage in him, he would not let them have the girl. He would turn their fury instead on the smallheads, who had driven him to use the hunger music, who had deprived him of his People, his deathward journey to the north, and now his very soul. He would find those smallheads, he would hunt down his hunters, and he would make them eat darkness.

Yaqut sneered. The bonesucker was coming for them, no doubt thinking he could surprise them, not realizing they had the tracking stone. Or maybe realizing it: The ul udi had supernatural knowing. Either way, he was coming, he was already here, somewhere in the violet light of dusk. The long waiting was over. The poison Yaqut had boiled from lethal toadstools— the black syrup condensed to a deadly tar that he had offered to the Beastmaker and had cursed with the names of all the Longtooth clanspeople slain by bone suckers—that toxin was ready now on his lance-tip. All it needed to kill was one cut, one doorway into the blood. For that Yaqut prayed to the Beastmaker as he peered into the gathering darkness.

At Yaqut's command, the fire had been left burning and the four of them had separated into the night shadows. There was only one ghost dancer; he would thus have to come for them one at a time, giving them a better chance to strike at him. The witch and the boy were useless, Yaqut knew, and he had sent them to the more open corners of the clearing, with instructions to cry out if they saw the bonesucker. Yaqut was not sure they would. But he could see them, though they thought they were hidden. If the bonesucker took out any one of them first, he would have a clear shot with his lance.

Hamr knelt in a holt of tall ferns. He watched Kir chi across the clearing, crouching alongside a fallen tree, arms hugging her knees to her chest. Timov stood in a thicket of switches that had sprouted from where the tree had fallen. His sling hung from his hand, but Hamr knew he could not use it. There was no room among the crowded saplings to swing it. Hamr kept his gaze close to those two. The bonesucker would not be stealing anyone else from him.

Timov hefted the stone in his sling, to show Hamr he was armed and ready to fight. He would stand by his clansman even though his dreamy memory of the ul udi inspired awe in him for the ghost dancer. To give himself more room, he edged over sideways, toward Kirchi, and stopped, catching his breath. A blue fire glimmered in the chest-high bracken beside Hamr, flashed abruptly closer, and then bounded through the ferns.

Hamr saw it too, and immediately turned the other way, remembering how the ghost dancer had deceived them when he kidnapped Duru.

"He's behind you!" Yaqut shouted. "There—by the ferns! It's not a ghost!"

Hamr was still looking away when the ghost dancer reared out of the bracken beside him, flames spinning from his body, swirling around him in the dark. With blazing hands, he seized Hamr's head and wrenched hard; there was a sharp crackle, and Hamr's arms jolted stiff, then went limp.

Baat snatched Hamr's spear and leaped over his slumped body, running right through the fire, scattering sparkling ashes in a blustery cloud and kicking chunks of flaming wood into the air.

The sight of Hamr so abruptly fallen under the fiery attack of the ghost dancer shocked Timov, and he stood numb, motionless, until the giant burst through the fire. With a mad scream, Timov leaped into the clearing, whipped his sling and let fly. The rock whizzed over Baat's shoulder; the ghost dancer stopped and raised Hamr's spear.

This was the opportunity Yaqut craved, and he bounded out of the darkness, lance held high. But before he could throw, Baat spied him, and twisted about with such vehemence that spits of blue fire jarred off him in pinwheels. His spear hurtled at Yaqut, but thocked into the maple beside the hunter.

Yaqut's scalded face split into a malicious grin. His lance had sagged before the hurtling missile but he raised it again. Baat hopped sideways, abruptly hit a knobby beech tree, where Yaqut aimed to impale him.

As the hunter flung his weight into his throw, the ghost dancer reached behind him and pulled with all his might, ripping up the misshapen tree by its roots from the soggy ground.

Yaqut had let his lance fly before he realized the giant was toppling the big tree toward him. With a startled cry he danced backwards. The falling beech groaned out of the earth and collapsed atop the hunter. But Yaqut's lance had glanced off the falling trunk and swerved, gashing Baat's left arm below the shoulder.

A gush of silver fire sprayed like spitting voltage from Baat's wound, and he yelped with the sting of the poison. The blue fire flushed bloody red, and the Dark Ones bawled in him, *Burn them! Burn the small-heads! You're poisoned! You're dying! Burn them!*

Baat swooped up a burning stick from the fire and pressed it to his cut, inhaling the stench of seared flesh.

You're dead, Baat! Kill the smallheads! Burn them!

Lightning seared his arms, crackled in asp-tongues from his fingertips. "No!" he yelled. He pulled the fire back into himself, and felt it retreating behind his eyes in a spasm of pain. Yaqut and the beardless one were dead. The hunt for him was over. No longer would he let the Dark Ones use him, no matter the suffering. He reeled across the clearing, scarlet fluorescence billowing out behind him.

Yaqut's spear had dropped beside Kirchi, but her eyes had been locked on where Hamr had fallen and she had not seen it. Her blurred gaze fell on it as the giant turned away. Numbly, her hands closed on the weapon. Her eyes followed the glowing hulk of the ghost dancer, rapidly listing away from her, and she raised the lance.

But as Kirchi threw, Timov collided with her, and

the short spear fell short of the giant. Looking over his shoulder, Baat saw Timov hugging a weeping woman. Pain closing in, Baat shambled off.

"You gawk of a milkless mother!" Yaqut cursed from where he lay under the beech. The branches had broken the massive force of the tree, and he scowled, unhurt, from under the thick boughs. He had kept silent, knowing the Dark Ones would kill him if he showed he was alive. Now, with a grimace of rage on his warped face, he pulled himself out from under the tree. He leaped to his feet and threw himself at Timov. "Why did you save him?" He grabbed the boy's lion-skin and shook him violently. "He killed Hamr!"

Timov wrenched free, and stared into Yaqut's broken face with defiant tears. Words balked in him, could not get past the hurt crammed into his throat. Hamr was dead— Any explanation was more than his grief would let him voice. He glowered at Yaqut, his lips trembling. With a frustrated cry the hunter slammed his fist against the boy's ear, felling him to the ground.

Kirchi shouted angrily at Yaqut, and knelt over Timov.

"Don't yell at me, witch! He should taste my poison for what he's done. You could have killed him! Here and now we could be done with that bonesucker!"

Kirchi shot a harsh glance up at Yaqut. Then her eyes went wide. Above the hunter, the canopy of the Forest blazed. Sparks from the campfire that Baat had kicked into the air had ignited among the autumnal leaves. All at once, sheets of flame dropped from the treetops. The fire spread quickly, shriveling the underbrush in its wake.

Yaqut picked up his lance and ran to where Hamr's body lay. Reaching under the dead man, he plucked the tracking stone from beneath his pelt, and dashed away.

Behind him, Kirchi helped Timov to his feet. Together, moving too quickly to talk or even reason, they carried as many of the pelts and satchels they could gather and fled into the night under a wall of fire.

Part
3

Masterings of the Beast

◆

I create evil: I the Lord . . .
—Isaiah 45:7

◆ 9 ◆

For the Dead, Who Live Us

Shooting stars glinted like needles in the north. Baat watched them briefly while he examined his pain, assessing how badly he had been hurt.

You will die!

The wound felt numb. *Poison!* His left arm tingled, as if it were going to sleep. Surely, if the toxin reached his heart, he *would* die. His heartbeat pulsed irregularly. Was that panic—or death?

Staring at the precise lines of the shooting stars, Baat confirmed that he suffered no blurred vision. But the cold fire of the ul udi steamed red from his flesh, as it did when the Dark Ones swarmed over a dying body and took the soul within for their own.

You are already dead, Hollow Bone! We are eating you!

Baat's heart bucked loudly in his chest. To calm it down, he reminded himself that the hunger music had invited the Dark Ones into his body: The poison and the killing had simply excited them. He decided his wound was not mortal.

Die, Hollow Bone! Curl up and die!

Baat shouted at the night, "Dark Ones, I will never obey you again!" Defiantly, he began to run. If the poison was enough to kill him, this would mercifully hurry his death; if not, the exertion would cleanse his blood. "You hurt me—you do not have me."

Baat ran back through the woods he had crossed before dusk, finding his way in the night by moonglow and the red light misting off his body. Silver hollows gleamed among the trees, where the lunar fire penetrated the treetops. "I did not burn the smallheads," he huffed as he ran, feeling a sudden chill stagger him. "I killed them with my hands. You did not use me."

You killed only one.

"Yaqut and the beardless one are dead. *I* killed them. Not you."

Yaqut lives. He will take your head after his poison drops you.

Baat pressed his run harder, though he had lost feeling entirely in his arm and he could not seem to draw his breath deeply enough. "Yaqut is dead."

No, Hollow Bone—your spear missed, his did not.

"But the tree—I dropped the tree on him."

The smallhead was too narrow to crush with a tree. He's no bison to be blindly smashed. You misjudged—twice, Hollow Bone. And now he will have your head for a trophy.

Ahead, the hawk-nut tree jounced into view, the numerous feathery burrs a haze in the moonlight, like the vision of atoms he had once shared with the Bright Ones. Or like an island of stars, a galaxy he had seen once on a journey to the upper air.

No more flights to heaven for you, Baat. Your

body will become mud, your atoms scatter among the roots. Die, Hollow Bone!

The air would not reach all the way into Baat's lungs. The poison slowed his circulatory system, famishing his blood. Now vision did blur, and the moonshot tree ahead wobbled, doubled, spun before him. His good arm swam, his legs shimmied, and he went down on his knees, straining upward.

Chill! Shiver! Spasm!

The air felt molten in Baat's gasping throat. The beat of his heart was irregular, and dizziness seemed to tilt his whole body. He dug the fingers of his hand into the ground, holding onto consciousness. Overhead, birds veered against the wind, away from the flaming shimmer in the west.

"Fire," he muttered to himself. "Autumn burn." He knew he should get up and move farther on. The webwork of creeks farther west, where he had left Duru, would stop this burn. He pushed with his legs and inched his back up the trunk, but a sickening weakness dropped him again.

From the cavern of twisted conifers, Duru watched. She was afraid to approach, seeing the bloodfire wisping off him, not sure if he would recognize her, or try to kill her. Swirls of red energy flared around him, fluttering like butterflies.

She absently picked at the remnant of vine still tied about her waist. Magpies and jays flashed through the murky air, and Duru turned to see what they were fleeing. The glow she saw in the west startled her. She stared at the brightening a long moment, baffled, thinking the auroras had fluttered to earth or that somehow the sun had climbed down, backwards—before she realized what she was seeing.

A group of elk galloped across a clearing and into

the dark, escaping the fire. Far off, she saw Baat trying to rise and then sinking back to the ground, an aurora of wingbeats of flame dancing around his head.

Spasm! Convulse! Die!

Baat tried to breathe deeply, to draw strength into his limbs, to stand and escape the approaching fire. But the taunting curses of the Dark Ones punished him for his awkward efforts.

He screamed, "Leave me be!"

His anguished cry jolted Duru to act. She had danced with the People. She had stood alone with Baat inside his mind and had felt his losses—so like her own, the sorrow no different. With a cry, she ran through the dusty moonlight between the tall trees. "You're hurt," she whispered, kneeling beside him. "How? What happened?"

Her words came to him as a breeze, delicate as pollen with its promise of life. "Doo-roo."

Duru pointed to the convulsion of flames just visible above the trees. "We have to get away." She looked around for a fallen bough that could brace the giant, and saw nothing suitable. "Use this." She placed her crutch in his good hand. "I don't need it anymore. It's short for you, but, well, come on. I'll help you."

Kill the smallhead bitch!

Baat swung the spruce pole up.

Do it! Brain the bitch!

He hooked the curved end of the pole to a lower branch of the hawk-nut tree and pulled himself upright. Duru helped support his hurt side, and the crimson haze on the ghost dancer's skin filmed over her. Dim, baleful voices pulsed in her: *You will die!*

Duru trembled and looked up fearfully at the giant. The gash in his upper arm crawled with bloodfire sparks. The energies whirling in the air exploded

slowly into clouds, that looked like fanged beast faces.
The girl shuddered and pulled away. But the look in the
ghost dancer's large face was hurt, not threatening.
She fought her fright, ignored the small, cruel noises
like rat faces flapping in the flames.

"Doo-roo." Baat grimaced through his pain, his
long eyes opening wider as he gazed down at her.
Where she held his numb arm, the red shine of his flesh
gleamed blue.

From a hillcrest nave of high-arched oaks, Yaqut
sat upwind of the burning and looked down on the
flight of flames. A webwork of creeks to the west and
south had already contained the fire there, and to the
east, the Big River gleamed like red snake-skins as the
conflagration approached. A few more hours of frenzied fire destruction remained. By dawn the blaze
would have retreated into ash.

Yaqut envied Hamr. The Beastmaker blessed only
the most rare hunter with such a pyre. Truly, he
thought bitterly, Hamr had been a Great Man—a
horsemaster, witchlover, lionslayer. Staring down into
the fiery portal to the afterworld, Yaqut remembered
when he had first thrown the oaf from his horse and
nearly killed him, not knowing that the beardless, inept
hunter was beloved of the Beastmaker. He frowned,
recalling the anger that had knifed into him inwardly
two days before, when Hamr held him on the ground
and made him swear not to harm the witch or the
boy—with the boy, all along, urging Hamr to kill him.

Ashes now, Yaqut thought. There would be no
need to avenge his pride on Hamr. Beloved as he was of
the Beastmaker, the horseman was no hunter of ghost
dancers. And as for the boy—Yaqut looked over his

shoulder into the darkness under the oaks, where Timov and Kirchi huddled, sobbing for Hamr. Yaqut had the tracking stone now. It chilled perceptibly when pointed northeast, and at dawn he would follow its icy guidance and finish the bonesucker off.

The witch would come with him. Neoll Nant Caw would want her vengeance for the ghost dancer's death. Far better that the sacrifice be Kirchi than himself. He would turn the young witch and the stone over to the hag once he had Baat's head. Meanwhile, she would warm him well on the chill nights to come.

As for the boy, Yaqut had sworn on the Beastmaker not to harm him—but that vow had died with Hamr. He would leave Timov to find his own way in the Forest. Before the moon was full, the boy would be bear scat.

That decided, Yaqut rose and strode through the fireshadows to the witch, jerked her to her feet. "Tonight, you sleep under me."

Timov rose, as Yaqut knew he would. The old hunter placed the tip of his lance under the crossed lionclaws at the boy's chest. "Hamr is dead. My vow to him chars with his bones. Leave us alone, boy. When morning comes, if you're still here, I will kill you."

Timov flinched.

Kirchi pushed away from Yaqut, her face slick with tears. "I won't have you, Yaqut."

"Flee, and I'll kill you too." The bad eye in the mangled face peered calmly. "You're coming with me, to get the ghost dancer's head."

The wet shimmer in Kirchi's eyes dimmed with alarm, and she looked to Timov. He stood small in the bulkiness of the lion's pelt; and she knew there would be no salvation from him. When she faced Yaqut again, her gaze was steady. "He comes with us."

Yaqut traced the line of Timov's jaw with the tip of his lance, saw in the boy's blood-smoked eyes the fright that had broken through his grief. The old man lifted the boy's chin disdainfully. "No."

"If you want any pleasure from me, he comes."

Anger flared out of Timov's fear. "Kirchi—no. He'll kill me anyway. I'll leave tonight."

"Where will you go?" the witch asked.

"There's only one place for him," Yaqut sneered. "The belly of the Beast."

Kirchi stepped closer to Yaqut. "I want him to stay with us. After you take the ghost dancer's head, I want you to let us go."

"You know your wants, witch."

"Timov has the inner sight. I promise if he comes with us, he will help find his sister—and the ghost dancer."

Yaqut squinted at Timov, hating the boy not only for wanting Yaqut dead but for the shiver now in his bottom lip, the nervous skittoriness of his dark stare, and the bonesucker blood with its fevered voices whispering in his veins. He wanted to stick him now, be done with him, and discipline this witch with terror. The flameshadows moving in and out among the oaks goaded him to do it. But the witch's promise held him in check. She *was* a witch. He knew he should kill her quickly.

"All right, the boy comes with us," Yaqut decided. "He may prove useful tending our camp."

Timov groaned. He knew the vengeful hunter would eventually kill him and Kirchi.

"You swear you will free us when the hunt is over?" Kirchi asked.

Yaqut nodded assurance—a mean joy knotting and unknotting in his belly—knowing that indeed he would free them, Timov to his death and the witch to Neoll Nant Caw. "But first, you must satisfy my wants."

"I will," Kirchi assured. "But not now. Tonight I mourn Hamr." She turned away and returned with Timov to where they had sat before.

Yaqut let them go. He went back to watching the fire, taking the twitchings of his little revenge plot with him.

Timov felt cold in his lion-skin despite the waves of heat reaching them from the holocaust below. He wanted to ask Kirchi to run away, tonight—but he knew that was hopeless: Yaqut would track them down before the sun crested the treetops. The boy took only one glance at the witch squatting in the dark under the trees, her face pressed to her knees, her masses of red hair bright even in the darkness. Then he looked away, not wanting to see her grief.

Hamr is dead, Timov told himself. Just the other night, Timov was the one who had died, dropped his body and flown into the sky. Now the fires of the auroras had come down to earth. They blazed below, reducing trees and shrubs and Hamr to ash, reducing them to the tiniest parts that once—and only once—had been put together in seed and in womb to build those lives. From the ash, he knew, more lives would be built—but never again Hamr. Never again Blind Side of Life. Or Cyndell. Or Aradia, Mother, Biklo, Father. None of the dead reduced to ash would rise again.

Kirchi sobbed herself toward sleep. She cried for the man the Great Mother had sent to save her. What remained for him now? What prayer could she give? That the Mudman honor Hamr? That Hamr's spirit watch over her and maybe even call Yaqut to join him?

The fear in those chants mocked the great man. Tears were all she could truly offer in prayer.

Ash from the burning Forest fluttered like moths through the red shadows. Those were the souls of all the animals burned up in the blaze with Hamr, accompanying him to the western kingdom. The smoke visible among the trees was the tide of the afterworld, the waves of shadow risen up for the dead hero of the Tortoise clan. When that tide went out, she would go with it. Only slavery and death awaited her in this world. Many deep woods separated her from her tribe, the Longtooth—Yaqut's tribe—where her sibyl mother, counselor of chiefs and hunters, would immediately return her to Neoll Nant Caw. She had broken too many tabus to ever go back to the witch. Death alone seemed plausible.

The roaring warmth of the blaze soothed those chill thoughts as sleep closed in. It was as though Hamr's body heat had gone out into the world and returned to comfort her. He wanted her to live, to struggle, as he had, to carry greatness with the same strength that he had carried death.

The Forest blaze ran through the dells and low hills to the west, looking molten to Baat from his high bluff, where he leaned against a scrubby yew. Long ago this scarp had been carved by the Big River, but since then the meander of the river had silted to a meadow, which at the moment was a smoky vat of moonlit fog. The fire ran farther on, burning to the very edge of the water, lighting the bend scarlet.

Baat kept his gaze on the distant flames, which quieted the gibbering voices of the Dark Ones. On the hurried passage away from the danger, the fear of the

wind shifting and bringing smothering smoke to them
had excited the ul udi, and their jubilant voices had
melted into each other and become a frantic yammering. But the wind had not turned. The fire retreated in
the distance, the spices of its burn sifting down to them
out of the hazy moonlight. Even so, the Dark Ones
continued to harangue him.

Yaqut's poison did not help. The venom had put
his left arm into a paralysis and hollowed out his chest
to a breathless cavern. The rush through the Forest and
uphill had only spun the toxin faster through his body;
he felt its chill coursing through the length of him,
blooming like a canker on his heart. He did not want to
be afraid—for then the Dark Ones' ravening din would
become unbearable—but the needle-stabs in his heart
told him he was dying.

Duru knew. She had smeared the gash with the
same healing tar that he had used to cure her leg
wound. She had diligently built a fire and heated rocks,
immersing them in his wooden bowl until the river
water there boiled and the sprinkling of herbs and
grasses became a brew. He had tried to drop several
red toadstools into the hot potion, knowing the amanita
would kill him faster than Yaqut's poison, but she had
caught him and thrown the toadstools out—as if she
thought he could yet live. But she knew. She heard how
shallow his breath had become, and she could see the
cold fire on his flesh giving up its strength.

"Drink," Duru ordered and held the burl cup to
Baat's lips. He sipped, and the liquid drooled from his
slack lips into his hackled beard.

"Don't bother anymore with me, Doo-roo. I am
dead. But I'm not afraid to be dead. Go back to your
brother. I did not let the Dark Ones kill him. And I
regret now—oh, I regret very deeply now that I let

them use me to kill the beardless one. I had thought only of killing Yaqut, but the Dark Ones filled me with murdering strength and I killed your clansman. When you learn that, you will be happy I am dead.''

Duru did not understand the ghost dancer's words. She wiped the spilled brew from his beard with a wad of dried grass and laid her hand on his forehead. He felt cool as stone. Where she touched him, the crimson light around his body patched blue. She took his hurt hand, lifted it in both of hers so that he could see the shine brightening to blue in her grasp. ''Baat— what does this mean?''

The blue fluorescence gleamed in Baat's drowsy eyes, and he stared. Could it be? he thought. The flutter of hope in him inspired the Dark Ones to a shattering blat of screaming. He closed his eyes, trying to retrieve the mental space he needed to fully grasp this perception.

Duru thought Baat had fainted. But when his eyes opened again, there was a sharper intent in his face than she had seen since he had danced down the spectral powers of the sky.

''Doo-roo.'' He pointed to the sky and then to her and offered his hand again.

Realization dazzled the girl. ''You want me to bring down the Bright Ones?''

Baat saw from her expression that she grasped his meaning. And though she would not comprehend him, he said anyway, to convince himself and to defy the tormenting voices battering the inside of his skull; ''Doo-roo—you can purge me of the Dark Ones. You can bring the Bright Ones down through you. Fulfill the bright calling. Just hold my hand. There's enough of the People in you to do it. Go on—take my hand and let the Bright Ones come down through you.''

Baat's fingers flexed for her grasp. When she took his hand in both of hers, the Dark Ones in him yowled, their voices merging into one massive roar. Stab-pain hit him in his heart, and his head jolted back, eyes squeezed shut.

Duru almost let his hand go, thinking she was hurting him. But his fingers clamped on hers. Then his eyes popped open, glaring with the intensity of his effort to stay alert against the battering voices only he could hear. His teeth clacked. "Doo-roo!" He raised her hands up, high enough to lift her to her toetips.

Looking upward, at the silver brow of the moon, her light steaming through the haze of the fire, Duru searched for the ul udi. But they were not there. They were already inside her, dimly calling. A patient voice spoke from far within: *Duru—be still. Be quiet as the oak that the lightning seeks out.*

Baat watched the azure light on Duru's hands climbing her arms, and he closed his eyes, knowing he had to hold out only a while longer. Already, their panic had splintered the Dark Ones' bellowing into distinct voices clashing between his ears: *You are already dead, Hollow Bone!*

Yaqut's poison eats your blood!

Convulse and die!

The voices gathered to a scream that faded abruptly to silence. Baat eased his eyes open a slit, glimpsed Duru standing rigid, face lifted to heaven, eyes rolled white, her small body sheathed in astral fire. He sat taller. His left arm was still numb, and the needles of pain in his heart had sharpened. But the terrible noise had vanished. He listened deeper, for the Bright Ones, and heard their whispery voices talking to the girl: *The Dark Ones are gone for now. But they watch. They wait. Baat is dying. Yaqut's poison has hurried his death closer yet. There is little time, perhaps too little for him to reach the door of the mountain, where his ancestors wait. He is listening. Baat, you were wrong to use the hunger music.*

"I know that now."

"Baat!" the girl's small voice broke in. "I understand you!"

"Yes—I hear you as well!" he cried into the darkness of his closed lids. "The Bright Ones have joined our minds."

"I'm afraid for you, Baat," Duru began. She seemed to be standing on the bluff among moon-ghosts, kelpy shapes that drifted between her and Baat. Baat himself looked like a ghost, more shadow than shape. "Sometimes I think you're dying."

"I am dying, young Duru. You heard the Bright Ones. I'm old—and Yaqut's poison has made me older yet. In a short while, this body will drop from me. This summer I had thought to journey to the door of the mountain for a vision, but I know now that if I ever get there, it will be to die."

"That's why you took me from my clansmen, to help you find the right place for you to die, isn't it?"

So now she knew that truth. "Among the People, my people who have opened themselves to the ul udi, the ghost dancers, must go north at the end of their lives, to the door of the mountain, where the Bright Ones come to earth. If I die there, Duru, I will be taken by the Bright Ones. Otherwise, my soul will belong to the Dark Ones, who will torment me for time beyond reckoning."

"I'll help you."

"You have helped me." Baat's shadow-shape leaned closer in her vision, and she discerned a sad gentleness in his heavy features. "I must tell you a thing. Hamr is dead."

Baat's ghostly shape became solid and larger, but his voice came out small: "I killed him."

Anguish washed through Duru, and she felt as if she were lifted away from herself, flying above the wind to find Hamr.

"You will not find him," Baat said. "His body is ash now."

"And Timov?"

"Your brother lives. I did not harm him. But Hamr is far from his old life now. I'm sorry. My fear used me."

Duru looked at the giant's hand held firmly in her small grip, the strange light of the ul udi joining them. Fervent emotion churned in her. She looked away to the great blaze of the moon-cast Forest. Hamr's death linked inside with all her other losses. Tears that had been burning in her since the fever took Mother burned hotter. She turned and pressed her face against Baat's hand. Grief and tears flowed through her, a current as strong as a river.

Baat had expected her to rage at him, and when she did not, his remorse deepened. He had wanted to end the hunt, not hurt this child. The Dark Ones chortled from far away and just behind his eyes, distant and close—haunting, yet not owning him anymore. Duru's bright calling had broken the spell of the hunger music. With this strong child to guide him, he would find his way past the Dark Ones entirely—away from the irreversible sorrows of this world. The Bright Ones had given her that power.

Duru cried until her grief settled into cold new thoughts. Hamr was dead. She was no longer a wife, no longer a clanswoman. Whatever the Great Mother wanted of her was right here with this ghost dancer, who might just as soon have killed her as Hamr. He was all the evil and all the good in the world; if she left him here she would only find him again in the first beast that came for her, as well as in whatever rock or club would defend her. She could not flee the Dark Ones and there was no life without the Bright Ones. Her destiny was clearly here with this dangerous friend. At least she could heal his pain and darkness. The blue fire shining from her to heal him showed her that. He needed her. Now that Hamr was gone, that need had become her whole life.

She stared up at the night. As the tears cleared from her eyes, mists of starlight brightened, teemed, condensed to the blue-white plasm of the Milky Way and the huge cobalt glints of individual stars.

The fire in the valleys had burned to a smolder. Smoke, phosphorescent with moonlight, churned in the hill-hollows and wafted in chalky smudges over the ridges. Out of a furl of woodsmoke, Timov emerged, his thin body looking smaller in the bulky lion-skin. He had wandered away from Kirchi and he hoped from Yaqut, too—to be alone with his grief. He thought he had come away to pray to the Beastmaker for Hamr, but as he ambled among the skinny, stunted trees on the stony shoulders of the river bluff, he realized that Hamr did not need anyone to speak for him to the Beastmaker.

Timov knew then that he had come to speak for himself. "I am the last man of the Blue Shell," he began, and his chant to the Beastmaker faltered. There was no need to say any more. There was no clan to hear him, no mysteries to be revealed. If he were going to be initiated at all, he would have to do it himself.

With his hands gripping the claws of the lion-skin, Timov called all of his grief back into himself. He withdrew all his mumblings to the Beastmaker and to Hamr's spirit. If they could help him at all, they would have to help him as himself, he grasped coldly. He was alone, the last of the men. Yaqut would certainly kill him. The hunter no longer needed him to find the ghost dancer. He had the tracking stone. To live—to make his self-initiation mean life and not death—Timov knew he had to make himself a man. No one else would. But make himself what kind of man? He did not have the strength of Hamr or the murderous cunning of Yaqut. How could he make himself into something more than a helpless and frightened boy?

"I am a man," Timov said to the night. "I am no longer a boy. I have put aside my childish fears. I will be brave. I will not disgrace the Blue Shell. If I am to be the last of our blood—I will be among the first in courage. Hamr showed me the way. I will walk it to my death."

But Timov felt foolish. He felt like the brine-flowers he used to see in the tidepools, their blind faces waiting for sustenance. He could say anything he wanted but still the fear persisted, the doomful solitude did not go away. He waited for some new power to come to him. But it would not come. He knew that. He had seen the curve of the world. He still vaguely remembered the beautiful music and the icy pain of the ul udi. Indeed, the world was far more strange than he could ever grasp. Yet, he was sure, no new power was coming to him that was not already in his hands.

Yaqut pretended to sleep, propped in the crotch of a stout oak, and watched Timov get up and slip into the moonlight. He thought the lad was fleeing, and he was glad of that. Kirchi lay under the neighboring yew, collapsed in her grief. She was the one Yaqut wanted.

She was not a beautiful woman, not as clansmen judged beauty—she was too skinny—yet Yaqut liked her vulpine stare, green as lit ice, and the way her cheekbones flared. She was a witch, and that stoked the heat of his desire. What a brutish joy he would know with her, for she would resist, certainly—just as the bonesucker had resisted the prick of Yaqut's poison. Let her resist. He wanted a good flesh-packed fight. He wanted the mixed delight of matching the cleaving ache in him, swollen from summer-long denial, with a biting, scratching truculence—enough pain to turn his desire into gleeful plunder.

Yaqut gritted out a curse between set teeth when he saw Timov return. The boy had merely gone off to empty his bowels. Should he kill him now? Or let him tag along until an accident found him? Sleep claimed him as he pondered this, and when he woke, the first rays of sun were riddling red through the smoke from the burned woods.

The charred spines of trees stood out above the brimming fog. Magpies shouted their loss from the surviving trees and hedges on the bluffs. Yaqut, after throwing to the ground his blanket of pelts and standing tall in the oak, stretching the sleep-cramps from his muscles, took the tracking stone from his hip-pouch and pointed it east. The crystal chilled with cold that faded as he aimed it north. He watched Timov and Kirchi relieve themselves in the bushes, then crept down from his night perch and emptied his bladder over the shackled roots.

East, the torn veils of fog revealed foliage, red, yellow, and patches of lingering green. There would be food. Deer, startled by last night's blaze, stumbled among the hedges, and one would be enough for several days. But first, he would claim his prize and get rid of the weakness Kirchi stirred in him. He sauntered to where the witch bent, gathering her pelts, lashing them with twine for the day's trek. When he stuck his lance in the ground and put his hands on her hips, she straightened as if stabbed.

"Here or in the bushes?" Yaqut asked. He caught Timov's alarmed stare, flicked his eyes to the side, telling the boy to go somewhere else.

But Timov stood, staring dumbly, as if trying to remember something.

"I'm mourning Hamr," Kirchi said, not even looking over her shoulder.

"You mourned him last night." Yaqut kept his hands on her hips, stepped close enough to smell the leaf-mulch scent of her matted red hair. "Time now to worship the life that remains. Let's go sing the Beast-maker's praises in the bushes."

"No, leave me be."

"We all need more time. But we only get what we have." Yaqut thrilled to feel the tension in her stomach muscles as she readied to twist about or flee. There would be a fight. He looked to the boy with a harsh stare, warning him off. If he had to speak to him, he swore he would do him some real injury. "Fight me if you want," he whispered into her bright hair. "I'll take you anyway."

For a stretched moment, they stood still. A black-bird screeched like a cat. Sunlight ripped through the creaking mists, and the rolling air carried the thunder of the Big River. Then Kirchi jumped forward, seized a club-sized bough from beside the burned-out campfire.

"Stay away from me," she said, with a threatening wave of the club.

Yaqut grabbed his lance, showed his brown teeth in a dread smile. With a swift twirl of his lance, he struck the club from Kirchi's hand and sent it winging away. She staggered backwards, and he lunged for her, grabbed her right arm, slipped his lance between her legs and with one push flopped her onto her back.

Timov leaned forward to jump, and Yaqut stopped him with a murderous shout. "Watch if you want—but touch me and you die."

Kirchi struggled ferociously, clawing for Yaqut's good eye. He blocked her arm with a bruising blow from the shaft of his lance, and pressed himself down between her legs, taking her awkward kicks gratefully. His scar-riven cheek took the force of her head-butts, one hand pressing his lance against her chest and arms. With the other he freed his turgid manhood from his loin-strap and groped for her cleft.

Timov swayed indecisively. If he attacked, he would die; he knew it. If he did not do something, he would want to die. What would Hamr do? No. He could never be Hamr. He had to do what he could do. But what? He looked for a weapon, saw nothing fatal. It had to be fatal—there would be only one blow.

Fear pounded in him as blood whipped through his inner ears deeper into his body—hiding from the fight to come, Timov thought, shamed. But he had spotted the pouch at Yaqut's hip. The tracking stone was in there. He started forward, stopped. What was he going to do? He pitted his whole body against fear, determined to do something. Timing alone would judge him now. He waited, watched with his heart soughing, as Kirchi bucked and fought and Yaqut rode her, trying to fit himself to her.

The moment opened: Kirchi's rise met Yaqut's thrust, and Timov leaped into the moment of the hunter's abandon. He snatched the hip pouch, squeezed it open, and tore free the crystal. Yaqut spun about with a curse of surprise and rage. But by then Timov had rolled away; he sprang to his feet, the tracking stone shaking in his hand.

As Yaqut rose, his member dangling through his loin-strap, his lance thrust forward, fury distorted his torn face. "You're dead, boy!"

But Timov knelt before an impacted rock; he smashed the crystal against it, again and again, until it shattered.

An involuntary cry drove through Yaqut, and, automatically, he cocked back his lance.

"Kill me and you'll never find the bonesucker." Timov stood up, streaming with sweat. To speak, he had to rock loose the muscles strapping his jaw: "You know I'm your only hope, Yaqut. Kill me and all you'll ever see of Baat are his droppings."

Kirchi lifted herself to her knees in amazement. The boy had mastered Yaqut. She could see the hunter's murdering lust subside, then disintegrate into embittered resignation, his lance-arm wilting, his cunning face hung forward in enraged submission.

But Yaqut was stalking toward Timov, menacingly.

Timov held his ground. The hunter stepped so close his blistered visage blocked out everything else. Timov noticed the blood tatters in the whites of his eyes, the roots of gray hair at the bony edges of his head.

Yaqut fixed him with a murderous glare. "Find the ghost dancer. That's all that's keeping you alive."

Timov's gaze wanted to slither away, but he held

it fast on the blue irises in Yaqut's eyes. Fear was needless now. He had found his strength, a strength stronger than Hamr's had been, and he had to use it—now. "You're not going to touch Kirchi anymore."

A laugh so toneless it was almost silent fell from Yaqut's slack mouth. A crazy willfulness rose in him—to gut this whelp and strangle him with his own bowels. But the ghost dancers' teeth tied across the hunter's chest harried him at the thought; his family's blood, soaked into these fangs, cried out to him. For them alone, he would tolerate this show of arrogance. He would not kill the boy, yet. He would let him live for the dead, who were living in himself and, for now, in the boy. He grinned like a skull. "You think you're man enough for the witch?"

"Just don't touch her again, ever." Timov held Yaqut's dire stare another moment, then strode past him to help Kirchi gather up the pelts.

"Thank you," Kirchi said with a soundless breath.

Timov managed a tremulous smile. He helped to fit the bound pelts to Kirchi's back. Then he picked up the satchels, and they left camp, following Yaqut east into the fire and smoke of the new day.

At the first painted light of dawn, Baat stood up to try his new strength, the stitched pelts he had slept beneath thrown over his shoulders against the dew-cold. His left arm felt weak, but at least there was feeling. The gash where Yaqut's poison had entered him itched and ached. He walked around the scrubby yew, where Duru lay curled in sleep, only her black hair visible under the deerskin. His legs swayed with the plunging motion of his knees, yet managed to keep him upright and moving. The painful needlework stitching in his heart was gone, and he could breathe deeply again.

Baat paused to gaze at the leakage of green light in the east, then scan north and, finally, west into the scorch and smoke of last night's wild fire. Thanks to Duru the Dark Ones were out of him now. Yet he knew what they would be shouting as he stared over the black spikes of the burned Forest: Yaqut moved relentlessly toward him with more of his poison; there was no escaping him.

North, the deep lanes of the Forest led to the Big River. He could hear the sliding water above the early racket of the birds. Through the slipping wall of smoke and fog, the abrupt end of the Forest came in and out of view. Unless Yaqut or other smallheads caught them, they would reach the grasslands today. Deep gratitude moved through him like a slow river for this child, who had forgiven him for killing her clansman. With her, he would see the north again.

An oceanic breeze lofted the river scent along the bluffs, carrying with it the daring smell of the open plains, the minty keen heather, purple and humming with bees. A thousand memories and their griefs littered Baat's heart in that drafty moment. He remembered his first summers on the tundra with the People—the solemn rituals and festive songs, the carousing and the careful hunting, and at night the men and women huddled in their circles and the cold fires of the sky blazing among them. All gone—yet everliving in his dreams.

This was supposed to have been his last sweet summer on the tundra, but it was stolen from him by the smallheads and denied him by the Dark Ones, who used him to kill the Longtooth and rape their priestess. No matter now. Summer was gone. Ahead, the short days labored under the long nights, naked to the sky and the hard stars. The sunlight, already frail, would only grow weaker.

Baat looked at the girl curled around her sleep and worried about what would become of her. Again, he knew what the Dark Ones would say: She would die. *Everything living dies.* What would the Bright Ones say? They had led him to her. They had selected her for his companion. They would not abandon her in the north after he was gone.

An echo of the Dark Ones' laughter mocked him for this thought, for even thinking he would survive today, let alone the trek across the tundra. He sighed and let his helplessness take over.

Duru sat up and peeked blearily into the lingering dusk. Baat watched her apprehensively, afraid of her grief. She took his hand and smiled at him. After she refreshed herself at a creek, they faced west, where Hamr had died and where his soul had gone, and Duru sang a lamentation she had learned from Mother. Behind her, Baat chanted. Even though he knew she could not understand him, Hamr's spirit could, and to him, Baat sang.

> Now you are dead.
> Now you are the secret part in us
> We meet in the darkness.
> You are the song of our wounds.

Baat wandered silently through the woods, Duru on his shoulders. They foraged as they traveled. By mid-morning, they reached the Big River, and there they found stream mussels and kelp to eat. Duru's leg gash had healed well enough for her to limp without her crutch, and they ate as they walked.

The land smoothed, and the Forest grew dense to the crumbly banks of the river. At noon, they reached a bend where the colorful trees fell back before a stony plain spiked here and there with conifers. Shallows wobbled with sunlight, trickling westward toward the grasslands, while the deep waters of the Big River swerved east in a stately arc that descended from the mountains.

Staring at the ghostly patterns of snow on the distant purple range, Duru wondered if she would ever see her Hamr again, or any of the dead. Baat read the dreaminess in her stare correctly, and spoke again his chant for the dead.

They waded west, leaving the Forest behind, and entered the wide-open flatlands that stretched north to the glaciers. Now that they were exposed, Baat sought out the deeply rutted migratory paths and the ravines carved by spring flood waters rushing to the Big River, which were more easily traversed.

Ahead, a herd of woolly rhinos nibbled the green shoots of the shallows. Baat knew that this red-shag herd was moving north, to winter at the spur of the icesheets, using their horns to probe under the snow for lichen. In a few days, they would pass their less hardy black-furred cousins trundling south, the dark-haired ones preferring the shelter of the Forest when the gale winds blew.

Baat carried Duru through a ravine that led upwind of the beasts. Along the way, they gathered a sheaf of hassock grass and bearded oat. Then Baat used a rock to crush the stems and paste their skin, hair, and pelts with the aromatic pith. He braided the oats to crowns for their heads and laced bracelets on their arms.

Bedecked in the fragrant mash, Baat and Duru rose from the ravine and let the wind waft their scents into the herd. Duru was frightened of the giant creatures, and lingered behind the ghost dancer as he ambled gradually closer, stopping frequently to sit and pick at the stones, finding grubs and sweet shoots and breathing the deep musk of rhino. A few of the behemoths raised their heads and with their tiny eyes watched the intruders, then lowered their lips again to their feeding.

"They're too big to kill," Duru whispered.

Baat smiled, not comprehending, and offered her a snail.

Slowly, Baat and Duru insinuated their way into the herd, not even disturbing the birds perched on the humped backs. Baat showed the girl how to hold out bunches of the oat mash for the rhinos to eat. At first she was afraid to extend her hand to the big animals, but after she saw that they accepted the grass docilely, she imitated Baat. Soon, the rhinos had eaten all their mash, and Baat demonstrated a way of digging in the mud of the shallows for the tubers and root mats the animals favored.

The wind changed, freighted with the mentholated scents of the north, and the herd began lumbering away from the shallows. Baat hoisted Duru onto the back of a still-feeding rhino. The beast twitched a conch-ear but otherwise did not seem to notice. Baat signed for the girl to hold fast to the thick fur. Then he laid a pelt over her and lashed it under with twine.

Baat climbed onto the back of an adjacent rhino and pulled a deerhide over himself. He waved to Duru as the animals began moving, following the others in

the herd, tramping north. The earth rumbled and jud-
dered, and Duru hung on with all her fierce strength
until the powerful rhythms of the beast became familiar, and she relaxed.

She smiled, waved at Baat, and hugged the animal
under her. The sun-rippled shallows fell away and lithe
grass wavered on all sides. Birds whizzed overhead,
the sky shook, and Duru laughed, riding the back of the
thunder.

◆ 10 ◆
The Door of the Mountain

The wind poured out of the north, blue with the smell of ice. At night, the full moon gazed through the auroras over the woolly rhinos drowsing in small groups, horned heads bent, lowing with dark, seismic music. Baat's glowing body interested the herd less than did the whiskers of autumnal grass among the cobbles. Their faces of living rock only occasionally looked toward his radiant dance.

Duru stared in wonder at Baat from inside the big reindeer skin she had pulled about herself. Out here, with no trees to block the view, she could see the spiraling trail of stardust glittering down the sky to the ghost dancer's body. In the distances on every side, similar funnels of sparks glinted, and Duru thought those must be other dancers.

Baat carried the cold fire to her. Shivering energy washed through Duru, and seraph-like forms waded out of the moonglare, weightless, faceless frost-bodies, almost human, mostly breezy rags of light rayed with darkness. These were the ul udi, come down to guide

Baat on his night journey. The rhinos had been a clever way of escaping the Forest, but their migration would not lead to where Baat must go. From here, Baat needed to carry Duru at night, and by day Duru would watch over the ghost dancer and prepare food.

"What about the others?" Duru asked, pointing to the numerous blue filaments along the horizon.

There are no others, a Bright One said. *Those are decoys we have lowered to distract hunters.*

"Then the tracking stone—"

Your brother destroyed it.

Duru looked to Baat, astonished.

"He's brave," Baat said, and in the glassy light of the ul udi, Duru understood him. "Yaqut would kill him if he knew."

Yaqut knows. But he has not killed him, yet. Timov has made himself useful to the Longtooth hunter. He is tracking you with his own inner sight.

Duru clutched Baat's hand. "Timov has spoken with the Bright Ones. I saw him. He won't lead Yaqut to you."

Baat smiled at her with sad understanding. "Yaqut can read spoor well enough to know if your brother deceives him. That is why the Bright Ones have let down other ropes of fire in places where we are not. Without them, Yaqut wouldn't need a tracker."

We must help Timov, the ul udi acknowledged. *The Dark Ones are in him, too. When Yaqut no longer needs him, the hunter will kill him. And if he dies now, the Dark Ones will own him.*

"Bright Ones, what will you do?" Duru asked beseechingly.

He has made himself useful to Yaqut. There is nothing more we can do. The Dark Ones are powerful.

You must move quickly. Hurry to the door of the mountain.

Baat lifted Duru and followed the ul udi through the docile herd and into the amethyst night. After the violent motion of the rhino, the motion of the ghost dancer's loping, tired run was gentle, rocking, like a dugout on a placid sea. And though Duru tried hard to stay awake and listen to the ul udi, she heard only a little before falling asleep: *The bodies of light never die. They are as timeless as the light that they are. When the body of flesh dies, its light is released. It belongs again to the freedom of the universe and to the mysteries of its own nature.*

The low voices of the ul udi lulled Baat, too, and he strode across the rocky, uneven terrain in a purposeful trance. He had heard the stories of the body of light many times before. All the stories had interested him once—how the stars were suns, how everything had once cooked in the stars and had been gathered into giant rocks that whirled about even more gigantic suns, and how the suns were gathered in enormous whirlpools and the whirlpools linked in long chains across the sky: All of creation held together by lightning.

The stories no longer interested Baat. He did not want to know any more. He wanted to experience for himself the celestial depths as a body of light and to feel the truth of those stories. As one of the People, his birthright was to have a place among the ul udi of the upper air. There, he would join with all the other People who had carried the cold fire while on earth, the other ghost dancers who had made this journey north to where the ul udi could walk with the animals.

Daylight streaks appeared as a soft rivulet of clouds in the east, and while its gray waters pearled brighter, Baat sought out a grassy swatch beside a

narrow lake. Under the thrust of a red sandstone boulder he lay down, and let his exhaustion claim him.
Duru woke as he put her down in the yellow grass. She
watched the moon set, a breath of mist in the cold blue.

Among the green sedges of the lakeshore, Duru
found sweet tubers that, even uncooked, were tasty.
There could be no fires, so she prepared the tubers by
mashing them and mixing in the insects and lizard meat
she spent the day collecting. Twice, beasts wandered
out of the stony ranges, big-shouldered hyenas and
wolves with long limbs, but a few thrown rocks suf-
ficed to drive them off, and she did not have to rouse
Baat.

From the top of the sandstone boulder, Duru
searched for Yaqut. The herd of woolly rhinos they had
ridden yesterday dotted the southeast. In the west,
bison rivered in long dark streams. White mountains
shone in the north like splinters of ice, and overhead,
below feathery ice clouds, wedges of geese flew south.

The day was short and charred to night swiftly.
Baat rubbed sleep from his face and dismissed his
dreams—more nightmares of the smallheads slinking
through the tall grass, their faces smudged with the
bone-ash of his dead clan. He ate the tuber-mash gratefully. Before he was done, the shine seeped from out of
the darkness and glossed the air around him.

"How far is there to go?" Duru asked, when the
dancing ultraviolet lace of the ul udi appeared around
them.

"We'll reach the Serpent Glacier before the new
moon," he said.

"Can you walk that long?" Duru asked, concerned.
"The days are too short to rest."

Baat smiled vacantly. "I only have to make this
journey once." His grateful eyes looked down at her.

"The ul udi will lead you back south. There, seek out the witch Neoll Nant Caw. She will find you a home among one of the northern tribes."

"And my brother?"

"Him, as well."

If either of us survives, she meant to add, but there was no need.

Baat nodded and said no more. The ul udi had begun their hypnotic stories. They spoke of the body of light's destiny, the illusion of time, unreal as the eerie perception of the sun and moon rising when in fact the world was an egg spinning in emptiness, whirling about the sun—and the body of light was in reality a broken piece of another dimension, deeper than depth, shorter than any height, thinner than width, and free of time. But she was not listening.

In Duru's mind, the image of her brother rose, and as sleep immobilized her body in the arms of the ghost dancer, her soul climbed into the sky to meet him. Baat felt her go and felt a pang of nostalgia for the caring that carried her. Years had passed since he had cared for anyone. The larger awareness of the ul udi engulfed his longing.

You are not alone. The People are with you.

"They are with you, in the sky," Baat responded. He watched his footing carefully. Duru was out of her body, and if he dropped her now, she could easily die.

The People are in your bones that make your blood. Have you forgotten the stories of the shells that make the body?

"Tell me again."

Smaller than you can see are shells, round and flat like the carapace of crabs. They link together to make your flesh, your bones. In each shell is a piece of your life—and each piece contains all the lives

*that have lived before you, every grandparent, every
distant animal ancestor of your oldest grandparent.*

"This is just a story."

It is a true story.

"It is a story, nonetheless. I am alone."

*Listen, Hollow Bone: Each piece of life in each of
the many, tiny shells of your flesh is an antenna.*

"As on insects."

*Yes, you remember this story. Like the antennas
on an insect that hear vibrations and feel changes, so
the antennas in the shells of your body feel the light
and the changes in the light. That is how we can be
with you. We are bodies of light far above in the
upper air—yet the antennas in the tiny pieces of life
in the shells of your body feel us, feel the changes
that are our voices and our thoughts.*

"Why do the smallheads not feel you?"

*Their antennas are not tuned to us. They hear
only themselves.*

"Then I'm not alone. The smallheads are alone."

*Yes. The smallheads are alone with themselves.
And when they grieve, they grieve alone.*

"I like the stories of the People better. I like the
one that says each star is someone who has lived
before, and when we die we appear in the sky."

*That is only a story. The stars are suns, far
away.*

"I know it is only a story. I know it is not true. And
that is why I like it."

Timov sat thinking of his survival, absentmindedly
spinning the disk of tortoise shell around a thin reed
and watching the markings blur. When Hamr had first
shown him the wheel, a lifetime ago, among the Blue

Shell, he had marveled at Hamr's words that the sun and the moon, too, were round as the wheel. Now, looking at the sun bloat red in the west while the moon lifted gigantically orange in the east, he knew they were round as giant berries.

"Hamr talked to me about the wheel," Kirchi said, as if she could read his mind. "He told me about Spretnak. He told me that destiny is the emptiness at the center of our lives, around which our lives turn."

"Yeah, Hamr loved that old man."

They were sitting among a cluster of low boulders on the tundra, the Forest a line of indistinct purple to the south. The land lay flat on all sides, clearly revealing the synchrony of the sun's setting as the full moon rose. Experiencing this balanced moment, Timov, Kirchi, and Yaqut, who sat apart, could hear each in their own memories the chants their clans sang to greet the sun's pale companion.

Yaqut hummed a moon-song he remembered and stared out over the fire at the dark flecks of a distant herd. Those were woolly rhino, he knew, the red shag giants who moved against the southern migrations of the other animals. Baat was using them to mask his flight from the Forest. Right now, he camped somewhere on the far side of that herd. Small flickers like heat lightning nibbled at the darkness in the north. Those would be the ul udi, coming down to comfort their monster.

With his inmost marrow, Yaqut felt the certainty of finding the bonesucker out here on the flatlands. The north was his home, its barrenness familiar to him. Here was where he had learned the Ways of Wandering from his elders. Here was where he had stalked and poisoned most of the tall bonesuckers. And here, among the rocks to the north, was where he had lost his

parents. Their spilled blood chilled the air more
sharply for him than the north wind.

The ghosts of his tribal past would guide him to
food and water, Yaqut knew. But to find Baat he needed
Timov's inner sight. He was glad now that the boy had
smashed the tracking stone. Watching the moon lift like
a grand skull, he was grateful not to have the witch's
crystal in his possession. Too well he remembered the
unnatural ferocity of the Moon Bitch, the way it moved
in eerie ripple-starts like a watery reflection, yet
flashed fangs and talons of keen reality and bellowed
like a pride of lions.

Yaqut was also pleased now that Timov had taken
the young witch from him. His lust to dominate the
woman had almost bested him. How corruptible is the
flesh, he thought, looking down at the blackening wood
the hungry flames fed upon. For his hunt of this most
wily of ghost dancers to succeed, Yaqut understood he
could not squander his power in sexual indulgence.
The tight confrontation with the bonesucker, the death
of Hamr, and the burning Forest had shaken his re-
solve, he realized now, and he had almost betrayed it
with the young witch.

With a sidelong glance, Yaqut watched Kirchi and
Timov playing with the tortoise wheel, smiling at each
other. Let them amuse themselves, he decided. That
would better enable him to focus on the hunt. Later,
after the demands of the dead had been met, there
would be time for the corruptible needs of the flesh.

Kirchi could feel Yaqut staring at her. She shifted
slightly, so she would not have to see anything of his
broken face. Her stomach tightened to think how close
he had come to taking her. With gratitude, she smiled
at Timov, who was reminiscing aloud about Hamr's
heroic deeds among the Blue Shell. In the broken moon-

light, his dark eyes and hair seemed black as night itself, and his youthful face floated apparition-like, the hollows of his cheeks and the breadth of his jaw hinting at the man he would be—if he survived.

Against the purple turbulence of the sunset, the ruff of his lion-skin fanning out in the steady breeze, Timov had looked almost as masterful as her Hamr had. But even though his resourceful courage and cleverness had saved her from Yaqut, he was not Hamr, not the one she had prayed to the Great Mother to save her from Neoll Nant Caw. Hamr had done that. Hamr had slain the Lion and the Moon Bitch. Hamr was the one she had wanted.

Timov saw sadness moving through Kirchi, and he put the wheel aside and brushed his knuckles against her cheek. So that she would not have to face Yaqut, he went to the fire and helped himself to pieces of the rabbit he had stoned earlier and that Yaqut had skinned and cooked. He expected some comment—perhaps a challenge—from the old hunter, but Yaqut simply stared at him with an unreadable expression on his raw face.

Kirchi and Timov ate in silence. The huge, crystal-bright sky lifted dream-shapes out of the landscape: Boulders shimmered like bearskin huts, shadow animals sneaked through the ditchgrass, and bats swerved against the eternities of the sky.

A shadow had edged closer. It ripped free of the darkness, billowed as a cloud of grassheads, then dissolved into a human form. "Duru," Timov said, almost afraid to breathe lest the apparition shatter.

Kirchi shrank into herself at the sight of the young girl, her black hair and onyx eyes glinting with moonfire, her small, round face waiting as if to say something. But as she moved to speak, her image scattered

like seed tufts in the wind, and there was only moonlight where she had been.

The next day, after following Timov's cold-fire
sense of his sister northwest over grass-stubbled land
rutted with numerous trails, they sighted bison moving
south. Though the herd was a horizon away, the wind
churned with the mulchy, drumming presence of them.

"Longtooth," Yaqut declared and pointed his
short lance into the dust shadows behind the herd.
Squinting patiently, Timov and Kirchi saw them: dots
of movement, hunters following the herd.

"How do you know they're Longtooth?" Timov
asked.

"They follow the Bison south. They're on their
way to join the other bands at Salamander Flats for the
Frost Moon rites. I had hoped to be there with them,
were it not for the trouble you've given me." Yaqut
shook his head with regret.

Now inspired by the sight of his clansmen, Yaqut
pressed their trek almost to a run. Kirchi faltered, then
disappeared into a ditch rife with rock-ivy and the tall
grass that had flourished where the herds could not
reach. When Timov went back for her, he found her
peeling the thick moss from the rocks at the soggy
bottom of the depression.

"I'm bleeding," she declared.

Timov started down through the profusion of nettles and ivy.

"It's moon-bleeding," she added, and he stopped
as though she had uttered a curse. "Let me attend to
myself and I'll be with you."

Timov retreated hastily. When he told Yaqut, the
hunter touched his genitals and waved his lance to
ward off whatever blood magic might have smirched

Timov. "I'm going ahead. If you're wise, you'll come with me."

During the moon-flow, among the Blue Shell, Timov had to leave Mother's cave and sleep in the cold, damp root cavern with the slave Biklo. Otherwise he would have been subject to the spirits that bled women to sate the blood-thirst of the Great Mother.

"I used to believe that, too," Kirchi said later, when they were gathering kindling for that night's fire. "That's what the Mothers say, but the witches say different."

The witches had spoken with the ul udi, Timov knew.

"And the ul udi taught me that this is nothing to be afraid of. My womb is cleansing itself, preparing to receive the next egg that I may grow into a child."

"No spirits?" Timov nodded. "No evil blood magic?"

"No moon-flow, either," Kirchi smiled. "I've been eating wonder-of-the-night berries to skip my flow this month. I just pretended to bleed, because I knew it would get us away from Yaqut for a while. I'm afraid of him, Timov. I know he wants to kill us."

"You're a witch," Timov said. "Isn't there something you can do, some magic—"

"I'm not like Neoll Nant Cow. I can't shape-shift. And I've only begun to learn about poisons. I'm sure Yaqut knows more."

"Then we'll just have to wait."

"For what? He's too cunning to deceive, too strong to fight. What can we wait for?"

Timov watched the way the fox-fine angles of her face absorbed her concern in a concentrated alertness. She never seemed to brood or frown, only to be more watchful, as if fear were something that existed only outside herself. When she talked about being afraid, she meant there was a real danger. Timov studied this with fascination, for it was so different from the continual dread that filled his body. For him there was always dread—unshakable and vivid. For this reason the Blue Shell's Panther men had not sponsored him when boys two years younger were already fully initiated. No one had wanted the contagion of his fear. And for this reason he had disliked Hamr before he had captured his horse and had become a great man. Hamr had laughed at fear. Fear was so much a part of Timov that he had felt Hamr was laughing at him.

Remembering Hamr, recalling all that he was, all that had been lost, left Timov numb. He caught a few voles, which they cooked with the insects and grassheads Kirchi gathered with the firewood, and they ate without talking. In the middle of their meal, the moonlight over the grass swirled, like flames on oil, and Duru appeared again, and floated closer.

Timov looked up startled and started to speak, but Kirchi stopped him, reached into her satchel and extracted one of her moonstones. She placed the pearly stone on the far side of the fire, and the wraith fluttered above it like a wavering thread of incense.

"Timov—" Duru's voice squeaked in the air, tiny as a bat's. "Follow if you must. But beware, brother. The Dark Ones are inside you. If you die now, they'll torment you."

"Duru, where are you? Are you alive?"

A blur of some object flew past Timov's face, and a lance struck the moonstone, sent it skipping into the dark. Duru's image wisped away. Yaqut jumped into the firelight and retrieved his weapon. "I warned you about the witch," he said gruffly. "There will be no conjuring of ghosts on my hunt."

Timov began to rise, a protest starting in him, and Yaqut thrust the tip of his lance at the crook of the boy's collarbones and forced him down. The hunter backed away and strode into the moonlit darkness.

At night, the far rim of the earth glowed as though the world burned. Banners of celestial flames unraveled green and yellow in the sky overhead, and their shreds fluttered on the horizon. Baat moved gingerly among the unseen potholes, grass-hidden fissures, and the malice of sharp rocks. Twice in one night his feet slipped from under him and he stumbled. Both times he took the force of the fall on his back and lay gazing up through the tears of pain and frustration at the lopsided moon, the sleeping girl cushioned against his chest.

Duru used Baat's cold fire to go into a flying trance so that she could visit her brother. The great danger was that she would be disturbed while out of her body; then her soul would be flung into the upper air, prey to the Dark Ones, who could keep her from coming back until her flesh died. Baat tried to talk with the girl about this. When the Bright Ones appeared at night, shining around them like formless man-sized snowflakes, the ghost dancer and Duru could understand each other. Duru agreed not to fly out of her body, just to rest. Yet even when she did not try, her concern for her brother carried her out of herself.

The only way Baat could protect her from being flung from her body was to keep the cold fire away from himself, so that Duru could not use it anymore. At nightfall, when the violent shine seeped from his skin, he raised his arms over his head and drew all the power into his hands. The energy burned in his grasp, hot as though he had thrust his fingers into the throbbing heart of a wood fire. Then, leaving him a burst of pain, lightning twisted off his hands and writhed upward into the spectral night.

Drained of his power, Baat carried Duru asleep in his arms through the night. At sunrise, he sought out kettle lakes and glacial streams, where the undergrowth was thickest and there would be water and food. Then he slept, and Duru watched over him and prepared their one meal of the day.

Each day the land became more strange to Duru. Spires of rock slanted out of the ground among silver ponds and waterfilled sinkholes. The ground itself became pebbly, strewn with smoothly worn gravel. Gradually, the rubble thickened, until the earth was covered with random pink loaves of frost-shattered rocks. At one site, stones clustered in perfect interlacing circles as far as she could see. She believed them to be spirit rings. But Baat knew from the ul udi that these magic rings were made by the freezing and thawing of the silty ground, which churned the thick soil like slow boiling water, arranging the rocks in the precise patterns of the circling heat.

Overhead, arrows of birds streamed south, stopping at the numerous lakes along the way, filling the chill opal air with their calling. Baat, seeing the ice peaks drawing nearer each day, broke his prohibition against fire, and they cooked duck and geese. Standing on a shelf of stacked boulders, staring north across mirror lakes bright with the reflections of the snow range, they spotted the blue vault of the Serpent Glacier.

Baat had dark memories of the People stoning smallheads here, but he also had the joy of remembering his initiation into this sacred place, thirty-five sum-

mers ago. This was where the old ones had brought him
and several other children to witness the Last Rites.
Only then could they be sanctioned to attend the ghost
dancing. The whole summer long, during the journey
north, the young boy Baat had been plump with pride,
for not all the People were chosen to call down the cold
fire. Many, like his parents and his brothers and sisters, feared the ul udi and wanted nothing to do with
them. But from his first awareness, he had yearned to
hold the cold fire, to be empowered by the ul udi, and
to know the mysteries the old ones whispered among
themselves.

Under the webs of stars, with the cold fire returned to the night, Baat remembered back to his boy-
days and his green heart, glowing with wonder.

In his sixth summer, Baat had secretly followed
the old ones when they left the camp with the older
boys. The boys, who had trekked to the Serpent Glacier
the summer before, were to be made men, and Baat had
crept after them, to witness the mystery for himself.
Glistening with the spiced nut-oil the mothers rubbed
over their young, he had been forced to crawl on hands
and knees through the thornscrub below the wind so
the others would not smell him. The thorns had cut his
back and pulled out tufts of his hair, yet he had pushed
on. He would see for himself the living fire the adults
spoke of in hushed awe when they thought the children
were not listening.

Baat had lain on his belly under the clawing bramble after he reached the high ground where the ceremonies were performed. Always before, he had been
forced to peer through the wicker of his mother's hut
when the ghost dancers came up here at night to worship, and he had seen little more than fireshadows
against the dark sky wavering in rhythm to the drum-

songs. But that night, while elder sister in the wicker hut thought the bundled straw beneath the buffalo skin was his slumbering body, he lay in the darkness outside the ritual grounds and saw the living fire.

Sunshine climbed down the night sky. Baat hid the fear in him and lay still, trembling inside, as heat lightning stood atop the high rocks above the men. He saw the fright in the faces of the older boys, saw the old ones looking up at the fire-tipped boulders with eyes as still as ice. Then he no longer knew what he was seeing. The fire, shapeless as brook-water, splashed over the gathered men; it clung to them, went blue all over the skin of their bodies, and sparked green in their long hair, green and slithery as eels. And the men did not cry out but lifted their flaming faces to the blue-black night and began to dance. Some beat the drums tied to their hips, others beat their chests and thighs and sent sparks gusting.

The older boys knelt before the burning, dancing men. The skin of the boys' bodies began to light up. The fire crawled green through their hair, flared whitegold in their eyes and filled their open, astonished mouths like fog. And soon they were uplifted, sheathed in flame and dancing.

One of the boys suddenly shrieked with a red rage, lurched about, and ripped off the ear of the boy next to him. Blood spat out like venom. The fathers grabbed the wild boy and struck him between the eyes; and the fire flashed—like sunlight in a tree-crown—and went out of him, leaving him dark and slumped in the arms of the dancers. But the cold fire continued to whirlpool above him: The Dark Ones had tried to take that boy, Baat would learn later. At the time he did not know what he had seen. Another man took the torn ear and slapped it against the wounded boy's head where it stuck. The fire burned brighter there a moment, white-hot along the rip, and the boy was whole again.

The boy Baat trembled with terror. He crawled backwards through the bramble. And the last he saw of that ritual was the violent boy's fire spinning back into him, lifting him into the dance—red as a dead day, and with eyes like giant snowflakes.

Later, when Baat was with the men, he asked many questions, so many that they called him Hollow Bone, good for noise and little else. "Who are the ul udi?" he asked many times before he was answered.

"They are the fiery ones who live in the sky. They come down to us at night and wear our bodies as we wear the bodies of the Elk and the Bison. Hollow Bone, you must not think of the ul udi until you are a man. You must concentrate now on learning the hunt."

The man Baat stood goat-footed on a boulder before the rosy gash of dawn. In the years since, he had learned the hunt. He had also learned grief. But he did not want to remember any more of that. Days without the cold fire in him, without the silent, penetrating music of the ul udi to entrance him, had allowed memories to congeal, and his body felt heavy with the weight of his past.

Ahead, between mountains of tormented purple, the river of sleeping water flowed, luminous even under the last sliver of moon. As the sky brightened, blue lights came on within the glacier. Clouds boiled over the snowcaps, and Baat woke Duru. Together, they wandered among the mighty boulders of the scree. With jaws set, Baat reviewed the glyphs the ghost dancers of former times had etched on the rock walls.

Duru saw the silver dazzle of an ul udi drifting among the weathered slabs, bright even in a slash of daylight. When the tall rocks opened to a pebbled clearing, a dozen of the Bright Ones came into view, ruffling in the dense sunshine, half-seen as jellyfish.

"The upper air comes to earth here," Baat announced, and she understood him. "The Bright Ones will guide us now."

"Welcome, Hollow Bone," a small voice said, and one of the Bright Ones dissolved to a swarm of golden insects, flashing octagonals. "You have been away a long time. Welcome to the door of the mountain.

The husks of golden light flitted ahead, across the clearing and through a crevice between joined granite monoliths. Baat and Duru followed, over the ice-polished stones to the granite wall. Using fractures for toeholds, they climbed into the dark cleft, and the lights of the ul udi directed them through the blackness. A blue star gleamed at the end of the corridor and they could see that it opened to a sun-blinding mountain of ice boulders—the face of the glacier.

Baat and Duru, their breaths smoking, trailed the sparkles of the ul udi into a crevasse. Walled in by ice, the air quivered aqua. Baat held the girl's hand firmly to keep her from slipping into the gaping cracks in the tunnel floor. When he stopped abruptly, Duru ran to his side, hugging herself against the cold. In the jellied blue light of the frozen wall, faces stared back—the corpse-stares of a dozen ghost dancers who had dropped their bodies here to climb into the sky.

The wind, blind and invisible, carried winter. The clear, furiously bright sky promised another clement day, yet the geese flew south in clouds. The horses, too, sensed the deepening meaning of the wind and were moving, not pausing to browse among the green wetlands between the finger lakes.

Yaqut lay flat on a rusty boulder, seeing men among the horse herds, riding atop their beasts. Those were Storm Riders, a rival tribe of the Longtooth. Anger flashed through him. He hoped that Timov and the witch stayed out of sight. Though, of course, they would think of Hamr when they saw the horsemen, and they might even leap and shout.

The last of the horsemen trotted into the migratory ravines and out of sight. Yaqut sat up, thought of doubling back to warn the boy, but his weariness cancelled out that intention. In the days since they had entered the tundra, he had begun to feel his age. Little as he liked the deceptions of the Forest, there at least he enjoyed ample shelter and rest. Out here, exposure stole a man's power. He tightened the pelts he had strung to the leather straps girding his wiry body and squinted into the glare from the snow-crags and reflecting lakes. If he lost the boy, he could not track down the bonesucker on his own. This close to the icefields, there were too many glacial erratics and boulder mazes in which the ghost dancer could hide. He needed sustenance to be strong for the coming confrontation.

Instead of going back for Timov, Yaqut used what strength he had to creep up on a band of antelope drinking at one of the waterholes. After he had lanced his antelope and skinned it, Yaqut carried the choice parts to the top of a clutter of boulders. There the hyenas, who had watched him from the far shore of the narrow lake, would have difficulty pilfering while he gathered tinder. As he stacked rocks atop the meat to fend off the birds circling overhead, he saw a long way out over the stony land, and his heart beat faster. He recognized the labyrinth of tilted boulders into which the ghost dancer had fled.

Surprise and a hard-edged grief sat Yaqut down heavily. He locked his gaze on the rough terrain to the northwest. All his life, he had followed the Ways of Wandering across the tundra, but he had not come here—not since he was a child, when the bonesuckers had ambushed his clan among those tumbled stones. Yaqut's breath ended in a sob. When Timov and Kirchi found him later in the day, he was still sitting there, rigid with impacted grief and anger.

From the time of the full moon, they had lingered behind the old hunter, seeing him only when he sought them out to confirm, by Timov's inner sight, what he already instinctively knew. Days alone together, Timov had come to know the witch better. Like him, she had ever wanted only simplicity and the blessings and comforts of the tribe. She had not wanted to be a witch any more than he had wanted to be a wanderer. But where he was perpetually scared, thrumming with dread, she endured an inviolable isolation, a solitude that had begun in her childhood. Her sibyl mother had set her apart from the other children by insisting her daughter be treated with the deference due the divine. Her isolation deepened after she matured into a rangy, thin-hipped woman—of no interest to the men or the Mothers. In her desolation, she had prayed to the Great Mother for help—and was given to Neoll Nant Caw. She thought her prayers had been mocked until Hamr came for her; but now that he was dead, her desolation was harder to bear than ever.

Timov felt her desolation as keenly, and when he saw the horsemen riding south he stood up in amazement, and the hope leaped in him that they were the answer to Kirchi's prayers. But when he jumped and waved, Kirchi tackled him. "They're Storm Riders," she cautioned. "Enemies of my people. They'll make a game of our deaths."

The two lay still against each other as the horse-thunder dimmed in the distance. The comfort of their embrace surprised both of them. Is he the one the Great Mother has sent for me? Kirchi wondered, looking with amazement into the deep black of Timov's eyes. Timov stared back, all the wished-for joy of his life rising into his heart. And he thought suddenly, this strange woman with the apricot hair was his destiny. Yaqut's threat had joined their lives; now they were one with only their gentleness to counter a harsh fate.

Kirchi pressed her lips to Timov's, smiling. "The Great Mother has thrown us together."

Timov sat up, his insides throbbing, his face pale. "Will we stay together?"

Kirchi's smile slid away, sadly. "I don't know."

"Do you want to stay with me?"

"Oh, yes." Kirchi hugged him, breathed deeply the fern-scent of his hair. "If we can escape Yaqut—if we can find your sister—"

Timov held her tightly, the fear of her departure clogging his breathing. He would not lose her as he had lost everything else. Yaqut could kill him, but Timov would not lose her to the Mudman.

After the Storm Riders passed, Kirchi and Timov hurried north, afraid their previous night's camp would be found and the horsemen would circle back for them. They found the butchered remains of an antelope and Yaqut sitting among buzzing flies. He looked at them with a blank stare, then shooed off the insects with a bloody hand and ordered them to build a fire.

"We saw Storm Riders," Kirchi said. "They'll spot our smoke and come back for us."

"They're not coming back," Yaqut mumbled. "Smell the wind."

The wind had the familiar heathery scent of the tundra, and the boy and the witch glanced at each other, not comprehending.

"Look at the geese," Yaqut added, wearily rising to his feet. He pointed to the flocks that peppered the blue distance. "They're not lighting in the lakes. The small fish and the insects they savor are still there."

"A storm is coming," Kirchi realized. "How soon?"

"Soon."

"There are no squall clouds anywhere," Timov said, wheeling around the open horizon.

Yaqut ignored him, pointed northwest toward the black mountains and their gleaming ice peaks. "The hunt ends there, less than a day's walk from here."

"How do you know?" Timov asked.

"Get the firewood," Yaqut said. "We need to eat well. Tomorrow, we walk hard."

◆ 11 ◆
Lightfall in the Stone

aat knelt before the dead ghost dancers, listening for their voices. With the Bright Ones sparkling in the chill air, he had thought to hear again the songs of the People, but there was nothing. He shrugged and stood up. On his journeys here as a child, he had been too young for the significance of this chamber, and he had not been shown the tumbled figures in the ice. By the time he had become old enough to participate in the rituals, the clan had thinned so greatly that only ghost dancers were coming up here, to die or to help their companions die.

Slots in the rockwall behind them admitted daylight, and by that radiance Duru examined the blurred faces of the corpses—thickbrowed men and women with worn-down chins, broad cheeks, and astonished hair standing out in red spikes. The people looked like Baat, and seeing them Duru realized sadly that this was his fate—to shuck off his body like a husk.

Baat read the consternation on her face, and said gently, "These are just hides. After the Bright Ones took their souls into the upper air, the People carried these bodies atop the glacier, to a sacred hole deep in the mountains and dropped them in. I saw that myself when I was a child. A stream under the glacier must have carried some of them here." He placed his fingertips against ice. The strength he projected into the wall did not come back, and by that he knew there were no souls trapped in there. "Even though their faces have not lost their features after all these years, they're just garments, Duru. Nothing more."

Duru reached up and put her fingers to Baat's lips, feeling the guttural sounds that he was making yet comprehending him in her own language. Each time she had experienced this she felt a frightful wonder, but it was more so here in the death chamber of Baat's clan, and she grasped that this would be very nearly the last time she could talk with him and his powerful spirits.

Baat touched a thick finger to her forehead. "It's here that you hear me. This is where the soft lightnings of the ul udi touch us."

"I will miss you, Hollow Bone." Duru's eyes filled with tears.

Baat nodded affectionately at this child, who, with her dust-gray face and mud-stiffened furs looked like a playful rock given life. "I could never have come even this far without you."

"What's going to happen now, Baat?"

Anxiety for this child's well-being tightened the ghost dancer's stomach muscles. He looked away, at the snowy daylight shining at the far end of the tunnel. Whatever good he could do for her would be done there. "Come. We must find the cairn."

Duru glanced again at the tumbled bodies in the solid freeze and followed Baat into the corridor of rock.

At the far end, a blue light gleamed. As they approached, it became the mountainous face of the glacier, a blue-white cliff crumbling into chunks and sheared wedges big as crags. Before it, the silt-black ground, strewn with smaller rocks, lay perfectly flat. Ul udi glinted before the blue wall, a sprinkling of stardust in the sunny air.

There were not as many Bright Ones present as Baat had hoped. As a child he had squinted against their glare. But that had been at night and earlier in the year, when the wise spirits were strongest. This late in the season of life, the air glowed darkly in the long rays of dim heat. Baat pointed to a heap of orange stones at the foot of the glacier, many of the rocks half-buried in ice. Above it, several ul udi glinted in the air, tiny as stars. "The altar of the Last Rite," he said with hushed breath.

Duru cocked her head, looking for some semblance of structure in the rocks.

"The ice has toppled it since I saw it last," he said and stepped out from the escarpment.

"Will it still work?"

Baat nodded. "The power is in the rocks, not in their arrangement. The power called iron."

"What's that?"

"Another of the ul udi's stories." Baat's hackles rose as he neared the fallen altar, and he signed for Duru to stop. The sky came down to the earth here. He could feel the luminous music of the Bright Ones growing in power in him the closer he got. Another step and he would plunge into trance.

He stopped and regarded the rusty rocks poking out from under pearly mounds of packed ice. Gloom of nostalgia claimed him, and he saw again the original structure: a dolmen slab of red iron braced by black granite monoliths, a doorway to the sky through which generations of ghost dancers had passed.

These orange stones were the shattered pieces of the slab. The vertical river still flowed through them. He felt its splendor lifting the small hairs at the back of his neck, ready to hoist his spirit into the heavens.

Build a fire.

The Bright One's voice had come from far away. They were only weak here in daylight—which meant that at nightfall the Dark Ones would thrive. He had to clear away some of the ice so that he could lay his entire body down inside the vertical river. He looked back toward the colossal boulders the glacier had shoved ahead of itself, searching the lichen-splotched scree for wood. Thorn shrubs peeked from among the shale, and mats of recumbent juniper lay on the pebbly ground where the tall rocks blocked the wind. With Duru's help, he culled the thick brush for dead branches and used stripped thorn-vine to tie up a large bundle of faggots.

At the edge of the glacier, among the ferrous rocks, Baat fed a big fire with bales of the dried tundra shrub. He dragged the scraggly hassocks from under shelves of rock, where the wind had wedged them, and threw them onto the flames. The fire watched the ice weep and shadows of orange stones appear in the bleary depths.

''Now what will happen?'' Duru asked apprehensively.

''While the fire does its work, I will talk with the ul udi. They'll show me where Yaqut is and your brother.''

''Let me see.''

''No. You must watch for danger around us. We

dare not rely on the ul udi to alert us. This is their weak season.''

Duru obediently sat in the buffeting warmth of the fire and observed Baat watching the stony shadows darken in the ice. He sat on a flat rock, his eyes narrowed as if he were about to fall asleep. He was sliding into trance. As before on their journey when Baat was unconscious, Duru selected a high point to watch for enemies, this time a tall rock at the spur of the glacier. From there she could see across the flat moraine to the door of the mountain they had come through. The enormous boulders crowded there defeated any attempt to see the tundra beyond them, and she sat staring at the lichen blotches on the wind-torn rocks.

The frigid air smelled empty of life as it flowed from the north over the glacier and tumbled into the dense thorn and shards of granite. Rising and falling with the wind came the sound of rivers, a murmur of torrents from inside the glacier, and every now and then a deep groaning of invisibly shifting ice.

Though there were no sounds or scents of trouble, Duru reminded herself that Yaqut was somewhere nearby, among the rock crannies, drawing closer each moment. Timov was with him—if he was still alive. That he, too, might be dead was something she tried not to think about. Still, the cold immensity of her aloneness closed in. Soon the ul udi would take Baat away, and if Timov were dead, then there was no one, truly no one left who knew her.

Duru looked back at the ghost dancer, saw him with his head hung forward, his shoulders slumped, and silver sparks glinting around him. He was with his spirits now, receiving their last instructions. And seeing that, the strangeness of the whole last season gripped her: She wondered if all this was a dream, a confused spirit journey such as the Mothers recounted in their fire-songs. Maybe she was still in a fever back among the Blue Shell. Maybe when the spirits took Baat away, she would wake up and find Mother and Cyndell laughing together, Aradia full with Hamr's child, Hamr in the vest he had taken from the Boar to avenge Father's death, and her brother lazing among the old women.

A cold wind blew over Duru. She relinquished her hope with a forlorn sigh and stared at the glaring snow peaks until her eyes hurt and she was entirely convinced she was awake. Sparkles wisped in the indigo sky. She thought they were ul udi until they flurried around her. The snow was slanting through sunlight, and Duru turned a slow, amazed circle on her tall perch, searching for clouds. The sky shone overhead like a deep pool.

In the cold eye of the wind, Baat floated. An updraft of magnetic current tugged at him, but he held back. If he soared now, he risked being out of his body when Yaqut came. Death then would give him to the Dark Ones. Their murderous yearning surrounded him in the cold: *Kill Yaqut. He will stab the eyes from Duru for helping you. He will leave her blind and bleeding for the wolves. Kill him first.*

"Where is he?"

Baat saw his body and the crackling fire swerve off, and he rose above the snake-length of the glacier. Broad desert, sere and vast, stretched away toward tumbled layers of mountain ranges and silver horizons. Beyond the ice ramparts from where the glacier descended storm clouds churned, coming closer.

Never before had Baat flown free of his body into

a day sky, and he marveled at the vistas. But the cold reminded him that he was vulnerable to the Dark Ones, and he focused his attention on the terrain near the door of the mountain. Immediately, he spotted his hunters. They were closer than he had feared. Already the tiny figures of their distant bodies flitted among the towers of rock that the glacier had shoved ahead of itself. That maze of boulders alone separated Yaqut from Duru and him.

You must kill Yaqut. Wickedness veered with the wind from all directions.

Evil faces watched Yaqut from the soft-edged shadows of the boulders. Necrotic shapes of half-rotted bodies wavered in and out of view like the crinkled air above a just-dead campfire. Those were the ghosts of the bonesuckers he had killed, come back to distract and baffle him. Since spotting the glacier, he had sensed them nearby. Now he could see them if he looked.

Yaqut tried not to look. He was not afraid of the dead. They could not harm him. He knew they had come close only because this was the demon land of the north, where the sun-power was weakest. As soon as the killing was over, their split-chestnut-shell eyes would be gone, their jaws without lips and their faces like slugs' underbellies gone.

For now, Yaqut ignored the dead bonesuckers lurking in the shadows and concentrated on following Baat without showing himself. Timov and Kirchi trailed far enough behind not to expose him, yet near enough for him to look back and get direction from the boy. They clattered noisily over the rubblestones, within range for him to turn and quickly slay them the moment he located the bonesucker; otherwise, they would surely try to kill him. Yaqut noticed that Timov kept a stone in his sling now. But the hunter did not fear him. The weather was far more deadly.

Flurries had begun earlier out of an empty sky and quickly thickened to a heavy snowfall. Footing had become tricky: The slicked surfaces among the cobbles and serried boulders, as well as his blurred vision, increased the chances of his twisting an ankle or toppling into a bone-breaking crevasse in the torn ground. Also there was a need to stay out of sight, so that the bonesucker would not see him coming and jump him from behind. That was how his family had died among these very monoliths. Yaqut kept his back to the giant rocks whenever he could and carefully peered up through the snowfall for signs of attack from above.

Fortunately, the air was still. Without wind, the cold was bearable and the snow settled evenly, without deceptive drifts. That could change at any time, however, and Yaqut was eager to stick the bonesucker with his poisoned lance and be done with the hunt.

Worry leads to hurry, a familiar voice spoke the ancient Longtooth adage.

Yaqut immediately crouched low and hugged his lance. At first he thought Timov had spoken, the voice had sounded so clear. But that was not the boy's voice. Yaqut looked about frantically.

Watching from the violet darkness of an overhanging rock stood the lean figures of his clansmen, who had been killed here when he was a child. A peculiar silver shine engulfed them, blurred their features yet left enough familiarity for him to recognize his mother and his older brothers, his uncles and their wives—and there was his father, who had spoken.

Who hurries, the hunt buries, his father completed the old adage.

"Father—I've come to avenge you."

Wet with radiance, Yaqut's dead clan nodded encouragement and faded into the dazzle of the snow. In their places, the dead bonesuckers appeared, putrid eyes staring, flesh-shorn jaws working with hate.

Yaqut looked away.

We are with you, son, his father's voice whispered from the back of his head.

Yaqut averted his glance from the dark crannies, reluctant to face again the family he had lost. His whole life had been given to avenging their deaths, yet he could not face them—not now. From the deathly day that he had crouched in one of these crevices and watched the bonesuckers stone his family—had heard their skulls crack, seen their bodies topple and the ghost dancers leaping down and braining them to be sure they were dead—then monstrously tearing the limbs from them and beating them with their own severed legs—the grief had stormed in him. Everywhere it went, it met rage. The rage had grown as he grew, not knowing where to settle except to rampage back into himself.

Yaqut's rage had knotted into a fierce will. It had made him a superb hunter, of beasts and of bonesuckers. Its invisible flames ate his heart and burned his face. No lightning had scarred his face—that, he well knew, was his own rage burning itself back into him. Now he could not face the specters of his family. His rage would not allow it, and he knew he was afraid that when they looked at him closely they would not recognize him for what his rage had made him.

Son, you are my flesh in the world, his father's

voice said. *Go and kill the bonesucker. Stab him with your poison. His head shall be your trophy.*

Yaqut looked up suddenly to where he had heard the voice, and saw not his father but a gray flutter of the air that blackened under his gaze to a mulch-face of hanging fangs.

"Who are you?" Yaqut yelled.

We are the dead.

"No! Not my dead." Yaqut jumped up and jabbed his lance at the grisly shadow; It shriveled to a dark blob, darkened again to a rooty body with a face like a dried leaf and tiny, needlefine teeth.

We are your allies, Yaqut. We know your grief and your rage, and we are here to complete them.

"You are the Dark Ones!" He stabbed the apparition again, making it curl up into a brown tremor. "Ul udi!"

Yes. We've come down from the night, down into the boreal day, to help you.

"Get away from me."

You need our help, Yaqut.

"You dare wear the likeness of my family and say you want to help? Get away from me." He turned and ducked into the shadow of a ledge-stone. This was truly an evil place. He clutched his genitals and then touched that hand to his forehead, imparting enough life-force to his senses to keep the Dark Ones away. Briefly, he considered falling back to the young witch and availing himself of her moonstones' protection. That was why he had kept her alive, to guard him from the evil spirits he knew haunted these northern ranges. But he was so close to his prey, he did not want to reveal himself to the bonesucker, who could be watching from any of these pinnacles. He muttered a prayer for the Beast-maker's protection and hurried on.

You need us, Yaqut, the Dark Ones persisted.

Yaqut hurried away, to search through the snow-fall, hoping to spot the bonesucker farther on, picking his way over the humped rocks toward the icefield ahead. Instead, he saw the gray emanation in the space beside him, the darkening rot-face appearing among the snow's flakes, a black leaf cankered with eyes and a weeping sore for a mouth.

"Get away!"

Hold out your hand, Yaqut, the Dark One spoke in an oceanic rumble. *Hold out your hand, and we will enter you.*

"Away!" Yaqut spun about to flee and faced a tattered corpse, a dead woman with arms like brown stalks and a body hacked out of shaggy peat. Her face, hardened and black as a beetle's shell, grimaced at him with the features of his mother. He staggered back, and moaned.

When we enter you, his mother said, *you will have the secret knowledge you seek. You will know where Baat is. Neither will he hide nor will he surprise you.*

Yaqut's heart beat like a club. "Mother! Do you want this of me?"

Oh, yes, Yaqut. I want this of you.

Why was he resisting? His mother was dead. His whole clan had been murdered before his eyes, and the Dark Ones would lead him to the murderer. He looked back at Timov and Kirchi, saw them huddled together in the falling snow, watching him nervously. Let them see his rage—let them see how much more death meant to him than life. He held out his left hand. "Come into me, Dark Ones. Come into me and let me be the weapon that will kill the ghost dancer."

Black lightning wove about Yaqut's extended

hand, and a hiss seared the snowy silence. He dropped to his knees under a spasm of spine-jolting pain; a scream clogged in his throat came out as a strangled cry.

Frozen in the posture of his agony, left arm up, mouth wrenched open, Yaqut suddenly was free of hurt. The ghosts were gone. Snow spun emptily in the windless air. No whisperings or haunting sounds troubled him. He rose, astonished, and an unfathomable strength pointed him northeast. The Dark Ones were in him now—but were they deceiving him? He dared not kill the boy and the witch until he was sure. Among the bison-shaped rocks, he moved slowly, cautiously, securing each step before committing himself to the next.

"You saw that?" Timov whispered, clutching Kirchi's arm.

"The Dark Ones have him," the witch acknowledged. "We should flee now."

"Duru—"

Kirchi nodded. "I know. We've come this far. We must try to save her. But Yaqut is no longer just a man."

"I thought only the Old People could carry the ul udi?"

"This far north, the sky power comes to the earth. I've heard it said that the Invisibles sometimes even ride animals up here."

"Can you drive the Dark Ones out with your moonstones?"

Kirchi stared harshly at him. "You saw the black fire. It would enter me. No, we should run while we can."

Timov looked desperately through the plummeting

snowflakes. "Maybe I can find Duru first. We can go our own way."

"No. If we lose sight of Yaqut, we'll be looking over our shoulders all the time. And he'll come for us, too. We have no choice, Timov."

Timov looked hard at Kirchi. For a moment she saw his fear as he recognized the inevitability. Then his jaw set, and he nodded. "You're right. We have to kill Yaqut. We have to strike first."

Yaqut had disappeared around a black shoulder of rock. Kirchi took Timov's hand, and they advanced, staying as much in the open as they could among the boulders jammed close together. The hunter's snow-prints climbed a gravel slope. Timov let go of Kirchi's hand and led the way, shifting the satchel from his back to his side so that he could whip his sling more effectively. Was Yaqut waiting for them at the crest of the slope? Was his lance poised to strike?

From the lip of the gravel rise, Timov spotted Yaqut ahead, slinking along the base of a towering slab. When the hunter reached a place where he had to choose which way to go, he no longer glanced back to Timov for direction, but moved unerringly among the maze of paths. Timov felt the accuracy of Yaqut's choice in his own body. Days of reaching inwardly for Duru had given him a sense of where she was: It pulsed like music in him at the very limit of his hearing. And now Yaqut heard it, too.

"He doesn't need me anymore," he said as Kirchi came up alongside. "The Dark Ones are guiding him right to the ghost dancer." They hurried to keep him in sight as he rounded another bend in the labyrinth. Again, Timov sidled into the opening first, sling ready. But Yaqut was already far ahead. "Why doesn't he attack us?"

"The Dark Ones want the ghost dancer," Kirchi huffed. As she spoke, an idea became clear. She reached into her satchel and took out a moonstone. "Timov, wait."

Timov looked back impatiently. He wanted to keep Yaqut in sight.

"We saw the Dark Ones enter him," Kirchi went on. "They're leading him. Why not have the Bright Ones guide us?" She held up the moonstone. "Take it. See if you can feel them."

Timov took the moonstone, felt nothing, and tried to hand it back. "We're losing him," he complained.

Kirchi took his hand and closed his fingers on the stone. "We saw the Dark Ones," she said. "The Bright Ones must be here too. You can feel them if you try. Then we won't have to keep him in sight. Try."

Timov closed his eyes. Fear moved sinuously through him, touching his thoughts toward Yaqut, toward Duru, who was in danger somewhere nearby. At the thought of Duru, the musical signature of her direction sounded louder in him.

Kirchi saw the frown relax on Timov's face; she knew he was feeling the strength in the stone. She had felt that strength before, in trances induced by a dreaming potion. From them she had learned how to call the Bright Ones by repeating the thoughts they had given her in previous trances. "Your bones were baked in stars," she whispered.

We are all children of the stars, a gentle voice opened in Timov's mind.

"I hear them!"

"Calm down and listen," Kirchi coaxed.

Timov listened but heard only tatters of a wistful music. Then, a new sense of direction took over in him, and his body turned. The stone dulled in his grip, and the music vanished. He opened his eyes and saw a path disappearing in the snowsmoke. "They want us to go this way. But I feel Duru this other way, where Yaqut has gone."

Kirchi took the moonstone and put it back in her satchel, then ran in the new direction, gravel under the snow crackling beneath her swift feet. Timov followed, and when they came to a mound of stacked rocks, he helped her climb. It was the only direction left, and they clambered silently, afraid they were wrong.

Near the top, an overhang forced them to duck into a cramped shaft, where the sun and snow penetrated in thin white rays. In the semi-darkness, Kirchi slipped, scraped her way down into a wedged pit, and lay there dazed until Timov lowered his sling and pulled her out.

Cold air braced them, and they gazed up into swirling snow. Pocks in the granite wall provided hand- and footholds, and Timov and Kirchi climbed up into the opening and ascended the flue. They emerged onto a stone-hobbled ledge in sight of the glacier. Below was a basin of rocks smooth as eggs and, below that, flat moraine. At the far end, on the spur of the glacier, a feather of black smoke rose from a small fire.

Kirchi pointed into the crevasse they had climbed out of. Down there, wending his way among the stand of rocks, Yaqut looked tiny. The Dark Ones were leading him through the maze, while the Bright Ones had shown them how to climb out; if they hastened, they could descend to the basin and reach the moraine before he did.

Lowering themselves from one ledge to the next, Timov and Kirchi dropped quickly down the face of the rockpile. At the bottom, Timov paused to select a round rock for his sling.

"Is that really Baat and Duru?" Kirchi asked,

squinting through the snow at the strand of smoke rising from the glacier.

When Timov did not respond, she looked behind and saw that he had wandered to the edge of the basin and had hunkered down to peer into the crevasse. "I can't find Yaqut," he said. "He must have seen us climbing down."

Kirchi stepped to his side and looked down into the wide chasm of cluttered boulders. Nothing moved in the sifting snowfall.

"He saw us," Timov breathed. "He saw us—and now he's coming after us."

Kirchi tugged at his elbow. "Let's meet him on the flat ground, in the open."

Trembling with fear, Timov met Kirchi's composed glance. "You're not scared?" he asked.

"I am scared." She took his hand and led him down the bank of clattering stones. "But the Bright Ones are here." She pointed toward the blue gorges of ice between the black mountains. "Baat has found the altar where the Bright Ones come to earth. We won't have to face Yaqut alone."

Timov let Kirchi guide him down the rockslope, while his eyes searched for Yaqut. She was a witch and could believe the spirits would help her. What else could she hope for? But he was a man, and he had learned by becoming a man that the spirits sometimes helped and sometimes killed. Hamr had shown him that. If they were going to survive Yaqut and the Dark Ones, only the slingshot would save them. He gripped the rock in his sling. It was hard and still. It, too, had been baked in a star, if what he remembered of the ul udi's music was true. Light had fallen from the sky to become stone. And now it sat in his hand, listening for death.

◆ ◆ ◆

Duru climbed down from her perch to warm herself by the fire. She had seen nothing living anywhere on the snow-hazy moraine, and she had decided that she could just as well watch for Yaqut from beside Baat. She sat alongside his upright, slumbering form and warmed her hands in the glow from the burning juniper branches.

A large facet of ice had melted, draining through the gravel and gathering in the shallow depressions nearby. Muddy pools like long dark fingers reached away from the fire, silvering at the edges where they had begun to freeze. The orange stones exposed by the fire seemed special only in their complexion. No carvings graced them, and no ritual objects were anywhere apparent. They were just a nest of broken stone which, when she looked closer, she saw were not really orange but a kind of ruddy brown.

Duru touched the nearest stone. It lay lifeless under her hand, neither energy nor music humming in it. She looked about for the ul udi, who were supposed to come down from the sky to these rocks, and in the teeming snowfall she did spy glints of star-sharp light. But the Bright Ones were not the fiery spirits she had expected to meet here.

Memories of her first nights with Baat brought back vivid images of his blue aura blowing off his giant frame in hot billows. She remembered her vision of Baat's people dancing in teeming throngs to the ul udi's music, jammed together like hiving bees. She recalled his solitary dance—whipping the cold fire around him like a cape, the blaze blurring to ghosts, to the spectral figures of his ancestors. That had awed her, had made her feel she was in the presence of something holy. Where were those ghosts now?

They were lost in the dayglare, she reminded herself. The power that had called them back was still here. She put her hand on the fur leggings Baat had cut from the deerskins and felt for the gash Bear had inflicted. Her fingers slipped through the seam of the leggings and stroked the smooth scar on her calf. The wound was entirely healed. Baat's blue fire had done that. Why did he not use that power to heal himself? Why did he choose to die now? He had never said to her he *had* to die. Maybe, she thought hopefully, he would use the ul udi's strength that was in these rocks to make himself stronger. Then he would take her south with Timov, and they would live together among other ghost dancers.

But there were no other ghost dancers, Duru remembered. Not like Baat. The ul udi had said he was among the last. Yaqut and men like Yaqut had killed the others. Sitting taller, alert with anxiety, she scanned the far wall of enormous rocks for Yaqut's approach, but saw nothing in the settling snow. The invisible threat bled into the landscape and transformed the sharp rockwall into ominous claws of granite, its shadowy seams and corridors into staring skull-holes.

Duru looked to Baat, whose chin was pressed to his chest, his eyelids twitching. For the first time, she noticed his age. Until this moment, he had simply been Baat the Ghost Dancer, long-boned and thick-browed, the only one of his kind she had ever known. But now she saw the squares of wrinkles on his cheekridges, where the skin had weathered to leather. She observed the gray strands in his spiky hair, the silver glints in the pink stubble along his jaw. Yes, he was old. The flesh hung loosely under his whiskery beard, and his shoulders, though broad, stooped with weariness.

She reached out to touch him gently on his knee, and suddenly compassion saturated her for this old man who, like her, had lost his tribe. All that was left to him of clan and continuity were the spirits of the sky. They were little enough to live for but, after her own journeys out of her body, she accepted that they were worth dying for. When Baat had danced the blue down from the sky at night and she had flown among the dancing ghosts of the People, she had heard the ul udi's music. The wailful, eerie beauty of their songs drifted through her memory, comforting as an imperishable blessing.

Baat's eyes opened. For a moment, the momentum of his flight outside his body continued in him, and dizziness made him squint and grab his knees. The Bright Ones had carried him into the windless sky and shown him the spoke of clouds freighting the snow. Blinking, he stared up at the overcast and realized he had been out of his body for some while. That thought made him anxious. On his flight, he had seen Yaqut nearby, across the moraine, in the maze of glacial erratics that was the door of the mountain.

Duru put a hand on Baat's arm. "What did the Bright Ones show you?"

Baat rubbed alertness into his face and looked at the child. Concern for her troubled him, muting the inmost music of the ul udi. Their drifting thoughts went on inside him, and he knew what they were saying. *Come away. Come with us into the sky, into the music of the stellar winds, the immaterial winds of nonbeing, pure light, timelost light, free of flesh and the strangeness of flesh, the hungers, the pain. Come away.*

When Duru saw the abstract look on his face, she got up and took the burl cup out of their satchel. Baat watched her walk over to the glacier and chip ice into the cup. He could not leave her here to die. He had let himself believe throughout the journey that the ul udi had selected her to guide him and that they would watch after her when he was gone. But he no longer believed that.

Duru placed the cup beside the fire to melt the chipped ice. "You're afraid for me, I can tell. What did you see?"

Baat saw that the fire had cleared enough ice for him to lie down among the sacred rocks. An idea came to him that required a lie. "I saw Yaqut. He is very close and will be here soon. But I did not see your brother."

Duru's face flinched with sorrow. "Is he dead?"

"I did not see him." Baat experienced a moment of regret that he had deceived her. She was such a child, ignorant of her own powers. Like the smallheads who had reared her, she thought she was locked inside herself. She did not know that if she tried, she could touch the ul udi. They would show her that Timov was near, just as they showed Timov where she was.

"What will happen now?" she asked anxiously.

Baat held up his hand, showing her the mauve glow between the spread fingers. "The power is in our hands. Yours, too. Look."

Duru opened her hands and saw nothing. Then, without her knowledge, Baat began drawing sky power through her, and her hands effused a blue shine. Her face brightened with recognition: This was the energy she had used to heal Baat, that had lifted her out of her body and had sent her flying through the night to visit Timov.

At Duru's thought of her brother, Baat's hand closed around hers and his lustrous eyes forced her attention. He did not want her to use this power to leave her body—not yet.

"Duru, the power is in your hands. If you want, you can come with me."

Duru blinked, bewildered.

"Your spirit can come with mine. I will take you with me when the ul udi carry me into the sky." He squeezed her hands gently. "Will you come?"

"To heaven?"

"To where the ul udi dwell."

"Will Mother and Aradia be there?"

Baat smiled sadly. She was just a girl, and that perception barbed him with memories of his own children. "No, Duru. The dead you know are not there. But there are many you don't know who know you, who live in your blood now. They are the People, your ancestors. They will welcome you."

Terror startled her as she grasped what Baat intended. He wanted her to die now, here on the glacier's rubble.

Baat saw her fear and released her hands. "I would never hurt you. I want to save you from Yaqut. If he kills me—and he most likely will—he will hurt you. Then he will kill you. And you will just be dead. I want you to live, free of pain, in a nimbus of joy vast as all creation."

Duru dropped her gaze, not wanting to see his lips moving differently than what she heard. "Joy?"

"Yes, more joy than you could ever know in this fierce world. That is what light is when we leave our bodies and rise to the music of the Bright Ones—inconceivable joy floating on the wind of the stars, drifting among islands of suns."

"But what about Timov? Can we find his spirit and take him with us?"

Baat looked over his shoulder for Yaqut. Through the roil of big flakes, he saw nothing at the door of the mountain. "Only you can come with me," he said softly, unhappy with his lie yet determined to get her away from Yaqut. She was not just a smallhead girl. She could carry the cold fire. Why should she be left to Yaqut—or, even if she got past him, why should he abandon her to a life of begetting and suffering? Never again would she have the chance to live as pure light, to go out into the immensities of life beyond the frenzy of animal cravings and wretchedness.

He listened for the Bright Ones, for their assurance that he was right to ask her to abandon this wasteland. But they kept the silence they had begun when he reached the altar. They were conserving their power to free his body of light. The life of one small girl was theirs to witness, not control.

"I don't want to be left here alone," Duru spoke, her voice reedy and small. The thud of her heart in her ears made her voice sound distant. "I'll go with you."

Baat searched out her eyes and held her gaze. "Come, then. Our journey has just begun."

Duru glanced nervously at the orange rocks. They looked glossy with snowmelt, like bones still wet from their meat. "How will we go?"

From the satchel, Baat removed a leaf-pouch and opened it, revealing a cluster of white berries, dried to silvery pebbles. "Night-wort berries. Four of these for you, the rest for me, and our bodies will let us go."

Duru took the four berries from the pouch and placed them in the palm of her hand to look at them more closely. They looked pearly as teeth. "Will it hurt?"

"No. The Bright Ones will carry us away from all pain."

Duru closed her fist around the berries and nodded at Baat. She was glad for this. Once she had gotten past the fear, this hope of becoming light—like the moon, the stars, like the sun—this storysong hope appealed to her. Everyone she loved in this world was dead. Why not travel with Baat and the bright spirits? Why not give her body to the Mudman and her soul to the sky?

She gazed down at the earth in prayer to the Great Mother and lifted the berries to her lips. But Baat stopped her. He was not looking at her, but staring through the floating snow at the door of the mountain. Figures had emerged from the rockwall. In a moment she would have noticed them herself. She dropped the berries and stood up.

The distant figures were a red-haired woman and a man in a bulky pelt. The man moved awkwardly under the huge ruff, which hung the length of his back, and Duru fixed him in a tight scrutiny before she recognized the gait of her brother.

The Dark Ones circled Yaqut like strange dogs—whispering evil thoughts: *The worms and grubs of this land ate the blood of your parents.* He ignored them and put all his alertness into his waiting. The Dark Ones were there, too, inside his physical senses, watching the world with the glare of the Owl.

From a crevice in the rockwall, Yaqut stared through the snowfall at the fire across the moraine. The bonesucker was in sight. Yaqut could see him standing with the girl he had kidnapped. But the hunter did not move. Before he stepped from the shadows of the rockwall, he wanted all his enemies in front of him and none at his back. He waited, hand curled around his lance, pulsing with killing intent, until he saw Timov and Kirchi walk out onto the flat terrain.

Timov had spotted his sister and shot both arms up in greeting. At the same moment Kirchi saw Yaqut slink out of a crawlhole between the boulders. He came swiftly toward them—lance raised in his right hand, his left gripping a large skull through the eyeholes, using the cranium as a shield.

Kirchi shouted in alarm. Encumbered by the lionskin, Timov lurched around. Fright flushed him with power, and he whipped his sling till it sang. He released his shot right into Yaqut's broken face, and the stone hurtled with lethal accuracy.

Yaqut blocked his face with his sheathed hand, and the skull took the impact. With a report that echoed from the rockwall to the glacier, the cranium splintered, and Yaqut rocked backwards.

Timov fumbled with another shot, fitting it to the sling as Yaqut bore down on him again. No time to whip the stone; he gripped it instead and hurled it at his attacker. Yaqut swept the missile aside with his lance arm, and Timov lunged.

To keep him from lowering his lance to thrust, Kirchi pelted Yaqut with stones. Her shots were stingingly accurate, and he dropped to a crouch as Timov swept over him. Wielding a large rock in his left hand, Timov swung to brain him, but the hunter did not stay still. He uncurled swiftly. One instant, the old man's head was bowed before Timov's raised weapon, and the next he stood upright, his lance blocking the boy's blow. Their eyes met. Timov had no chance to recoil from the murderous blue stare. The bruise-pain arrived from where the lance had hit his left wrist just as the shaft slammed hard against the side of his head.

Timov's long hair splashed outward and his eye-balls rolled white. Limbs, collapsed, he lay unmoving under the dark mane of the Lion.

Duru shrieked. "Timov!"

Baat stepped backwards, closer to the sacred rocks and their vertical river of power. He felt the trembling updraft gust at his back as the Bright Ones called: *Come away.*

Eat the night-wort berries. Cross over into the light.

Hurry. Leave the smallheads to their own furies. Return to the peace of your ancestors.

Quickly. Eat the berries. Come away from the Beast.

"The Beast," Baat whispered to himself, violence coiling tighter in him. "Of course it has come to the Beast. Will I feed this child to the Beast—as I fed it my own children?"

You are thinking like the Dark Ones, Hollow Bone.

Baat cast the poison berries into the fire, and strode away from the altar rocks, his fists clenched. A blind roaring of anger filled him. He knew his rage was not rooted in the Dark Ones. Their punishing voices were absent from the hot surge of force in him; yet their strength filled him. He was infuriated by all that he had lost to the smallheads. The Bright Ones sensed that; sensed, too, the reservoir of black energy behind Yaqut.

Come back! The Dark Ones are drawing you away. They want to kill you outside the updraft, where we cannot help you.

"It's not the Dark Ones," Baat spoke defiantly, breaking into a lope. "This is the will of my blood."

Duru seized a club of burning juniper and ran across the moraine after Baat.

Stay here child, an alarmed voice spoke. *He has gone to the Beast.*

Duru disregarded the spirit warnings. She ran hard, determined to spend all her strength attacking Yaqut. But he was already too far away to reach. In moments, Yaqut would slay him. "Baat!" she cried in despair.

The ghost dancer stopped running and lifted his hands over his head. He did not know that he could strike Yaqut at this range. A colder part of him willed him to wait, to sacrifice the smallhead youth to Yaqut for a sure kill. But anger choked him. He would not have Duru suffer the death of her brother if he could stop it.

Transparencies of sky-fire flashed between his arms, and pain ripped through him. With a blast, the air around Baat jagged with lightning, and a piece of the sun seemed to arc across the snow-hung moraine as he flung the fire.

Yaqut had pulled his lance back to stab Timov as Kirchi dashed toward him, clutching a moonstone in each hand. She had thought to drive the Dark Ones out of Yaqut. But the moonstones burned her fingers; she threw them into the air, and they tracked like shooting stars. Baat's lightning struck the flung stones with a peal of searing heat, hurling Kirchi to the ground, eyes blind, hair singed.

Yaqut dropped his arms from his face, surprised to find himself unharmed. He saw the witch sprawled unconscious before him, her face red from the heat of the blast. The Dark Ones had diverted the bolt from him to the moonstones.

Stick the bitch!

Yaqut stepped over Kirchi and ran toward the ghost dancer, who had dropped to his knees. The hunter would not listen to distracting voices now, nor waste his poison. He had only one purpose. *Kill the bonesucker.*

Baat grimaced with the pain of his miss, and pressed his brow to the stony ground. Futility immobilized him. As Duru rushed to his side, he waved her away. No power remained for another try; he barely had the strength to stay on his knees. "Go— He wants only me. When I'm gone, beg for his mercy. Do this for me."

Duru did not understand his thick words without the Bright Ones to translate. She looked for them, but they were nowhere in the ravelling snow. Baat gestured toward Yaqut sprinting toward them, and Duru dropped the juniper bough beside Baat and hastily began gathering rocks.

Baat stopped her and waved her aside. He struggled to his feet, pushed her away when she came close. Tottering dizzily, he scanned the ground for a suitable rock. When he bent to lift a large, flat rock for a shield, he nearly toppled.

"Die, bonesucker!" Yaqut yelled.

The smallhead's screech made Baat flinch behind the rock he clasped in both hands. But Yaqut did not throw his lance. He stopped and stared at the bonesucker, wrath chilling him as he caught his breath. Looking upon the monster that had defied him so long, he was surprised to see how old it was. The thing was older than he had thought, its large face and splotchy beard haggard.

It could easily have been among the monsters who killed his family.

Gut the bonesucker!

Baat heard the echoing voices of the Dark Ones squeaking around Yaqut, and he squinted with malice at the smallhead.

Yaqut's half-face smiled; and the twisted side of his mouth grimaced with delight. "You hate me, don't you? I want you to die hating me. I want you to die knowing that I killed you. I, Yaqut." He thrumped the haft of his lance against his chest and pointed it at Duru. "Before I give your eyes to the crows, bonesucker, I'm going to prop your head on my lance so that you can watch me take my pleasure with your women—the witch and the girl."

No more talk! Kill the animal!

Baat did not comprehend the smallhead's words, but he recognized the noise of the Dark Ones and Yaqut's lewd stare at Duru.

"Yes, yes," Yaqut said when Baat lurched in front of the girl to protect her. "She will suffer. Her anguish is the song she'll sing for having helped you."

Baat shambled forward and dropped to one knee, with the weight of the stone in his hands. Duru moved closer, and he shouted, "Stand back!" The girl hopped backwards, startled by the venom seething in Baat's voice; then she snatched up a rock and threw it at Yaqut. He ducked, and the rock clattered behind him.

"Hate me, bonesucker." Yaqut gasped a laugh. "Hate me for killing you. Hate me for killing the witch and little Duru—for, surely I am going to kill them both."

In mid-breath, the hunter flung his lance.

With a mighty heave, Baat lifted the flat rock to protect his heart, and the flint blade smashed against it. The force dropped him to his side, where he floundered, stretching feebly to reach the lance. But it had fallen too far away.

Spry as a spider, Yaqut pounced. Duru tried to block him, but he flung her aside and slashed at the ghost dancer with his knife. The sharp flint tipped with poison scored Baat's upper arm. With a victory cry, Yaqut snatched up his lance and bounded out of reach.

Baat cried out, rocked himself upright, a clod of earth in his hand, smashing the earth against his wound and glowering at the evil smallhead.

With the tip of his lance shattered, Yaqut cast it far out of reach. Then, one pace closer to his prey, he sucked a sharp breath through his teeth. ''Feel my poison biting your heart. Feel it rotting your insides. Die, bonesucker. Chill, spasm, and die!''

Duru recognized that sinister voice from a nightmare. ''The Dark Ones are inside you, Yaqut!'' she called out.

The grizzled head bobbed and grinned. ''I gave myself to them—and they gave you to me.''

''They'll kill you!'' Duru knelt beside Baat, but he would not look at her. He was listening inwardly, past the pain congealing in his wound and the poison already lacing his heart with ice, to the unbodied vastness within, from where the Bright Ones spoke when they came.

Yaqut sneered. ''He's the one the spirits want. The bonesucker's the one they'll hurt forever.''

''You, too, Yaqut,'' Duru spat. ''The evil spirits are in you now!''

Yaqut frowned impatiently. He was eager to take this head now, and be on his way before the wind came and drifted the snow. ''Die, bonesucker. Spasm and die!''

Baat meshed his teeth and sucked hard at the air, his lungs suddenly tight, the pain re-doubling with his effort.

Hopping from foot to foot, stabbing the air, too wary to step any closer and deal the death blow but too excited to just walk away; Yaqut shouted with glee. He ranted with spiteful merriment, "I see the shadow in your face, bonesucker! I see death widening the holes of your eyes! Your tongue is too numb to curse me now. Every breath stabs like my lance. I'm stabbing you again and again! With every breath you suck, I'm killing you. Spasm and die!"

Yaqut leaped forward suddenly. "More poison, bonesucker!" He slashed again with his knife, cutting Baat across the backs of his hands. "Die!"

Baat swung out his huge arms to protect himself. But he was too weak from throwing fire and from the poison to find his target. He slumped to the ground.

As Yaqut spun away, chortling, Duru swung at him with the juniper bough. The bough snapped across Yaqut's legs. He lost his footing, scrabbled hard on the flying gravel for a moment, then misstepped and snagged his foot in a crevice. Jerking himself sideways, he tripped and sprawled before Duru.

She struck him fiercely behind the head with the broken bough until he reared up furiously. He grabbed her throat and would have torn her windpipe out but for the amazement on her beautiful childish face. He glanced down at where she gazed so intently and saw blood in the crook of his elbow. Fright pierced his heart, as he comprehended: He had stabbed himself in the arm with his poison-tipped knife.

He spat out a curse at the knife, still fisted in his right hand. He sheathed it quickly, not taking his eyes from the puncture wound. The blade had gouged into the crease of his elbow; already he could feel the poison moving upstream, up the bloodways of his arm. Wildly he tore off the pelts covering his torso, and snapped free the chest-strap studded with the teeth of the bone-suckers he had killed. Weeping sweat, he wrapped the strap about his upper arm and, with his teeth holding one end in a panic, jerked it tight.

Baat watched him coldly. Duru backed away to the ghost dancer, and crouched beside him. Together they watched Yaqut tighten the tourniquet frantically around his arm. But muscle after muscle froze in deadly rictus. It was clear his efforts were useless. Yaqut whimpered, the unmarked side of his face trembling with his effort to save himself, the ruined side locked in terror.

He looked to Baat, the black deepening in his eyes, his mouth widening around a scream that never came.

Baat watched him until the poison in his own body blurred his vision. The sky darkened, the chill deepened. He squinted for clarity, saw Duru gaping at him in alarm, and tried to smile—to show her he had no fear now that she was safe from the Beast. Her small hands urged him to rise. But he felt frozen fast to the gravel, and the altar stones seemed far away in the swirling snow.

Duru shouted angrily at him, then turned away and gazed across the moraine to where her brother lay beside the witch. Baat, too, wondered if they were alive, or if Duru was completely alone out here on the tundra in the snow. For her sake, he had to get up and eat enough pain to reach the Bright Ones. They were the only strength that could avail her now.

The poison swathed his heart with thorns. His effort to rise pierced him cruelly, and he sat back down and rested his sick head in his hands. Duru spoke close to his ear, her small hands on his arm, coaxing him to get up. Her meaningless words carried the softness he had loved in his children and he had come to love in her.

Da! It hurts! The memory of his helplessness while his children convulsed in his arms enlarged around the pain killing him. This was their suffering. Now he was making it his—and he would use it to help this other child.

Baat meshed his teeth against the hurt and wrenched himself upright. Pain-weeping and dizzy, he staggered two steps and almost fell down before Duru braced him. He listed to one side, afraid of falling on her, and she clung to him, gummy with his blood.

At the heap of orange rocks, the fire had died, clearing a wide enough space to hold Baat's full length. He toppled onto the altar shards and rolled to his back. The vertical river of energy sluiced through him, carrying away his pain and leaving him glistening with strength. He sat upright—and found that he was sitting atop his body.

Duru had stepped back when Baat fell, and she stood at the edge of the updraft, her hair standing out from her head. "Baat—I see your spirit!"

Baat smiled and lifted his hands. The gashes of his wounds glowed silver as lightning. From above, the voice of thunder spoke his name, and he gazed up through a vortex of shining power and blinked into a sun-blinding joy.

"Baat!" Duru called. "You're fading!"

Baat's wraith looked back at her, his eyes straining. In the dark of the world, she was hard to see. But beside her, in the world of light invisible to her, Timov and Kirchi stood. "Don't be afraid, Duru," he said, his body of light brightening as he spoke. "Your brother will wake soon. And the witch. Go south with them, quickly as you can."

Duru understood and stepped closer, against the buffeting force of the spirits. Her black hair swam in the air and sparkled with blue motes of static. "I want to go with you!"

Baat shook his head benignly. "Go south. The others need you. Go south and live."

"The others don't need me," she pleaded. "You need me. Only you have ever needed me."

"I still need you, to lead the others back. I don't want them to die for me." Her shadow bled into night, and he saw only Timov and Kirchi on either side of her darkness, guiding her backwards. "Will you help me do that?"

His head fell back, too heavy now to move, and he swallowed with difficulty.

Come away, Hollow Bone

The call of the Bright Ones came to him as a seraphic music he remembered from his childhood. He began to slip, to float into a radiance that had its own shapes.

"You're fading," Duru cried weakly. "Baat—I . . . I can't bear to lose you too."

Baat whispered to the darkness. "Don't be afraid for me, little Duru. Everything passes away. As my people have passed away, so will yours someday. And the Old Ways will pass and pass again, till nothing of this earth will remember us, you and me. Yet nothing living is destroyed. We all go on. We all go on as light. Remember that."

"Baat!" Duru reached for his hand, but already it was growing cold, and when she called out his name it reverberated in the emptiness above the ghost dancer's body. She breathed desperately on his fingers to keep them warm. "Baat—I need you!"

Baat wanted to answer, to tell the child to let him go. There was nothing to fear, even in the world of shadows. The light was indestructible, immortal. The inconceivable truth of that widened in him with the upsurge of the ul udi's music, and he soared toward the brilliance of the sun.

The world's edge gleamed blue against the night. Baat rose effortlessly as an air bubble from the sea's bottom, feeling himself expanding, his body of light becoming more diffuse. Far off, he saw little Duru weeping over his body. Then, a ravenous cold penetrated him, and by that he knew he was trespassing the savage domain of the Dark Ones.

Bonesucker!

A dazzle of freezing energy stymied Baat's ascent, and fear crisped in him again and with it the pain of his wounds as he recognized Yaqut's voice.

Ghost dancer! Help me!

"Yaqut? Where are you?"

I'm here! Right here before you. Don't you see me?

Baat searched around him. Against the azure glare from the Earth, he barely discerned a sullen green spark. "Yaqut?"

Your light, ghost dancer! Touch me with your light! Hurry! I'm falling apart from the cold. Help me!

The emerald spark zipped closer, but a sudden gust of blizzard force shook Baat. In the freezing energy that cut through him came evil voices: *Now you are ours! And we are going to bake you in our cold—*

cut you with our knives—and eat you, eat you, eat you!

Yaqut's scream shattered.

Baat reeled away, but the icy pain went with him and the voices, booming like drums.

You grew out of the dirt. The light touched you, and you rose from the mud. But you turned your back on the Light and rejoiced in your shadow.

Bone-needle pain stabbed and ripped, again and again. Baat and Yaqut screamed as one. The cold clamped tighter, sharpening and monstrously expanding their anguish.

Baat searched the stars, saw them cringing in the darkness. One of them shone brighter, and he rose toward it, leaving his suffering behind. The grotesque voices of the Dark Ones dimmed too, yet Baat still heard Yaqut bleating: *They're eating me! The stars are eating me!*

Baat stared back at the Earth, saw the auburn crusts of land, the sapphire sea, and the long fleeces of cloud, all turning, slowly, majestically, under him. He saw no sign of Yaqut's green mote or the tortuous realm of the Dark Ones.

He must stay below, a gentle voice spoke. *He belongs to our dark brethren. Remember, they are ul udi, as we are, and so, too, do they occupy a place in this world. While we thrive on the solar wind, they listen to the grinding of the continents and the vast electrical storms in the mantle of the planet.*

The Bright One's soft voice layered into echoes, and Baat felt sleepiness spin him into a long, long tunnel. Behind him, the blue shine of the Earth shrank away, tightened to the dimensions of a distant star. Darkness funneled ahead to where all the stars clumped, fusing into one white dew-star shining in the quivering darkness.

Peacefulness amazed Baat. He flew serenely toward the most radiant light he had ever seen. And something like homesickness healed in him, comforted by the dim figures appearing out of the tranquil glare.

Empty of all grief, calm as the dark silence that held the stars, Baat flew into the light at the end of the world, toward the frail shadows of those he loved.

◆ 12 ◆
South

The vertical river disappeared, and Duru's hair fell limply to her shoulders. A dull heaviness pressed down around her, and she staggered back from where Baat's corpse lay, not wanting to see the ghost dancer this way.

From the glacier, an etheric wind flowed and set the snowfall roiling. Duru darted across the moraine to where Timov lay, and crouched over him. With her warm breath in his face, he came around groggily, still dreaming of floating in the sky, staring down at the blue turtleshell of the planet. Then he remembered Yaqut's murderous stare, his last image before the blow that knocked him unconscious. Timov sat bolt upright, and Duru clasped herself to him.

When the stiffening wind finally unlocked them, they found Kirchi sitting up, blinking with astonishment. Timov's head ached from Yaqut's blow. Otherwise he was unharmed, and wanted to see Baat. Kirchi, too, was sound enough to walk with him to the altar stones. Duru followed reluctantly, Baat's last instruction still ringing loud in her ears: *Go south, quickly.*

They weaved drunkenly around Yaqut's stiff corpse and hurried away from it, against the mounting wind.

Baat lay on his back in a sprawl, the snow already half-covering him. Timov regarded the face intently for some time, then reached under his lion-skin and took out Cyndell's calendar bracelet. "From the last of the Blue Shell," he said softly and placed it in the giant's hand.

"To the last of the Old People," Kirchi murmured.

A green spark whirled among the snowflakes, and the three huddled together before the fallen ghost dancer. In the distance, a lunatic voice squeaked: *Tree-houses fall—dungpiles rise. You will die!*

The three shared startled glances and bolted from the broken altar. They did not look back or glance again at Yaqut's corpse, but ran for the door of the mountain. Tumbling through a rock crevice, they clung to each other, exhausted, as the wind cried about them.

A short while later, the gust quieted; they crawled out and clambered over snow-slick granite blocks and stacks of shale. By the time they reached the far side of the rockwall, the western sky had cleared. There, the gaseous sphere of the sun swelled crimson among the citadels of boulders.

Timov, Kirchi, and Duru stood irresolute before the snowblotched expanse of the tundra. No inner sight gleamed with direction, and no Bright Ones shimmered, speaking out of the wind to guide them, as Baat had promised.

Timov considered—he knew they wanted to go southeast, but what was the best way through the jumble of erratic boulders and snow-drifted trenches torn

into the earth by the herds? Duru was frowning, trying
to recall the land she had watched while Baat had slept.
To her relief, the images came. "I remember the way
Baat brought me," she announced.

So Kirchi and Timov followed Duru south, as she
followed her memory backwards. Everything she had
seen on her way to the door of the mountain had been
changed by the snow, altered in dress as if for mourning. They picked their way slowly, in stunned silence.
They had seen Baat's body of light, had heard the
lovely vaporous music of the ul udi; but already each
felt subtly changed, muffled in their senses like the
landscape, as though what had happened that day had
occurred long ago and to someone else.

The snow began again that first night. The travelers huddling among the rocks found enough bramble to
burn through the long cold darkness. Mice and voles
zipped through the grass-jammed crevices, and provided an ample meal. With the obsidian knife from
Duru's satchel, Timov cut the oversize lion-skin to
make leggings and headgear for the women and himself. But the next day few promontories offered themselves as landmarks, and Duru guided them by the
sun's shadow in the overcast.

Storm Riders appeared from behind a boulder and
came crashing toward them through the snow. Their
horses huffed jets of snowy breath, laboring under riders, pelts, poles, and the butchered haunches of caribou. None of the three attempted to hide. Two days in
the bone-penetrating cold, and they were ready to be
slaves to the Storm Riders.

But when the horsemen got closer, they stopped.
Perhaps it was a bad omen finding three people alone

on the snowy tundra. Or perhaps the fierce serenity with which the wanderers faced the horsemen seemed unfamiliar and eerie. The Storm Riders approached only to stare, then threw down a haunch of caribou, made abject warding signs, and rode off.

The caribou meat lasted several days. Each night, they found shelter among the rocks piled high by older icesheets, and thawed the meat over twig fires and flares of dried grass. Blizzard winds bellowed through the crevices, and they slept clutching each other for warmth. At dawn, they had to burrow through the snow to get out.

The day their meat ran out, they found the Storm Riders again. The horsemen, seven of them, sat mounted on steeds that had knelt into the gale winds and frozen. Crusty with snow, they had become one with the earth.

Timov dislodged two more haunches of meat and dragged them through the snow as the storm grew worse. Swirling snow blinded them by day; night closed in with no shelter in sight. The force of the wind had sharpened, and their numbness became a burning pain.

The sky opened, vast and blue. Neoll Nant Caw gazed up into empty space from a snow-laced glade in the Forest. Her mind was as empty as those cloudless reaches. The death of the Moon Bitch had taken all power from her, and she had spent the moon period since then staring blankly from a cold place inside her skull.

The witches she had called on to help her build the Moon Bitch had all fled back to their tribes before the snow. They had taken her crystals with them, after preparing for her three days' food and firewood and leaving her in the care of the Great Mother. In the spring, they would return to honor her bones.

Neoll Nant Caw had wandered from her burrow days ago, tired of waiting for death. She had walked into the woods to give herself to the Beast, and had surprised herself by living among the rotting leafdrifts for days without food. She walked through dark hollows and briar groves, where the Beast lurked. But Bear was already asleep, and Lion and Panther had gone to the herd trails. She lived for days with only sleep and sips of stream water. Now she stood, wispy from hunger and distracted, staring at the shining sky above the white spires of the Forest.

A cry startled her. At first, she believed it was a hyena. The Beast had found her at last. But then the cry came again, and this time she knew it was a baby crying. The unlikeliness of that helpless sound so far from the nearest tribe lured her back into the Forest. She followed the infant's wailing among the trees, past twig-snags that showered her bedraggled head with clumps of snow and through a frosted thicket. In a clearing trampled by footprints into slush, she found the baby.

He was naked, smudged black from the ashes of the fire where he had been placed. His mother lay beside him, the snow crimson with her blood loss. She lay on her side under a bloodstained pelt, mouth slack, hapless eyes open, staring lifelessly.

Neoll Nant Caw gasped at the sight of her, recognizing even in death the haughty countenance of the Longtooth priestess. Without thinking, the witch charged into the clearing and swooped up the child. The ash was still warm. She removed the pelt covering the dead priestess and swaddled the baby, while casting around a harsh-eyed search for those who had abandoned them here.

The witch saw pug marks in the snow, smelled the musk of Cat. Shadows flitted beyond the icy hedges. "Thundertree!" she cried out, and her voice croaked. "You are cowards!"

The shadows slunk away. Neoll Nant Caw turned to all sides, searching for beasts that might have smelled the blood and heard the crying. Wind shed a glitter of snow-motes from the high trees but otherwise, nothing moved. The witch held the infant close in her trembling arms and stared into its screaming face—the ghost dancer's issue.

In the black belly of the night, without fire or shelter, Duru, Timov and Kirchi slept. But when they woke at dawn they found the snow melted around them in a large circle. Their breaths smoked, yet the land felt warm, a mire of sunken stones and dew-glinting bramble. Beyond the perimeter of the thaw, snow blanketed the land to the horizons under a vivid blue sky.

Ul udi, they all knew, but no one said it. No one had spoken since they had found the frozen Storm Riders. Duru got up and walked to the edge of the thawring. She took two steps into the knee-deep snow and stopped. "We've been here before," she said, but her voice was too thick to be understood. She turned to the others, with astonishment. "Hamr found the black knife here."

Timov and Kirchi looked around at the smothered landscape, bewildered, amazed to be in the world at all.

Climbing to the top of a nearby slope, Duru cried out, "The Forest!"

The others scrabbled after her. When they reached her side, they gazed south at a horizon glistening with the gossamer veils and filigreed shrouds of the Forest. Timov shouted out loud, laughing, and waded through the snow with Duru. Only Kirchi paused, suddenly fitting the muted terrain to her memory of the trance-time, moons ago, when she had witnessed evil here.

"Duru," she called. "The Moon Serpent."

Duru understood, and drew the black-glass knife from her satchel. She had not seen it used since Timov had cut down his lion-skin to share with them, and she regarded it soberly. It had not really been a knife at all, but an emblem. Of what? Of all that had been cut away? Of all that cut?—Time's fang? It belonged here, she realized; it belonged here, where the journey to the land of the dead crossed its own tracks. She held it up for the others to see. Their ice-burned faces nodded consent, and she placed the knife in the snow.

Timov looked south to the treeline, where their fates awaited them. From his tattered bag he removed the tortoise shell and spun it on its reed axle. The hunt had completed its cirolo. Yet the sky continued to turn—or the world turned under it if the Invisibles were to be believed. Either way, new journeys were already beginning. He held the spinning wheel over his head, and the bearded trees watched, secretive and wise under the blue blast of heaven.

Squinting into the ice-light, Neoll Nant Caw stared north across the flat terrain. A herd of woolly mammoths milled around in the rocky bed of a frozen stream, probing with their tusks and trunks for lichen under the snow. They began to move away suddenly, and the crone watched them until the baby beneath her mantle squirmed. He flexed awake but did not cry out. A grin relaxed the witch's squint. Yesterday, she had gone to the Beast to die. Today, she was a mother.

Without milk or tribe, Neoll Nant Caw could give the child only Fire to warm him and maple sap to quiet his hunger. A dream had led her to this spot. She had seen Baat dancing on the spine of this ridge, at the edge of the Great Forest and the tundra, and she had come to show him his son. Now she found herself squinting against the snow-glare again, wishing her eyes were not so old. The mammoths had lumbered off, and three figures moved slowly along the stony margins of the stream—a man, a woman, and a girl.

In a moment, the witch recognized them; and stared harder, gaping until she was sure hope had not tricked her. A gasp of laughter shook her bent frame, and the baby startled, and wailed.

The crone smiled down at the child and opened her mantle so he could see the cold world. "Cry, little one. Cry to the wind and your song will be heard." She lifted the screaming infant to her shoulder and carried him up the rock crest, to where the wanderers below would see her and surely hear him.

In a burst of lucidity, the witch understood that these wanderers were why Baat's ghost had danced on this ridge in her dream. Her time was done; the Great Mother had sent the baby, the dream, and the wanderers to grant her last acts power. With exhilaration, she saw that she would give the child to them, to the young strangers from the south and to wayward Kirchi. Timov, who had soared with ul udi in the celestial sphere, could parent the ghost dancer's boy—and Kirchi would have her chance to be a simple mother, at last.

Another laugh coughed its way out of her: The

pattern of her life had come clear so abruptly that now death seemed welcome. She would die, but her work with the Invisibles would still have life. The child of spirits—Baat's last companion—Duru would take her place. There was time yet to show her how to make and use the crystals—time yet and hope for the future, for capturing more fire from the sky and setting it ablaze in the minds of the people, time yet to light up the whole, wide, motherly world.

Neoll Nant Caw lifted the infant above her head and held him up with her quavery strength. She wanted the wanderers below to see how tiny and powerful the future really was. And she wanted the child to see.

"Look, little one," she called to the wailing baby. "Look below at those young people, who have found their way to us through every grief. There is your family."